FLASHPOINT

THE **IRON KINGDOMS** CHRONICLES

ACTS OF WAR I
FLASHPOINT

AERYN RUDEL

Copyright © 2016 by Privateer Press, Inc.

All trademarks herein including *Privateer Press*®, *Iron Kingdoms*®, *Full Metal Fantasy, Immoren*, *WARMACHINE*®, *Steam-Powered Miniatures Combat, Convergence of Cyriss*®, *Convergence, Cygnar*®, *Cryx*®, *Khador*®, *Protectorate of Menoth*®, *Protectorate, Retribution of Scyrah*®, *Retribution, warcaster*®, *warjack*®, *HORDES*®, *Circle Orboros*®, *Circle, Legion of Everblight*®, *Legion, Skorne*®, *Trollbloods*®, *Trollblood, warbeast, Skull Island eXpeditions, SIX, Dogs of War, Exiles in Arms, Iron Kingdoms Excursions, The Warlock Sagas, The Warcaster Chronicles*, and all associated logos and slogans are property of Privateer Press, Inc.

Published in the United States by Skull Island eXpeditions, a division of Privateer Press, Inc.

ISBN 978-1-943693-17-7

Printed in the United States of America

www.privateerpress.com
www.skullislandx.com
facebook.com/skullislandexpeditions

First Paperback Edition

Book design by Richard Anderson
Cover illustration by Grzegorz Rutkowski

The text of this book was set in Adobe Garamond Pro

— CONTENTS —

PART I

●

— 1 —

LIEUTENANT LONAN DUFF WALKED DOWN the gangplank of the Ordic frigate *HMS Maiden's Wrath* and breathed in the unlovely scent of Five Fingers. Although the mingled aroma of coal smoke, cooking pots, and the stale sweat of humans was not pleasant, it was what the smell represented that really bothered him most. It was the smell of shore, where he was most vulnerable.

He was the last to leave the ship; the rest of the crew had long since departed for a few days of leave and the revelry that entailed. Soon enough, they were bound for Zu, the mysterious land far to the south, serving as an escort for two House Mateu frigates carrying supplies and men to their outpost in that exotic land.

It would take two days to acquire all the supplies necessary, and Captain Vanus of the *Maiden's Wrath* had ordered his crew to rest and enjoy themselves. They would be at sea for three months after Five Fingers and would have few chances for such things in the immediate future.

Lonan had lobbied the captain to be allowed to stay aboard, but Vanus would have none of it. The captain thought it was merely social awkwardness and a devotion to duty that made Lonan reticent to go ashore. He couldn't tell the captain the real reason: that his name was not Lonan Duff, that it was *Prince* Lyan di la Martyn, perhaps the sole living heir to the throne of Llael, a country now occupied by the Khadoran Empire. He couldn't tell his captain that his father, King Rynnard di la Martyn, had died under mysterious circumstances, that the king's power had been assumed by a corrupt government, and that nearly everyone with a claim to the throne had been killed or forced into hiding. No, he couldn't tell *anyone* that, so he'd left the captain's cabin, gathered his pistol and cutlass, and forced himself to walk down the gangplank into a city filled with thieves and murderers, a city where agents of the enemy could be lurking around every dark corner.

Lonan stepped onto the bustling and noisy pier. The city loomed ahead, a seemingly endless collection of buildings fading into the horizon like a grey carpet over Captain's Island, one of the many islands over which Five Fingers spread like and infection. The *Maiden's Wrath* was moored in the Rivergrav District, one of the city's busiest. Men and laborjacks—massive, steam-powered automatons—swarmed the pier, moving cargo to and from the many ships and riverboats anchored there.

He'd become adept at getting lost in a crowd, and he let himself be pulled along by the stream of people moving down the pier. The dockside was a place of constant motion; people were either coming or going, and there were few destinations beside a handful of taverns or one of the many moored ships.

He pulled his hat down low and pushed up the collar of his jacket, hiding his face. His long coat was too warm for the climate, but it hid the shirt of chainmail he wore beneath it. These days, he never left the ship without some form of body armor. He had no destination in mind, but wandering could be dangerous. The longer he was visible, the more likely it was he would be seen by someone who knew his true identity.

He wasn't normally so cautious, so afraid. After the war in Llael had reached a fever pitch, the search for King Rynnard's heirs had hardly been a pressing concern. Lonan had been hiding in Ord since his father's death, and the war had made it easier to move around. He'd joined the Ordic Navy under an assumed name almost ten years ago, working hard but deliberately rising only to the rank of a second lieutenant. The middling rank hid his true abilities and intelligence beneath a cloak of feigned awkwardness and professional indifference and afforded him some anonymity while granting him enough authority to occasionally avoid dangerous situations.

He still retained a few contacts in Llael, but they had been silent for years. He assumed they had been killed in the fighting or had fled the country as he had. So, he'd been shocked to receive a missive from one of them in his last port of call, a letter suggesting the search for the king's heirs had been resumed but not by agents of what remained of the Llaelese government or even the Resistance fighting against the Khadoran invaders. The note had only one line, and it had chilled him to the bone. It said: *Khador searches for surviving heirs.*

The Khadorans controlled huge sections of western Llael, including the capital city of Merywyn, and they had no interest in seeing the return of a Llaelese king. The Resistance might wish it, as a legitimate heir could galvanize the populace, but no one had ever contacted him, most likely thinking him dead. The Khadorans could only be searching for him for one reason: to remove him and remove the possibility of a son of Rynnard ever sitting on the throne of Llael.

He'd seen no sign of assassins in the various ports he had visited over the last month, although his fear mounted each time his ship came to shore. His recent assignment to the *Maiden's Wrath* had been a godsend, and its journey to the new frontier Zu would see him on the open ocean for months, well beyond the reach of Khador. He just had to survive the next two days in Five Fingers.

He knew the city intimately; he'd been stationed here for nearly seven years with the Royal Navy. It was a place where he could hide and become lost in the teeming crowds of the sprawling city, a known haven for pirates and smugglers, but now it seemed the perfect place for assassins to strike. The only safe haven for him was the Naval Fortress. There he could find relative safety among the sailors stationed at the Royal Navy's garrison.

The only problem was the garrison was on Bellicose Island, meaning he'd have to traverse a fair portion of the city, passing though Chaser Island and Doleth Island to reach it. He glanced around at the bustling crowd of people on the dock. Hundreds of sailors and laborers went about their business all around him. Most were human, though a few trollkin and he could see the occasional towering ogrun among them.

No one was paying attention to him, and he blended in with the crowd. Lonan quickened his pace, moving with the flow of people. He'd need to cross one of the many bridges connecting the islands of Five Fingers to reach his destination, and the first wasn't too far away.

He stuck close to the many dockside warehouses that lined the pier, avoiding the bulk of the crowd. He made good progress after that, moving away from the huge marina toward the more commercial portion of the docks. Here fishmongers and other merchants hawked their wares, and the crowd changed from sailors and seamen to a more cosmopolitan mix. Lonan didn't like that; his naval uniform made him stand out.

He hurried through the market area, ignoring the cries of merchants and the dull susurrus of the crowd. The bridge to Chaser Isle wasn't far now. He exited the Rivergrav into another section of Captain's Island that was more sparsely populated. This was the Spiritgrav District, the center of industry on the island, where looming factories belching smoke into the sky and countless warehouses where goods were stored dominated the horizon.

He was more vulnerable here. He wasn't alone, but the crowd was thin, and there were many dark, narrow alleys between buildings that could easily harbor an assassin. He wove around the people in his way, eyeing each as he passed, looking for any hint that they were something other than just faces in the crowd.

He could see the bridge now, a massive thing of stone and steel arching up and over the channel between Captain and Chaser islands. That was a relief. Chaser Island was primarily a marketplace, and the city watch had a larger presence there as a result.

Just the same, he was overly cautious as he neared the bridge. There were people going to and fro across it, but standing in front of it were two men clad in grey long coats, the telltale bulge of swords or pistols visible beneath them. They looked out of place not because they were armed or because of how they were dressed. It was the way they watched the crowd that terrified him. Their eyes lingered on everyone who passed them—a penetrating, searching gaze.

Lonan stopped, his heart thundering in his chest. It was possible the men weren't looking for *him*. They could be employed by one of the infamous High Captains, powerful criminals who were the true power in Five Fingers, and whomever they were searching for had nothing to do with an exiled prince of Llael. He rubbed his mouth and looked behind him. The way was clear, and there was another, lesser-used bridge to Chaser Island back through the Rivergrav. He could turn around and go back the way he had come.

He glanced again toward the bridge. The two men were staring directly at him. One of them nodded to the other, and they began moving toward him.

He considered pulling his pistol and gunning down one of them immediately. It would likely bring the watch, which might provide some measure of safety, but he dismissed the idea quickly. The watch was as corruptible as everything else in Five Fingers. He began walking in the other direction. He wasn't running. Not yet.

He was moving against the flow of people on the dockside, pushing past them. He glanced back over his shoulder. The two men were still behind him, moving swiftly.

Lonan realized he had seen them too easily, as if they were placed there to force him to move in the other direction. Spook him toward—

He slammed into a wall of muscle, a wall wearing a grey coat with a square jaw and dark eyes. The wall was also grinding a short-bladed knife into his ribs.

The blade pierced Lonan's coat, but the mail shirt beneath stopped it from penetrating his flesh. Still, the strength behind the blade was immense, and he gasped in pain as one of his ribs cracked. He stumbled backward, and his attacker's eyes widened in surprise—he hadn't been expecting the armor—and advanced on him. This time Lonan did pull his pistol, a heavy repeater he'd spent almost a month's salary on. He fired at point blank range, two shots: chest, head. Blood splattered, and the man went down. Cries of alarm rose up from the crowd on the docks, and people scattered. Ahead, Lonan could see more grey silhouettes moving toward him. He wanted to fire at them, but there were too many people between him and his targets. Panicked as he was, he didn't want risk wasting the bullets on unnecessary targets.

He looked over his shoulder. The two men behind him were closer. He was outnumbered and likely outgunned. To his left was the entrance of a huge warehouse, and he could see laborjacks moving within while workers stood and stared at him. Some of them had weapons of their own. Most citizens of Five Fingers were well acquainted with violence.

He turned and ran into the warehouse, past two workers, one of who shouted something at him. The interior of the warehouse was a maze of crates and boxes, and he tried to maintain his direction, hoping he'd find an exit on the far side.

The towering walls of boxes made it impossible for him to see if his attackers had followed him in. Who were they? His contact said Khadoran agents were looking for him, but these men weren't soldiers, at least not in the normal sense.

He pushed on, transferring his pistol to his left hand and drawing his cutlass with his right. The crates and boxes thinned, and he had reason to feel hope when the other side of the warehouse presented a clear open space and a set of great double doors leading to a wide thoroughfare.

He wanted to sprint toward the exit, but again he had that

unquiet feeling he was being herded along a path chosen for him. The prospect of an escape route was too tempting, however, so he raced toward the open door.

As he emerged onto the street, the first thing he noticed was how empty it was; the next was the tall stone building directly across from him. He didn't even have time to glance up before the first shot rang out.

Something struck his left shoulder and spun him around. His pistol flew from his hand, and a deep burning pain stabbed deep into his shoulder. He stumbled back into the warehouse, throwing himself to the left as another shot ricocheted off the concrete floor.

Lonan ran toward the first row of crates to his left, the tall stacks creating a narrow alley-like path. Blood ran down his left arm, and trying to move the injured limb only intensified his pain to searing agony. The bullet had passed through his chain mail without slowing and had likely driven some of the links into his wound.

He listened as he moved, but the warehouse had grown quiet. Only the distant rumble of laborjacks' boilers pierced the silence. He was nearing the end of the row of crates, which opened in another row running left to right in a T-section. He wasn't remotely surprised when another of the grey-coated assassins appeared in the intersection, a long curved saber in hand.

He glanced backward. Another assassin was moving toward him. A strange sense of calm settled over him. His death was imminent; there were more than enough of these men to murder him. He took some comfort that it would be an end to the running and to the hiding. He'd never been an overly devout man, but perhaps there was a place in Urcaen for him, a place that offered some semblance of peace.

But he would not go meekly to his death.

"I am Lyan di la Martyn!" he shouted, giving voice to a name he had not spoken in over a decade. "Which of you lowborn curs shall be the first to die?"

He charged toward the assassin armed with the saber. The man shifted his feet and took up high guard, right arm held out, blade pointed at the ground.

Lyan rushed forward then sidestepped while making a wide backhanded slash. He'd been trained as a swordsman in his father's court, with the finest instructors, and he had not let his skills lapse in the ten years since. He was faster and more skilled than his foe, despite his wound. His blade slammed against his opponent's, and his heavier weapon knocked the saber off line for a single heartbeat, long enough for him to riposte and turn his first blow into powerful cut. His blade slashed into the assassin's neck, cutting through the flesh and lodging against the man's spine. Blood sprayed, and Lyan jerked his weapon free as the man crumbled to the ground.

He whirled to face the next attacker, who was not rushing him—he had waited calmly for Lyan to finish with his compatriot. The killer's hand was thrust out, and a ring of runes circled his fist in motes of arctic blue.

There was no time to avoid what was coming. Lyan thrust his arms up over his face. A blast of bone-cracking cold followed as he was enveloped in the Khadoran sorcerer's spell. His muscles locked, the breath froze in his lungs, and it felt as if every inch of his exposed skin was assaulted by numbing pain. His chainmail was no protection for this attack—and the steel rings simply fused together in a sheet of icy metal.

The supernatural cold ripped the strength from his limbs, and Lyan fell to his knees. He'd held onto his sword and brought it up as the man approached. His killer was tall with sharp features and dark thinning hair. His eyes were blue, cold and merciless, and his lips were drawn up in a tight smile. He carried a heavy battle axe in one hand, its blade flickering with shining runes.

Lyan tried a clumsy slash at the arcanist, who casually stepped aside, then lashed out with a booted foot and kicked the blade from Lyan's hand.

"You are brave, Prince Lyan," the man said. His Khadoran accent wasn't thick, but it was unmistakable. "I did not expect you to be . . . so spirited."

Lyan opened his mouth to speak, but his body was shaking so violently from the cold he could barely get anything out. "Do it," he said. "I've had enough of pretending . . . hiding who I am."

The man nodded, his face twisting into a mockery of sympathy. "Yes. Those days are over for you," he said, and to Lyan's surprise, he let the axe drop to his side as he reached beneath his coat. He pulled out a long, straight dagger with a wickedly sharp point. "But I will not cut you down like a common dog. You deserve a better death than that. A noble death. Can you stand, Prince? Can you die on your feet?"

Lyan found he did have the strength to stand and that he did not want to die on his knees. He climbed to his feet, gasping as pain lanced though his body. The supernatural cold had done grave damage to his internal organs. His vision greyed.

"Do it," he whispered.

"With pleasure." The man put one hand on Lyan's shoulder and placed the point of his dagger against over his heart. "Goodbye, Prince Lyan. I promise your death will usher in a new era of greatness for your nation."

He jerked Lyan forward, driving the blade through his mail and into his heart.

The shock of the blade entering his body gave way to a spreading warmth, and Lyan di la Martyn welcomed the darkness that rose up to swallow him.

— 2 —

North of Corvis

LORD GENERAL COLEMAN STRYKER walked at the head of a long procession of Storm Knights. His weathered face was creased with worry, making him look older than his thirty-five years. He ran a hand through his shock of red hair and looked behind him. He led a smaller force than he was comfortable with, but they would only be exposed for a short while.

They were on their way to Merywyn, the capital city of wartorn Llael, where Cygnar's fiercest enemies awaited them, but they didn't go to continue their decades-long conflict but to usher in a new era of peace. He'd been fighting the Khadorans for years, and in his experience, peace was not a concept the northern nation of Khador regarded with much enthusiasm.

They had left Corvis a day ago and had followed the Black River north in a small fleet of ships filled with Cygnaran soldiers and dignitaries, but they'd now reached a portion of the river known to be plagued by gatorman attacks from the nearby

Bloodsmeath Marsh. The savage reptilian humanoids had a nasty habit of sinking ships passing through their territory. So, it had been decided while the rest of the Cygnaran envoy continued ahead by ship, Stryker and a small force of Storm Knights would escort the king by land. They only needed to march ten miles down the Great Northern Tradeway to reach the point where the Cygnaran fleet would pick them up, but it meant passing close to the Glimmerwood, a forest that lay near the domains of the enigmatic Iosans, xenophobic elves who took supreme umbrage at any humans entering their territory.

"I don't like this; we're too damned exposed, and too few in number," Stryker said to the muscular Storm Knight walking next to him. Captain Garvin Tews had removed his helmet, exposing his blunt, square-jawed features. He was pushing fifty but was still in top fighting condition, and the weight of his heavy Stormblade armor and the great voltaic storm glaive he carried didn't seem to bother him a bit.

"You already know our king thinks a smaller force will be less noticeable," Tews said.

"And what do you think of that, Captain?" Stryker said with a weary smile.

"Begging your pardon, sir, but I think King Julius should leave matters of strategy, especially where they concern his own safety, to those with more . . . experience," Tews said and chewed on his lip.

Stryker's smile widened. Tews had been a military man for the better part of thirty years. He was a knight, as all those in the Stormblades were, but he was also a soldier, a grunt at heart. "The scouts are overdue," Stryker said. He'd sent a squad of rangers ahead to see if the road offered any potential danger.

"Not by much," Tews replied with a shrug. "What's worrying you, Lord General?"

"Probably nothing, but we're nearing the Glimmerwood, and it's close to the road. We'd be hemmed in by it and the river to the west."

"Are you afraid of an ambush?" Tews asked.

"It's where *I'd* put it," Stryker said.

Tews rubbed his chin. "Now you've got me worried about it," he said. "But by who? Iosans?"

"There's worse than elves in that forest," Stryker said. He'd made his decision. He held up one armored fist. "Company, halt," he said, and the clatter of armor and weapons sounding behind him told him one hundred knights had followed his order immediately. He looked back down the ranks of knights to where two towering Ironclads stood looming over the humans there. One of them was his personal warjack, Ol' Rowdy. The other Ironclad was controlled by another warcaster, Captain Kara Sloan, who, along with eight members of the royal guard, were guarding the king. Julius rode on horseback nearby, towering over his knights. Stryker mentally reached out to Rowdy, and the warjack's mechanikal brain became a low buzzing in the back of his skull. Rowdy was irritated, anxious. He wanted a fight, but there was not one to be had. Stryker clamped down on the 'jack's emotions and calmed him.

"Lieutenant Archer," Stryker said to a nearby Storm Knight. "Inform the king I think it best he and Captain Sloan stay where they are while half our force scouts forward. Tell him it will delay us approximately three hours."

"Yes, sir," Lieutenant Archer said, hurrying away toward the center of their short column.

"What are you thinking, Coleman?" Tews said stepping close. Stryker had known the Stormblade captain for fifteen years; they'd fought and bled together on countless battlefields. That he used Stryker's first name didn't bother the lord general in the slightest. They were more than brothers in arms—they were friends.

"I can't put my finger on it," Stryker said, "but something doesn't feel right."

"You don't think the Khadorans would attack us on the eve of our peace treaty, do you?".

Stryker shook his head. "No, that would be foolish, and one thing Empress Vanar is *not* is foolish."

"Well, your hunches usually mean violence is on the horizon."

Tews set his helmet on his head and lifted his heavy storm glaive, a wide-blade two-handed sword empowered with galvanic energy. In the hands of a man like Tews, such a weapon could easily cut an armored man in half. "It's been awhile since we had a good scrap. And the king isn't half bad with a blade himself. Still, I hope he doesn't do anything rash if it comes to blood."

Stryker grimaced. "Sorry, Captain, but the king's mood, desires, and plans in general are not something he confides in me. I don't have his trust like I had Leto's."

It had been two years since the costly civil war that had seen Julius, the son of the infamous tyrant Vinter Raelthorne IV, take the throne of Cygnar. Julius' uncle, Leto, had abdicated to prevent further bloodshed, and a new era in Cygnar had begun, an era in which Stryker was more and more alienated from his new king.

Lieutenant Archer returned shortly. "Sir," she said, her face creased with worry.

"Spit it out," Tews said. "The Lord General isn't the type to shoot the messenger."

"The king will continue moving behind you but keep a healthy distance," she said. "He believes a three-hour delay would not be, uh, politically prudent."

"Hard to protect a man who won't listen to you," Stryker said, "but he is the king. Archer, can you command a warjack?"

She nodded. "I've had training in the basics."

"Good. Bring up the two Sentinels under Captain Sloan's command," he said, naming a type of light warjack armed with a stout shield and a high-speed chain gun. "I want them near the king. Rowdy will come forward with me."

"Yes, sir," she said and hurried to carry out her orders.

He reached out to Rowdy and urged the big warjack to join him at the head of the column. The Ironclad reached him quickly, venting a shrill blast of steam in greeting. Rowdy gripped his gigantic quake hammer in one metal fist and was opening and closing the other. The warjack sensed Stryker's anxiety through their connection.

"All right," Stryker said, turning to address the fifty or so Storm

Knights that made up the head of the column. "I want storm glaives powered up, and I want eyes on the tree line. Understood?" A chorus of "yes sir" responded. He pulled his own weapon, the mechanika great sword Quicksilver, from the magnetic clasps on the back of his armor and balanced it over one shoulder. "Then move out."

. . .

THE GLIMMERWOOD WAS A THICK tangle of gnarled oaks and elms, stretching far to the east. It was a wild place between the nations of Llael and Cygnar and the barren stretches of The Bloodstone Marches to the east. Tribes of trollkin still lived in these woods, and the proud warrior race had had a patchy history with Cygnar, but Stryker didn't expect an attack from them. Other, more feral creatures were said to dwell in the Glimmerwood, but Stryker's forces were too large in number to present a tempting target for a raiding band of Tharn. What, then, had him so unnerved? He couldn't shake the feeling he was missing something as they approached the edge of the woods.

The king and half his Storm Knights had extended the distance between them and Stryker's portion of the column, though they were still too close for Stryker's liking. If there was an attack, he wanted to take the brunt of it before the rest of his men arrived. He glanced behind him. The king stood in the middle of a tight group of Storm Knights. Julius wore similar armor, and its blue coloration would make him difficult for an enemy to pick out among his knights. The hilt of Julius' father's sword, Kingslayer, jutted over the young man's shoulder—he was a gifted swordsman, though far from being as ruthless and savage as his father, who had been singularly terrifying with a blade.

The road they were following, hard-packed earth that provided stable footing for both soldiers and warjacks, ran close to the Black River. It narrowed considerably against the encroaching presence of the Glimmerwood, as if the ancient forest were trying to devour the road.

Soon enough, they'd be forced into a narrow column, no more

than thirty feet between the river and the edge of the forest. All eyes were on the gloom amongst the trees, searching for movement. Stryker let his senses drift into Ol' Rowdy, giving himself a better vantage point from ten feet off the ground.

There was nothing . . . then a flash of white, and Stryker's muscles quickly tensed. What came next was no surprise, and he swiftly summoned his magic to cast a protective field of energy over himself and the Storm Knights nearest him. The sight of the runes forming around his body was more than enough to alert his men that battle was imminent, yet he shouted the order anyway. " Storm Knights, form ranks!"

There were fifty Storm Knights in the forward part of the column and another fifty farther back, guarding the king. The men around him quickly formed a line, their storm glaives projecting toward the trees, a deadly hedge crackling with voltaic energy. Stryker was at its center with Rowdy next to him, the big warjack pounding his hammer into his open fist, nearly quivering with excitement for what was coming.

"Steady!" Tews called out from where he stood near Stryker.

The forest suddenly came alive with white shadows and the telltale snap of crossbow strings hitting their prods, then a hail of bolts burst from the trees.

Stryker had expected the Storm Knights nearest him would be protected by his spell, but the bolts were neither slowed nor deflected by magic.

Out of the corner of his eye, he saw one of his knights fall forward. A crossbow bolts had found its mark. Whoever was attacking them was skilled enough to find the weak points in a Stormblade's armor.

"Fire!" Stryker shouted. His Storm Knights thumbed the firing studs on the hafts of their storm glaives, and bolts of electricity arced into the trees. They were firing blind, but Stryker still heard screams of pain from the forest.

The wooded area then disgorged dozens of white-armored warriors wielding wide slashing swords and carrying shields bearing the loop and cross icon of the Menofix, the holy symbol of the god Menoth. These were knights of the Protectorate, the theocratic nation east of Cygnar, which had recently expanded into northern Llael. Stryker had no time to consider their presence here as they slammed into his line of Storm Knights with a clatter of steel on steel.

Rage and disgust boiled up within him. He'd fought these zealots many times, and their blind and violent adherence to their religion had cost many lives.

He met a charging knight with Quicksilver, knocking askew the Protectorate warrior's sword thrust with his much-heavier blade, then riposting and bringing Quicksilver down in a powerful slashing arc. The heavy blade ripped through the enemy knight's breastplate, splitting him to the breastbone. The knight was dead on his feet, and Stryker shoved the body away.

He reached out to Rowdy and sent the warjack charging into the middle of the enemy, swinging his quake hammer in wide arcs. There was no deflecting such a blow, and Protectorate knights were smashed away, their armor crushed, their bodies broken.

Stryker glanced to both his left and right; his Storm Knights were not faring well. The Protectorate warriors were skilled, and their light quick blades were finding the gaps in Stormblade armor.

Tews was shouting and slashing with his storm glaive. He cut down a Protectorate knight then killed another charging at him with a blast of electricity.

Rowdy was taking damage, but so far it was light, and armored corpses were piling up around the big warjack's feet.

Stryker was about to move to Tews' position when two thin, curling plumes of smoke appeared above the tree line. That meant only one thing: warjacks. The Protectorate 'jacks burst from the forest some thirty yards from Stryker's position. They were smaller than Rowdy, their armor painted white and red, Menofixes prominent on their hulls. The two warjacks gripped long slashing blades in each fist and moved quickly and gracefully. Worse, they were not alone.

The man who emerged from the forest behind the warjacks wore little armor, and his massive upper torso was naked, exposing slabs of muscle and scar tissue. His face was obscured by a golden mask, and he carried a long, heavy flail in one hand, the bulk of its chain wrapped around his arm. Stryker knew him: he was Amon Ad-Raza, a warcaster like himself and one of the Protectorate's deadliest fighters.

The reason for the attack was painfully clear. Peace between Cygnar and Khador would mean either or both nations could turn their attention to a mutual foe: the Protectorate of Menoth. This would threaten the Protectorate's holdings in Llael. Cygnar had considered that the Protectorate might answer the treaty in some way, but an attack on the road, so close to the border of Cygnar and against the king himself, had been the least likely.

Stryker had listened to his instincts, which had led him safely though more danger than he could remember. Julius was not in the forward part of the column where Amon-Ad Raza had likely assumed he would be. The Protectorate warcaster had tipped his hand too early, and it gave Stryker a chance.

He looked back to where the king was positioned about fifty yards from Stryker's own position; the king's guards had formed a protective ring around him, storm glaives in a lethal wall. A surge of panic coursed through Stryker as Julius stepped away from the protection of his guards to engage a pair of Protectorate knights who had made it down the road to his position. Yet Stryker needn't have worried. The king's blade was a living thing, a striking serpent of blood and steel, and he moved Kingslayer with such speed that it seemed to weigh nothing at all. Julius checked a strike with his sword from the first knight, then cut the enemy down with a riposte so fast, Stryker didn't actually see it. One moment, the Protectorate knight was standing; the next, he was lying at the king's feet in two pieces. Julius killed the remaining knight with a lunging thrust, driving Kingslayer through the man's breastplate, his body, and then out his armored back. Julius pulled his blade free and calmly returned to the protection of his knights.

Stryker focused his attention back on his immediate surroundings, cut down another enemy knight charging at him, and summoned Rowdy to his position. He'd need the big Ironclad to handle the enemy warjacks. He felt Rowdy's eagerness and then the warjack's thundering footfalls as he raced toward Stryker.

Amon Ad-Raza had engaged the nearest Storm Knights, and his warjacks scythed through them in a flurry of steel and blood. Stryker charged forward, heedless of the enemy, cutting them down when they got in his way or letting Rowdy smash them aside.

Amon looked in his direction as Stryker approached, and bright yellow spell runes formed around the Protectorate warrior's heavy fist. Scorching heat surround Stryker as the spell took effect, and his power field flared as it tried to compensate. His warcaster armor ended up taking the brunt of it, and the heated steel scorched the skin on his arms and legs. He gritted his teeth through the pain and ran, summoning a spell of his own. Lightning shot forth from his outstretched hand, a fan of blue-white energy that lanced toward his foe. Amon was unencumbered by armor, and his training with the monastic Order of the Fist made him incredibly nimble. He leapt away from the lightning, avoiding the bolts with what looked like childish ease.

The Storm Knights behind Stryker were still battling the Protectorate knights, and those ahead were trying to fend off Amon's warjacks. Stryker ordered Rowdy at the enemy 'jacks while he pursued Amon. The thrilling sensation of the Ironclad's first blow with his quake hammer came through their connection, followed by Rowdy's satisfaction as the first Protectorate warjack's hull crumpled.

Stryker glanced down the road toward the rest of the Cygnaran forces and the king. Figures in blue armor were moving now in his direction. The king was among them; he would no doubt throw himself into battle beside his men. Stryker could not allow this, could not allow Amon Ad-Raza to get that close to Julius.

Stryker was twenty feet from his enemy when Amon snapped his flail forward, the heavy ball at the end coming at Stryker like a great golden meteor. He twisted to the side, and the weapon missed him by mere inches. Amon snapped his arm back. The weapon returned to him.

Stryker was now close enough to lash out with Quicksilver. He was fast and skilled, and he'd channeled his will into the blow, but Amon danced away. Quicksilver struck empty air.

Again, Amon's flail whipped toward him. This time Stryker attempted to knock it away with his weapon. He succeeded—partially. He smashed the head of the flail off line, but it still struck him a glancing blow and sent him staggering back, his breastplate dented above his abdomen.

Amon looked to where the rest of the Cygnaran forces were advancing up the road. He clearly realized his target was not where he'd initially thought. Stryker attempted to close again, and Amon sent his chain flail arcing in his direction. This time, Stryker stood his ground and held Quicksilver up in front of him. He sidestepped as the head of the flail sped toward him, and he slashed at the chain connecting it to Amon. The consecrated steel was too strong to cut, but the blow changed the direction of the flail's head so that it wrapped around Quicksilver. The force of it nearly tore the weapon from Stryker's grasp. But he had Amon's flail pinned, though the Protectorate warcaster would yank it free any second. Stryker depressed the firing stud on the base of Quicksilver's hilt, triggering its voltaic blast. Lightning arced up into the sky *and* along the flail's chain, its metal haft held in Amon's right hand.

Amon's body went rigid as the galvanic energy raced through his body. The effect would not be enough to kill the warcaster or even cause him lasting harm, but it gave Stryker the opening he needed. He shook free of Amon's flail and charged forward, leveling a wide, sweeping cut at his foe. Amon had recovered enough, but his reactions were slowed. He tried to spin away from Stryker's blade a fraction of a second too slowly. The tip of Quicksilver bit into Amon's side. Though Amon wore no armor, Stryker's blow encountered resistance as if he were. The strange ways of the Order of the Fist protected their bodies from harm. Still, the blade connected, cut flesh, and ribs snapped beneath its impact.

Amon stumbled away, jerking his flail behind him. Blood ran

down his side, but Stryker could not tell the extent of the injury. He took a moment to check on Rowdy. Through the warjack's eyes, he saw that both Protectorate 'jacks were down, destroyed by Rowdy and the concentrated attacks of the remaining Storm Knights.

Stryker turned back to Amon, ready for another attack, but the Protectorate warcaster inclined his head toward Stryker.

"Do not think this is over, Lord General," he said, his voice deep but still distant behind his mask. "You cannot stem the tide of those who follow the True Law, no matter what alliances you make."

Before Stryker could reply, Amon turned and sprinted back into the Glimmerwood, one hand clamped to his injured side. He disappeared into the tangled gloom of the forest in seconds. Amon had confirmed the reason behind the attack, as Stryker had suspected. Yet there was nothing he could do with the information now, and what remained of the Protectorate knights were falling back. He heard Tews giving the order to let them go.

Stryker drew in a deep breath and let his body relax, let the adrenaline rush leak out of him. Tews moved to join him.

"How bad?" Stryker said to the Stormblade captain.

Tews shook his head. "Hard to tell yet. At least five dead, ten more wounded. I assume the scouts we sent ahead are dead as well."

"Damn it," Stryker said under his breath. It was the price of command. Even victory cost you something.

The rest of the Cygnaran forces had reached them, led by Captain Kara Sloan. The warcaster was tall and thin, with short-blonde hair and a spray of freckles across her nose. She carried a mechanika long rifle in both hands. Stryker had fought alongside Kara many times, and he knew she could be relied on to wreak havoc with her weapon.

"Lord General," Kara said, "the king is safe. I advised he stay behind."

"Thank you, Captain Sloan," he said. "I think we're done here. Bring more men up to see to the dead and wounded."

"Was that Amon Ad-Raza?" she said, her eyes wide.

Stryker nodded. "I'm as surprised as you are."

"What in Morrow's name was he doing here?"

Stryker offered her a tired smile. "Failing to kill our king."

— 3 —

Merywyn, Khadoran Occupied Llael

STRYKER AGAIN WALKED at the head of a procession of Storm Knights, Tews beside him, his broad face grim.

"By Morrow, this feels wrong," Tews said.

Stryker again walked at the head of a procession of Storm Knights, Tews beside him, his broad face grim.

"By Morrow, this feels wrong," Tews said.

Stryker said nothing, but he could hardly argue with that. He was leading his Storm Knights not into battle but through a huge courtyard toward one of the grandest building in all of the Iron Kingdoms. The Great Cathedral of Ascendant Rowan in Merywyn beggared just about every other Morrowan structure in the world, save for the Archcourt Cathedral in Caspia, the seat of Morrowan power.

Arrayed before the mighty cathedral and flanking the white stone path that led to its entrance were two full regiments of soldiers: one Cygnaran, one Khadoran. It was a shocking contrast of red and blue before the pristine white of the chapel. Storm Knights, sword knights, and three warcasters stood at attention on the Cygnaran side. Captain Sloan had traveled with Stryker; the third warcaster, Captain Jeremiah Kraye, and a contingent of sword knights had come from Point Bourne to join them in Merywyn. Stryker couldn't help but think that had Kraye been with them on the road, they might have lost fewer men to the Protectorate ambush. In addition, four warjacks—two Ironclads and two Sentinels—stood front and center before the array of Cygnaran troops. The warjacks' cortexes were a buzzing presence in the back of Stryker's skull, one stronger than all the others. He smiled as Ol' Rowdy turned his head toward him. Stryker's trusted, battle-scarred warjack vented steam in a shrill whistle in greeting, causing the 'jack marshal next to the Ironclad to jump in surprise.

Calm down, old friend, Stryker thought at the warjack. Rowdy's aggression and instinct to seek battle were made stronger by the trouble they'd encountered on their way to Merywyn. Stryker couldn't blame the warjack.

Across from the Cygnarans, the Khadorans had assembled their own display of martial strength. Rows of Man-O-War shocktroopers, stout soldiers encased in huge suits of steam-powered armor, stood next to ranks of the more conventionally armored Iron Fangs, their broad shields resting against the ground, pikes planted, points reaching up to the heavens in a thicket of spikes. There were two Khadoran warcasters Stryker recognized among the troops. First was Forward Kommander Sorscha Kratikoff, a warrior as cold and merciless on the battlefield as any he'd faced, tall and chilling like an icicle, one given form and murderous function. Also among the Khadorans was Kommander Strakhov, square-jawed and dark haired, he was a rugged battle-scarred soldier loved by his nation and hated by its enemies. Stryker had faced both in battle many times. And, of course, there were Khadoran warjacks, hulking monstrosities of steel and iron that always appeared primitive to Stryker, but he'd faced them in battle, and their effectiveness was without question.

Ahead of Stryker and Tews walked two men, each stately and regal. The first was the former king of Cygnar, Leto Raelthorne, who had recently abdicated the throne to his nephew and the son of his brother, the tyrant Vinter Raelthorne. At nineteen, Julius Raelthorne resembled his father more than his uncle. Tall and lean with black hair and sharp square features, the young king moved with a warrior's grace and confidence. There was a predatory coldness to the young king that made Stryker repress a shudder. *Just like his father.*

Stryker was still adjusting to the concept of the son of Vinter Raelthorne, a tyrant he had helped remove from the throne over fifteen years ago, a man he had helped defeat in Vinter's recent bid to return to Cygnar as the rightful king. Leto had abdicated to avoid a protracted civil war that would have cost Cygnar dearly, and Stryker could understand his former king's reasoning. But there was so much of Vinter in Julius, and unlike his relationship with Leto, Stryker did not have the young king's trust.

"Just grit your teeth, Captain," Stryker said, finally remarking on Tews' comment. "It'll be over soon enough, and then we can go home."

"Yes, sir." Tews was staring at the Khadoran troops to his left, and if Stryker knew his friend's mind as he thought he did, Tews was likely trying to figure out how many Khadorans he could kill if things went sour.

There was little chance of violence, however. They were here at the invitation of Empress Ayn Vanar herself to sign a treaty that would end the fighting between their two nations. After a costly civil war and with a new king on the throne, Cygnar needed time to heal, and an end to the decade-long war with Khador would give them that time.

On the grand marble steps of the Cathedral awaited their host, Empress Ayn Vanar, a stately, raven-haired woman with ivory skin and dark eyes. She seemed small, even fragile, but there was steel in her blood, and she had ruled the fractious nation of Khador with an iron fist for over a decade. Beside her was a man Stryker recognized at once. Darkly handsome and clad in baroque crimson armor, Great Prince Vladimir Tzepesci was a powerful noble who ruled a vast stretch of Khador and whose lineage could be trace to the very founding of his nation. Vladimir was no soft noble, however; like Stryker, he was a warcaster. He was also a brilliant and ruthless military leader. Stryker had crossed swords with Vlad on more than one occasion, and the Khadoran was both skilled and devious. His presence here did little to quiet Stryker's doubts.

"Empress Ayn Vanar," Julius said as the small procession of Cygnarans stopped at the foot of the stairs. He inclined his head but did not bow; he was, after all, speaking to an equal. "Thank you for agreeing to meet us here at the Cathedral. It is a magnificent building, somehow untouched by all the . . . strife this city has seen of late."

The empress smiled, though it did not reach her eyes. "Of course, King Julius. It was only fitting we meet in a place where you would be most comfortable, since you have graciously made the long trek to our city."

"Their city?" Tews whispered.

Stryker threw the captain a reproachful look, but he'd had the same reaction to the empress' statement. The Khadorans had seized Merywyn when they invaded Llael, and they now occupied a large portion of that nation. Cygnar was allies with Llael and had aided the Llaelese Resistance in fighting the invaders. That was all over now—at least Cygnar's hand in it-though the Resistance was very unlikely to recognize the treaty his king was about to sign.

"Your Majesty, may I present to you Great Prince Vladimir Tzepesci," Empress Vanar said and placed her hand lightly on Vlad's armored shoulder.

Julius dipped his head to the warcaster. "Prince Tzepesci, I have heard much about you," he said. "You have been a mighty foe to Cygnar, and I now look forward to counting you among our allies."

"You honor me, Your Majesty," Vlad said, bowing. "I, too, am eager to call you friend and ally." His accent was more noticeable than the queen's, the consonants sharper, certain words more pronounced.

Stryker had been present for many formal negotiations, and he knew the dance of feigned pleasantries well enough, but it still grated on him to hear the king speak so kindly to a man who had likely slaughtered hundreds if not thousands of Cygnaran soldiers.

"I see Lord General Stryker has accompanied you, Your Majesty," Vlad said, looking over Julius' shoulder.

Julius glanced back at Stryker and his honor guard of Stormblades. "Of course, the lord general is a valued member of my council."

"I have no doubt," Vlad said. "It is good to see you again, Lord General, under . . . more pleasant circumstances."

Stryker nodded. "And you, Prince Tzepesci. Our last meeting was far less . . . agreeable than this one."

There was a tension in the air. Men who had once called each other bitter enemies could not put aside their differences so easily, and they would resort to the weapons available to them: in this case, barbed words and forced pleasantries.

"I understand you encountered some trouble on the road," Vlad said.

"We were attacked, yes. An assassination attempt on our king by the Protectorate of Menoth." Stryker was surprised Vlad already knew about the attack.

"They fear the strength we both will gain from our alliance," the queen said. Anger flashed across her face. "But to attack a sovereign in such a fashion is unthinkable and beneath even the zealots of the Protectorate." Stryker was impressed at the Empress' acting skills. Her sincerity would have fooled many, but not Stryker. He wondered how angry she'd be if Amon Ad-Raza had succeeded. She herself had very recently attempted to kill Leto Of course, all that had been forgiven in the name of political expedience.

"I was well protected, Your Majesty," Julius said. The king had spoken little about the attack and hardly seemed troubled by it. "The assassins were no match for Lord General Stryker and his Storm Knights."

"Of course," Vlad said. "The lord general's battle prowess is well known." The tension returned, and before Stryker could respond to Vlad, High Chancellor Leto cut it cleanly.

"Your Majesty," the former king said, "we have much to do. Perhaps we should begin."

Julius looked back at his uncle and smiled. Something flashed across his face, a minute tightening of his lips, a barely perceptible creasing of his brow. Irritation? Stryker wondered. Then it passed, and the young king said, "Of course, Uncle. This is a momentous occasion, and I am eager to begin."

"Please, follow me, Your Majesty," Empress Vanar said. The grand doors of the Cathedral opened behind her, revealing a vestibule with white stone walls, each wall bearing the symbol of Morrow worked in gold into the stone. Beyond lay the chapel proper.

The empress and Vlad entered the cathedral, and Julius and Leto followed.

"Honor guard, fall in," Stryker said and motioned the dozen Stormblades that made up the king's honor guard to follow him.

The interior of the cathedral was breathtaking, its soaring majesty a fitting tribute to Morrow and the ascendant to whom it was dedicated, one of the eleven mortals raised up by Morrow to serve him personally.

The empress' own honor guard was waiting in the nave, a dozen Iron Fangs in red armor chased with gold standing in front of the grand altar. A marble pedestal had been placed in the center of the nave, and a single sheet of parchment lay atop it. This was the treaty Julius and the Empress would sign.

The nave was filled with people, mostly nobles drawn from both nations, and Stryker recognized men and women from the Cygnaran Royal Assembly as well as more prominent figures, such as Duke Kielon Ebonhart, one of the first to support Julius Raelthorne as he took the throne. It was quiet in the cathedral, the pregnant hush that often preceded great events.

Of course, all the details of the treaty had been worked out weeks ago by the inner councils of both rulers. The signing was simply a spectacle for the masses, a way for Julius to highlight the beginning of his rule and find favor among his subjects for ending the war. Stryker had had little to do with the terms of the treaty; the new king rarely called on him, and Stryker's presence on the inner council was no more than token. The thought of this monumental turnabout, just one of many he had endured over the last three years, sent pangs of doubt through him. He had been King Leto's lord general and an integral part of the Cygnaran war effort. The former king had often sought his advice and counsel had often, but now it seemed he was little more than a figurehead.

He had been briefed on the terms of the treaty. Peace between the two nations rested largely on Cygnar recognizing Khador's claim on the parts of Llael it had seized and then the restoration of lucrative trade lines to ease Khador's strained economy and the promise of future trade endeavors, among them unmolested passage to the exotic land of Zu. Julius had argued for and had successfully inserted a proviso in the contract that stated if a true heir to the throne of Llael were to come forward, Khador's claim would be nullified, and they would remove their troops. Of course, there was little danger of that. None of the progeny of Llael's last monarch, King Rynnard, had been seen for over a decade, and all were assumed dead. Julius' addendum to the treaty was simply to show the Llaelese people—Cygnar's allies—that they hadn't been completely abandoned. Stryker struggled to understand how the people of Llael could not feel betrayed by Cygnar's new monarch.

The treaty's others provisions included Khador removing troops from Cygnaran lands seized in battle, such as the Thornwood Forest, and the reestablishments of valuable trade routes on the Black River, a major waterway that ran through Cygnar and into Khador-occupied Llael.

It all seemed too easy to Stryker. Of course, they all wanted an end to the war. Khador and Cygnar had been fighting off and on for years, and some of the bloodiest battles had been fought in the neighboring nation of Llael, beginning when Khador invaded. Stryker had personally led thousands of men and spilled more blood in Llael than he cared to remember in an attempt to repel the Khadorans. He had also witnessed firsthand their brutal subjugation of the Llaelese. So, to let them simply keep their war prize galled him. The return of a forest currently filled with Cryxian horrors and a few lucrative trade arrangements hardly seemed a fair exchange.

He had raised his concerns with the king but had been shouted down by others on the inner council, many of whom had ancestral lands in areas of the Thornwood seized by Khador. Whether this had been a factor in their decisions made no matter; they had far more influence with Julius Raelthorne than Stryker did.

He pushed these thoughts from his mind as they neared the pedestal. He raised a hand, and the Storm Knights behind him spread out, matching the positions of their Iron Fang counterparts.

The empress waited at the table, Vlad a step behind her. Julius approached, and Leto stood back, matching Vlad's position. There was a ceremony to these proceedings, part of the spectacle, and it all seemed overwhelmingly hollow to Stryker.

The rulers of the two most powerful nations in the Iron Kingdoms looked at one another. The fates of millions rested on the strokes of their pens.

There were two silver inkwells next to the treaty as well as a pair of white quill pens. Julius picked up his quill first and waited for the empress to do the same.

Empress Vanar picked up her quill, and the two rulers dipped them in the inkwells.

"To peace, friendship, and a lasting alliance," Julius said as he scrawled his name across the bottom of the treaty. It was not lost on Stryker that the empress had waited for the young king to sign first.

"May Cygnar and Khador be as brothers from this day forward," the empress said and signed her name below Julius'.

The cathedral erupted in a round of applause and a few scattered cheers. Stryker did not add his own voice to the rising din; he couldn't help but wonder if disaster was more often heralded by willing applause than the pained cries of the oppressed.

— 4 —

Five Fingers, Ord

ASHETH MAGNUS SAT AT A LOW TABLE, resting the heavy bulk of his prosthetic mechanika arm across it. Around him in the squalid but spacious riverside room was a collection of hard-looking men, mercenaries all, armed and ready to fight and kill at his command. The worst of these men—or the best, depending on how you looked at it—waited in a small adjoining room across from Magnus' table.

"What's taking him so long?" A gaunt, bird-like Ordsman named Xavius Marlowe asked from where he stood next to the room's only window, likely to escape the reek of Magnus' warcaster armor. Magnus had turned the boiler down to its lowest setting, but the trickle of smoke coming from the stack on his back had filled the room with a smoky haze. Magnus smiled; the smell from the dockside street below couldn't be much better.

"Harrow knows his business," Magnus said. "Let him work."

Xavius lips curled in irritation, and he turned back to the

window. He was a former member of the Order of the Golden Crucible, a well-respected group of alchemists and arcanists. But he had fled his order, largely due to his obsession with poisons and explosives and his willingness to test them on the townsfolk in the Ordic city of Corbhen. He was irritating, erratic, and very, very skilled, so Magnus tolerated him. In fact, most of the men in this room were deeply flawed and dangerous, the kind of men that followed strength and had no place for compassion or even real loyalty.

The door across from Magnus opened, and Sebastian Harrow emerged. The other mercs in the room were dangerous, but Harrow was the only real killer among them. He was gaunt and ugly, his face a network of scars from which shone two ice-blue eyes. He wore a heavy pistol holstered on one hip and a saber on the other. He was wiping his hands with a bit of cloth; the cloth came away stained crimson.

"I'll give those Section Three bastards credit; they're tough," he said.

"What did he give you?" Magnus asked.

Harrow smiled, showing a mouthful of straight white teeth, a predator's gape. "The prince is dead and they dumped his body in a 'jack forge."

Magnus grimaced. Julius had hoped to find the Llaelese heir alive and keep him that way, if he was amenable to the young king's plans. "Does he know about the girl?"

Harrow shrugged. "Couldn't get that out of him. And believe me, I tried."

The man closest to Harrow, a former Steelhead named Silus, shuddered. They'd all seen Harrow interrogate a prisoner, and his methods were brutally effective.

"Do you think the prince knew about her?" Silus asked. "She was his cousin, right?"

"Hard to say," Magnus said. "The royal family has been so fractured. Either way, he likely thought her dead along with the rest of his kin."

"Then I say we operate under the assumption that *he* did know and that he told the Khadorans before they killed him," Harrow said.

Magnus considered that for a moment. It made sense. The Cygnaran head of the CRS, Scout General Bolden Rebald, had assured him no one in the Khadoran government knew about the princess. What he didn't and couldn't know was if someone outside of Khador's intelligence agency—someone *not* looking for a Llaelese heir—knew about her. The most likely person to know would be someone in her family: her cousin Lyan di la Martyn, recently slain by Khadoran operatives. Since Magnus couldn't speak to Lyan, he had to agree with Harrow and assume the dead man had given the Khadorans information about Princess Kaetlyn di la Martyn, who now appeared to be the sole living heir to the throne of Llael.

Magnus glanced around the room. "We have to assume the Khadorans know about Katelyn, but we have to make sure that information doesn't leave this city." They still had a problem, though, he realized. Rebald had said there were six Section Three operatives. They'd captured one, but where were the others?

"I do have *some* good news," Harrow said, smiling. "He told me where the others are holed up. They spooked when we grabbed Ivan here." He cocked a thumb back toward the darkened room from which he'd just come. "They're likely looking for a ship to get them out."

"Then we don't have any time to waste," Magnus said. He let his consciousness drift down into the empty warehouse below them, to the slumbering cortex of the light warjack they'd brought with them. It was one of Magnus' own designs, cobbled together from pieces of other warjacks, though no less deadly for its composite construction. He could sense a small spark within the cold darkness of its mind, a spark he would soon fan into a roaring flame.

"Is this a capture or a kill mission?" Silus asked. He didn't look like either would bother him much.

"We're tying up loose ends," Magnus said and pulled the short scattergun from its holster at his hip. He checked the load and then put it away. He narrowed his eyes at Silus. "So what do you think?"

"A kill mission then," Harrow said. "You'll get no complaints out of me. Simpler that way. What about our guest?"

Magnus glanced over the merc's shoulder at the room behind him. A slight whimper or maybe a gasp drifted out from the darkness.

"Loose end," he said.

Harrow grinned.

"Make it quick, Harrow," Magnus said, then added, "and painless."

Harrow drew his saber. The blade made a menacing hiss as it scraped the metal throat of the scabbard. "He won't feel a thing."

The merc walked into the room behind him. After a moment of grim silence, Magnus heard a sudden outburst of Khadoran in a wavering, terrified voice. He understood the language: the man was pleading for his life.

The soft hum of a blade slicing the air cut short the Khadoran's pleading. Magnus heard a solid thump, as if someone had dropped something heavy onto the floor. Seconds later, Harrow emerged again, this time wiping blood from his saber.

"Tied it up in a nice little bow," he said.

...

THE SHIP WAS CALLED *The Sea Raven*, and it was an old Ordic trader that sat low in the water. It was moored in the Captain's Prow District of Captain's Island, which catered to merchant vessels. Magnus was pleased to see it was the only ship in its berth—they would have the isolation they needed. That was not to say they were alone; you were never alone on Five Fingers. Even in the dead of night on a pier at the ass-end of Captain's Island, there were people going about their business. Of course, that business, like Magnus' own, was the kind best done in the dark anyway. None of the few figures they passed let their eyes linger long on the four armored men and the looming form of the Renegade, its upper half cloaked in a sheet of burlap to hide that it wasn't a simple laborjack. Its shredder saw jutted from beneath the shroud, and this would occasionally whir to life as the warjack's impatience grew. It *wanted* to fight. Magnus clamped down on these urges; it wouldn't help their mission if the Renegade sawed a passerby in half.

"Why this ship?" Xavius asked as they approached *The Sea Raven*. The former alchemist wore a brace of alchemical grenades around his chest, and everyone was giving him a wide berth because of it.

"It's a small merchant ship," Magnus said. "Not the kind of thing anyone would look for."

They were coming at it from between two big warehouses, hidden from the lookouts—likely hired guns—the Khadoran spies had on deck. It wasn't as if they could simply call in military support; they were a kill squad, intentionally cut off from any military backup to promote plausible deniability. They were cornered, and it would only make them more dangerous.

The sailors aboard *The Sea Raven* were preparing to cast off. Likely the remaining Section Three operatives had decided their wayward member was not returning and it was time to flee without him.

They were still thirty yards from the ship when they stopped in the shadows between buildings. "My guess is they'll be in the hold," Harrow said. "Are we fighting our way through all these men to get there?"

Magnus smirked. "No, we're taking a more direct route." He turned to Silus, who was carrying a long rifle, hidden under a heavy cloak. "I want you and Harrow to keep the men on deck occupied while Xavius and I make a hole."

Harrows eyes widened, and then he grinned. He had some idea of what Magnus had planned. "That's gonna make a lot of noise, and the watch, even in Five Fingers, is likely to notice."

"Then we'll be quick," Magnus said.

Harrow nodded. "You ready, Silus?"

The former Steelhead put his rifle to his shoulder. "There's two on deck that are obviously gunmen," he said. "See 'em?"

"I do," Harrow said and drew his heavy repeating pistol. "I've got the one near the forecastle. You take the one near the port gunwale."

"Xavius, you're with me," Magnus said and summoned his magic. He turned away from the ship so his body would shield the bright circle of runes forming around his left hand. The runes winked out, and the Renegade became insubstantial, its outline blurring. That, the dark, and Magnus and Xavius' natural abilities to conceal themselves would make them hard to spot or shoot.

"Go," Magnus said, and he and Xavius sprinted from between the buildings. Magnus urged the Renegade to follow, and it cast aside its tarp and followed eagerly.

They were halfway to the ship when they were spotted, and cries from the deck of *The Sea Raven* rang out, followed by a pair of gunshots from behind Magnus. Two of the men above, both aiming rifles at the Renegade, jerked and crumpled to the deck.

Magnus and Xavius ran toward the pier, crossing the remaining distance in a few seconds. More shots rang out, but Magnus couldn't tell if they were coming from the ship or from his own men. They reached the side of *The Sea Raven*, a wall of slatted wood, and Magnus urged the Renegade closer. A bullet ricocheted off its hull and struck the power field Magnus' warcaster armor generated. The invisible wall of energy flared as it slowed the bullet, rendering its impact against his breastplate harmless.

"Xavius, get down," Magnus said, squatting on the pier, his head down. The Ordsman did the same, and Magnus ordered the Renegade to use its most potent weapon, the obliterator rocket attached to its left arm. A surge of glee flowed back through his link with the machine, and he heard the deep whine of the rocket launcher priming to fire. A bullet hit Magnus' power field, throwing sparks, and the slug bounced off the iron plating across his back harmlessly, robbed of its kinetic energy.

The obliterator rocket was ready, and Magnus let himself see through the Renegade's eyes, choosing the spot on *The Sea Raven*'s hull.

Fire.

The rocket went off with a thunderous roar and a bright yellow flash. A burst of white-hot energy struck *The Sea Raven* and blasted a hole nearly six feet in diameter into her side.

Magnus surged to his feet, pulling Xavius up next to him. "Grenades!"

The alchemist looked stunned, but it quickly faded. He plucked a pair of metal cylinders from the bandolier across his chest, thumbed their clockwork triggers, and tossed them into the hole the Renegade had made.

Magnus caught movement within the belly of the ship just as both grenades went off, double blasts of noise and light. More gunshots rang out from behind him and overhead. Magnus ignored them. He leaped from the pier and into the hole in the side of the ship.

He landed in an abattoir. Bodies and pieces of bodies were scattered across the hold, and the walls had been painted a garish crimson. He saw two of the Section Three operatives immediately, or what was left of them.

Two more.

The hold was low ceilinged, roughly twenty feet wide and thirty feet long. Stairs leading up to the deck stood at the far end. It was dark and smoky, but movement near the stairs drew his attention.

Magnus drew his sword, the mechanika blade he'd named Foecleaver, and the rune plate providing its arcane power filled the hold with an eerie blue glow. The figures near the stairs became clearer: three men in dark clothing. All were still reeling from the concussive blast of the grenades. He couldn't give them time to recover. Magnus moved away from the hole in the side of *The Sea Raven* and summoned the Renegade. The leap from the pier into the ship was dangerous; if the Renegade missed and fell into the bay, its boiler would be doused and it would sink straight to the bottom.

The Renegade leaped, guided by Magnus' will, and landed inside the hold of the ship hard enough to make the boat rock. Its saw whirred to life, a frantic metallic scream that heralded destruction.

Gunfire erupted from the other side of the hold, and bullets struck the hull of the Renegade, igniting a surge of rage within it. Then the hold lit up with fell blue light and the telltale sign of magic, as runes formed around the outstretched hand of one of the men, who had stepped behind his compatriots. Magnus could see the spellcaster clearly now: tall, sharp-featured, with thinning black hair. He held a heavy single-bitted war axe in one hand. But this man was not merely a Section Three operative. He was something much more dangerous than his simplest title: he was also a Greylord, one of the infamous Khadoran ice sorcerers and seekers of ancient magic.

The spell went off before Magnus could get out of the way, and a blast of chilling frost arced across the hold. Most of it struck the Renegade, and Magnus sensed the damage to some of its internal systems as they seized up beneath the icy spell.

His power field and armor protected him from the worst of it, but he clenched his teeth in agony as the cold sent what felt like daggers of ice into his exposed flesh.

"Go," Magnus said through clenched teeth, ordering the damaged Renegade forward. It barreled through the hold, its saw howling in the gloom. Magnus pulled his blunderbuss and aimed at one of the men trying to climb the stairs to the upper deck. He pulled the trigger and poured his will and magic into the shots, guiding the heavy slugs' trajectories. The man, likely one of the Section Three operatives, took the bullets in the back and toppled over backward.

The Renegade had reached the other side of the hold. Its saw licked out, ripping through one man's midsection and out his back, spraying the walls with fresh blood. The Greylord stepped back, and another spell formed around his right hand as the Renegade yanked its weapon free and turned toward him.

Ice and rime suddenly appeared on the hull and limbs of the Renegade, and it stopped moving, held immobile in a thin cage of ice.

Magnus charged, flinging his blunderbuss away and taking a two-handed grip on Foecleaver. The Greylord brought his axe up.

Blue runes flashed across the weapon's blade as Magnus brought Foecleaver down in a powerful cut.

The Greylord was a skilled fighter. He managed to turn Magnus' sword aside, but the force of the blow staggered him back against the wall of the hold. He recovered instantly and launched himself forward, winging the axe in a wide swiping cut.

He was faster than Magnus had anticipated—he couldn't get Foecleaver down in time to intercept the blow. The axe, enchanted with powerful runes, cut through Magnus' power field in a shower of sparks and into his breastplate and the flesh beneath. He gasped as the icy metal cut his skin, but the axe had become lodged in his armor. And then the Greylord made a crucial mistake.

He tried to pull it free.

The split second of effort left him with no defenses, and Magnus swept Foecleaver through the Greylord's neck. His head came away from his body in a gout of blood, and his corpse toppled backward to join the others.

Magnus wrenched the axe free from his body, and a stream of blood ran down his armor. He grimaced, not with the pain of his wound, but at the fact Bolden Rebald, Scout General of Cygnar, had not told him the Section Three operatives were working with a Greylord. Maybe he hadn't known—but maybe he had.

Xavius had come through the hole now. The Ordsman wasn't much use in a standup fight. He had a sheaf of papers in one hand and was looking from them to the corpses on the ground. Rebald had provided them with sketches of the Section Three operatives' faces so they could be easily identified.

"Bloody hell, this one doesn't have any face left," he said. "I think it's one of the red bastards. This one definitely." He pointed to a corpse missing both arms and one leg, though its face was perfectly intact.

"Come here and look at these two," Magnus said. "Quickly." He turned his attention to the Renegade as Xavius moved to join him. He channeled more of his magic through the machine's cortex, breaking the spell that held it in place. Anger, hot and fierce, flowed back through his connection with the warjack. It had been cheated out of a kill.

"Yes, these are the remaining two," Xavius said. "Who's this one?" he pointed at the headless Greylord.

"A complication," Magnus said and grunted in pain. The wound might be a bit deeper than he thought. Gunfire was still echoing outside the hold. "We're done here. Let's go before Harrow kills the whole damn crew."

— 5 —

Caspia, Cygnar

THE INNER COUNCIL CHAMBER of Julius Raelthorne, first of his name, suited the young king. His father, Vinter Raelthorne, had rarely used the room, preferring to hold council meetings in the throne room in Castle Raelthorne. Stryker had witnessed many of them as a member of the royal guard almost fifteen years ago. Vinter's son, however, preferred a less grand meeting place. The chamber was behind the throne room and was once reserved for private meetings with important dignitaries. It was small, and the u-shaped table of polished iron-wood took up most of the space. The walls were painted the royal blue of Cygnar and decorated with portraits of the various kings who had ruled the nation. Stryker noted Vinter's portrait had recently been returned to its place on the wall.

The table was large enough to accommodate all the members of the council, of which Stryker was a member. Though his inclusion by the king was allowed reluctantly at best. Most of the men who made up Julius' closest advisors had either pledged their support to the young king during the recent civil war or, in the case of Orin Midwinter, were exiled criminals, once loyal to his father, whom he had pardoned. Stryker grimaced as he stared across the table to where Midwinter sat—Midwinter was to the right of High Chancellor Leto, who in turn was closest to Julius in the center of the U. Once a senior inquisitor under Vinter Raelthorne, Midwinter had been forced to keep a very low profile when his former liege was ousted from the throne. He'd supported Vinter and then Julius in exile, and the young king had pardoned him when he'd taken the throne, granting Midwinter the title of Arcane Advisor. The man was an accomplished wizard, but the rumors about his activities during and after Vinter's reign were disturbing, to say the least.

To the left of the king was Scout General Bolden Rebald, a master spy and the man in charge of the Cygnaran Reconnaissance Service. The next man at the table was Warmaster General Kielon Ebonhart, a powerful duke and a man Stryker knew well. Stryker had trained under Duke Ebonhart over a decade ago when the man had been head of the Stormblades. Ebonhart had been one of the more prominent nobles to support Julius in the civil war.

The remaining two men on the council, seated on the arms of the U, were the Navarch Galten Sparholm III, head of the navy, and Lassiter Polk, a master mechanik and the head of the Cygnaran Armory. Stryker had had little association with either man, but he knew them by their reputations, and they were both capable.

Then there was Stryker himself, seated as far from the king as possible. He was a Lord General in the Cygnaran Army, his rank second only to the Warmaster Kielon Ebonhart. He attended every council meeting, though the king rarely called on him for advice. Julius listened primarily to his uncle Leto on matters of state, to his warmaster on matters military, and, Orin Midwinter on nearly everything else. Since the battle at Fharin, Julius seemed to have put considerable trust in the former inquisitor's hands. Perhaps it was the connection to his father that drew Julius to

Orin. Stryker didn't understand why the king would place so much faith in someone who had been part of an organization so universally maligned.

Stryker was an outsider, a stranger whose opinion was nether sought nor well regarded. His true place was on the battlefield, leading soldiers and warjacks. That he was on the council at all likely had to do with Leto. The former king and he had been close, and it pained Stryker to see someone else on the throne, no matter how legitimate the young man's claim.

"Your Majesty," Leto said, his voice pulling Stryker back into the conversation, "we have received a copy of the signed treaty from Khador's envoys, and it has been officially entered into the record." The former king smiled. "We are at peace."

"Hear, hear!" Warmaster Ebonhart cried, and applause filled the chamber. Stryker reluctantly added to it.

"But there are many matters that still require your attention, of course, Your Majesty," Midwinter said after the clapping subsided.

"Without doubt, Midwinter," Julius said. "But there is a pressing matter we must discuss first. Something I have kept from you all for some time out of necessity, and you will soon understand why. Scout General Rebald will inform you of the details." The king nodded at the Scout General.

Rebald cleared his throat and sat up straighter in his chair. A strange expression passed across the spymaster's face. He looked nervous. Stryker had worked closely with the man for years, and he'd never seen the Scout General so much as ruffled. It was an odd fit on a man who had pulled the strings of a vast web of spies and assassins for years.

"Yes, Your Majesty," Rebald said as he stood. "I won't keep you in suspense. An heir to the throne of Llael has been found."

Stunned silence.

Stryker looked at the faces of each council member. There were wide eyes and ashen faces all around. He too was shocked. An heir to the throne of Llael had major repercussions. For one, it nullified Khador's claims in the country per the treaty they had just signed—assuming Khador accepted the claim.

Stryker found his voice first. "Who is this person?"

"Her name is Kaetlyn di la Martyn," Rebald said. "Her mother was one of King Rynnard's mistresses, a woman of minor noble birth."

"How long have you known about this, Rebald?" Leto asked. The former king's face was pinched with irritation.

Rebald glanced at Julius, his eyes darting, tense. Again, Stryker was struck by the man's lack of composure. It was completely out of character for him.

"The Scout General located the girl shortly after I took the throne," Julius said.

Two years! Stryker thought. They'd been sitting on this monumental secret for two years, and they'd maneuvered Khador into signing a treaty that would nullify their claims to Llael. It was devious and brilliant...and incredibly dangerous. The empress was too smart not to smell the sour stench of political maneuvering here, and her reaction once the heiress was revealed could throw both nations back into war.

"Rebald had discovered the heiress in Ord," Julius continued, "and he informed me of his discovery right away, seeing the potential leverage it might grant us some day."

"Julius, this is a dangerous and foolish game you have played," Leto said. The High Chancellor had obviously been kept in the dark along with the rest of the council.

Julius' eyes narrowed, and anger flashed across his face. Stryker saw Vinter's wrath behind his son's eyes. "You forget yourself, Uncle," Julius said. "You no longer speak with a king's voice."

Leto looked away. "My apologies, Your Majesty," he said, his voice slow and measured. "But as your High Chancellor, I cannot properly serve you if you keep such things from me."

Julius nodded. "I agree, Uncle, and I promise you this is an isolated incident."

"So, we are going to set this girl on the throne of Llael then?" Stryker asked. "Khador will not acknowledge her claim as legitimate."

Leto turned to Stryker. "Lord General," he said, "the treaty they signed is legitimate, as is the girl's claim to the throne. They will be obliged to honor it or violate the treaty."

"Then you will invite them to war?" Duke Ebonhart said, putting voice to Stryker's next question. "My apologies, Your Majesty, but we have just attained peace. Why throw it away?"

"I understand your reticence, Warmaster Ebonhart," Julius said. "And I would not embark on this path if it did not serve to make Cygnar stronger."

"How will another war make Cygnar stronger, Your Majesty?" Stryker asked. It seemed ludicrous, but if Rebald and Midwinter were involved, there was an angle here, an advantage to be gained.

Julius turned to Stryker deliberately, fixing him with his dark gaze. For a man so young and so unaccustomed to rule, there was an undeniable strength to the king. It was the same steel his father had had. Stryker hoped for the sake of Cygnar it was better tempered.

"I will marry her," Julius said.

"And add Cygnar's claim to the heiress'," Rebald said. "Julius and his sons and daughters would rule both nations."

It was an aggressive move, one the king's uncle would not have taken or approved of, but if successful, it would substantially increase the size of Julius' kingdom and add what military might remain in Llael to Cygnar. They would become the greatest nation in the Iron Kingdoms, controlling more rich arable land and resources than any other.

"What of the Resistance?" Leto said. "They may have their own ideas about what do with this heir."

"If they wish to continue to enjoy the military support of Cygnar against Khador, they will follow where we lead." Julius chuckled. "I hardly expect them to seek aid from the Khadorans."

It was a cold stance to take toward the beleaguered Resistance and its leaders. Stryker had fought alongside Llaelese troops and warcasters many times against the Khadorans. Their military leader, Ashlynn d'Elyse, a Llaelese noble and warcaster, was a passionate but reasonable woman, and her opinion could sway the rest. "If you can convince Ashlynn d'Elyse to acknowledge the heiress, you could gain the support of the Resistance," Stryker said. "But we should notify her at once. She won't like being kept in the dark about this."

"Thank you for your counsel," Julius said, "but my future wife does not require the backing or approval of Ashlynn d'Elyse. She demands her loyalty, as do I."

"In addition, the Resistance has been working with the Protectorate of Menoth," Rebald said, naming the nation of religious zealots to the east who had laid claim to some parts of Llael. "We should consider them compromised."

"What choice did they have?" Stryker said. "They can't fight both Khador *and* the Protectorate."

"Enough," Julius said. He did not raise his voice, but there was iron in his tone. "I did not assemble my inner council to discuss the Llaelese Resistance."

He was being scolded like an errant child, silenced by a king who had been nothing more than bastard in exile not more than three years ago. Stryker's voice had always been heard in Leto's court. His counsel had been sought, his experience relied upon. "As you wish, Your Majesty," he said, biting down the anger and resentment rising up his throat like a tide of vomit.

He caught Leto's eyes, and the former king's expression stung him more than his nephew's rebuke. He'd brought pride, joy, and even anger to Leto's noble face on many occasions, but never pity. It was subtle now, but it was there.

Stryker sat back in his chair and let the rest of the council members hammer out the details of the king's plans. He listened, but he did not speak again. It was clear he was an outsider, and his voice carried no more weight than a shout into a windstorm.

— 6 —

PRINCESS KAETLYN DI LA MARTYN, heir to the throne of Llael, was a tall girl of no more than seventeen, Stryker guessed. She had long dark hair, high cheekbones, thin lips, and bright blue eyes, her most striking feature. Her dress was long and flowing and worked with gold and purple beading, a beautiful thing that only enhanced her regal appearance.

She walked down the center of a bright blue and purple carpet trimmed with gold, mingling the colors of Cygnar and Llael, toward Julius Raelthorne's throne. The king stood before his seat of power dressed in his military uniform; his father's sword, Kingslayer, was sheathed at his side. At his left stood his Uncle, Leto Raelthorne, to his right, Orin Midwinter. The rest of the inner council, including Stryker, stood to the right and left of the throne. There was no one else in the chamber except for members of the Royal Guard. The news of the heiress' discovery had not been relayed to the Royal Assembly, as it was vital to keep her existence a secret until the time was right.

Princess di la Martyn was trailed by two men Stryker did not know, her personal guard. Both were dangerous-looking men dressed in black greatcoats and high black boots. Each wore a dual magelock pistol at his hip, and the a bright purple pin in the shape of a rose was affixed to each man's lapel, marking him as a former gun mage of the Loyal Order of the Amethyst Rose. Some of these men and women were sworn to protect the royalty of Llael, much in the way the Royal Guard did in Cygnar. Their order had largely been disbanded after King Rynnard's death, but some remained, and apparently these two had been protecting the heiress for most of her life.

The princess stopped ten paces from Julius and bowed. Her guards stood silently behind her. "King Julius," she said. "I am overjoyed to finally meet you. Your Scout General"—she glanced at Rebald—"has told me much about you."

Julius smiled, showing his straight white teeth. It was a genuine smile. He stepped forward and gently took the princess' hand. He bent, lifted her slim hand to his lips, and kissed it softly. "No more overjoyed than I, Your Highness," he said. "I have looked forward to this day since I learned of your plight in Ord. Living in exile is a hard life and one with which I am well acquainted."

"You are kind, Your Majesty," she said. "I am grateful for your support as I am sure the people of Llael will be."

Julius smiled again and stared at the princess for a moment.

Stryker repressed a smile of his own. His king rarely showed his youth, but he *was* a young man, and the princess *was* a beautiful young woman. Stryker wondered if the king had been afraid his future bride would be homely. Perhaps he was relieved. Perhaps he was smitten.

"Let me you introduce you to the members of my inner council," Julius said. "This is High Chancellor Leto Raelthorne, my uncle."

Leto gave a small bow. "Your Majesty."

"My Arcane Administrator, Orin Midwinter."

Orin also bowed, showing the top of his head. A slight grimace passed over the princess' face, but her smile quickly covered it. *Maybe she can smell the man for what he is,* Stryker thought, hoped.

On down the line Julius went, introducing Duke Ebonhart, Navarch Galten Sparholm III, and Lassiter Polk. Then he came to Stryker. "And this is Lord General Stryker," Julius said. "One of our bravest and most experienced military leaders."

"Your Majesty," Stryker said, inclining his head. He expected she would turn back to the king, but her gaze lingered on him.

"I am told you have personally fought in Llael, beside our brave soldiers, against Khador," the princess said.

"Yes, I have had that privilege. The Llaelese are a strong and courageous people, and they deserve to be free from tyranny," he said, touched by her recognition.

"I thank you, sincerely, for that, Lord General, and I am glad to have such a noble ally."

"Your Highness," Stryker said again, somewhat embarrassed.

The princess turned back to the king, and Julius opened his mouth to say something, but a loud rapping on the great throne room doors sounded. Julius frowned and shook his head. He glanced over his shoulder to where one of the royal guardsmen stood and said, "Please go and see why we are disturbed on such a momentous occasion."

The guard hurried to the doors. He opened them a crack, revealing another member of the Royal Guard standing outside. The man wore a captain's pauldron, which meant whatever reason he had for disturbing his liege was important.

A short whispered conversation passed between the two guards, then the first guard closed the door and walked briskly toward Rebald. He placed an envelope sealed with wax in the scout general's hand then returned to his post behind the throne.

"Your Majesty," Rebald said, "this letter comes from one of our senior spies in Khador."

"Open it then," Julius said.

Rebald glanced at the princess and her guard and pursed his lips. "Perhaps some privacy, Your Majesty?"

Julius waved a hand in irritation. "She will one day be my queen," he said. "I see no reason she must be excluded from matters of state."

The princess held her composure at Julius' blunt announcement of their future nuptials. She had to be aware of the king's intentions, but to hear them so plainly spoken on their first meeting must have been shocking.

Rebald opened the envelope and quickly scanned the letter within. He said nothing, and his expression gave no hint as to the contents of the letter. He handed it to Leto, who read it quickly. The former king's eyes narrowed, and he drew a deep breath when he finished.

"Tell me," Julius commanded.

"It seems while we have been making wedding plans, the empress has been making her own," Leto said. "She is now betrothed to Vladimir Tzepesci, which will soon make him the prince regent of Khador and bind his house and all the influence he commands to hers."

Stryker well understood the empress' reasons for marrying Vlad. He was the ruler of Old Umbrey, the head of an ancient and powerful family that could trace its roots back to the founding of their nation. He represented the old ways, tradition, and most important, the more independently minded people of eastern Khador. There were many in Khador who believed he was a threat to her sovereignty, but now she had removed that threat and added his power and influence to her own.

Julius said, "An unexpected development but not exactly a grave threat."

"I disagree," Leto said. "She is consolidating power, and now Vlad's claims in Llael will have the full weight of the empress behind them."

"It seems we have underestimated the empress, and we have been caught flat-footed, Your Majesty," Midwinter said.

"Wait," Ebonhart said. "I agree with the high chancellor that the empress and Lord Tzepesci's marriage strengthens her position, but it doesn't mean they are necessarily preparing for war."

"We have seen Khador break treaties before," Midwinter said and turned to the king. "Your Majesty, this is a precursor to Khadoran treachery."

"War is inevitable," Julius said. "Khador was never going to accept the princess as the rightful heir to Llael." It suddenly struck Stryker that this was likely Julius' plan all along—his and Rebald's, and possibly Midwinter's. Julius simply needed an excuse to go to war, and the princess gave him a situation where Khador must refuse the terms of the treaty, especially now that the empress had solidified her claim to Llael.

"And you've known that all along," Leto said, giving voice to what Stryker had been thinking. "Which is why you've kept the princess a secret from all of us."

"It is the right course of action, Uncle," Julius said. Stryker noted that he did not deny Leto's accusation.

"We should announce the heiress," Rebald said. "Though it is sooner than we would have liked."

Leto said, "Your Majesty, I agree, but we must wait for the empress' reaction. We cannot be seen as the aggressors by the Cygnaran people *or* by the Royal Assembly."

"Wait," a soft feminine voice said. Everyone turned to the princess. Her face was a mask of anger, her blue eyes flashing like icy daggers. "I will *not* marry you."

"Your Highness?" Julius said. It was the first time he had looked surprised during any of today's events. "Surely, you must see that our marriage is of utmost importance if we are to strengthen our nations against what must surely be forthcoming Khadoran aggression."

"No, Your Majesty, what I see is that my people are going to suffer further degradation from Khador while you and your council wait for the empress to act."

Stryker stifled laughter. Julius and Rebald's well-crafted plan was about to fall apart at the whim of a seventeen-year-old girl. She *was* a queen, that much was now apparent. The steel in her tone brooked no argument, and her chastising of the king was pointed and on target.

"Your Highness, be reasonable," Rebald said and stepped toward Kaetlyn. "This is the best course of action."

"It is *not*, Scout General," she said. "The best course of action results in the immediate freedom of the Llaelese people." She turned her gaze back to Julius. "If you want to marry me, if you want to gain all that entails, then you will remove the Khadoran scourge from my country immediately."

"Your Highness," Julius said softly and stepped toward her as well. He reached down and took her hand in his. She flinched but did not stop him. There was a moment of tense silence, and the men in the throne room sworn to protect their rulers stiffened. "I promise you, I will do all in my power to free Llael from Khadoran control and put you on the throne. But I agree with my uncle— we should let Khador show the world that it does not honor its treaties, that the empress' word is worth nothing more than the breath that creates it. The empress will waste no time in denying your right to the throne, and then, I swear to you, I will bring the full might of Cygnar thundering into Llael to crush the invaders."

The passion in the young king's voice was moving, and here was something in the man that *was* unlike his father. He had already learned there were ways to motivate people other than fear or the edge of a sword. A king who spoke plainly to his subjects with passion could gather a nation behind him just as easily as a tyrant who demanded their support.

Julius' words had the desired effect, maybe more so than the king or anyone else in the room could guess. The princess leaned forward. She kissed Julius softly on the cheek, then pulled away. "Thank you, Your Majesty."

— 7 —

"SHE HAS DENIED THE CLAIM," Julius said and put the letter from the empress of Khador down on the table. He'd just finished reading the letter aloud, and he did not look angry; in fact, he looked satisfied. Ayn Vanar had taken little more than two weeks to deny Kaetlyn di la Martyn's claim to the throne of Llael.

They were back in the inner council chamber with all members in attendance. In addition, Princess di la Martyn was present, sitting beside the king. She'd become a regular fixture in their meetings. She rarely spoke, but she listened, and it was clear more and more every day that she had the king's ear. Stryker actually approved of this. Despite her youth and inexperience, Kaetlyn had a good head for matters of state, and she was honest and forthright. Perhaps she would counteract the influence of creatures like Orin Midwinter on the king.

"She well knows she is in violation of the treaty," Leto said. "And the consequences of that."

"Just so," Warmaster Ebonhart added. "She leaves us with little choice but to enforce the princess's claims." There were nods and voices of agreement around the council table.

"Uncle, draft a declaration of war immediately," Julius said. "I want it presented to the Royal Assembly within the week."

Leto nodded gravely. "Yes, Your Majesty." Stryker couldn't imagine how his former king must feel. His own rule had been marked by near constant warfare and strife, and he'd done his best to do what was right for his people. He'd seen peace settle on Cygnar for a brief moment, only to see it consumed once again by the flames of war.

"Warmaster Ebonhart, Navarch Sparholm, Lord General Stryker, you will begin planning the invasion of Llael at once," Julius said.

The word invasion struck a sour note with Stryker. In all his years in the Cygnaran military, he'd fought to defend Cygnar or Llael, reacting to the aggression of enemy nations. Now, Cygnar would become the aggressor and begin the fighting instead of weathering it.

"Rebald," Julius continued, "when will Asheth Magnus arrive from Five Fingers?"

It was if someone had kicked Stryker in the stomach. His eyes widened, and he opened his mouth to give voice to the outrage boiling within him, to cry out against the sheer lunacy of the king's words. But he checked himself. "Your Majesty, you cannot be serious," he managed at last.

The council chamber grew silent, and Julius' eyes narrowed. "Lord General, I am well aware of your history with Asheth Magnus, but he was and is one of the finest military minds in the Iron Kingdoms. Additionally, I would not be sitting on this throne if not for Asheth Magnus. I owe the man a debt."

"He is a criminal and a bloodthirsty killer," Stryker said, clenching his fists at his side. Asheth Magnus had served Julius' father and had been one of his most ruthless servants. He had also been Stryker's mentor, fostering his warcaster talents and leveraging a place for him in the Royal Guard. When it became clear how dangerous King Vinter was and that Magnus followed him blindly, Stryker had joined Leto Raelthorne's side in overthrowing Vinter in a short, bloody battle called the Lion's Coup. Magnus had been severely injured in the fighting but had escaped. He'd then spent the next fifteen years working to restore Vinter to the throne. He'd also served as Julius' mentor while the boy was in exile. Granted, in the final moments of the civil war, Magnus has slain Vinter, striking the killing blow while the former king had battled Leto and Stryker. But Vinter had also tried to kill Julius, and the new king had pardoned Magnus when he took the throne.

All eyes were on Stryker, and he could see that he was not alone in his opinion of Magnus. Leto, Rebald, and Ebonhart all looked concerned, worried even, but none of them said anything.

"Lord General Stryker," Julius said and sighed exasperatedly. "I expected a reaction from you at this news, but I did not expect that you would forget you place and insult your king."

Again, the rebuke. Julius did not shout at him nor threaten; instead, his calm, almost parental tone was far worse, far more humbling.

"Your Majesty, I beg your pardon," Stryker said and stood. He locked eyes with each member of the council. "Council members, Asheth Magnus is a dangerous and duplicitous man. You all know this. You all know how many Cygnaran deaths can be laid at his—"

"Hold your tongue, Lord General," Julius said and surged to his feet, knocking his chair over with a clatter. Beside him, the princess visibly recoiled at his outburst.

Visions of Vinter Raelthorne slammed into Stryker's mind as if the tyrant sat the throne once more. He was shaking with fury, and his gift, the magic that made him a warcaster gathered in the back of his skull, a desperate buzzing, an electric storm aching for release. The Royal Guard in the room stiffened, their hands creeping down to their pistols. Was he so close to violence they feared he would actually attack the king?

"Lord General Stryker," Leto said, standing as well. His voice was calm, measured. "You may not trust Magnus, and truthfully"— he looked at his nephew—"I have my doubts as well, but it is the will of your king. My nephew has insight into Magnus' character that none of us possess."

Stryker was baffled. How could Leto even entertain the idea of Magnus resuming his place in the Cygnaran court? During his reign, Leto was bent on finding Magnus and bringing him to justice. Worse yet, Magnus had nearly slain Leto after he'd killed Vinter, and only the presence and quick-thinking of a warcaster named Allister Caine had prevented it. Now Leto would welcome the man back into the capital, back into the throne room, where he could influence *another* Cygnaran king. The eyes of the new king were on him still, penetrating and cold. Stryker was more alone now than he'd ever been. The thought of resigning his post came to the fore of his mind—he had no doubt Julius would accept such a resignation—but there were still people who depended on him, men and women who had followed him into battle because they trusted him. He could not abandon them to Magnus, who would almost certainly be promoted to Lord General once Stryker was gone.

"Forgive me, Your Majesty," he said and bowed his head. It was a show of respect, but it also hid the clench of his jaw.

The king said nothing for a moment, but he sat back down, smoothing his jacket. "You are forgiven, Lord General," he said at last, breaking the long and uncomfortable silence that had settled over the chamber. "I know your history with Asheth Magnus is difficult, and, in truth, I too have taken issue with some of his . . . methods in the past. But I expect you to put that aside for the benefit of Cygnar. Can you do that?"

Stryker drew in a deep breath. "I will do everything in my power to work with . . . him." He couldn't bring himself to say something as simple as "yes;" the situation was far too complex and emotionally charged for that.

"Good," Julius said. "Then let us return to more important matters. We have a war to plan."

...

STRYKER WALKED DOWN THE MAIN HALL of the royal residence, a wing of Castle Raelthorne that housed the king as well as members of the royal family. He'd heard enough from the king, enough of war, and there was only one man who could turn them from the course Julius had set.

The royal guardsman outside High Chancellor Leto's chambers acknowledged Stryker as he approached. One of them, a short grey-bearded man named Harken had been serving when Stryker had first been a member of the guard nearly twenty years ago.

"Sergeant Harken," Stryker said. "It's been awhile."

The old guardsman's face seemed carved from stone—he'd spent nearly thirty years standing at attention, still and alert—but a slight smile creased his lips. "You have business with the high chancellor, Lord General?" he said. "He's not expecting you."

That was true, but he still hoped Leto would speak with him. "I don't, but it's a pressing matter. Please inform the high chancellor I wish to speak with him."

Harken grunted and frowned but turned to the door and knocked twice.

"Come." Leto's voice drifted through the door.

Harken opened the door and stepped inside the chamber. "Lord General Stryker waits in the hall, my lord. He seeks an audience." There was a time when Stryker might have simply walked past the guards and demanded an audience, but he needed to keep a level head. He was not on the battlefield, and this was a war of a very different type.

"Send him in," Leto said.

The old guard turned to Stryker. "The high chancellor will see you."

Stryker walked past the guard and into Leto's chamber. It was spacious and well-appointed but not cluttered. Leto was a simple man, and the chamber reflected his tastes. The high chancellor was seated at a broad desk near a window, and the waning sun was streaming in, catching on the brilliant blue of Leto's uniform. He looked regal, kingly.

Leto put down a quill pen and stacked a sheaf of papers in front of him. The former king of Cygnar doing paperwork for his nephew; it was beneath the man Stryker had followed for so long. "I thought you might come and speak to me," he said and motioned to a plush chair in front of the desk.

"I wished to speak in private, just for a moment, Your Highness" Stryker said and sat. It was still strange not to say *Your Majesty.*

Leto steepled his hands in front of him on the desk. "Then speak."

"I want to know why you are backing the king's plans to invade Llael to start another war with Khador."

Stryker's bluntness didn't seem to faze Leto, and he stared at Stryker for a moment before speaking. "I think you want to ask a different question," he said. "I think you want to ask why I follow my nephew so willingly, blindly even."

"My lord, I would never—" Stryker began, but Leto raised a hand to silence him.

"Has it occurred to you that I actually agree with Julius?" Leto asked.

Stryker was at a loss for words. The high chancellor was right: Stryker had believed Leto was backing the king out of obligation, loyalty, maybe even guilt. He hadn't entertained the idea that Leto was actually in favor of a war that could cost them everything.

"I don't understand," Stryker said. "You—we—fought Khador for so long, saw so many lives lost, and now we have peace, for the first time in over a decade. Why throw that away?"

Leto stood and turned to face the window. The former king's shoulders were tight, as if his next words were painful to say. "We fought them, yes, he said. "We defended Cygnar and Llael where we could, but we did not remove Khador. We fought, we fell back, we lost men and land, and then we settled for this treaty." He turned to face Stryker. "I know you fought bravely for Cygnar, for me, and I will be forever grateful for your loyalty, but let me ask you: what did we gain in all those years?"

"What did we gain?" Stryker said, taken aback. "We protected Cygnar. We kept our people safe."

"But our enemy remains, and now they are stronger," Leto said. His eyes had become hard, bitter. "My nephew has much of his father in him. I know that troubles you, but my brother was not always the monster he became. He had strength. His son has strength, perhaps a strength I do not possess."

"That is not true, my lord," Stryker said and stood. "You were a good king, a man I followed without hesitation, a man I would have followed to my death."

Leto smiled. "You are a good man, Coleman, and a good soldier, but I simply defended, and in doing so, we lost ground as a nation. Julius has the strength to take what we've lost back, to make Cygnar stronger than it has ever been, to take the fight to our enemies. He is a king worth following."

Leto was a man who Stryker had looked up to, admired, strove to emulate. It was strange to hear him speak about himself this way. "My lord, the risks are too great. If we invade Llael and are repelled by Khador, it may embolden them to invade Cygnar. The losses we suffered in the war against your brother have not been replenished, and further losses would make us vulnerable."

"You are right, of course," Leto said. "It is a risk, but it is one we must take or else lose Cygnar bit by bit to its enemies." He walked across the room and placed his hands on Stryker's shoulders. "I'm recommending that you lead the invasion force. You are Cygnar's best chance, and if you ever loved me as your king, then give Julius the same loyalty, the same courage you gave me."

Stryker couldn't look Leto in the eyes, and he turned his head. "And Magnus? Do you approve of this as well?"

Leto released him and stepped back. His face hardened. "I will never trust him, but the king *does* trust him, and Magnus has been loyal to him. I do not think he would willfully undermine Julius' goals."

"The world I knew is gone," Stryker said, more to himself than to Leto. "I do not know my place in this one."

"You are a lord general of Cygnar," Leto said. "Cygnar exists today because of *your* actions. Men like Magnus cannot take that away from you if you do not let them."

"You're right, Your Highness," Stryker said. "I apologize if I have overstepped." It was good to hear that Leto still valued all he done and sacrificed to protect Cygnar. "I am sorry to have disturbed you," he said. "I will leave you."

Leto nodded as Stryker walked to the door. He opened it, but before he stepped through, he heard Leto's voice. "You are an important part of Cygnar's future, Coleman. Remember that."

— 8 —

THE CASPIAN GARRISON HOUSED nearly two hundred members of the Stormblade infantry as well as a fair number of their cavalry counterparts, the Storm Lances. Most of these troops were drawn from Stryker's own Storm Division, which had no fixed headquarters and had been largely removed from the structure of Cygnar's four armies; therefore, they could theoretically be deployed anywhere. The truth of the matter was that most of the Storm Division was garrisoned on the border between Khador and Cygnar, though a large portion of its Storm Knights and warjacks would be recalled for the invasion of Llael.

When it was far smaller, the Storm Division had once been housed in Caspia as part of the general garrison, and Stryker used the old Stormblade compound as his general HQ and personal quarters.

His favorite section of the garrison was the training yard set aside for the elements of the Storm Division. He'd spent many long hours in places like this during his youth, training with newly formed Stormblades and receiving instruction from men like Garvin Tews. The yard was small but still serviceable. It was a fifty-yard square of packed dirt with wooden pells at one end for blade training and earthen berms at the other for practice with thrown lightning

The was only one other person in the training yard, and Stryker smiled at the bear-like form of Garvin Tews slashing at a wooden pell with a blunt practice storm glaives. Tews watched him approach, put the tip of his sword in the ground, and leaned on it.

"Rough day, Lord General?" he said as Stryker approached.

Stryker snorted. How much did Tews already know? "You could say that, Captain."

"Bloody Magnus," Tews said with a shake of his head. So, he had heard. Stryker wondered from whom. He decided it didn't matter. "Hard to believe that back-stabbing son of a bitch will enter Caspia as a free man and at the king's request to boot."

Stryker fought down a spike of anger at the mention of Magnus. "I'm not here to talk about Magnus," he said. "I'm here to thrash you like a one-legged gobber in the sparring circle." He flashed the Stormblade captain a wide grin. "That is, if an old man like you can still lift a storm glaive."

"Oh, is that a fact?" Tews said and set his practice glaive across one broad shoulder. "Perhaps you've forgotten who it was that taught you how to use a storm glaive in the first place."

"No, I haven't," Stryker said. That part was true, but a troubling memory of Magnus teaching him to use the Caspian battle blade along the road from Fisherbrook to Caspia came to mind instantly. It had been Magnus who'd shown him the basics of swordplay. He pushed the memory away and forced a smile. "I'm just better than you now."

"Care to put that to the test?" Tews said. He'd dropped the sirs and the lord generals. They were friends, and here, now, their ranks didn't matter.

"What, with Quicksilver?" Stryker said, and tapped the haft of his mechanika blade still affixed to the back of his warcaster armor.

"You might have a bit of an advantage there," Tews said and pointed to nearby rack of practice storm glaives.

"Fair enough," Stryker said and took a blade from the rack. He removed Quicksilver from his back and set it in the practice weapon's place.

"Ready," Stryker said and walked to one of the sparring circles nearby. Tews grinned and joined him there.

Tews lifted his blunted practice blade in both hands. Like all storm glaives, it had a long haft and was wielded more like a great sword than a pole weapon. Tews wore a suit of battered plate, his practice armor, well dented and scratched from countless hours of practice.

It had been a while since Stryker had used a storm glaive; it had the size and heft of Quicksilver, but his own weapon was patterned after the more traditional two-handed Caspian battle blade. Stryker wore his warcaster armor, but he'd deactivated the arcane turbine; the power field it generated would give him yet another an unfair advantage.

He raised his weapon into a high guard, angling the point toward his opponent. "Ready?" he said.

Tews nodded and took up a more defensive stance, holding his own weapon with its hilt close to his belly, blade projected out. They'd sparred many times, and in truth, Tews was the superior swordsman. Stryker was an expert with the blade, but his ability to channel his warcaster gift into his strikes, increasing their accuracy, speed, and impact made him more than a match for even the best swordsmen who lacked his gift, assuming he fought with his unique weaponry. Of course, it was an unspoken rule between him and Tews that he would not use those weapons and those gifts to sway the odds in his favor. It would be unsportsmanlike. That usually meant he would end up with a set of new and painful bruises by the time their sparring session ended.

"Three touches?" Tews said.

"Like always," Stryker answered.

"Come and get it."

Stryker wasted no time and rushed forward, his blade flashing down in a powerful diagonal slash. Tews lifted his weapon and moved to the side with a grace and speed most would think such a large man incapable of. Their blades came together in a ringing clash, and Tews deflected Stryker's blade away, missing his right shoulder by inches.

Tews used his sidewise movement to launch a riposte, a quick forward cut around Stryker's blade that lacked the force of a full swing, but with a swordsman of Tews' considerable size and strength, it hardly mattered. Had Stryker's arcane turbine been activated, the power field generated by the device would have robbed Tews' weapon of some of its kinetic energy, possibly even stopping it cold. Without that protection, however, the tip of the Stormblade's weapon smashed into Stryker's breastplate with a hollow clang and sent him stumbling back, grimacing.

"One," Tews said and held up a finger.

"Morrow, you're too damn fast for a man your size," Stryker said, knowing he'd have a bruise on his chest for the next week. "And age," Stryker added with a wry grin.

"Speed is one of many, many gifts, and with age comes wisdom and skill," Tews said.

Stryker resumed the high guard, and Tews took his blade in the middle guard again. They came together once more. This time, Stryker threw a feinting cut at Tews' head, causing him to raise his blade to intercept. Stryker pulled the strike at the last second and reversed its direction into a low sweeping blow. It was a difficult technique with such a large blade, but he was not without his own gifts.

The blade struck Tews' left greave with a satisfying crunch, denting the steel and sending the big Stormblade stumbling sideways.

Tews chuckled. "I never see that one the first time you throw it," he said, shaking out his left leg.

"Which is why I throw it every time," Stryker replied. "Oh, and that's one for me."

"Tied, then," Tews said, and brought his glaive up in the high guard, mimicking Stryker. That meant Tews was going on the offensive, and Stryker groaned inwardly. There were more bruises to come.

They fought for another ten minutes, and Tews won the match, as he usually did, three touches to two. The last "touch" had been another riposte from one of Stryker's own blows, and it had come so hard and so fast he'd been unable to slow it, or even touch it, with his own blade. Tews had knocked him completely off his feet, breathless and gasping. Had it been a real storm glaive, Stryker would have been cut neatly in two. Of course, there had been moments when, had Stryker been dueling with Quicksilver, he could have channeled his will into his attacks with it, using his innate gifts to add speed and accuracy to his blows. But Quicksilver was out of reach for this practice. After all, he and Tews had an agreement.

Tews approached Stryker where he sat on the ground, trying get his lungs to cooperate again, Tews grinning ear to ear. "That's three. You want to go another round?"

Stryker looked up at his old friend and shook his head. He held out his hand, and Tews pulled him up. He winced as the sudden movement brought fresh pain to his battered ribcage. "No, Captain, I've had enough," he said after he managed to get enough air into his lungs for the task. "Sparring bouts with you make a man look forward to something easy, like invasion and full-scale war."

Tews chuckled. "We both know I'm no match for you if you used even a smidgen of your real ability."

"Maybe so," Stryker said. "But Morrow above, man, I'm glad you're on *our* side."

Tews face grew serious. "I'm always on *your* side, sir. No matter what comes."

Stryker smiled tiredly. "I've never doubted it," he said. "Now, will you tell me how to throw that damn riposte you clocked me with at the end?"

"You'll have to ask Major Maddox, sir," Tews said with a sly grin. "She's the one who showed me."

"Ask me what?" a voice said from behind them.

Stryker turned and saw a warcaster, seemingly about his age, walking across the training yard toward him. She was tall, lean, with short straw-colored hair, high cheekbones, and blue eyes. She moved like a warrior, graceful and with a certain economy of motion that all skilled swordsmen seemed to acquire. Major Elizabeth Maddox wore armor similar to Stryker's—it too was powered by galvanic energy rather than steam—though built somewhat lighter. She carried a massive two-handed mechanika blade casually in one hand. It was patterned after a storm glaive, but it hid a number of surprises for Cygnar's enemies. Stryker had seen the weapon, Tempest, in action many times.

"Beth," Stryker said. He'd known Maddox for over fifteen years, and they had served together on many battlefields, beginning with the first conflict in Llael. She had been a member of the Stormblade infantry and a seasoned veteran by the time her warcaster talent had been discovered, and now she was one of the finest warcasters in the Cygnaran Army.

Maddox offered him a rare smile, and it momentarily removed the touch of sadness that always seemed present on her face, a detachment that made her appear cold. Maddox had good reason for her pain, as Stryker knew. She'd spent three years as a prisoner of war in the hands of the Protectorate of Menoth. She'd been liberated years ago, but the torture she had endured. . .

"Hello, Beth," Tews said. He smiled at her, but there was a distinct sadness in his eyes. They had been together before she had been captured by the Protectorate; that relationship had obviously ended.

She nodded at Tews and then turned quickly to Stryker, as if she couldn't bear to look at the big Stormblade. "I heard you were hiding here," she said. The smile had vanished, but there was a wry tone to her voice. Like Tews, she didn't bother with formal protocol; they were all friends here.

"I have *not* been hiding," he said. "Just getting a little exercise."

"I saw," Maddox said. "Care for a little more?"

Stryker considered the proposal. It had been years since he'd sparred with another warcaster. He'd certainly *fought* more than a few enemy warcasters in battle, but he was long past the need for training in a full-contact sparring session with one of his fellow gifted. He hadn't done so with Maddox since their days together in the Stormblades, well before his talent had been made public and hers had even manifested. He suspected her proposal had an ulterior motive behind it. Maddox had never been shy about sharing her opinions with her superiors, and Stryker allowed her much more latitude than most. A lecture from her was certainly coming.

"Grab a practice blade," Stryker said. "You still remember how to use a storm glaive?"

She snorted over her shoulder. "I think I can figure it out." She selected a practice blade and set Tempest on the rack next to Quicksilver.

She returned to Stryker holding the blade in one hand. Her warcaster armor, like his, increased the strength of the wearer when the arcane turbine was powered up. He activated his, taking comfort in the whirring hum of voltaic energy as it flowed through his armor. The practice storm glaive he was holding instantly weighed almost nothing at all.

"Before we begin," Maddox said. "I'd just like to say that you are full of buffalox shit, sir."

He knew her bluntness shouldn't surprise him, but it always did. Since her return to Cygnar, she had assumed a position of command in the Stormblades, and Stryker had come to rely on her for counsel—she was skilled, honest, and unafraid to tell even a superior officer what was on her mind. That always had its uses—if the superior officer wasn't too egocentric to handle the criticism. Sometimes, Stryker wondered if he was up to the task.

"Well, that's my cue that this conversation is above my pay grade," Tews said and returned his practice blade to the rack. "I'll leave you two to sort this out."

Stryker watched Tews disappear into the main garrison building, and then said, "Thamar's teeth, Beth. Tell me what you *really* think."

"Glad to. You need to accept that Asheth Magnus is part of

your life again, and more important, part of the king's." She didn't give him a chance to reply as she rushed forward, her blade flashing out in a low, rising cut.

She'd caught him off-guard and flat-footed, but he managed to snap his own blade down to parry hers. The impact jarred the teeth in his head—she'd used her arcane talent to add speed and power to that blow. Before he could riposte, she sprang back, lithe and nimble.

He circled to his left. "Goddamn it, you were *there*. You saw what a monster he was, how willing he was to serve a tyrant, how willing he was to *kill* Cygnarans."

"Yes, I was there, and I remember very clearly the kind of man Magnus was," she said matching him step for step. "But it really doesn't matter. We have a new king, and *he* is *not* a tyrant."

This time Stryker went on the offensive and lashed out with his weapon. He took his top hand off the hilt and swung it with his bottom hand while lunging forward. Swinging a storm glaive one-handed was no easy task, even with warcaster armor, but the move gave him nearly a foot of extra reach. The move surprised Maddox, and she leaped back but not quickly enough. Her power field flared as Stryker's blade smashed into it then through it. The tip of his storm glaive caught her above the right hip. Her power field had stolen some of the force of his blow, but it was still hard enough to send her reeling sideways. She recovered instantly and slapped away his next strike with the flat of her blade.

"That remains to be seen. He is his father's son," Stryker said, breathing hard. "There are already questionable influences on his council."

Maddox shook her head. "He's young, and he might be a little rash, but he is not Vinter Raelthorne. Plus, there are others on his council who can counteract the influences you're talking about. His uncle, Duke Ebonhart, and, if you'd pull your head out of your ass, you."

Stryker made a disgusted sound. "Does everyone know you speak to a lord general this way?"

She grinned, but her answer was a sudden lunge, as she used

her storm glaive like a great rapier. She was faster than him, faster than Tews, and Stryker's parry was nowhere near in time. The point of Maddox's weapon slammed into his chest with the force of a train—she really wasn't taking it easy on him. That blow, too, had been augmented and knocked him back three steps and down to one knee. Only his power field had saved him from being completely knocked off his feet.

"He doesn't listen to me. The only reason I'm on the inner council is because of Leto," Stryker said and struggled back to his feet. Maddox let him get up.

"Coleman, this isn't about *you*; it's about what's right for Cygnar," she said. "Come on. You're better than that. I know it. What's taking you so damned long to know it yourself?"

Stryker smiled in spite of the rebuke. "You're as tactful as an Ironclad's fist."

"I'm not cut out for diplomacy, I guess. And frankly, if I thought it'd knock some sense into you, I'd let Rowdy smash you a good one. But I can still probably do it myself." Again she launched herself forward, this time with an overhand cut, but Stryker had been expecting her this time. She'd telegraphed the move by putting weight on her lead leg. He snapped his blade up and caught hers high, leaving her midsection completely exposed. He threw a crisp front kick into her armored belly, putting his magic into the blow. He caught her flush and sent her crashing backward three steps and then down onto her backside.

"I've gotten rusty," she said grimacing as she climbed to her feet. "Should have seen that one coming."

He stepped back and let her rise, just as she'd done for him. "I hear what you're saying," he said. "But I don't think anyone knows Magnus the way I do. Nobody really knows how dangerous he is."

She bent over at the waist, getting her breath back. "That may be true," she said after a moment. "More the reason you should keep your mouth shut and stay in the king's good graces."

He let out a long ragged breath. "So I can watch him. I know."

"Exactly." She brought her sword up. "What is that, two touches to my one?"

"Yeah, do you want to call—" She did not telegraph her next attack. It was a charge, but it came from an oblique angle—she'd juked left and then rushed forward virtually at the same time. It was a degree of agility and speed he simply lacked.

He whirled to meet her attack, which had culminated in a back-handed cut at his midsection, and brought his own weapon up to intercept hers. Too slow. His power field flashed, and then he was on the ground, his ribs thrumming with pain.

Maddox stood over him, triumphant, and extended her hand. "That's two for me. Let's call this a draw."

"Fine by me," he grunted as she dragged him to his feet. "They'll need me somewhat intact when I get to the battlefield."

— 9 —

THE TONE OF THE CITY CHANGED over the next few weeks. Once the declaration of war was drafted, it was ratified swiftly by the Royal Assembly, and then the unavoidable information creep into the general populace began. An official announcement to the people of Cygnar had not been made, and the various nobles had been sworn to silence until the king gave them leave to tell the people who lived in their provinces and holdings. But with over a hundred nobles in the Royal Assembly, there were bound to be loose lips.

Stryker heard whispers of war on the streets, in the taverns, and, generally, anywhere he traveled within Caspia. His presence alone was likely to prompt those around him to discuss the likelihood of war.

He'd spent the last few weeks in the Caspian garrison, where members of the Storm Division were stationed, spending time among the friends and comrades he'd found over the last fifteen years. He hadn't spoken much in these weeks, preferring to wrestle with the doubts and fears clouding his mind on his own rather than burdening his subordinates with it. He spent long hours in the training yard with blade and pistol, the rote, mechanical repetition and physical strain serving to clear his mind, at least for a while.

Today, however, he would face the source of his consternation. He'd received word that Magnus had arrived in the city. Though the warcaster had not yet sought him out, Stryker could not avoid him any longer. More galling still was the fact that Magnus had been given an official rank within the Cygnaran military: a general, no less. Stryker refused to dwell on that; there were far more distressing things about Magnus' presence than his rank.

The king had called a war council to outline the invasion plan, a plan he had contributed to in private meetings with Warmaster Duke Ebonhart and other vital members of the Cygnaran Army. All they had decided would likely be challenged or changed by Magnus; Stryker had no doubt the man would want to make his presence heavily known upon his return to Caspia.

Stryker left the garrison early, looking forward to the long walk to the palace as time to gather his thoughts. Maddox was waiting for him outside the palace gates, and he was grateful to see her. It would be good to have a friend by his side during what was going to be a challenging ordeal.

"Major Maddox," he said, as he neared the main gates.

"You ready for this, sir?" She said and fell in beside him.

He nodded. "Of course," he said. "I will do my duty. I was recently reminded, and rather painfully, that I shouldn't act like a snot-nosed cadet whining about . . . How would you put it?"

"Perhaps not being allowed to eat at the officers' table, sir," Maddox suggested.

He grimaced. "That's pretty good. Well, when I *do* eat with the other officers, it appears *General* Magnus will be joining me."

• • •

Asheth Magnus had also arrived early to the castle, and he was standing in the large antechamber outside the throne room. The war council would be held there instead of the smaller inner council meeting chamber. Seeing him woke a storm of emotions for Stryker: anger, betrayal, and more than anything else, a surprising fear.

Asheth Magnus was more or less as Stryker remembered him. He was tall and dark haired, though his hair was now peppered with silver. His face was lean and hawkish, his eyes dark and penetrating. Magnus wore a suit of warcaster armor, but unlike those crafted by the Cygnaran Armory that Stryker and Maddox wore, Magnus' kit looked cobbled together, salvaged from whatever he could find. It looked crude, but Magnus had a gift for mechanika—the potent technology that combined the arcane with machinery—and his creations were often lethally effective. His engineering skill was reflected in the mechanika prosthetic that had replaced his right arm. The limb had been crushed by a falling warjack, a warjack toppled by Stryker's magic when he'd turned against his former mentor. The mechanika limb was an ugly thing of steel and bronze, and looked every bit as ramshackle as the man's armor.

Magnus was not alone. He had two men with him, and neither looked like they were part of the regular Cygnaran military. In fact, they had the look of mercenaries, likely drawn from the hard men who had served Magnus while he was in exile. Reports indicated he had consorted with all manner of unsavory characters, including some of the most infamous criminals in the Iron Kingdoms.

"Try to keep it civil, sir," Maddox said to Stryker. The fact that she'd called him *sir* meant protocol was back in place—for both of them.

He gave a stiff nod and gritted his teeth. Even speaking to Magnus turned to his stomach, but Maddox's counsel during their sparring session, especially her urging that he needed to remain on the council to keep an eye on Magnus and counteract his influence as best he could, was first and foremost on his mind.

Stryker walked across the antechamber toward Magnus, who turned to greet him, a slight smile on his face.

"General Magnus," Stryker said, his stomach twisting at uttering those two words together.

"*Lord* General Stryker," Magnus said. "You've done well for yourself. Not quite the boy I plucked out of Fisherbrook all those years ago."

Magnus had fired the opening shot, reminding everyone present that it was *he* who had brought Stryker to Caspia, *he* who had once served as Stryker's mentor. The shot landed, but Stryker had one of his own.

"General Magnus, I am aware you have been outside of a standing military structure for some time, but, as I'm sure you'll remember, it is proper to call a superior officer sir when addressing him."

Magnus' smile widened, perhaps in appreciation of Stryker's rebuke, perhaps just so he could show his teeth like the predator he was. "Of course, *sir*," he said. "As you say, I have been outside of a standard military for some time. While I was away, I was forced to resort to a more . . . meritorious system of command."

One of the men with Magnus, a brutish fellow with a bald head and a thick chest and arms, chuckled. He wore a breastplate, battered but perhaps shined up a bit for the occasion, adorned with the fading symbol of the mercenary outfit known as the Steelheads. Stryker doubted the man had served in that well-regarded organization in quite some time. He also wore a lieutenant's bar—a *Cygnaran* lieutenant's bar—on his right pauldron. Before Stryker could question why this obvious former mercenary had been given an officer's commission in the Cygnaran Army, Maddox stepped in front of him.

"General Magnus," she said. She must have felt the tension between them. In fact, everyone in the antechamber was looking at them, including six members of the Royal Guard standing at attention outside the throne room doors. "My name is Commander Elizabeth Maddox."

Magnus nodded at her, though his eyes remained on Stryker. "Yes, I remember you from . . . before. You were one of Leto's Stormblades." He glanced over her warcaster armor. "I see you are more than that now."

"You have a good memory, sir," Maddox said. "I look forward to working with you."

Stryker tried not to roll his eyes and only partially succeeded. Maddox was only doing what he should be doing—that is, hiding past grievances and maintaining professional decorum—but the fact she had to call this man *sir* galled him.

Before any of them could say more, the doors to the throne room opened, and High Chancellor Leto stepped out into the antechamber. When he saw Magnus and Stryker standing next to one another, his eyes widened. Stryker couldn't blame him.

"Lord General Stryker, Major Maddox . . . General Magnus," he said. "The king is ready to begin as soon as the other members of the war council arrive. Please take your places."

"All right, everyone. Let's go," Stryker said and headed into the throne room.

"Yes, sir," Magnus said from behind him. "I'm looking forward to getting back to work."

— 10 —

THE THRONE ROOM HAD BEEN ALTERED since the last time Stryker had seen it. Three large tables had been brought in, their surfaces polished onyx. They were arranged in a U-shape with the throne in the middle. Stryker, Magnus, and Warmaster Ebonhart stood at the center table—it was preferable to sitting in warcaster armor. Other members of the inner council sat at the remaining tables, and they were joined by other important men and women, who, while not part of King Julius' inner circle, made up his larger advisory council. This included the Lord Treasurer; the two most prominent leaders of the Mercarian League, Duke Waldron Gately of Mercir and Lord Ethan Starke, chief alderman; Arland Calster, head of the Caspian branch of the Fraternal Order of Wizardry and former arcane advisor for Leto; and Commander Birk Kinbrace, Chancellor of the Strategic Academy. Stryker was happy to see Kinbrace there—he knew the aging warcaster well, and Kinbrace was an honest, forthright man who'd also helped overthrow Vinter Raelthorne.

The only person who seemed out of place was Major Maddox, but her presence was likely due to her current role as the centerpiece of a propaganda campaign designed to promote support for the military and the new king.

"I say again, an attack on Merywyn, the seat of Khadoran power in Llael, is the most direct way to break their power in the region," Stryker said. He'd outlined the plan he and Ebonhart had devised, which included a siege of the former capital of Llael. Unsurprisingly, Magnus thought it was the wrong course of action.

"Your Majesty, you've been to Merywyn recently," Magnus said, addressing Julius. The king had said little. He had sat quietly on his throne, listening to his advisors. Stryker was loath to admit it, but it was another trait where Julius differed from his father. Vinter had rarely heeded anyone's counsel but his own.

"You saw how strong it was," Magnus continued. "The Khadorans have spent much time and effort restoring the city, and its walls are thick and well defended. A siege would be protracted and its outcome uncertain."

"I agree, Your Majesty," Chancellor Kinbrace said, disappointing Stryker. He couldn't imagine the man agreeing with Asheth Magnus about anything. "It is too well fortified."

"Yet we have reliable intelligence that only a single division defends the city," Ebonhart said. "That is not a lot of men, and if we strike quickly, and in force, we may overwhelm them."

Magnus shook his head. "There may be only a division there at the moment, but remember that the Khadorans control the Umbrean Line, which connects directly to Rynyr and Laedry. They could get troops to Merywyn in hours."

"The military presence in Laedry and Rynyr is minimal," Stryker said. "You should know that, General, if you'd studied the reports you were given."

"Lord General," Magnus said, and turned to Stryker. Duke Ebonhart stood between them, dwarfed somewhat by the two armored warcasters flanking him. "I have read yours and Duke Ebonhart's reports, and they were thorough . . . where it concerned the Khadoran military."

"What are you getting at, Magnus?" Ebonhart said. He was obviously growing frustrated with the challenge to his plan, though he had more tolerance for the man than Stryker did. Ebonhart had thrown in with Julius early in the civil war three years ago.

"What I'm getting at is the fact that the Prince Regent, Vladimir Tzepesci, has been amassing his liegemen and their household troops in Laedry. He has ten thousand heavy horse there: Iron Fang uhlans *and* drakhun."

"How do you know this?" Leto asked. He stood beside the throne and had been listening to the exchange, his brow creased with worry.

"Your Majesty," Magnus said, and then stopped, and smiled. "My pardon, High Chancellor. I am more accustomed to thinking of you as *King* Leto."

Rage boiled up within Stryker. Magnus' slip was no accident. It was another subtle jab to remind those who had once been his enemies, those who had forced him into exile, that he had weathered their storm, and their power had diminished while his had increased.

Leto held his composure and waved away the faux pas. "Continue."

"I was going to say that I have had loyal men in Laedry for quite some time. No one notices a mercenary, and they can get into places even the scout general's spies cannot."

"Rebald," Julius said, "what have your spies told you about Laedry?"

Rebald cleared his throat and rose. He was at the table to the left of Stryker, sitting next to Orin Midwinter. The two never seemed far apart these days. "Your Majesty, I have some reports of Vlad's men gathering in Laedry but not in the numbers General Magnus suggests."

"I trust the men I have in place there," Magnus said. "And it only follows that the Prince Regent would take steps to enforce his recent claim to the region."

Stryker frowned. Magnus' logic was hard to argue with. The

man had a keen mind, of that there was no doubt. Still, he could not let Magnus turn his plans aside so easily. "Your Majesty, while there is some logic to General Magnus' arguments, the men he has associated with these past years are hardly the kind I would call trustworthy or reliable. If what he says is true, Rebald would surely know about it."

Julius stared at Stryker, his face unreadable. There was no indication that he trusted Magnus' report. Stryker allowed himself to hope the young king might listen to him and Ebonhart. But that hope was quickly dashed.

"May I remind you, Lord General, I was one of the men with whom General Magnus associated," Julius said. He looked at Magnus. "General, if what you say is true, do you have an alternate plan of attack?"

Magnus nodded. "Of course, Your Majesty."

"Please relate it to the war council."

Magnus stepped out from behind the table and walked to the middle of the room, standing in front of the throne to address the assembled war council. "My plan is simple," he began. "We march our army through free Llael to Riversmet." He looked at Stryker and Ebonhart. "*There* you will have your siege."

The city of Riversmet sat on the confluence of the Black and Oldwick Rivers in northern occupied Llael. It was an important mercantile city, but it had been all but destroyed by Khador during the initial invasion.

"Why Riversmet?" Stryker asked, genuinely curious. "That's a long way to march a sizable army."

"Yes, but the walls of Riversmet were almost completely destroyed, and they have not been rebuilt. In addition, the city is currently garrisoned by no more than two battalions," Magnus said. "If we take it, we have access to the Black River and the ability to move troops quickly down to Merywyn when it is actually time to assault the capital."

"It is Kommander Harkevich who commands there, correct?" Leto asked.

Rebald answered. "That is correct, High Chancellor. He is

a skilled leader and a warcaster, but his talents lay more toward taking cities than holding them."

Stryker had never faced Harkevich in battle, but the Khadoran was known to be skilled with artillery and often used his warjacks as gun emplacements to great effect.

"Warmaster Ebonhart, Lord General Stryker," Julius said. "Tell me, how feasible is General Magnus' plan?"

Stryker looked over at Ebonhart, but the warmaster was looking straight ahead. He was Stryker's commanding officer, and it would improper for Stryker to speak first. But he knew what Ebonhart was going to say before the man opened his mouth, because Magnus' logic was unassailable. His plan promised a quick victory, which was vital for morale, and then a strategic holding in occupied Llael to conduct the rest of the invasion. Regardless of Stryker's personal thoughts about Magnus, the man had a talent for military strategy.

"It . . . is a sound plan," Ebonhart said. His jaw worked, as if he was chewing something particularly tough and vile tasting. "And, truthfully, a better plan than mine."

Stryker wondered if he would have been able to say that, no matter that it was true.

"I appreciate your candor, Duke Ebonhart," Julius said. "Lord General Stryker, are you in agreement with the warmaster?"

It was a pointed question, a test after his outburst in the inner council. The question was not if he agreed with Ebonhart, it was whether he could bring himself to publicly agree with Asheth Magnus. The weight of the question settled on him, and he was keenly aware that everyone in the throne room was looking at him.

He glanced at Maddox. She gave a minute shake of her head, a subtle urging to maintain his composure. He tried to push away that black, pulsing tangle of emotions that revolved around his memories of Asheth Magnus and think like the Lord General of the Cygnaran Army, someone concerned with the safety and well-being of his men and his nation.

He surprised himself by succeeding.

"I do, Your Majesty," Stryker said, though the words tasted like vinegar on his tongue. "Now that I have heard General Magnus' plan explained in greater detail, I see it is a sound one."

The tension in the room seemed to drain away, and the king nodded. "Good, then my most seasoned war leaders are in agreement. We shall execute General Magnus' plan, and he shall serve under your command, Lord General, when you lead the invasion force into Llael."

"Of course, Your Majesty," Stryker said. He glanced at Magnus. The older warcaster's face was passive, inert. If the king's decision bothered him, he wasn't showing it. "I would like to request that Major Maddox be assigned to the invasion force as well."

Julius considered this, then said, "Duke Ebonhart, have we further need of Major Maddox in Cygnar?"

"She has become quite popular with the people, Your Majesty, and her story does inspire support for the military and the crown," Ebonhart said. "We may need that more than ever in the coming days."

Stryker wondered how Maddox felt having her career discussed this way, as if she were a piece on game board, moved at the whim of powers greater than herself. He knew how it would make *him* feel.

"That may be true, Warmaster Ebonhart," High Chancellor Leto said, "but I think Major Maddox will serve us far better in Llael. Another war with Khador will not be well-received by the people of Cygnar, but if Major Maddox is with the invasion force, it may soften the public reaction."

Julius considered. "I agree, Uncle. I like the sound of the recently liberated Major Maddox going forth to liberate the oppressed people of Llael and hoist the flag of freedom over Riversmet."

"Just so, Your Majesty," Leto said.

There was the logic in that, but it pained Stryker to hear Maddox discussed in such a way. She was more than a propaganda piece, more than a symbol; she was an experienced warcaster. "Let us not forget that Major Maddox is a skilled battle leader and a talented warcaster. I agree that her presence will inspire, but make no mistake, my request for her inclusion is based on her *martial* prowess."

"Of course, Lord General," Leto said, and then turned to Maddox. "My apologies, Commander, if it appears we have made light of your accomplishments on the battlefield. That was not my intent."

"There is nothing to forgive, High Chancellor," Maddox said, inclining her head. "I am happy to serve Cygnar in any way I can."

She is a far better diplomat than I am, Stryker thought.

"Excellent," Julius said. His face was glowing, and there was excitement in his voice. It was clear to everyone in the chamber: the young king was eager to make his mark on the world. "Then let us discuss the particulars of our liberation of Llael."

— 11 —

THE WAR COUNCIL WENT ON for another three hours, revolving around the composition of the invasion force, allocation of resources and supplies, and moving the necessary troops from all over Cygnar to the fortress of Northguard on the border of Cygnar and Llael, the most logical mustering point.

The invasion force would be drawn largely from the Fifth Division garrisoned at Corvis and would include large numbers of trenchers, the versatile workhorses of the Cygnaran military. The 31st Storm Knight Company, commanded by Maddox and Stryker's old friend Captain Tews, would add heavy infantry and warjack support, as would with the 21st Sword Knight Company. It was a formidable assembly of some of Cygnar's finest military assets, though as they worked out the details, the weight of what they were actually doing—planning an invasion—settled on Stryker. He'd wrestled with the notion for weeks, and it was still alien to him.

He was relieved when King Julius finally called a halt to the proceedings, to be resumed the following day. He was weary, physically and emotionally, and completely unprepared for the spectacle that awaited him outside the throne room.

He heard raised voices at first, and a deep bellowing shout he recognized. Tews. He'd ordered the Stormblade captain to meet him here with a small contingent of senior Stormblades so he could begin briefing them on the battle plans.

Stryker hurried to the doors, Maddox and other members of the council close behind.

The doors opened and Stryker saw Tews, in full armor, standing inches away from a man Stryker had long thought dead. His name was Sebastian Harrow, and he had been a mercenary in service to Magnus long before the warcaster's exile. Stryker had had more than one run-in with the man, the last of which had incited him, young and brash, to take control of a warjack in the Fisherbrook jack foundry to protect his father. He'd lost control, and the damage the jack had caused had almost ruined Joseph Stryker. All of it had been engineered by Magnus, who had used Harrow to manipulate Stryker.

Harrow was tall and gaunt, his face a weathered network of scars and ugliness. He wore a long sword and a heavy pistol, and Stryker had seen firsthand how fast he was with his gun. His hand hovered over the butt of the weapon now. He also wore what looked to be trencher armor with a captain's bars on his breastplate. It seemed General Magnus had *promoted* some of his most trusted mercenaries to positions in the Cygnaran military, surrounding himself with men he could rely on.

Three senior Stormblades stood behind Tews, all three lieutenants. They did not have their hands on their weapons, but their faces were pinched with uncertainty. They'd likely never seen Tews in such a state. Harrow was not alone, either; the two mercs that had been with Magnus stood behind him. They did not look uncertain or even worried—instead, they looked eager.

"You will take that back, you mercenary dog, or I will cut you down," Tews said, practically roaring.

Harrow smirked, unfazed by the giant Stormblade. "I only

spoke the truth, Captain. Khador smashed you out of Northguard with little effort."

Tews face was crimson. "Good men *died* there, you miserable cur," he said. His hand was on the grip of his storm glaive, the mighty voltaic-powered sword of the Stormblades. Stryker had seen Tews cut armored men in half with that blade.

Royal Guard were gathering around the pair, and it would get ugly if Stryker didn't intercede, though he'd like nothing more than to see Tews remove Harrow's head.

"Captain! Stand down. Right now."

Tews turned toward Stryker, and the rage seemed to drain out of him at the sight of his commanding officer. He took a step back, away from Harrow, and let his hand fall away from the hilt of his storm glaive.

"Captain Harrow, what happened here?" Magnus said from behind Stryker. The older warcaster walked around Stryker and approached his man. Leto and Duke Ebonhart had followed them out, and Stryker could hear the rest of the council emptying behind them. He hoped the king had retired to his chambers, accessible through the rear of the throne room.

Harrow took a step back, though he did not take his hand from the butt of his pistol. "Just a friendly debate," he said, and flashed a grin at Tews. "Seems I inadvertently struck a nerve."

Tews threw a murderous glance at the mercenary and then turned to Stryker. "I'm sorry, sir," he said. "He was insulting the 31st and the men who died at Northguard. He said we were cowards."

Tews had lost people close to him there. So had Stryker, and he understood the captain's anger, but all eyes were on them, on him. "Tews, return to the compound at once; we *will* discuss this further."

"Yes, sir," Tews said and stalked off.

"My apologies, Captain," Harrow called after the big Stormblade. "Seems I got you into a spot of trouble with the brass."

Rage boiled within Stryker, hot and acrid. He wanted to

maintain his composure and show Magnus and the rest of the council he would not be provoked, but the last few hours had thinned his defenses. "Magnus, if don't put a muzzle on that dog, I will have him beaten from the city."

Magnus said something to Harrow that Stryker couldn't hear, and the merc nodded and then walked away. Magnus said, "I will deal with my subordinate, Lord General, just as you will deal with yours."

It wasn't enough. Stryker had weathered the storm of Magnus' overriding him in the council chamber, but seeing Harrow again dredged up old hurts he could not ignore. "How could you bring that man to court?" he asked. "Harrow is a thug and a killer. You know that."

Magnus shrugged. "He's loyal, and I have had need of thugs and killers in the past fifteen years. *We* may have need for them now."

"Like attracts like," Stryker said. "That you would let such men serve you tells me you are no different than they are. You never were."

"Oh," Magnus said, "I believe you have employed mercenaries yourself, Lord General. Did you vet them all to make sure they were of strong, moral character?"

Stryker stalked up to Magnus. "You are a traitor and a liar," he said. "You always were. I don't know what spell you've cast over our king, but I know you for what you are. You do not belong here. You belong at the end of rope."

"Stryker, that is enough," High Chancellor Leto said.

Stryker turned to the former king, wanting to shout *you, of all people, KNOW what he is*, but he held his tongue, biting the inside of his cheek hard enough to draw blood.

"Don't fret. I do not take offense, High Chancellor," Magnus said. "Coleman—pardon, Lord General Stryker—and I have a . . . complicated past. I am sure we will soon move past that."

"Let's go, sir." Maddox's was hand on Stryker's forearm. "We need to brief the men."

"Listen to the major, Stryker," Duke Ebonhart said. "That's an order."

Maddox was pulling him now, and he wanted to resist, to remain and rail at those who would accept this traitor back into their midst. Perhaps it was Maddox's presence that swayed him. He drew in a deep breath, ragged and cold, and swallowed down his rage.

"Yes, sir," Stryker said. "My apologies for the outburst, High Chancellor." Each word was grinding acquiescence. Magnus had made him look the fool, and he'd done it easily enough.

He turned and walked away, Maddox beside him. She didn't say anything until they were out of the palace. Once they were beyond all ears, she turned to him and said, "Permission to speak freely, sir?"

He grimaced. That only meant one thing. She wanted to berate him for making an ass of himself. He could refuse her. He had that right as her superior officer. But he respected her too much for that. "Go ahead."

"Thank you. What in the name of Morrow were you doing in there?" she said.

"You don't know that merc, Harrow," Stryker said. "The fact that he's here, with Magnus, speaks volumes about our new general."

Maddox sighed. "The only one speaking volumes of anything back there was you. In front of the High Chancellor and your superior officers, I might add."

"I *know*, but I feel like everyone is turning a blind eye to Magnus, overlooking what he really is."

"What he *is* right now is one of the king's favorites, a man Julius trusts probably more than anyone else on the council. You have to know you won't convince anyone by confronting him directly."

Stryker stopped and put his hand on Maddox's armored shoulders. "Do *you* believe me?" he asked. "Do *you* think Magnus is dangerous?"

She stared at him unflinchingly. After a long pause, she said. "I don't know. That's the truth. I want to, actually. You have a history with the man that gives you insight into his character that no one else has, but it's been fifteen years. Who knows what he is today."

"People don't change like that," Stryker said.

"He's lived a hard life since Vinter was deposed, and I *do* know that can change you. A lot."

There was no doubt her time as a prisoner of the Protectorate had changed her, and not for the better, but Stryker couldn't bring himself to equate her misery to whatever had happened during Magnus' self-induced exile. "It's not the same. In his heart, he's still the ambitious, power-hungry monster he was before."

"Well, let's say he is," Maddox said and stopped. A group of trenchers walking up the road toward them saluted as they went by. Stryker and Maddox returned the salute, and then began turned in the other direction. "So, my point still stands. Julius may be blind to it, and that means he needs you more than ever, even if he doesn't realize it. You have got to at least give the appearance you can work with Magnus if for no other reason so you can watch him."

She was right, of course, as she often was, but Magnus awoke such a storm of emotion in Stryker that it was hard for him to think straight. He'd managed it at the war council, thanks in part due to her advice, but the thought of holding his anger in check day in and day out on the march to Llael seemed an almost impossible task.

He drew in a deep breath and let it out slowly. "You're a good officer," he said. "I wish I had your level-headedness at times."

She laughed. "Well, being rash and headstrong has served you . . . at times."

"Here and there," he said. He wasn't the planner that someone like Magnus was, but he'd always trusted his instincts, and they'd rarely steered him wrong. He strove to be the kind of man other men wanted to follow. That had always been his primary goal.

"Look, I don't like what Rebald and Ebonhart have made out of me," she said, her face hardening. "I'm little more than a recruitment poster these days, aren't I? But I have to follow orders, and you do, too."

"There's more at stake here than the chain of command," Stryker said.

"Of course there is," she said, "but you have to set an example for the rest of the men. You have to show them you can buckle down and accept a situation you don't like, that you hate even, if that what's it takes to get the job done."

"I'm not denying any of it. I just can't forget what he is."

"Try *harder*," she said. There was steel in her voice.

"I will. I promise. But make no mistake, when Magnus reveals what I know he is, I also promise I'm going to be there."

She nodded. "Good. Make sure of that."

It was clear Maddox was done talking about Magnus. They walked in companionable silence, but as they neared the garrison, she spoke up again. "By the way, thank you for getting me out of here. I think I might have gone mad if you'd marched to Llael without me."

Stryker smiled. "I meant everything I said in there. You're one of the best warcasters in Cygnar, and I want you fighting by my side."

"I appreciate it, sir. So, what are you going to do about Captain Tews?"

"Say pretty much to him what you just said to me," Stryker said. "I can't blame the man for wanting to kill Harrow. I've wanted to kill him for over a decade."

She snorted. "Seems fair to me."

PART II

—12—

Outside Corvis, Cygnar

THE RAILCAR BOUNCED AND ROLLED over the countryside, and the jostling, the constant sense of motion, soothed Stryker. He'd ridden in the more comfortable troop car with the other officers from Caspia all the way to Bainsmarket, overseeing the loading of troops and gear at stops in King's Vine and Fharin. Now, on the last leg of their journey to Corvis, he'd sought out one of the heavy, reinforced cars carrying the army's warjacks.

He sat in the dark, his warcaster armor humming, its galvanic relays painting the walls with flickering blue light. There were four heavy warjacks in the car with him—two Ironclads and two Stormclads—all secured with heavy chains to the railcar walls. They were dim, hulking shadows, hunched and silently menacing, like brooding steel gargoyles. All were powered down but one.

He'd powered up Ol' Rowdy during the stop in Bainsmarket, and the old warjack's eyes blazed crimson in the darkened car. Stryker was connected to the warjack's cortex, Rowdy's mechanikal brain, and he was drifting through its memories. Rowdy had been with him for fifteen years, assigned to him during his journeyman tour. He had served other warcasters for thirty-five years prior to that and was one of the first Ironclads to be assembled. The warjack was unpredictable, cantankerous, and devastating in combat, a combination that made him difficult to control for everyone but Stryker. The two had a bond; some suggested they were kindred spirits, if such a thing could be said about a warjack and its warcaster.

Stryker had been through many battles with Rowdy, and the warjack's memories were filled with blood and fire. Stryker did not shrink from these images—he embraced them. They would steel him against the chaos of the battles to follow. But there was another reason Stryker often visited the limited stored experiences in Ol' Rowdy's cortex. The faces of friends and men he'd commanded sometimes drifted up, men who had given their lives to protect Cygnar and all it represented. Before every campaign, he subjected himself to the ghosts of these fallen, their slack faces and torn bodies serving as a reminder of what was at stake each time he stepped onto yet another battlefield.

Stryker knew it might be grim, and he could not deny that revisiting the ethereal graveyard in Ol' Rowdy's cortex took a toll on him, but it also galvanized him, reminding him of his duty as a leader of men. Every decision he made on the battlefield cost lives, and it was his job to mitigate those losses as best he could.

The memories were usually colored by Ol' Rowdy's perception of the events. Warjacks had rudimentary personalities that could become stronger and more defined the longer they remained in service. And a warjack could develop simple emotions like anger, aggression, even grief over time, which could make them harder to control. Some warcasters saw the development of a warjack's personality as an impediment to their use on the battlefield. But Stryker didn't agree with that. His warjacks were soldiers like any others, and the bonds that developed between them only made warcaster and warjack stronger, more in tune, increasing the efficacy of their symbiotic relationship.

Stryker was jarred out of his memories by the sudden lurching halt of the rail car. He pulled away from Rowdy's cortex and let his mind drift into the mechanikal brains of the other warjacks in the car. They were inert, akin to a human sleeping, but he pulled each one out of its mechanikal slumber, bidding it power up. Soon the railcar was lit by six pairs of luminous eyes.

The railcar door opened abruptly, letting in the light and noise of one thousand men and machines. This was only the first of more troop trains to come; they would all meet up at the same mustering point near Northguard. Soldiers set a heavy ramp in place, wide and sturdy enough to take the multi-ton weight of offloading warjacks.

Stryker spun up the arcane turbine on his armor, pushing more energy into the suit and lending himself enough strength to easily handle his weapon, the giant two-handed mechanikal blade Quicksilver. It was based on a Caspian battle blade, a heavy two-handed sword favored by the knights of Cygnar, but it was scaled up significantly, longer and heavier. Its mechanikal augmentation made it lighter and more nimble, but it still weighed nearly sixty pounds and was impossible to wield without the added strength from his warcaster armor.

Stryker set Quicksilver across his back, magnetic patches holding the blade in place, and ordered each warjack to fire its boiler and begin building the steam that gave power to its limbs.

"Rest well, sir?" Maddox asked and walked up the ramp into the railcar. She wore her warcaster armor and her mechanika blade Tempest across her back.

"Needed to spend some quality time with Rowdy," he answered. "He gets lonely on long trips."

In response the big warjack vented a shrill whistle of steam and looked in their direction.

"Yeah, we're talking about you," Stryker said. "Now get up."

"You sure you're not trying to avoid something or someone, sir?" Maddox suggested, smiling.

"No, Major, I'm not," he said, faintly irritated. She didn't know about his pre-battle ritual with Ol' Rowdy, and he didn't want to share it with her, but her accusation stung him a bit just the same. "Take the three Stormclads and move them out. I'll take Rowdy and the other Ironclads."

"Yes, sir," she said and the subtle buzz of magic stirred the air as she connected to the warjacks he'd indicated.

The warjacks' boilers were sufficiently hot to provide locomotion, and all six stood, their tether chains rattling, smoke belching from their stacks.

Together, Stryker and Maddox led the great machines down the ramp and out into the bright afternoon sun. The rail line ended some thirty miles from Corvis, and they would need to march the rest of the way to Northguard. He looked down the long row of rail cars at the hundreds of soldiers disembarking. It was chaos at the moment, but he trusted his officers, and they'd have the men ready to move out soon enough.

There was a small town at the end of the railway, and hundreds of townsfolk had gathered to get a look at the Cygnaran Army. News of the invasion was widespread now, and the reaction from the populace had been better than Stryker had anticipated. This had a lot to do with one person in particular.

"Major Maddox! The Liberator of Llael!" he heard someone cry from the crowd of Cygnaran citizens, a cry that was echoed throughout the gathering. They'd seen Maddox, and they'd instantly recognized the new face of the Cygnaran Army.

Maddox forced a strained smile and turned to wave at the crowd. A bright chorus of cheers went up.

"You're bloody famous, Beth," Stryker said and chuckled. He'd seen similar reactions in the other towns they'd stopped at. The "Liberator of Llael," as she'd been dubbed, had become somewhat larger than life, a symbol for justice and an end to Khadoran tyranny.

"With respect: eat shit, sir," she said through her clench-jawed smile, still waving.

He threw his head back and laughed. "All right, then. If you're through with your fans, let's get this army moving."

"Morrow above, please," she said. "Wagons from Corvis should meet us here in the next couple of hours. They'll take the warjacks while we march the troops north to the mustering point outside Northguard."

"All right. I know I'm going to regret this, but where is Magnus?"

She turned and pointed.

The older warcaster was moving through the crowd of troops swarming around the train. Trenchers and even sword knights moved out of his way without a word. He wore the same cobbled-together armor he'd worn back in Caspia, though he'd added a coat of blue paint to it, and a Cygnus had been added to the breastplate. His own mechanikal sword, Foecleaver, was sheathed across his back next to a holstered scattergun.

Harrow walked beside Magnus, and to Stryker's perpetual disgust, the man wore a suit of trencher armor, a *captain's* armor, to be exact. He'd been given that rank shortly before they'd left Caspia. The rest of Magnus' officers followed behind him, all of them former mercenaries.

A sudden surge of anger spiked Stryker's mind. Ol' Rowdy was standing close by, and the warjack had reacted to the sudden shift in Stryker's emotions at seeing Magnus. He reached out and put a hand on the big warjack's hull, drawing strength from its bulk and heat.

"Lord General," Magnus said as he approached. He glanced up at the towering warjack next to Stryker. "Good to see Rowdy's still in service."

The big Ironclad vented steam, a low, irritated hoot, and took a step toward Magnus.

"Easy, Rowdy," Stryker said and clamped down on the warjack's aggression. "He's a loyal soldier," he said to Magnus.

"No doubt." Magnus hadn't flinched when Rowdy moved toward him, though the warcaster would have felt the surge of animosity from the warjack. He looked back at Stryker. "I suggest we gather senior officers to coordinate the march to Llael."

It had been Stryker's next planned move, and he hated that Magnus had suggested it before he could give the order. He didn't want to appear petty, so he nodded. "Agreed, General. Maddox, gather the senior officers. We'll meet by the engine."

"Sir," Maddox said. Her gaze lingered on Stryker for a moment. It was obvious she didn't want to leave him and Magnus alone.

"Now, please, Major," Stryker said. Maddox turned and moved down the railway.

"So, it's a march to Northguard then up the Great Northern Tradeway into Llael," Magnus said. "Should take us three weeks to reach Riversmet."

"That's what I've calculated, General," Stryker said. Why Magnus thought it necessary to reiterate these well-known details to him was a mystery. "How are your men adjusting to serving in a proper military?" He glanced at Harrow. The man wore the same conceited smirk Stryker had seen outside the throne room in Caspia—Harrow also wore trencher armor with a captain's bars on the right pauldron. Stryker couldn't wrap his head around the fact that Harrow was giving orders to Cygnaran soldiers, but the king had granted Magnus' request that some of his men be allowed to serve him in an official capacity.

"Well enough," Magnus said. "Like me, they're shaking off the rust a bit."

"I'm sure."

"It suits me," Harrow said, his smile widening. "I quite like giving orders to men who fight for something other than coin. Makes a man feel . . . proper."

Stryker ignored him. He couldn't bring himself to speak directly to Harrow. He was relieved to see Maddox returning with the senior officers, Captain Tews among them.

Once they'd gathered, he gave a brief overview of their marching orders. "Once transportation for the warjacks arrives from Corvis, we'll march to the mustering point outside Northguard. We'll hook up with Colonel Bartlett and elements of the 82nd heavy cavalry regiment. Then we'll move up the Black River and into Llael."

Nods all around. None of this was new information; that was next.

"We will march to Greywind Tower, where we will rendezvous with Colonel Stoyan Jarov of the Llaelese Resistance." Stryker paused, letting that sink in. He had sent word to Greywind Tower not long after they'd left Caspia. Though it has been decided the Resistance would not be an official part of the Cygnaran invasion force, it would be stupid to ignore the potential value they represented to this war effort.

"I thought we weren't involving the Resistance," Captain Tews said, giving voice to what everyone else was likely thinking.

"Officially, we're not," Stryker said. "But the colonel has vital intelligence about Riversmet that we cannot do without."

"He'll want to send troops with us," Magnus said. "How far does this unofficial involvement go, sir?"

"I expect to use some of his scouts, if he'll let us, but no front line troops."

Magnus said nothing more as Stryker briefed the rest of the officers on what to expect in the coming weeks. By the time he'd dismissed them all, the wagons from Corvis could be seen moving across the flat northern plains toward the railway. The officers hurried to get their men and equipment ready for the long march. Magnus, however, lingered.

"You surprise me, Stryker," he said, a strange look on his face.

"How's that?" Stryker suspected he was taking bait of some kind.

"That you'd involve the Resistance surprises me," Magnus said. "Do not misunderstand. I agree with you. The Resistance likely has vital intelligence that is far more important than the political ramifications of involving them."

Stryker said nothing.

"You surprise me because it's exactly what I would have done," Magnus said, saluted, and walked away.

Stryker watched him go, hating the pride he felt at the faint praise from his former mentor.

— 13 —

THE BATTLEMENTS OF GREYWIND TOWER ROSE over the rolling hills of eastern Llael, a grim sentinel, weathered and battle tested. The tower was eighty feet high and large enough to hold several hundred soldiers. The Resistance had done some repair work to the crumbling three-hundred-year-old fortress, so the ancient grey stone was pockmarked by lighter-colored rock that had been quarried in the nearby hills.

A small town had sprung up around the tower, a town composed primarily of refugees fleeing Khadoran tyranny. The township was a ramshackle conglomeration of tents, shacks, and a few proper buildings. The people here supported the Resistance fighters fervently, providing for the soldiers within the tower by performing various necessary tasks: cooking, mending uniforms, repairing weapons, anything to help.

The town seemed empty as they approached. Stryker could

hardly blame them. These people had come to distrust any army that did not fly the Llaelese flag, and eight thousand Cygnaran troops, supported by warjacks and heavy horse, had no doubt frightened them away.

Stryker had ordered the bulk of their army to make camp two miles south of the tower, and he had chosen a small delegation to meet with Colonel Jarov. The delegation included Major Maddox, Captain Tews, and General Asheth Magnus. He'd wanted to leave Magnus behind, but he couldn't exclude the general from such important meetings without jeopardizing the mission.

They passed through the town outside the tower in silence and found Colonel Jarov and two other men standing outside the tower gates. Soldiers looked down on them from the battlements above. Jarov was a short, solidly built man in his mid-fifties. His blunt features and his surname suggested Khadoran descent, though his lineage had not affected his rise to prominence in the Resistance. The two men standing next to the colonel caught Stryker's eye immediately. The man to the right looked to be in his early forties, was tall and lean, even gaunt, with a thin mustache and sharp features. His black hair was long and tied into a loose tail behind his head. His black greatcoat was drawn back at the waist, exposing the double-barreled magelock on his right hip and a long mechanika saber on his left. The gun left little doubt in Stryker's mind as to the man's profession, but the stylized rose pinned to his lapel confirmed it. He had clearly been a gun mage of the defunct Loyal Order of the Amethyst Rose, and a veteran one at that.

The man on Jarov's left clashed with the silent menace of the gun mage opposite him. The second man was of middling height, pot-bellied, with his face obscured by an unkempt dark beard. Stryker might have taken him for a refugee if not for his armor, which was not of Llaelese manufacture. It was Cygnaran trencher armor, much repaired, and though bits of it had been replaced, it was still recognizable for what it was. Many Cygnaran soldiers had been left behind after the withdrawal from Merywyn, and some had chosen to fight on with the Resistance. Technically, these men and women were deserters, but Stryker could sympathize with their positions, though it was brave—and a bit foolhardy—for this man to expose himself this way.

"Welcome, Lord General Stryker," Colonel Jarov said as they drew near. He stepped forward and offered his hand. Stryker had never met the colonel, though Jarov had a reputation as a skilled leader and tactician.

Stryker gripped Jarov's hand. "Thank you, Colonel. I appreciate you meeting with us, especially in light of my government's refusal to involve the Resistance in this invasion."

Jarov grimaced and released Stryker's hand. Stryker wanted to get the ugly truth of the situation out of the way first before they spoke further. "Yes, it is unfortunate that your new king does not trust us to liberate our own nation . . ." He paused, then gave Stryker a tired smile. "But we are soldiers, yes? And we must do what we are told. At the end of the day, we want the same thing—a free Llael."

"When this is over, Llael and Cygnar will be brothers, bound together by the bonds of battle and marriage," Stryker said.

"We will be a vassal state of Cygnar, you mean," the gun mage behind Jarov said. "With a puppet queen on the throne."

Jarov glared back at the man, then returned his attention to Stryker. "Lord General, this is Captain Vayne di Brascio of the Loyal Order of the Amethyst Rose. He is a ferocious fighter, but no diplomat, I'm afraid."

"It's quite all right," Stryker said. "I have long admired the skill of your order, Captain. And I am grateful for your assistance. Have you met Princess Kaetlyn?"

The gun mage shook his head slowly.

"Then trust me when I say that girl . . . that *woman*, will be no man's puppet. She is a di la Martyn, make no mistake."

"I have heard much about you, Lord General," Captain di Brascio said. "And I know you have been a friend to Llael. You have fought valiantly for her, but your king insults us, and some say he is too much like his father."

"This is enough, Captain," Jarov said. "This is not the time or place for such discussions, if you please."

Stryker said nothing, but the man was perceptive, and he echoed Stryker's own fears about Julius.

"As you wish, sir," the captain said.

"Let me introduce you to my senior officers, Colonel," Stryker said, eager to change the subject. "This is Commander Elizabeth Maddox."

"The Liberator of Llael," Vayne said under his breath with a sour laugh. Stryker ignored him, but Maddox grimaced in reaction.

"This warjack-sized brute is Captain Tews. He commands my Stormblade infantry." The big Stormblade nodded at the colonel. Stryker steeled himself for the last introduction. "And this is General Asheth Magnus, my second-in-command."

The man in trencher armor behind Jarov drew in a sharp breath, his eyes wide. He stepped to the colonel's side. "Sir, this man is a traitor and a criminal," he said. "We cannot treat with such as this."

The man was undeniably former Cygnaran military, and his blunt and undiplomatic assessment of Magnus was not surprising.

Jarov frowned. "My apologies, Lord General, but Captain Gibbs is right. Why is Asheth Magnus among you?"

"I have been pardoned by King Julius," Magnus said before Stryker could answer. "And I am once again a loyal subject of Cygnar."

Stryker's stomach roiled. He could relate to their mistrust of Magnus, but he needed their information, and so he found himself in the unenviable position of defending a man he loathed. "This is true, Colonel. King Julius has the utmost faith in the general, and the general's military experience will serve us well here." The words were ash on his tongue.

Jarov shook his head. "I promised you I would give you what information I have, and I will do so." He was visibly unnerved by Magnus' presence, but Stryker was relieved the colonel was a man of his word. "Follow me."

The gates of Greywind Tower opened. Dozens of soldiers were arrayed in the courtyard beyond. They stood at attention, rifles against their shoulders. Whether it was meant to be a subtle threat or a display of Llaelese discipline, Stryker couldn't say. He looked back at Magnus, whose face was stony and unreadable.

"After you, sir," Magnus said, and Stryker stepped through the gates.

...

COLONEL JAROV LISTENED INTENTLY as Magnus outlined for him in broad strokes of their plan to attack Riversmet. They sat in the colonel's relatively lavish chambers, seated around a roaring fire, glasses of good Llaelese wine in hand. They would spend the night at the tower, one last chance to sleep in a bed and eat a hot meal before the long march to Riversmet.

Captain Vayne di Brascio had joined them, and the gun mage's expression grew more and more dour as Magnus laid out his strategy. Captain Gibbs was not present; perhaps he was afraid of spending too much time among men who might cart him back to Cygnar as a deserter, Stryker imagined.

Maddox added small details to Magnus' explanation, largely the logistics on troops and how they would be deployed. Stryker and Tews were both silent. Stryker found himself growing uncomfortable that Colonel Jarov had said nothing to this point.

When Magnus finished, Jarov cleared his throat and said, "Your plan is sound. In theory, that is, but the reality of the situation is much different than you have anticipated."

Magnus frowned. "Please explain, Colonel."

"I'll let Captain di Brascio explain. He has led a number of patrols in that area, and he has seen the situation in Riversmet firsthand. Captain."

"You're right, General, that the western portion of the city is still weakened, and they would expect an attack to come from that direction, which is why you've chosen to attack the eastern portion of the city."

Stryker said, "But?"

"The eastern part of the city is heavily fortified," di Brascio continued. "That part of Riversmet was largely left intact after the initial Khadoran assault, and Harkevich has spent nearly all his men and resources rebuilding it."

"Of course, we expected Kommander Harkevich would not be completely unprepared for an assault," Magnus said, an edge of irritation creeping into his voice.

"He is more than prepared," di Brascio said. "He is all but impregnable from that side. He's demolished every bridge across the Black River save one, The Great Gate, and it is the only way across. He also has a small fleet of gunboats patrolling the river to discourage anyone foolish enough to attempt a crossing elsewhere."

"Understood," Maddox said. "So, we take the bridge. What are its defenses?"

"Considerable. The Great Gate is a fortress unto itself, heavily fortified, and manned by an entire battalion of Man-O-War. But that's not the worst of it. Harkevich has recently taken delivery of a pair of Conquests, and they stand guard at the far end of the bridge."

That was a problem. Conquests were gigantic warjacks, often called colossals. They were walking artillery batteries, armed with massive double-barreled cannons that could fire explosive shells up to a mile.

Tews glared at Magnus and clenched his huge fists. "We'll be bottlenecked on that bridge, and those damn colossals will take out our people on the bridge, regardless of what our Stormwalls do in return," Tews said, naming the Cygnaran counterparts to the Conquest, gigantic galvanic warjacks that could fill a battlefield with their immense destructive capabilities.

"That's right," di Brascio said. "The Conquests are supported by batteries of heavy artillery, and trust me, Harkevich knows how to use them."

Magnus rubbed his mouth and stared at di Brascio. It was the first time Stryker had seen the man flustered since he'd returned. He took grim satisfaction in Magnus' perfect plan coming apart at the seams, but there was much more at stake here than just seeing his old enemy humiliated.

"We could cross farther south of Riversmet and attack the city from the east," Stryker said.

"No, that won't work, either," the gun mage said. "Harkevich has destroyed every bridge large enough within a hundred miles of the city. Once you cross into occupied territory, he'll know you're coming, and you'll be hounded the entire way. Not to mention, it will give him time to secure reinforcements from Rynyr."

"Then what do you recommend, Captain?" Magnus said. It was quite obvious it pained him to ask the question, but he was no fool, and di Brascio was their only chance now.

"I think your plan is still sound," di Brascio said. "Attacking from the west affords you the element of surprise. You can reach the city largely unmolested *and* without alerting Harkevich. But once you're there, he's going to be a hard nut to crack . . . unless you have help from the inside."

Magnus cocked his head. "What do you mean?"

"As you are no doubt aware, Kommander Harkevich is the military commander in Riversmet, but powerful kayazy merchant princes have interests in the town as well."

Stryker didn't like where this was going.

"A man named Lord Pytor Aleshko oversees mercantile interests in the city."

"Wait. How does this help us?" Maddox asked. "Do you know something useful about this man?"

di Brascio sat back in his chair and folded his arms across his chest. "Truthfully, I'm not certain," he admitted. "What we have heard are only rumors, though they are intriguing enough to listen to. We hear he is as corrupt as Harkevich is patriotic, a man always looking for an advantage, always looking for a way to increase his wealth and power. He took over all operations when the man before him was executed by the Protectorate."

Magnus said, "Such men are easier to deal with than idealistic patriots like Harkevich." Stryker did not miss the sidelong glance Magnus cast his way.

"Yes, my thoughts exactly," di Brascio said. "He may be approachable."

Stryker considered their choices. "If this man is as untrustworthy as you've heard, why would we contact him? He's not stupid enough to throw open the gates for us, no matter what we pay him."

"I give you this information only because I have it, and because you cannot take the Great Gate in a frontal assault."

"Captain, I have an army behind me and enough firepower to *level* Riversmet."

"Is that your intention, Lord General?" Colonel Jarov said. "There are still many loyal Llaelese citizens living under the yoke of Khadoran oppression in Riversmet."

Heat rose to Stryker's face. "No, of course not," he said. "I simply mean that we may be able to take the Great Gate without resorting to Lord Aleshko."

di Brascio shook his head. "Even if you do take it, you will lose a lot of men, and you may not be able to hold the city afterward. Of course, if you had the Resistance involved . . ."

"But I don't," Stryker said. He would not go down that road; it was too tempting. "I will not defy my king further than I already have."

"Then what you do recommend, Lord General?" Magnus asked. The question was dagger-sharp.

"We need to see the bridge and its defenses for ourselves," Stryker said. He looked at di Brascio. "I do not doubt your assessment, but it is only one piece of the equation. *You* do not understand the capabilities of my men as well as I do."

"As you say," di Brascio said, "but I have fought for Llael for twenty years. My experience tells me Harkevich will hurt you badly if you attack him straight on."

"I appreciate your candor," Stryker said and meant it. The gun mage was growing on him. The man was obviously experienced, disciplined, and knowledgeable. "And you have given us valuable information. If I might ask one more favor, Colonel?"

"Ask," Jarov said.

"Your scouts have provided you with good intelligence on Riversmet and likely the road between here and there. Would you loan me some of your men to see us to the city?"

"I had anticipated this request," Jarov said. "Captain di Brascio and a unit of my best scouts will go with you."

"I will not put them in harm's way if I can avoid it," Stryker said.

di Brascio laughed. "With respect, Lord General, you can't avoid that."

— 14 —

Ten Miles from Riversmet, Occupied Llael

STRYKER LOOKED DOWN AT THE HUGE MAP spread out in front of him. It was a detailed blueprint of the city of Riversmet, provided to them by Colonel Jarov. It also showed a good portion of the Black River on the eastern side of the city. They were assembled in his command tent in the center of the Cygnaran camp. It was large but not lavish, providing enough room for his armor, weapons, and the big, low table for the map. The presence of Maddox and Magnus made it crowded.

"The Great Gate," Maddox said and pointed to a wide bridge on the eastern side. "If di Brascio is correct, these"—she pointed to a number of smaller bridges—"have been destroyed."

"And if he's right, then we must discuss other options." Magnus let the last word hang in the air between them.

"I need more information before I reach out to this Pytor Aleshko," Stryker said, making no attempt to hide his irritation. Magnus had made it very clear he thought the kayazy was an avenue they should explore immediately.

"I know men like this. Greedy, without loyalty," Magnus said. Stryker suspected Magnus had just described himself. "I know how to manipulate such men. I know what motivates them."

Stryker was about to reply when one of his guards, a young Stormblade, stepped into the tent. "Sir, di Brascio and the rest of the scouts have returned."

Stryker nodded. "Thank you. I'll speak with them outside."

All three of them left the tent and stepped into the noise and stench of the huge camp. Rows of tents stretched in all direction, and men and warjacks moved among them preparing for the next day's march and the battle that would soon follow. It was a huge operation; he couldn't let the army sit for much longer. They had considerable stores of food and water, but an army this large could eat a small city's worth of food every day.

di Brascio and four of Stryker's best scouts were waiting for him. The Cygnaran scouts were all experienced men, but two of them—recommended by Major Tobias Johnson, who commanded the small force of rangers, Cygnar's best scouts—were a strange sight, even to Stryker. Swift Sergeant Sharp and his mate, Corporal Horgrum, where an odd pair. Sharp was a lean, haggard man of middling height. He had a ranger's lean build, and he looked quick and hardy. The other half of his two-man team stood out like a cannon among pistols. Corporal Horgrum was a trollkin who stood at least seven feet tall. He wore customized light trencher armor and was a walking wall of blue-leathery skinned muscle. His face was broad with a wide mouth, a huge lower jaw, and no indication of a nose. Thick patches of rocklike scales covered his chin like a beard, and his head was crowned with a thicket of spiny quills. The trollkin gripped a truly gigantic rifle—a Raevhan Express, a sniper rifle too large for a human to fire and with an effective range of over half a mile.

"Corporal Horgrum," Stryker said. "I'm glad to have you along with us. I've heard a lot about you and that rifle of yours."

The big trollkin returned a smile. "I call her Dhunia's Mercy," he said, naming the goddess whom trollkin worshipped.

Sharp looked horrified and elbowed the big trollkin in the ribs. "Say *sir*, you big lout," he said. "That's a bloody lord general you're speaking to."

"Uh, sir," Horgrum added. "My apologies. Still adjusting to life among you . . . the military."

Stryker chuckled and waved away the breach of etiquette. "No offense taken, Corporal. You're here to shoot, not to bow and scrape after me."

It wasn't unheard of for non-humans to serve in the Cygnaran military. Gobbers made up a fair portion of the mechaniks' corps, and trollkin and even ogrun had been taken and trained as trenchers. Most trollkin, however, were tribal people who lived in the wild places of western Immoren, though some had settled in Cygnaran cities, and a handful of those served in the army. Trollkin were brave and loyal fighters, and Corporal Horgrum was said to be one of the finest snipers in the army.

"Okay, Sergeant," Stryker said, turning to the trollkin's companion. "Report." He wasn't ignoring di Brascio, but he needed to hear it from his own men.

"Yes, sir," Sharp said. "It's like Captain di Brascio said. That bridge is a bloody castle and guarded by enough Reds to make me more than a little nervous, I don't mind saying."

"And the other bridges?" Magnus said.

"Gone, sir," Horgrum said, his voice the low rumble of grinding stones. "They tore them all down."

"We couldn't get too close," Sharp continued. "Riverboats patrol near the shore, but we saw the colossals, and I counted eight Destroyers on the bridge." He named one of Khadoran warjack chassis armed with a long-ranged mortar.

To run that many warjacks day and night would eat up a lot of coal, Stryker was well aware. Harkevich had to be getting supplies from the mining town of Rynyr to the west. It was good information—if they could cut that supply line somehow.

"Not that I doubted your word, Captain," Stryker said turning to di Brascio. "But . . ."

"I understand, Lord General," di Brascio said. "You should

know the bridge has three fortified towers. One at each end and one in the middle. Each holds a garrison of Man-O-War shocktroopers and snipers. They also provide cover and force an enemy army through a series of narrow gates."

That wasn't good. It was as Captain Tews had said at Greywind Tower: they'd be bottlenecked and picked to pieces if they tried a frontal assault. "Sharp, you're dismissed. Get some food into you and your men, then I want you back out there."

"Sir," Sharp said. He and the rest of the Cygnaran scouts went in search of the nearest mess tent.

"Captain, if you'd join us in my tent," Stryker said.

di Brascio dismissed his own men and followed Stryker.

"I need options," Stryker said once everyone was gathered around the map.

Maddox said, "I agree with Captain di Brascio. A frontal assault on the bridge, even with our Defenders and Stormwalls, is going to cost us badly." She named two of their best warjacks for siege work.

"No fortress is impregnable," Magnus said, "though it's sometimes more prudent to go *around* an obstacle than to go *through* it."

Stryker knew what Magnus was intimating, and he hated that it might be the only route available to them. "Captain, do you know how to get a message to this Pytor Aleshko?" he asked. Magnus' smile gaped like a slit throat.

"Possibly," the captain said. "I have one man on the inside, but I haven't received any reports from him in some time."

Magnus said, "We could send some of my men, led by Captain Harrow perhaps. They won't be recognized as Cygnaran soldiers, just mercs looking for work. They know their business; they could get it done."

di Brascio nodded, as did Maddox. "It makes sense," she said. "A town like Riversmet is going to attract mercenaries like flies, and no one else can avoid notice like they can."

Stryker clenched his jaw. He hated fighting like this. He wanted to face his enemy, look into his eyes, and bring him down with courage and steel. But he was no fool, and he understood that war was not always won on the battlefield. "Not Harrow," he said to Magnus.

"Why? He's my best," Magnus said. "He's been getting into and out of tight and dangerous spots for the better part of a decade. I've given him missions like this before, and he's never disappointed."

Maddox was staring at Stryker. "He's the best choice, sir," she said. "We could send some of di Brascio's men along as well. Assuming you're willing, Captain."

di Brascio looked from Stryker to Magnus, his eyes quick and appraising. "I will go myself," he said. "After my order was disbanded, I was little more than a mercenary. I know the life and the lingo. I won't be suspected."

Stryker was grateful to the Llaelese gun mage. Even if di Brascio didn't quite understand Stryker's mistrust of Magnus, he was aware of the man's reputation, and he would keep an eye on Harrow.

"Very well," Stryker said. "Get Harrow in here. I want to brief him immediately. We'll reconvene in one hour."

— 15 —

Outside Riversmet, Occupied Llael

IT WAS GOOD TO BE IN THE FIELD AGAIN, even for a short time. The ceaseless tedium of his position often made Stryker feel more like an administrator than a soldier. After Harrow had been briefed, it had been decided a small team of scouts would escort him and di Brascio across the river. Against the counsel of both Maddox and Magnus, Stryker had chosen to lead that team.

They were moving up the wide, sandy shore on the eastern side of the Black River. Riversmet was a few miles ahead. He had a half a dozen rangers with him, including the sniper team of Sharp and Horgrum. They needed to move swiftly, so Stryker had chosen a warjack capable of both speed and stealth. The Hunter light warjack that followed behind his small team was still a large machine, standing over nine feet tall, but it moved with an economy of motion uncharacteristic of most warjacks. It was armed with a short-hafted axe, though its primary armament was a long-range cannon that fired armor-piercing shells capable of penetrating the stoutest armor. Its smoke stack was small, producing little smoke, and upgrades to its cortex allowed Stryker to command it at double the normal range. It could scout hundreds of yards ahead if needed, providing valuable intelligence to its controlling warcaster.

The final members of Stryker's team were the former mercenary Captain Harrow and the Llaelese gun mage Captain Vayne di Brascio. Though Stryker had been convinced to let Harrow be part of the team to infiltrate the city and get a message to Lord Pytor Aleshko, he still wanted to see the city for himself. More than that, he wanted to make sure di Brascio and Harrow made it to Riversmet without incident. Maddox had disagreed with his decision to accompany their escort, but, at least this once, he hadn't listened to her.

They would get Harrow and di Brascio within a mile of the city, though Sharp and Horgrum would shadow them a bit farther as a final measure of support before they entered Riversmet.

The Black River was wide and fast moving, and this close to the shore, it emitted a constant dull roar. The noise would hide sounds of their passage if they encountered any Khadoran patrols. There was no doubt Harkevich was aware of their presence now; it was hard to hide an army of ten-thousand men, and, of course, Khador had their own scouts and spies.

Ultimately, Harrow and di Brascio needed to approach the city from the western side, the most likely direction from which a mercenary looking for work would come. That meant getting them across the river, a difficult proposition, as there were no intact bridges save the Great Gate. They'd passed the shattered ruins of three smaller bridges already; all three had been destroyed by explosives, leaving little but scorched stone and wood.

They needed a boat to get Harrow and di Brascio across, which was easy enough for the horde of mechaniks with the Cygnaran Army to provide, but Stryker had a different idea, one that was not popular with Major Maddox. In fact, she'd called it "surprisingly stupid." His aim was to take one of the small Khadoran riverboats that patrolled the Black River, accomplishing two objectives at the same time. First, he would gain valuable intel on one aspect of the Khadoran defenses, and second, he would secure a light, fast craft that would not be instantly noticed by the enemy while Harrow and di Brascio crossed.

"How far south do their patrols travel?" Stryker asked Sharp, who was walking beside him.

"From what I've seen and from what I've heard from the Llaelese, just a couple of miles. They tend to stick pretty close to the city, and there are numerous checkpoints downstream. But we're getting close to the outer reaches of their patrols."

"What do you have in mind, Lord General?" Harrow asked.

"We need to draw one close to this side of the shore, give it a reason to land, then take the crew," Stryker replied. Harrow had largely been silent since they'd left camp, for which Stryker was grateful.

Harrow rubbed his hands together. "Maybe we set out some bait then."

Stryker eyed the merc. "That was my thought. Suggestions?"

Harrow pointed ahead. "There. That stand of trees about fifty yards from the shore. Good cover. The gun mage--uh, Captain di Brascio—and I will stand near the water and wait. When a boat comes along, we'll wave it down. We don't look much like soldiers, and they might stop to investigate."

"And if that fails to get their attention?" Sharp asked.

Harrow shrugged. "Then I'll shoot at them."

"The point is to get you and me across the river in one piece," di Brascio said. "not to get us both shot."

"Oh, don't you worry. I've been shot at an awful lot. I'm pretty hard to hit."

"I can do something about that," Stryker offered.

Harrow's eyes narrowed for a moment, then he understood. "Right, you've got the gift. I remember."

"I'm sure you do." Stryker had first tapped into his magic fifteen years ago in the city of Fisherbrook. He'd had a run-in with Harrow then, a fist fight he'd won despite his youth and lack of experience. "Sharp, how long do you think we'll be waiting?"

The ranger considered. "An hour or two. From what I can tell, that seems to be the length of their patrol loop."

"All right, but I don't want to risk *both* of you," Stryker said to Harrow and di Brascio. "Harrow you're out front. di Brascio, you're with me."

"All by my lonesome, then, eh, sir?" Harrow said. "You wouldn't be hanging me out to dry for past grievances, would you?" His tone was casual, even friendly, but the question scraped at Stryker's every nerve.

"Are you asking me if I'm intentionally putting you in harm's way for petty vengeance?"

"I didn't say it was petty, sir," Harrow replied with a grin.

Stryker stepped close to the merc. He was taller than Harrow, and his armor mad him considerably bulkier. "You're new to a proper chain of command, Captain Harrow, so I'll give you some leeway, but I don't put my men—and, yes, as sorry as I am for it, you're one of mine—in danger without good reason. Captain di Brascio is a skilled gun mage, a leader of the Llaelese Resistance, and an honorable man. You are a former mercenary of highly questionable character and intentions, who, for the moment, serves some purpose. In short, I'd rather lose you than him, but even so, I wouldn't put you out there if I didn't think you had a good chance of surviving. Understood?"

The rest of his men were silent, and even di Brascio looked surprised. Harrow, however, was unfazed. When he smiled next, it was like a fat eel had crawled across his face. "Oh, it makes sense to me, sir. I *am* just a humble merc, as you say. I thank you for taking the time to explain my expendability."

"I'm glad you understand. Now let's get into position."

• • •

THE KHADORAN PATROL BOAT was larger than Stryker had anticipated. It was forty feet long, fifteen feet wide, and sat high in the water. It was powered by a single paddle wheel aft, and Stryker could hear the rumble of its steam engine. The deck was largely open, but an armored pilothouse sat aft. He could see four men on the deck, one behind the small stern-mounted cannon and two more armed with long rifles standing port and starboard. The final member of the Khadoran crew stood like a great red sentinel in the middle of the deck. The Man-O-War shocktrooper was eight feet of steel-clad menace, a brave solider encased in a suit of steam-powered armor armed with a devastating mechanikal axe and a shield mounted with a short-range cannon. The Man-O-War were the Khadoran answer to the light warjack, as the northern nation lacked the resources to produce cortexes at the same rate as their enemies. Stryker had to admire this particular Man-O-War's courage. If he were to go overboard in that armor, it would be straight to the bottom and an ugly death.

Harrow was standing near the shore, waving his arms at the boat. Stryker and the rest of his men were fifty yards away, concealed in the trees. He'd turned down the Hunter's boiler so its smoke would not be visible to the Khadorans.

One of the Khadoran crewmembers pointed at Harrow and shouted. The boat veered toward shore. They didn't make landfall, and Stryker could hear the boat engines working as the pilot held the boat steady against the current ten feet from shore.

Smart, Stryker thought. They'd be able to get away quickly if there was trouble, and that changed Stryker's game plan. The Khadorans were shouting at Harrow; the cannon swiveled in his direction. Stryker wondered if they'd open fire—part of him wouldn't mind seeing Harrow take a cannon shell to the chest. And after all, he still had di Brascio. They didn't fire, however, and Harrow shouted back at them. Stryker couldn't hear what they were saying, but it didn't matter. The boat was as close as it was going to get, and it was time to act.

Stryker reached out to Hunter, pushing his will into its cortex. There was a moment of confusion as he experienced the world through his own eyes and the Hunter's optic relays at the same time, but it passed quickly enough. He'd done this many times. He aimed the Hunter's cannon at the pilothouse. It was small enough that any shell penetrating wouldn't fail to miss the man inside. The Hunter's eagerness for that shot flowed through their connection—this was what the warjack was meant to do, and it wanted to get to it.

"Horgrum," he said to the big trollkin. "You take the Man-O-War. Can you one-shot him?"

The trollkin grinned. "Yes, sir, no problem."

"The rest of you focus your fire on the others. I want to take them all clean. We're only going to get one good shot at this."

Nods all around and the telltale sound of rifles being readied. "Pick your targets," Stryker said, and the tension rose around him as the rangers aimed. Magic stirred in the air as di Brascio ensorcelled the rounds inside his magelock.

Shouting pulled Stryker's attention back to Harrow. One of the soldiers on the deck was shouting at Harrow and pointing. Harrow shook his head and made negative gestures.

Then things went bad.

The hollow thunder of the Man-O-War shocktrooper's cannon went off, and the sand in front of Harrow plumed into the air. The round had missed, but the shockwave hurled the former merc backward hard. He landed in a heap ten feet away.

Worse yet, the boat was pulling away from the bank, its single paddlewheel spinning faster; they'd smelled the trap.

"Damn," Stryker said and returned his senses to the Hunter's cortex. The boat was farther away and moving, making the shot that much harder. "Fire," he said.

The Hunter's cannon went off, a thunderous blast from overhead. Stryker poured his will into the shot, guiding it to its destination. The armor-piercing round tore through the pilot's booth, shredding it and whatever was inside.

Horgrum's rifle went off half a heartbeat later, followed by the staccato burst of the trencher rifles. The Man-O-War's helmet disappeared along with its owner's head in a volcano of gore and shattered steel. The rest of the boat's crew were struck multiple times by rifle bullets, and the cannon operator was blown clean off the boat by di Brascio's enchanted bullet.

All of this happened in the blink of an eye. The boat, now with no pilot, lurched forward, and Stryker aimed the Hunter's cannon again and fired. This time the round struck the vessel aft, putting a hole in it well above the water line. The force of the impact knocking the boat askew—its nose was now pointed at the shore. Its engines roared, and it cut through the river and up onto the shore in a spray of water and sand—beached, as he'd hoped.

Stryker let out a long breath. "Nice work, team," he said. "It couldn't have gone cleaner than that." He turned to Horgrum. "Hell of a shot."

The trollkin shrugged. "Only fifty yards. I could have made that shot with my eyes closed."

"Damn it, Horgrum," Sharp said, aghast. "The lord general just paid you a bloody compliment."

Stryker snorted. "Don't worry about it. I think Horgrum has cause for a little ego. All right. Let's go look at our boat."

They left the trees and made their way down to the beached riverboat. Harrow was trying to get up. "Help him," Stryker said, somewhat reluctantly, to two of the rangers, and they went to pick him up.

"What happened?" Stryker said once Harrow was on his feet again.

The former merc spit sand from his mouth and grimaced. "Tried using the few Khadoran words I know to get them closer," he said. "But they didn't buy it."

Stryker nodded. It wasn't a bad idea, even if it hadn't worked out. "I appreciate the strategy. See to the ship, Captain."

Harrow made his way to the boat, clambered aboard, and went to the pilothouse. "Gods, it looks like someone dumped a bucket of raspberry jam on everything," he shouted over the idling engines.

"Shut them down," Stryker called out. A few seconds later, the engines dwindled and then died, leaving the site of their short battle quiet and still.

Harrow emerged from the pilot's booth with a disgusted look on his face. He wiped his hands on his pants. "I tell you, I'm not driving that bloody thing. It smells like the inside of a slaughterhouse in there."

Stryker ignored him and pointed at two rangers. "Gather the bodies quickly and hide them in trees. Sharp, can you pilot this vessel?"

"I think so, sir," he said.

"Good, because you and Horgrum are going with them. I want you to take Captain Harrow and Captain di Brascio to the other side, at least as close as you can. Then you'll shadow them up to the gates. Once they're in, you hustle back, hide the boat as best you can, and wait for them to return."

di Brascio spoke up. "Once we reach the city, it shouldn't take long to get a message to Vasko and set up a meeting."

"Or get caught and end up at the end of a rope," Harrow added with a grim chuckle. "But I agree with the captain. We're looking at a couple of days, a week tops."

"Understood," Sharp said. "Horgrum and I have enough rations to last that long, and we can hide from or deal with any patrols that happen by."

"I'm sure the Khadorans have supplies on board as well," Stryker said. "You and Horgrum get aboard. Harrow, di Brascio, you, too. We'll get the boat off the beach."

He let the others board but pulled di Brascio aside before the gun mage could get on the ship. When the rest were out of earshot, Stryker said, "Watch Harrow closely." Harrow could see them talking from the ship, and that was fine with Stryker; he wanted the former merc to know he was being watched.

"I will," di Brascio said. "The man is competent, but there is dirt on him that does not wash off."

"I'm glad we're on the same page then."

The gun mage patted his magelock. "Trust me, Lord General, I know how to clean hard-to-remove dirt."

Stryker waited for the odd collection of soldiers to board: a Llaelese gun mage, a ranger sniper team that included a trollkin, and a man he'd once considered an enemy—though, if he were truthful with himself, he still did. It was a motley group, but he had faith in three-fourths of it. He hoped Magnus was right about his man and that Harrow could be trusted, but he had a backup plan: di Brascio would put a bullet in Harrow's head if he betrayed them. It seemed like a solid plan.

Once the team was aboard the riverboat, Stryker reached out to the Hunter and urged it approach the stern. "Push it," he said and relayed his command into the warjack's cortex.

The Hunter's boiler revved and smoke poured from its stack as it transferred steam-powered strength to its limbs. It put its body against the hull of the boat, leaned forward, its wide feet digging into the sand, and shoved. The boat moved slowly, but it moved, and the Hunter began to inch forward, pushing it back out into the water.

The warjack had to move into the river to completely free the vessel, a dangerous proposition for a warjack. Submersion would quench its boiler and shut down its cortex. But the Hunter was nimble, and with Stryker guiding it, there was no real danger.

The boat was soon free, and its engines fired up, revving against the current. The boat made a fairly clumsy U-turn in the middle of the wide river—Sharp was not an experienced pilot by any means—but soon righted itself and was moving downstream toward Riversmet and what would hopefully be the first step to victory.

●

— 16 —

North of Riversmet, Occupied Llael

THEY WERE CLOSER TO RIVERSMET than Stryker liked, but the kayazy prince, Lord Pytor Aleshko, would meet nowhere else. They had actually passed the city going north into territory controlled by the Protectorate of Menoth. A smart gambit—Aleshko knew they would not risk bringing a large force into Protectorate holdings.

"He's got ships," Magnus said with an appreciative tone.

They were moving up the Black River again, along the shore, skirting the water's edge for the cover of the tree line. Ahead the masts of four large galleys rose over a small port. The port itself looked hastily constructed, little more than a collection of wide wooden piers.

"*That* could be useful," Stryker agreed. "If he's willing to part with them."

So far, the warcaster's plan had worked. Harrow and di Brascio had returned four days after they'd entered Riversmet under the guise of mercenaries looking for work. They'd gotten word to

Aleshko, and the kayazy had agreed immediately to a meeting. The quickness with which the kayazy had accepted surprised Stryker and worried him, but Magnus chalked it up to the man's eagerness to make a profit *and* avoid the risk of open battle. Stryker could see the wisdom of that, but something still bothered him.

He and Magnus were alone; those were Aleshko's terms. He would meet only with the heads of the Cygnaran Army: no warjacks, no guards. Maddox had again petitioned to be her who met Lord Aleshko, and again Stryker had refused. He wanted to be there, with Magnus, ready for the aging warcaster's duplicity, should it exist.

Stryker wasn't about to leave without insurance, however. He'd been impressed with Swift Sergeant Sharp and his trollkin sniper companion, so he'd brought the two along with them, though they were following well behind, hidden by the dark and the trees. They would observe the meeting from afar, and Horgrum's Raevhan Express would be their first response to treachery.

They were approaching the pier, and on the nearest dock next to one of the big ships stood a small group of men. Stryker counted eight. They were big men, muscular, and armed with an assortment of knives and pistols. He'd heard many lurid tales of the thugs who served the kayazy, men drawn from vicious Khadoran street gangs called *bratyas*. Many were reputed to be skilled assassins.

"Welcome, friends," a commanding voice called out in Cygnaran when Stryker and Magnus were a few yards from the dock. One of the eight men stepped forward and into the light of a single lantern hung on a pole. Lord Pytor Aleshko was a viciously ugly man in his late-forties. His full head of black hair was greying at the temples, lending him an air of dignity that he likely didn't merit. He had large eyes that reminded Stryker a wild animal cornered and prepared to fight its way out of a trap. He was short but well built, a muscular man who seemed comfortable with confrontation.

"Lord Aleshko," Stryker said. "I am Lord General Commander Stryker, and this is General Asheth Magnus."

The kayazy's lips formed into a tight smile. "Of course, I know you both. Warriors of great renown . . . and some infamy, eh?" He glanced at Magnus. "Your men said you wished to meet with me, but they did not say why. Perhaps I can guess, yes?"

Stryker was curious to find out what the man already knew. "Why do you think we have come then?"

"You need to get into the city," Aleshko said. "Simple. Your army would like to cross the bridge and occupy Riversmet."

Magnus smiled. "And how do you feel about that, Lord Aleshko?"

He shrugged. "I am a man of business; I look for profit, not conquest. Kommander Harkevich has not been as eager as I to reap the many rewards Riversmet has to offer."

I'll bet, Stryker thought. From what he'd heard about Harkevich, the man was a fierce but honorable fighter. Having to put up with this brute of a man likely turned his stomach as much it did Stryker's.

"And you think we might, eh?" Stryker said.

"Arrangements could be made, yes," Aleshko said. "Once Riversmet is taken, you could perhaps allow me to retain my position—not publicly, of course, but I have grown fond of overseeing the wellbeing of the citizens."

"Wellbeing, huh?" Magnus said and chuckled. "You mean extorting every red cent you can from them while you keep squeezing. That's not going to work in a Cygnaran or Llaelese city."

Stryker was surprised. Magnus sounded genuinely disgusted, and he had answered Aleshko's request just as Stryker would have.

"As you say," Aleshko said with a shrug. "But there are other ways to make money. When the city is restored, trade along the river will resume—food, spirits, weapons. A man could do well overseeing such matters in the city. My masters in Korsk do not care who holds the city, as long as the money continues to come in."

Stryker weighed his choices. Letting this man graft from honest merchants was distasteful, but if it would get them into the city, the good they could do for the people there would outweigh this petty evil.

"I need some proof you've got something to trade," Stryker said. "Otherwise, we're done here."

Aleshko grinned. "Of course, Lord General. Of course. Here is what I will tell you. You have seen the Great Gate, yes?"

"I have."

"Impressive, yes? So many men and machines to guard it, but this is not its greatest danger. Harkevich knows he cannot let anyone cross the bridge from the east, and he has taken steps to ensure no enemy ever does."

"Get to the point," Magnus said.

"There are explosives under the bridge, at weak points. Even if you defeat his men and machines, he will destroy the bridge out from under you."

It was the final nail in the coffin, Stryker knew. Attacking the bridge was a no-win scenario.

"But I know where the explosives are, and I could get a small group of your men inside to disable them," Aleshko said. "Is that valuable enough, Lord General?"

Stryker opened his mouth to reply, but Magnus cut him off. "Lord Aleshko, these are some impressive vessels you have here. What is their purpose?"

Aleshko frowned. He was on a roll, he was in command, and he didn't like the change of direction. "Supplies and men go to and from Rynyr from the Oldwick. My ships make this possible."

"Men, you say?" Magnus said and took a step forward. The thugs Aleshko had brought with him moved in tune with Magnus, taking one step toward their leader, their hands dropping to their weapons. "How many men could you get on a ship like that? Sixty? Seventy?"

Lord Aleshko's eyes narrowed and his frown deepened. "My ships are not available, General. I have told you what I can offer. If I gave you my ships, that would be obvious treason; I could not remain in the city after that. No, you have my offer."

Magnus looked over at Stryker who caught a thrilling and

terrifying glimpse into what was about to happen. Both he and Magnus wore their warcaster armor and were armed with mechanikal blades and heavy pistols. They faced eight hardened killers who were lightly armed and armored. Magnus had gauged the situation and its outcome, and he was about to take action.

Aleshko was no fool. The negotiations were over, and a decision had been made. He took hasty step back. "Kill them both," he said, his hand darting for a pistol at his waist.

Aleshko's thugs rushed forward, but the kayazy had chosen his meeting place badly. The pier was narrow enough that his men could not overwhelm their foes and were forced to come at them no more than two or three at a time.

"Damn it, Magnus," Stryker said under his breath and ripped Quicksilver from his back as Aleshko's thugs closed in. This was not what he had wanted. It might be necessary to force Aleshko's hand, but he had hoped to avoid bloodshed.

Magnus drew Foecleaver in one smooth motion, whipping it up into a high cut at the first thug to meet him. The man had a pair of wide-bladed daggers, and he shoved them down in a crossed X to halt Magnus' attack. Stryker had seen Foecleaver in action before, and the kayazy's skillful parry would not save him. Foecleaver flashed up, clanging against his foe's paired daggers and smashing them aside. The mechanikal blade plowed a furrow up the man's midsection, splattering Magnus and Stryker with wet red warmth. The man fell away, and the battle began in earnest.

Stryker's first act was to summon his magic and cast a protective arcane shell over him and Magnus. Shots rang out, but the bullets were deflected harmlessly away from the two warcasters, flaring uselessly against Stryker's arcane barrier.

Stryker held Quicksilver low at his side, aiming its tip at a charging thug. He depressed a stud on the big sword's handle, and a blast of azure lightning flared from the weapon, catching the kayazy in the chest and hurling his smoking corpse from the pier.

Stryker and Magnus each stepped back, letting the enemy come to them. Stryker parried a high dagger thrust to his head, and then let the man's second dagger scrape harmlessly against his armor. He lashed out with the hilt of Quicksilver, ramming its pommel into the man's face, shattering his teeth and sending him reeling back. He killed the man with a wide, slashing cut that opened his opponent up from neck to navel.

A shot rang out from behind them, low and thunderous, and another kayazy thug pitched over backward, the huge slug from Horgrum's Raevhan Express removing most of his skull.

Magnus maneuvered effortlessly in the tight quarters, and it was clear that the man's age and his many wounds did not hinder him in combat. He skewered one enemy with Foecleaver, leaving the man twitching on the end of his blade, then drew his scattergun with his left hand and shot another through the chest.

Aleshko had backed up to the end of the pier, and his remaining men clustered around him. Stryker and Magnus advanced, two gore-splattered warcasters who had ripped through five of his men in a matter of seconds. Aleshko had nowhere to go, so he did what he did best: he bargained.

"Enough!" he cried, gesturing at his remaining men. "Throw down your weapons."

His men seemed quite prepared to die for their master, or if not for him, then for their own honor, but they did not move for several moments, seemingly confused. Magnus strode forward, raising his weapon, but Stryker put a hand on his shoulder and pulled him back. The warcaster threw a venomous glance behind him—his blood was up—but he stopped.

Weapons clattered on the pier as the thugs realized there was no point in fighting further.

Stryker raised one fist and summoned another spell. He sent an arcane bolt into the air, a crackling blue orb of energy that cast a wan glow over the water. It was a signal to Sharp and Horgrum to join them.

"On your knees," Magnus said, and the Khadorans complied.

"This is not necessary," Aleshko said. "You have made your point. We can include the ships in further negotiations."

Magnus laughed. "The negotiations are over, my friend. We'll take the ships and you. I'm sure there's a lot you haven't told us about that bridge."

"Your reputation for duplicity is well earned, General Magnus," Aleshko said and spat.

Stryker couldn't help but agree with the man.

• • •

"YOU GAVE NO ORDERS TO THE CONTRARY, Lord General," Magnus said. "I only acted as I thought best, an appropriate response to the situation."

"I gave no orders at all," Stryker said, glaring across the wide table at Magnus. They were in his command tent, and there were guards outside, guards who might take Magnus in custody in the very near future. "You acted without my leave, and you put us both in danger."

"Danger?" Magnus waved his hand dismissively. "Two fully armed and armored warcasters with one of the best snipers in the army watching their backs against a handful of kayazy thugs? You know better than that, sir. We weren't in any danger."

Magnus was right to some degree. Aleshko and his men had been sorely outmatched. Stryker chalked it up to the man's overconfidence that he had agreed to meet with two warcasters with only minimal guards in the first place. But that wasn't the point. Magnus had acted alone, just as he'd done for the past two decades.

"I am your commanding officer," Stryker said, grating the words through clenched teeth. "And as much as that must pain you, you will follow my orders, and you *will* inform me of *all* your plans henceforth."

Magnus' eyes narrowed, and his jaw clenched. He was angry, and Stryker took some satisfaction that he could provoke that kind of response from the man. But Magnus nodded slowly. "Yes, sir," he said.

"Gentlemen." Maddox had been all but forgotten in the tent. Stryker had summoned the commander to brief her on what had happened. "Though I do not agree with the general's methods, we have a favorable outcome here. Let's focus on that."

Stryker drew in a deep breath. "Very well," he said. "We have Aleshko in custody, and I agree he may know more about the city's defenses than he's told us."

"I think there's little doubt of that," Magnus said. "The man is like a rotten onion—each layer you peel, the worse it stinks."

Stryker was struck again by Magnus' obvious distaste for Aleshko. It was palpable, and to Stryker it seemed out of place. There were more than a few similarities between the two. Perhaps it was motivation and not methodology that rankled Magnus. He had fought for a cause, as misplaced as that might have been, and Aleshko did everything for power and greed.

"What of the ships?" Maddox asked.

"They're an asset, no doubt," Stryker replied. "Each can hold nearly fifty men, but they're not warships, and we dare not sail them downriver."

"Do we have men who can sail them?" Magnus asked.

Maddox nodded. "A few. Enough for a skeleton crew for each ship."

"We could use them to get a small force across the river and possibly hit the city from the west," Stryker said.

"We can't do anything, on either side of the river, until we learn more about the explosives on that bridge and whatever else Lord Aleshko knows," Magnus said, rubbing his chin.

"How do you propose we extract this information?" Stryker asked. "He's a tough man and stubborn. He's not going to buckle to interrogation soon."

"Who do you have with him?" Magnus asked.

Stryker thought that an odd question, but he answered. "Lieutenant Dayton Sims," Stryker said. "He's been with the CRS for some time, and he's a skilled interrogator."

"We need that information fast," Magnus said. "And I don't think Lieutenant Sims' methods will get us there quickly enough."

"You're talking about torture. We'll go hard at Aleshko, but there's a line I don't want to cross."

Magnus laughed. "If you think Cygnar is too noble to use *alternate* interrogation methods, I have a rude awakening for you.

They've been using them for years. Some are not as squeamish as you, Lord General."

"I'm not naïve, nor am I squeamish. There are simply lines civilized men do not cross. I know in your day, under Vinter, torture was just another tool in the toolkit, but not under my command."

"So, you'd risk the lives of Cygnaran soldiers because you're too bloody civilized to seize the one advantage that might save them . . . sir," Magnus said. His tone was mocking, incredulous.

Stryker considered the guards outside. How easy it would be to have them take Magnus away, lock him up for insubordination, and have him out of the way. Part of him wanted that badly, but no good would come of it. Magnus' men had no loyalty to anyone but him, and once that fetter was removed, they'd desert. Or worse.

Stryker looked at Maddox. She was staring at Magnus, her lips in a tight line, her gaze as jagged and piercing as a knife in the guts. It wasn't difficult to tell what *she* thought of Magnus' proposed course of action."

"You have heard my decision, General," Stryker said. "And you *will* abide by it."

"You're making a mistake," Magnus said. "We need that—"

"You are dismissed," Stryker said. "I will inform you what course of action we will take with Lord Aleshko tomorrow."

Magnus bit his lip, maybe to keep from saying something he'd regret. It pleased Stryker that he could anger the man. "As you wish, Lord General," Magnus said and stepped out of the tent.

Maddox lingered. It seemed she wanted to say something, and Stryker waited. Finally, she said, "You made the right call, Lord General." She paused, and seemed to gather herself. "And I say that not because of what happened to me."

"Thank you," Stryker said, and a wave of compassion for Maddox washed over him. He wanted to say more, to comfort her if he could, but that wasn't what she wanted and, besides, Maddox was through talking.

"Good night, sir," she said and stepped out into the night, leaving Stryker to ponder the difficult decisions to come.

— 17 —

South of the Cygnaran Encampment

"YOU KNOW, LORD ALESHKO, I have your countrymen to thank for adding a whole new set of skills to my repertoire," Harrow said and set a rubber truncheon on the short table next to Pytor Aleshko. The truncheon joined a ballpeen hammer on the plain wood.

The kayazy prince was tied securely to a stout chair. He had been stripped to the waist, and his shoes had been removed. He was an impressive physical specimen, and the scars across his broad chest suggested he was no stranger to pain. He glared up at Harrow, his wide eyes full of hatred.

They were in one of the more permanent structures within the Cygnaran camp, a heavy steel railcar that contained many of the tools and equipment for the warjack mechaniks. Its steel walls would dull the screams that were sure to come, but Magnus had had it pulled to a location nearly a mile south of the camp and had set guards—his own men—to keep anyone from approaching.

The fewer who knew what was going to happen here, the better.

The rectangular car was large enough to hold Aleshko and Harrow and still give the merc room to work. Magnus stood at the other end of the structure, near the door.

"That's right," Harrow continued. "I was working for General Magnus"—he stopped, looked back at Magnus, and winked—"Well, he wasn't a general then, but you get the point. We were working with the Steelheads in Ord, and I was gathering some intelligence on Khadoran activity on the border, near Midfast. Well, I wasn't as sneaky as I thought I was, and a patrol of Winter Guard put a rifle slug through my shoulder and dragged me back to their kapitan for interrogation."

Aleshko sat silently, but Magnus noticed his eyes had taken on a curious look. He still looked defiant, resolute, but he was beginning to look frightened. It was something about the pleasant, almost sing-song quality of Harrow's voice that conjured a sense of dread. The man's cheerful demeanor was so out of place here, so jarringly inappropriate, that it made what was about to come that much worse. Magnus had seen Harrow do his work many times, and though he was familiar with torture techniques, the former merc's obvious pleasure at his task was more than a little unnerving.

Harrow squatted down in front of Aleshko, his hands on the man's knees. It was a shockingly intimate gesture, an invasion of Aleshko's personal space, and the prisoner's lips skinned back away from his teeth in anger and revulsion.

"Anyway, the kapitan was one hell of a skilled interrogator, and Morrow, he worked me over good," Harrow said. "I had a fair amount of skill at the occupation at that point, but through the pain and the blood, and, I'm not afraid to admit, the screams, I learned I was just an amateur in the presence of a master."

"I will tell you nothing," Aleshko said. It was the first time he'd spoken, and despite the bravado it was meant to convey, it had the opposite effect. Aleshko had already broken a little.

Harrow patted the kayazy's knee. "Hush now," he said. "We'll get to that. Anyway, this kapitan—Yeltzin, I think his name was—knew his business, and he had me singing pretty as a songbird before too long. Hell, I would have told him anything just to make the pain stop, just for a few minutes so I could weep and bleed."

Harrow's admission to something most men would consider shameful created a dark tension in the room. It was the intimacy that strangers avoided, yet it was so casually spoken. Magnus was keenly aware the interrogation had already begun, and Harrow was using the best tool at his disposal: his mind and his complete lack of empathy.

Harrow rose and went to the small table that held his tools. "You see, Lord Aleshko, Kapitan Yeltzin was an artist because he believed in simplicity. There were no hot pokers, scalpels, thumbscrews, or anything so sophisticated, or, if I may be so bold, unnecessary. No, Yeltzin needed only three things. The first was his fists." Harrow held up his right fist, the knuckles scarred from countless fights and likely beatings he'd given to bound men. "The second was this." He picked up the rubber truncheon. It was just a length of rubber hose, thick enough to serve as an effective club. Harrow set the truncheon down and picked up the ballpeen hammer, a simple blacksmith's tool given terrible presence in this situation. "And this was the last thing he needed."

Magnus could see small beads of sweat on Aleshko's face despite the chill air inside the car.

"Harkevich will have your head for this," Aleshko said.

Harrow laughed. "From what I hear, Kommander Harkevich might pin a medal on me for getting you out of his hair." He put the hammer back down on the table. "Now, let's set some ground rules. Here's what's going to happen. I'm going to ask you some questions, and no matter how you answer—truth, half-truth, or outright lie—I'm going to hurt you."

The tension in the room grew thicker, and Aleshko's fear was almost palpable now.

"But here's the catch, Lord Aleshko," Harrow said. "You get to decide how I hurt you. If you give me a good answer, you get this." Harrow held up his fist. "If you give me a bad answer, you get this or this." He put a finger on the truncheon and then on the ballpeen hammer.

Aleshko's response was surprising. He threw his head back and spat directly in Harrow's face. He was braver than Magnus had suspected. Harrow smiled and wiped the spittle away. "You get that one for free, Lord Aleshko," he said. "Do it again, and—"Harrow drew a long, needle-pointed dirk from his belt"—we'll expand on Yeltzin's technique a bit."

He held the dagger up for a moment so Aleshko could see it, then he sheathed it again.

"Okay, first question," Harrow said. "Are you ready?"

Magnus had briefed Harrow extensively on the information Aleshko might possess, and the merc had been instructed to prioritize his questions depending on Aleshko's responses to the interrogation.

Aleshko did not reply.

"I'll take that as a yes. How many patrol boats does Harkevich have?"

Aleshko glared at Harrow, his lips trembling with either rage or terror or both, but he said nothing.

"Lord Aleshko," Harrow said, "I'm going to count to three, and if you haven't said anything by then, I'm going to consider this a *bad* answer. One."

Aleshko was silent.

"Two."

Nothing.

"Three."

"*Eske morda,*" Aleshko said, his eyes blazing with hatred.

Harrow looked back at Magnus.

"Eat shit," the warcaster answered.

Harrow chuckled. "Now *that* is impolite, Lord Aleshko." He picked up the ballpeen hammer. "It's also a very bad answer."

Harrow moved to stand behind the kayazy, and the man whipped his head back and forth trying to see the merc. Harrow looked at Magnus and cocked his head. The question hung in the air, and Magnus was pleased that Harrow was at least attempting to adhere to military protocol.

"Proceed," Magnus said.

Harrow's left hand shot out, snake fast, and grabbed a hunk of Aleshko's hair. He yanked the kayazy's head back so the man was looking up at the ceiling, and before the Khadoran could shake loose, Harrow brought the hammer down in a quick, forceful blow. He struck Aleshko in the mouth. Magnus heard the man's teeth shatter, and shards of them burst from his lips.

Aleshko loosed a long, screeching howl, and Harrow released him. The man's head snapped forward, and blood sluiced down his face and onto his bare chest. He had stopped screaming, but he was breathing in ragged, wet gasps.

Harrow walked slowly back to the table and put the hammer down. He waited for a few minutes then moved to stand in front of Aleshko. "How many patrol boats does Harkevich have?"

Aleshko raised his head and Magnus saw the hammer had removed his front teeth and split his upper lip nearly in half. He spit blood on the floor—not at Harrow, Magnus took note—and his lips moved. A faint whisper.

Harrow bent down next to the kayazy. "What was that?"

"Twelve," Aleshko said, his words slurred by his broken teeth.

Harrow stood and smiled. "Excellent. That is a *good* answer, Lord Aleshko."

He drove a short, hard punch into the Khadoran's midsection. The breath left Aleshko's chest in a rush, and he spit blood, splattering Harrow's uniform. The merc took no notice of it and stepped back. "There, you see the difference between a good answer and a bad answer? Which one is worse, do you think?"

Aleshko was still struggling to breathe, and Harrow let him alone for another few minutes.

"Next question," Harrow said. "This is an important one, so you need to get it right. What type of explosives has Harkevich rigged the Great Gate with?"

Aleshko groaned. "I don't know.".

"Now that can't be true, Lord Aleshko," Harrow said, his voice dripping with mock chastisement. "I mean, you told General Magnus and Lord General Stryker you *did* know. In fact, that was what you brought to bargain with. Do you want to rethink your answer?"

Aleshko said something in Khadoran, and again Harrow looked back at Magnus.

"Something about your mother and a goat, I think," Magnus said.

Harrow threw his head back and laughed. "Well, you couldn't have known my mother, so I'm going to call that a lucky guess." He moved to the table. "But that's not a very good answer to my question, now is it?" He picked up the rubber truncheon. Aleshko whimpered.

Magnus had seen men tortured before—he'd even endured it himself—but the way Harrow went about his business was chilling. He wasn't enjoying Aleshko's pain, at least not directly, but he was enjoying himself in the way a man good at his work enjoys a day's labor. There was a level of detachment from what he was doing that Magnus had strove for in his military career but had never quite attained. It had occurred to him that Harrow might be insane—he was certainly unstable—and perhaps that's what allowed him to excel at this kind of work.

Harrow approached Aleshko with the truncheon, smacking it into his palm, the sound a sharp harbinger of what was to come. "Now, Lord Aleshko, I'm going to hit you with this, and let me tell, you it's going to hurt. But if you want to give me another answer to my question, I'll give you a choice of *where* I hurt you."

"I . . . don't . . ." Aleshko said, trying to stay resolute in the face of absolute terror and helplessness. He failed. "He found the explosives in the city. In the ruins. I don't know more than that."

Harrow looked back at Magnus. "Did the Llaelese Army have much of a presence here?"

"They did, and Harkevich might have found a stockpile of munitions. Why he would use Llaelese explosives instead of his own, I don't know." Magnus took a long look at Aleshko. "He's probably telling the truth."

Harrow turned back to his prisoner. "There, you see? Not so hard. You told me the truth, now you get to choose. Nuts or knees."

Aleshko looked up at Harrow in horror. "I . . . can't," he whispered.

"If you don't choose, I'm going to choose for you," Harrow said.

"Knees," Aleshko blurted out.

Harrow clucked his tongue. "You know, you wouldn't think it, but that's the worse of the two." He slashed the truncheon through the air once, twice. The wet slap it made against Aleshko's body was shocking loud in the tight space, and the kayazy's pained screams echoed off the steel walls, lingering for instant time even after the screams had dissolved into faint sobbing.

And there were still many questions that needed answering.

— 18 —

"WHAT DO YOU MEAN HE'S GONE?" Stryker said to the three terrified CRS agents standing in front of an empty tent, the empty tent where Stryker had left Lord Vasko Aleshko.

"General Magnus and some of his men came a few hours ago and ordered the prisoner's release into his custody, sir," said Lieutenant Drayton Sims. He was the ranking CRS officer, and Stryker had left Aleshko in his custody.

Stryker clenched his fists at his side and turned away. Sims was a good officer, and he did not want the man to see the fury in his eyes and think it was directed at him. When he had himself under control, Stryker turned back. "Did General Magnus tell you where he was taking the prisoner?"

"No, sir, he didn't," Sims said. "I've cocked this up, haven't I, sir?"

"No. You only followed the orders of a superior officer, and I left no instructions that you should do otherwise," The relief in Sims face was palpable. "But I need to know where Magnus has taken Lord Aleshko. I want you and your men to find out and report to me at once."

"Right away, sir," he said. "We'll find him." He turned to his men. "With me." And they moved off into the Cygnaran camp.

Stryker drew in a deep breath to steady himself. His mind was reeling. He'd known Magnus was going to be a challenge, but he was still surprised the warcaster would openly defy him. There was nothing he could do but wait and hope Sims would discover where Magnus had taken Aleshko before it was too late. The CRS agents were well equipped to ferret out information, but there wasn't much time, and Stryker desperately wanted to catch Magnus in an act that would get him court martialed. He ached for it.

He turned and headed back to the command tent to wait.

• • •

"WHAT ARE YOU GOING TO DO when you find him?" Maddox asked as they both sprinted through the early evening gloom toward the outskirts of the camp. Sims had discovered where Magnus had taken Aleshko, and Stryker had acted immediately. He had wanted to go alone, but Maddox wouldn't have it, and he didn't want to deal with *two* of his officers disobeying direct orders.

"It's a hanging offense, Beth," Stryker said as he ran. "He disobeyed a direct order during a time of war."

"I know, but I'm just asking that you get all the facts before you act, sir," she said. She was doing what she often did for him, adding a cool and rational counterargument to his more emotional one. He wasn't in the mood for it now.

"You can't agree with what he did," Stryker said. "He may have jeopardized everything, for all we know."

"Of course not, but you need to control your emotions," she said. "I know this is what you were afraid would happen. Maybe you even hoped for it. But our primary goal is to secure the prisoner."

"I'm well aware of what needs to be done," Stryker said. They were nearing the river, and their destination lay ahead. Magnus had dragged a railcar away from the camp—likely appropriating some of the army's warjacks to do it—and was using it as a makeshift interrogation room. It was visible near a small copse of trees, maybe thirty yards from the edge of the river. Two men stood outside of it, both wearing trencher armor.

The two guards started as Maddox and Stryker neared. They were not expecting to see two warcasters in full armor running toward them at full speed.

"Step away from the railcar," Stryker said as he came to a stop ten feet from Magnus' guards. Both had that rough-around-the-edges look that all of Magnus' men seemed to have. They were likely former mercs who had served him while he was in exile. That Julius had allowed Magnus to give them positions in the military still astounded him.

The two guards hesitated, and one of them even let his hand fall to a pistol at his side.

"If you don't move your hand away from the pistol and step away, I will kill you where you stand," Stryker said. He hadn't drawn Quicksilver, but it wasn't an idle threat. A warcaster in armor didn't need a weapon to kill.

The eyes of the two guards went wide, as the peril they were in finally registered. They both stepped aside. One of them even offered a hasty, "Sorry, sir."

The door to the railcar was closed and likely locked from the inside. It didn't matter; Stryker wasn't about to knock. He moved up, grasped the door by the long locking bar on its front, and pulled. The galvanic coils along his back flared bright blue as the armor's arcane turbine poured strength into his limbs. The metal began to groan, and then the door came away from its hinges with a satisfying shriek of tearing steel. He tossed the door away and sprang up into the car.

Stryker saw what he'd expected. Aleshko was bound to a chair at one end of the railcar, slumped and bleeding. Harrow stood behind him, a rubber truncheon in hand. Magnus stood in front of the prisoner, a small trickle of smoke escaping from the stack on the back of his warcaster armor.

Magnus's face was impassive, stony. This infuriated Stryker, that Magnus wouldn't even give him the satisfaction of looking surprised. It looked like he'd even *expected* Stryker's presence. The warcaster opened his mouth to speak, but Stryker rushed forward and grabbed Magnus around the waist, pivoted, and hurled him through the open door of the railcar. Stryker heard Magnus land with a crash outside, and he leapt out after him.

Magnus lay in a heap with Maddox standing over him. *She* looked surprised. "Sir, I—"

"Secure the prisoner, Major," Stryker said through clenched teeth. "And if that *thing* of his gives you any problem, cut him down."

For once, Maddox didn't argue with him. "Yes, sir," she said and moved to the railcar.

Magnus was climbing to his feet. His breastplate was dented where he'd landed on his belly. His power field had likely absorbed most of the impact. "Coleman, wait, I need to—"

Stryker charged him, lashing out with a crisp right cross. Magnus' power field flared as Stryker's fist made contact, and it slowed the punch somewhat; otherwise, it might have broken Magnus' neck. The blow still had enough force to knock him off his feet and onto his back.

The rage Stryker had felt moments earlier had changed to something else: vindication. Old hatred bubbled up from the dark place he had hidden it away, and he let it take over, let it drive him. This man deserved to die for so many reasons, and Stryker would end it all right here.

Magnus was trying to stand again, and Stryker slammed his knee into the warcaster's chest, crushing him back to the ground. He held Magnus down with the considerable weight of his armored body and drew his fist back, channeling his magic into the strike that would crumble Magnus' skull. Then something struck him hard in the back, and he was hurtling forward through the air. He hit the ground on his belly, his power field flaring blue as he landed.

Stryker rolled over to see Maddox standing over Magnus, her

face clouded with shock and anger. She'd kicked him in the back. "What in the name of Morrow are you thinking?" she asked.

"He's a traitor," Stryker said, climbing to his feet. "I'm within my rights to execute him."

"With your fists? He wasn't even fighting back," Maddox said. "You're better than that."

When it came to Magnus, Stryker wondered if he was, but Maddox's words drained some of the wrath from him, and he shook his head. Magnus simply stared at him.

"I didn't fight you because I was hoping you'd come to your bloody senses at some point," Magnus said, wiping at a trickle of blood running from his nose. "So I could tell you what we learned."

"I don't care what you learned," Stryker said. "You disobeyed a direct order, and I'll see you hang for it." Harrow had emerged from the railcar, a smug smile on his face. "And he'll hang right beside you."

"You and I both know you're happy for the excuse," Magnus said. "Lord General Stryker, so moral, so just. I know you better than you think I do."

"Then it's a means to an end," Stryker said. "Even without the rules and the orders, it's wrong. *You're* wrong."

"You should listen to what Magnus has to say," Maddox said softly. "Then decide what you want to do with him."

Stryker stared at her, gritting his teeth. She was trying to calm things down, trying to get him to think. Part of him hated her for it, hated her for derailing the rage he felt so justified in feeling. But she was right, and another part of him was grateful to her.

"Speak," he said.

"He told us about the explosives at the Great Gate," Magnus said. "They're more than explosives—they're some kind of alchemical agent."

That shocked Stryker, and the implications of what it meant drained away the last of his murderous wrath. "Aleshko told you that?"

"He did," Magnus said. "And more. Do you want me to brief

you, or would you rather just throw a rope around a nearby tree and get on with it?"

Harrow and the pair of men who had been guarding the railcar moved to stand next to Magnus, perhaps to protect him or perhaps to seek protection from him. Stryker wasn't having it.

"You men, back to camp immediately," he said.

Harrow looked questioningly at Magnus. The warcaster did not meet his gaze.

"Or you can be shot where you stand. Which will it be?"

The threat worked. Harrow and the two guards walked off silently into the night.

Once they were gone, Stryker turned back to Magnus. "Will Aleshko survive?"

"Harrow didn't do any permanent damage," he said. "He'll recover."

"There were other ways to get this information," Maddox said, addressing Magnus for the first time.

"Not quickly," Magnus replied. "I did what had to be done. What the lord general was unable to do."

"Damn you, Magnus," Stryker said. He didn't think his loathing for the man could get any more intense.

"Yes, damn me, so you don't have to dirty your hands, Lord General," Magnus said, his eyes finally showing some hint of emotion. Anger. "Men like you need men like me. You want war to be honorable and clean, when we both know it isn't." He gestured toward the railcar. "That's what war sometimes looks like, and sometimes it saves more lives than all the glorious battle on Caen."

Stryker had done things in the name of war that he wasn't proud of, but he'd always felt there was a line that couldn't be crossed. To men like Magnus, however, that line did not exist. Part of him, however reluctantly, conceded that Magnus was right. The information he'd gotten out of Aleshko would likely save Cygnaran lives, but he could never condone his methods.

"I think you're wrong," Stryker said. "I think men like you make the choices you do because it's easier to let yourself sink to the same level as your enemy and call it necessary rather than stand as an example of what men can and should be."

Magnus smiled. "Agree to disagree, sir," he said. "Now, do you want me to brief you or not?"

"You disobeyed a direct order," Stryker said, and then, "Ask for forgiveness."

Magnus' smile faltered. "What?"

"As for my forgiveness, or I'll invoke my right to execute you." It was a gamble. Magnus was already chafing at serving under his command, but to admit to his authority so openly, so *meekly*, was a blow from which he would not quickly recover. Of course, Stryker had put himself in a corner; if Magnus refused, he would have to kill him.

"You can't be serious." But Magnus hesitated, glaring at the lord general, the two of them silent for a long minute. Then Magnus said, "You just want to drag me into your self-serving temple of morality."

"You will at the very least pay lip service to regretting your disobedience *and* your immorality." Stryker touched Quicksilver's hilt. "Ask for forgiveness."

A trickle of sweat ran down Magnus' forehead to mingle with the blood from his nose. He clenched and unclenched his fists.

"Forgive me, Lord General," he finally said. He looked away.

"Forgive you for what?" Stryker said. A subtle shift in the tension surrounding them had happened; the balance of power had changed. Stryker was in command again, not simply reacting to Magnus.

Magnus' eyes narrowed in fury, but he checked himself. "For my disobedience."

"For torturing Aleshko," Stryker said. His tone, patronizing but firm, clearly enraged Magnus, but the cold pragmatism that was his defining trait kicked in.

"For torturing the prisoner," Magnus said. "And attaining information vital to our mission." It was a small defiance, but Stryker let it pass. He had what he wanted. For now. "Can we get back to the business at hand now?"

"This isn't over, Magnus," Stryker said.

"No, probably not," Magnus replied. His mouth turned up in a tired smile. "You and I will be a thorn in one another's side until one of us is dead."

For once, Stryker agreed with the warcaster completely.

— 19 —

Cygnaran Camp, Free Llael

THE GRAND TENT IN THE CENTER of the Cygnaran camp was spacious, large enough to accommodate all of Stryker's senior officers and a number of their important aides. They stood around a large table, the map of Riversmet spread across it.

"We have gathered vital intelligence on the Khadoran defenses in Riversmet, and General Magnus and I have constructed a plan of attack," Stryker said, locking eyes with the men and women around him.

"Sir, how did you come by this intelligence? Did Aleshko crack?" a tall robust young commander asked. This was Major Tobias Johnson, a rising star in the Cygnaran military and the ranking member of the CRS, the Cygnaran Reconnaissance Service, in the Army.

Stryker had kept the business with Lord Aleshko off the record, though his officers were aware a number of kayazy had been captured. He didn't want his men to know what Magnus and Harrow had done to get the man talking. In truth, he wanted to forget it himself. Aleshko had survived Harrow's interrogation, and his wounds were relatively minor.

"Yes, one of General Magnus' men is a skilled interrogator, and Aleshko's information to be valid," Stryker said. His chest tightened roiled at naming Harrow anything but a brutal and uncaring killer.

Major Johnson nodded; it was clear he understood the word *interrogation* meant a lot more than questioning here, and he said nothing further.

"We know Harkevich has rigged the bridge with explosives that carry an unknown alchemical agent," Magnus said, picking up where Stryker had left off. Aleshko hadn't known what type of agent Harkevich was using, only that it was something the prisoner had never seen before. Magnus had assured Stryker that one of his men, a former alchemist with the Order of the Golden Crucible, could likely identify the substance. It was yet another reason Magnus was not in chains; Stryker doubted he could get the men loyal to the warcaster to follow his orders if he'd taken Magnus into custody. They'd likely desert the first chance they got. "What we do not know is exactly *where* these explosives are located on the bridge."

"Then we're back to square one," Captain Tews said. "We can't assault the bridge."

"Not exactly, Captain," Stryker said. "Lord Aleshko had a small fleet of merchant ships, which we have appropriated. Each of these ships can hold fifty men and all of their gear *and* get them across the river."

Tews nodded. "Then what?"

"The best way to disarm those explosives is to get to them from the other side of the bridge," Magnus said. "I will lead the force crossing the river, and we will enter the city from the west. They won't be expecting an attack there, plus the Khadorans will be distracted. My man can identify the alchemical agent once we're there."

Stryker hadn't been overly enthusiastic about this part of the plan. He hadn't been overly enthusiastic about working with Magnus at all, but he had to keep up appearances. For now, however, Magnus was still a general in the Cygnaran Army, and Julius had chosen him personally to lead part of the invasion force.

Hitting the city from both sides made strategic sense, but Magnus had insisted the small force crossing the river be drawn from his own men, those who had served him during his exile. There was no doubt many of these men were skilled at covert operations, as Magnus had had little choice but to move in secret when the former Cygnaran king, Leto Raelthorne, was hunting him, but all were little more than jumped-up mercenaries whose loyalties lay with Magnus and not with Cygnar. He didn't think Magnus would betray him—but only because if either of them failed, it meant destruction for the other. His men, on the other hand . . . Magnus put too much faith in men like Harrow, men with no masters but coin and their own urges. Stryker needed something to balance that out.

"Captain Tews, you will accompany General Magnus, along with four of your best."

The big Stormblade's eyes went wide, then a look settled over his face that was equal parts disgust and resignation. "Yes, sir," he said.

"Happy to have you aboard, Captain," Magnus said evenly. He had to know why Stryker was including the Stormblade captain, but perhaps he *did* see Tews as an asset and not a watchdog.

Stryker continued with the briefing. "While General Magnus enters the city from the west, Colonel Bartlett and I will lead an assault on the bridge. We're going to throw everything we have at them, giving Magnus' force time to reach the bridge and neutralize the explosives."

"Morrow, our timing better be right on the mark, or Harkevich is going to drop us in the river," Bartlett said. She was a tall woman in her mid-thirties, her black hair streaked with gray. She was a knight with a noble lineage, and a fine battlefield commanders for the Cygnaran Army.

"You're right, of course," Magnus said. "Timing will be key.

If he drops the bridge, my men will be trapped in the city and slaughtered. So, let's get it right the first time, eh?"

"This is it, people. Our one shot," Stryker said, answering the questioning stares from his officers. "Harkevich very likely knows we have Aleshko, so we've got to hit them before he can shore up his defenses or get reinforcements from Rynyr."

A murmur of assent passed through the gathered officers. They were all good soldiers, and he had the utmost faith in them.

"And what will my role be in this attack?" Vayne di Brascio said. He'd been quietly listening to the briefing. Stryker had invited him to attend more out of respect for the man than anything else, but di Brascio was a soldier too, and he wouldn't appreciate being left behind.

"Captain di Brascio, I am grateful for the aid you and the Resistance have contributed thus far, but I cannot ask you to risk your life and the lives of your men in a frontal assault," Stryker said.

"Do you remember what I told you at Greywind Tower?" di Brascio said with a crooked grin.

"I do. And you are not under my command."

"Then I'll see you in Riversmet." the Llaelese gun mage walked out of the tent. Many of the officers cast confused glances after the Resistance captain; he was a bit of an enigmatic figure, but Stryker liked their chances a little better with the skilled Llaelese gun mage at his side.

"All right. Magnus and his men will move out tonight and cross the river. The ships are crewed and ready to go. The rest of us will march at dawn and hit the bridge at midmorning." Stryker looked over at Magnus. "Once we hit the bridge, I figure you've got about three hours to remove the explosives."

"We'll be there," Magnus said. "But I won't complain if you could make my job easier by killing as many Khadorans as you can before we get there."

Stryker ignored the humor, mostly because he knew how many Cygnarans would join those Khadoran dead. "You all know what needs to be done. So, let's get about it," he said. "Dismissed."

The tent emptied quickly, as the officers hurried to make

preparations for the assault. He'd be inundated with reports in the next couple of hours regarding their progress.

Magnus lingered behind, as Stryker thought he might. "You still don't trust me, do you?" he said when they were alone.

"If you're asking if I think you'll ignore my orders when it suits you, then, no, I don't. If you're asking if I think you're stupid enough to commit high treason again with a king you support on the throne . . . Well, I don't think you're stupid," he said.

"Treason, eh?" Magnus smiled thinly. "If you recall, I was supporting the rightful king, defending against a coup, when I was labeled a traitor. I still support the rightful king. The only difference is my opinion and loyalty are now the popular ones."

"He was a tyrant, and Cygnar lived in fear with Vinter on the throne. I remember you being an architect of that fear, spreading it, nurturing it," Stryker said. He wasn't shouting, but his words came in a forced whisper, low and urgent. "Can you really say that Cygnar wasn't better off under Leto?"

"That's not my place to judge, nor is it yours," Magnus said. "We are soldiers. We do our best to serve our kings, even when we disagree with them."

It was the first time he'd heard Magnus even hint that he had disagreed with Vinter's methods. It surprised him. "No, you're wrong. It is our duty as soldiers and as servants of Morrow to protect Cygnar and fight to protect the innocent."

"Is that what we're doing here? Protecting the innocent?"

Stryker looked away. It was a fair point. They were an invading army, and even if their cause was just, he couldn't say for certain that its purpose was. "That's what *I'm* doing," he said, "to the best of my ability. And while you wear that uniform under my command, you'll damn well do the same."

Magnus stared at him, his eyes appraising. Finally, he said. "He's not his father, you know. Julius."

Stryker had to consider his next words carefully. Magnus knew his feelings about the young king, and he could be luring him into seditionist talk. His position with Julius was tenuous already. "In my experience, the apple does not fall far from the tree."

"Is that right? Tell me, is the man standing before me now anything like his father? I fought with the man for over a decade. He was skilled and brave, but his heart was not a warrior's."

The mention of his father struck him hard. Joseph Stryker had been a warjack mechanik, serving in the Cygnaran Army under then-Commander Magnus. Joseph had taken a terrible wound in the infamous Scharde Invasions, when the Nightmare Empire of Cryx had invaded the shores of western Cygnar, and he had been discharged from service. He'd never recovered and had developed a loathing of warfare as well as the men who practiced it. "He wasn't the same after he came back, after fighting under *your* command," Stryker said. "And he never recovered from my mother's death."

Something passed across Magnus' face, momentarily softening its wolfish severity. Was it regret? Sorrow? "Her death affected us all."

Stryker waved a dismissive hand. "General, I am done dredging up the past. You are dismissed."

Magnus lingered for a moment, and Stryker wondered if he would disobey him. Then he smiled. "Good luck to you tomorrow, Lord General."

Stryker said nothing and stared at the map on the big table until Magnus had gone. *He is not his father.* Julius was fierce and headstrong, but he hadn't yet shown his father's penchant for cruelty. Would it come in time? Would Magnus foster tyranny in the young king?

He dismissed this and struck out for his own tent. He needed to sleep, though the specters of the past would keep him awake long into the night.

— 20 —

Cygnaran Camp, Free Llael
Solesh 28th, 611 AR

STRYKER RODE AT THE HEAD of a long column of soldiers and warjacks. They wound behind him for over a mile across the battered Llaelese landscape. Though the Resistance controlled this part of the country, evidence of the Khadoran aggression could be seen everywhere. They often passed the ruins of small villages, and there was an abiding sense of emptiness that made Stryker uneasy.

Maddox rode next to Stryker, struggling to control her horse and cursing under her breath. She was not a skilled rider, and her mount was merely for transportation. She, like most Stormblades, fought on foot.

He, too, has spent much of his military career among the infantry, but in the last few years, he'd developed an appreciation for the cavalry. He'd fought many times among the Storm Lances, the heavy Cygnaran horsemen equipped with deadly electro lances that could generate dangerous blasts of lightning. His own mount was specially bred to carry the heavy barding that protected it from this, along with the considerable weight of a warcaster in full armor. As much as controlling a warjack thrilled Stryker, there was something to be said for swinging a blade from the back of a fully barded warhorse.

They were following the river, and the city of Riversmet loomed to the northeast. The triple towers of the Great Gate Bridge rose into view, great heavy stone monoliths reinforced with steel plating strong enough to turn aside light cannon fire. Stryker looked back at the column—looming over it were the two Stormwalls, thirty-foot-tall warjacks powered by a combination of traditional steam and galvanic energy. Each was armed with two heavy cannons, a pair of high-speed chain guns, and voltaic-charged fists capable of leveling a building. They were impressive, terrifying to the enemy, but he had get them close enough to be effective, and Harkevich's Conquests had better range with their own cannons.

They could already hear the dull thud of Khadoran cannons, as well the shrill whine of descending artillery shells. Elements of the Cygnaran Army, primarily trenchers, had gone forward, preparing artillery emplacements and getting heavy warjacks armed with long-range weapons—like Defenders and Hunters—into position. Their job would be simple: throw enough lead at the Khadorans to give Stryker and his Storm Lances a chance to get close enough to charge onto the bridge. Behind him would come Maddox leading more Stormblade infantry and trencher riflemen, all to keep the Khadoran snipers in the towers busy.

Stryker reined in and signaled the Storm Lances behind him to do the same. Each rode a heavily barded warhorse like his own, and all were knights of the finest skill, both with their devastating lances and with the twelve hundred pounds of horseflesh beneath them. One of the knights disengaged from the rest and rode up next to Stryker.

"Colonel," Stryker said, "they're going to throw everything they've got at us when we go for that bridge, and you and I need to make a hole big enough for Maddox and her Stormblades to charge through."

Bartlett said, "As long as the 'jacks can make a hole for *us*, it's all in a day's work, Lord General. Ride straight into the teeth of cannon and sniper fire, and try not to get killed." She smiled.

Stryker chuckled. He'd always liked the colonel; she had a grim sense of humor that made her very popular with the other knights. She was also absolute murder with lance and sword. "Don't worry; Maddox and I will make that room for us."

"Do you think General Magnus made it through?" Maddox asked, shifting uncomfortably in her saddle. "I don't fancy a swim in the river. Looks cold."

"No way to tell," Stryker said. "But I'll say this, despite my misgivings about his character, General Magnus is one of the most resourceful fighters on the face of Caen."

Bartlett snorted. "When he's fighting for Cygnar; otherwise, he's a bloody dangerous mercenary killer." It was the other reason Stryker liked the major—she shared his loathing for the recently pardoned general.

"As I said at the briefing, if he fails, we're all in trouble. I at least expect him to work at saving his own life."

Maddox threw him a disapproving glance. It was clear she didn't think it was proper to be speaking about another officer, even Magnus, in front of his subordinates. He choked back the rest of what he wanted to say—she was right, as usual. "Maddox, ride ahead and make sure the rest of the Stormblades are prepared for the assault."

"They will be, sir," she said, then spurred her horse and rode off.

"Ready for this, Colonel?" Stryker said to Bartlett and looked behind her at the twenty Storm Lances awaiting their orders. Their helmets were up, lanced held high, bright blue armor gleaming in the morning sun. They were sharp and eager, just like their commander.

"Absolutely, Lord General. Let's bring the thunder."

...

STRYKER HAD OFTEN HEARD the phrase, "in battle, there is no law." He'd never agreed with it; there were plenty of laws and rules to warfare. What was missing was the sense of time. In battle, there is no time. He'd determined that the world shrunk, and the flow of minutes and seconds seemed to disappear, leaving one in a timeless void where life and death were measured by skill, reaction time, and luck.

The last part of that equation made itself known twenty yards from the bridge. He and Bartlett charged up the short berm in front of the great bridge, the Storm Lances flowing behind them in a tight wedge, Cygnaran artillery shells whistling overhead. He could see one of the Conquests at the far end of the bridge through the double portcullises of the towers that blocked their way. The huge machine—a monster of red steel and black cannon barrels—turned, the double cannon on its back swiveling in their direction. He heard the thunderous blast of its discharge, heard the shrieking whine of the discharge's descent, and then nothing.

He had braced for the impact, expecting a rush of heat and pressure. Instead, he heard Bartlett laughing as they covered the last few yards to the bridge. She pointed ahead of them. The huge shell from the Conquest stuck out from the ground like a short fat javelin. A dud.

"If that isn't a sign from Morrow, I don't know what is," Bartlett called out.

Stryker hoped she was right. He turned his attention to the three warjacks moving up ahead of them, two Defenders armed with long cannons and heavy shock hammers and Rowdy armed only with his fists. Stryker had had the 'jack's quake hammer unbolted from his right hand. It was just too dangerous to have such a weapon on a bridge rigged with explosives. Rowdy's disappointment at losing his hammer was evident as he swung his right arm back and forth in irritation.

There was a hundred yards of bridge between them and the first tower. The portcullis was down, and behind it, Stryker could see the hulking red forms of Man-O-War shocktroopers, skilled fighters encased in steam-powered armor that increased their strength and durability tenfold. They were ready and waiting should the Cygnarans breach the tower. The tower rose high overhead, squat and steel-shrouded. Gun barrels protruded from the many slits that dotted its surface. Bullets from those guns rained down on the Defenders, but their armor was too heavy for small arms fire to affect them, and they shed the projectiles in whining ricochets.

The warjacks had reached the bridge now with Stryker and his Storm Knights right behind them, and the Conquests wouldn't fire on them any longer for fear of hitting the bridge and collapsing it.

Stryker reached out to the Defenders and ordered them to pull up thirty yards from the gate. *Fire!* he urged, and the double blast from their cannons sounded. The heavy slugs smashed through the portcullis and three Man-O-War behind it; they came apart in chunks of armor and bloody flesh.

"Get 'em, Rowdy," Stryker said under his breath, and the Ironclad loosed a triumphant blast of steam and charged at the gate. The Man-O-War were still recovering from the Defender's blasts, allowing Rowdy to reach the gate. The warjack wrapped his hands around the bars of the portcullis and pulled. The steel groaned and bent beneath Rowdy's titanic strength, and the gate ultimately come loose.

Push it, Stryker encouraged and Rowdy slammed his weight into the loose portcullis, knocking it down and into the courtyard beneath the tower beyond. He summoned his magic and cast a shielding spell over Rowdy, just as the Man-O-War beyond opened up on the warjack with their shield cannons. Half a dozen rounds struck Rowdy, but his thick armor and Stryker's spell turned aside most of the damage. Stryker now sent the Defenders rushing in, and behind him he heard the staccato bursts of Cyclone chain guns as Maddox peppered the tower with bullets, forcing the snipers there to duck inside or be torn to pieces.

"Lances down," Stryker called out, straining his voice to be heard over the cacophonous din of the artillery shelling. Beside him, the Storm Lances lowered their electro lances into position.

He didn't carry a lance, but he dropped Quicksilver into a similar position.

They were ten yards from the portcullis, and they spurred their mounts into a gallop.

The cycling whine of voltaic mechanisms inside each Storm Lance howled in unison, and twenty-one bolts of brilliant blue electricity lashed from the charging knights. Stryker added Quicksilver's electric discharge to the volley, pushing his will into the blast, increasing its power with arcane might. The bolts flashed around the warjacks inside the courtyard and slammed into Man-O-War, killing or wounding half a dozen of them.

And then they were through, hammering through the archway of the tower and into a wide courtyard. The Man-O-War had locked their shields in a tight line against the three warjacks, but they were simply overmatched. Rowdy replaced his missing hammer by snatching up a Man-O-War in one hand and using the unfortunate Khadoran like a club, smashing the soldier's armored body into the enemies surrounding the warjack, and quickly turning his makeshift weapon in a pulped wreck.

The Storm Lances struck next, and Stryker was the first to reach an enemy. He flashed by Rowdy and brought Quicksilver down in a brutal overhand cut, putting all his considerable strength and the horse's momentum into the strike. The Man-O-War he targeted brought his shield up to ward off the blow, but Quicksilver sheered clean through it, its arcane edge slicing through the steel and into the Khadoran's helmet, cleaving his head in two.

The lances of the knights behind him were nearly as effective. He glanced to his right as Bartlett skewered a Man-O-War, lifting nearly five-hundred pounds of man and armor off the ground. It was a mortal blow, but it snapped her lance in half, leaving her only the bladed, axe-like hilt to defend herself.

They had passed through the ranks of Man-O-War, killing many. They'd taken casualties as well; three Storm Lances had been cut down by the fearsome Khadoran annihilator blades, weapons designed to penetrate warjack armor. Above them, shots from the snipers resumed as Maddox, ranks of Stormblades, and the two Cyclones moved up the bridge behind Stryker's initial charge.

There was a moment of red chaos as the courtyard churned with combat. Men and horses screamed, the clash of steel on steel echoed, and the stench of voltaic discharge mingled sickeningly with the coppery tang of blood. The warjacks took a devastating toll on the enemy, and soon, crushed bodies of slain Man-O-War littered the courtyard.

Maddox and her forces made the courtyard soon after the battle ended, though her Cyclones remained outside, peppering the tower above with chain gunfire. "They're going to start shelling this tower," she said. The Conquests and half a dozen smaller Destroyer warjacks were visible at the far end of the bridge through the portcullises of the remaining towers. "I guarantee they're discussing how valuable the lives of the men inside are." She pointed at the floor of the tower above them, where there could be as many as fifty Khadoran soldiers and snipers.

Stryker nodded. "Then let's get warjacks up here. I want Defenders in this courtyard right away to give those Conquests something to think about. Bartlett, we're going to ride on to the second tower. Maddox, I'll leave the Defenders with you, so you can lob shells over the towers at the Conquests. I'll take the Cyclones and Rowdy to give us some cover. Guide your shots; I don't know where those explosives are, and an errant shell on the surface of the bridge might bring the whole bloody thing down."

Maddox's eyes took on a vacant, faraway look. She was connecting with the cortexes of the warjacks assigned to her. After a few seconds, she returned to herself. "Understood, sir."

Stryker looked out at the next tower. Like the last, the portcullis was down, and he could see red shapes moving behind it. Farther back, he could see Khadoran troops, Winter Guard by the look of it, heading across the bridge to the second tower.

There were Trenchers coming up the bridge behind Stryker. They'd secure this tower, root out any remaining snipers, and then help hold it while Stryker pushed forward. "Reinforcements are on the way," Stryker said to Maddox. "Once we take the second tower, move up, and continue shelling the Conquests from there."

"We're gonna leapfrog our way into the city, huh?" Maddox said. "Does it seem a little too easy to take this tower, sir?"

"Yes," Stryker said. "Harkevich wants us on the bridge. If things go south at the next two towers, where he's bound to have the bulk of his forces, he can blow the whole damned thing, dump us in the river, and cut his losses."

"My thoughts as well," Maddox said.

"Hopefully, Magnus will put a wrinkle in Harkevich's plan." He tried to sound like he believed it. The knights around him needed to hear that. He turned to Bartlett. "Let's mount up."

— 21 —

Eastern Riversmet, Occupied Llael

ASHETH MAGNUS FELT NAKED AND VULNERABLE without his warcaster armor. He'd left it behind because it would be immediately recognizable for what it was, and stealth was key now.

They'd found a section of the outer wall on the western side of Riversmet that had not been repaired. They'd waited until the sound of artillery splintered the morning air, and then moved in, he and ten other men. He'd brought nearly three hundred with him across the river, but they were waiting in reserve about a mile from the city, waiting for the signal to assault the city after the explosives on the bridge had been disarmed.

He had with him nine of his best, including Harrow, and a single, angry Stormblade captain Lord General Stryker had shackled him with. Tews was a skilled soldier—he'd served as a Stormblade for the better part of two decades—but he was with them for only one reason. He was Stryker's watchdog. Magnus understood the Lord General's motivations, but he wished he'd sent that Llaelese gun mage di Brascio instead. *He* at least had some notion of stealth and covert operations. With speed and stealth paramount, Tews had discarded his bulky Stormblade armor and storm glaive and wore non-descript boiled leather and carried a Caspian battle blade. The weapon was similar in weight and size to his storm glaive.

They were inside the city, crouching in the ruins of a small house. He'd sent Harrow and three of his best scouts out to reconnoiter the area and determine how many soldiers were present.

His knees ached, his back hurt, and only the heavy brace on his right leg made walking without hobbling possible at all. It was just some of the toll years of warfare and exile had taken on his body. His armor provided some support to his battered limbs, but without it, the full weight of his fifty-five years settled on his shoulders. He flexed his mechanikal hand, frowning at slight squeaking noises it made. One of the galvanic relays needed adjustment; he'd need to see to that soon.

Magnus looked up and noticed Captain Tews glaring at him from across the rubble-strewn room, his deep set eyes filled with a mixture of anger and disgust. It was a look Magnus had become accustomed to since his return to Cygnar. "Something on your mind, Captain?"

"I remember when and why you got that arm, General," Tews said.

"Is that so?" he said evenly.

"I remember because you were seconds away from gunning down me and my entire squad," he said, his voice rising.

Some of Magnus' men stirred, and their hands went to their weapons. They were all former mercenaries, promoted to various ranks among the trenchers at his request. They were loyal to him, and they'd kill for him without question. He held up his hand, the one that was still flesh and blood. Tews needed to get this off his chest. Best to let him do it now than during the more sensitive work ahead.

"You were supporting a violent overthrow of the rightful king, Captain Tews," Magnus said, smiling.

He might as well have struck the big Stormblade. Tews shot to his feet, his fists clenching at his side. Magnus held his stance. "Do you remember that part?"

"We overthrew a tyrant," Tews said, his jaw clenched. "A tyrant you served without question. We made Cygnar better, stronger."

Magnus climbed to his own feet, refusing to wince at the dull spike of pain that shot through his joints. "Did you really make Cygnar better?" he asked. "I think you merely started a sequence of events that led to a civil war and more Cygnaran deaths."

"That's not true." Tews' eyes blazed. "Vinter was a monster. We saved lives by removing him and *you* from power."

Magnus sighed. He'd had this same argument more times than he cared to admit. No matter what he did now or that Julius trusted him, he would never be accepted by men such as Tews. They'd been through too much, lost too many friends, to put aside their hatred. It was tiring, a heavy burden Magnus just wanted to set down so he could get on with the business of making Cygnar great again.

"Fine," he said. "You've said your peace. Do you feel better? Are you going to follow my orders like a proper soldier now?"

"I follow the orders of Lord General Stryker," Tews said. "Not yours."

"Do I need to reacquaint you with the chain of command? I am a general appointed by the rightful king of Cygnar. *Your* king. You will follow *my* orders when the lord general is not present. You can hate me, you can curse my name. Hell, if it makes you feel better, you replace 'sir' with 'traitorous bastard.' I really don't care. But what we're doing here is bigger than all this petty horseshit you and . . . others in the Cygnaran Army seem so obsessed with. Would you agree with that, Captain?"

Tews glared at him, but after a moment, he nodded slowly.

Movement drew Magnus' eyes away from the Stormblade. Harrow and the three men he'd sent with the former merc had returned. They moved quietly into the ruined house.

"Report," Magnus said.

"Just like you said, General," Harrow replied. "The attack

across the river has most of the troops in the city clustered in the eastern half of Riversmet."

"Good. We'll move out immediately. Stryker will have taken the first tower by now."

Harrow cocked his head. "You think so?" The question was not one a lifetime military man would ask; it was a mercenary's question. It conveyed doubt, even scorn. Magnus wasn't the only one with scars gained at Stryker's hand.

"The lord general is a capable battle leader," Magnus said. He believed it, but Stryker could have been so much more than that. "He'll succeed."

"Well, he did learn from the best, sir," Harrow said with a crooked grin.

Tews uttered a short, sharp laugh at that, drawing Magnus attention back to him. Magnus sighed. "So, Captain, are you going to follow my orders or do I need to leave you here?"

Tews lips curled up in disgust and he clenched his fists, but he responded, "I will follow your orders."

Magnus smiled. "'I will follow your orders' what?"

"I will follow your orders, you traitorous bastard . . . sir."

"Excellent," Magnus said. "Let's move out."

• • •

THE THUNDERING SOUNDS OF ARTILLERY and the shrill whine of their lethal descent filled the air as they drew closer to the Great Gate. They'd reached the portion of the city that was largely intact and provided little immediate cover. However, the streets were choked with townsfolk moving away from the fighting. It was not difficult to move among the panicked citizens and avoid the notice of the many Khadoran soldiers. With the group's nondescript armor and weapons, they looked like mercenaries, of which there were many in Riversmet.

The Khadorans had constructed a perimeter wall around the entrance of the Great Gate, and they had fortified the gatehouse itself so that it became an imposing structure of steel-clad stone.

Khadoran troops swarmed around it, and three towering

Juggernaut warjacks, a lethal deterrent, stood near the entrance. Rising above the perimeter wall were the gigantic forms of two Conquests. Magnus had never seen one of the mammoth warjacks up close; they were impressive. To punctuate that point, both colossals fired their hull-mounted twin cannons. Even from a hundred yards away, the pressure wave from the discharge rattled his teeth.

They were close enough now the Khadoran troops would notice them if they approached. There was a definite no man's land between the city proper and the great gate.

"There," Magnus pointed at a narrow alley between two buildings. His small group pushed through the crowd and disappeared into the alley. It was mid-morning, but there were enough shadows to hide them from a casual glance.

"Gods, we're not getting through that wall," Harrow said.

"That's not our objective," Magnus said. "The explosives are *under* the bridge."

He turned to one of the men in his group, a tall, spindly Ordsman with a badly burned face. His name was Xavius Marlow, and he was another exile like Magnus, a man who had been forced to make a living outside the bounds of the law. Xavius had been a member of the Order of the Golden Crucible, a group of arcanists who studied alchemy, mechanika, and other esoteric lore. Xavius' specialty had been explosives, and the charred rubble of the order guildhall in Corbhen was testimony to his skill and the reason his membership had been forcefully revoked.

"Xavius, let's have a look at that map," Magnus said.

The alchemist reached beneath his breastplate and pulled out a scrap of rolled paper, spread it out, and flattened it against a nearby wall. It was a sketch taken from the blueprint of Riversmet, and it showed the bridge of the Great Gate. A number of Xs had been marked on the bridge—the most likely place for the explosives to be.

"If I wanted to bring down the bridge, this is where I would put the explosives," Xavius said. His voice trembled, but it was not from fear. It was excitement. Xavius loved his work, perhaps too much. Also, the prospect of a chemical agent attached to the explosives only made the man's eagerness more apparent.

"How do we get to them?" Tews asked. "They're under the bridge."

Xavius seemed confident. "We don't need to get to all of them, just one. Harkevich has to detonate them remotely, so they're likely linked together and wired to a central detonating device across the bridge. If we can get to the first one, we can disable the linking device and disarm all of them."

"That's a lot of ifs," Tews said. "What if he has multiple detonators?"

Xavius chuckled. "Another 'if'? Khadorans aren't that smart."

Tews did not look satisfied. "Magnus, this is too big a gamble; we're risking everything on this man's hunch."

"I've come to trust Xavius' hunches, and he knows his business," Magnus said. "If he says they're all linked, I believe him. You should as well." It was a half-truth. Xavius *did* know his business, but the crazy Ordsman would likely be just as satisfied with detonating the explosives as disarming them.

"That one, right there, is closest," Harrow said, pointing at an X on the map denoting an explosive under one the main support pillars closest to the shore. "The climbing kit is sturdy enough, but we need to get Xavius up there without him getting shot to pieces."

"I can do something about that," Magnus said. "I'll go with him. The rest of you, find some cover near the shore. We might need you to create a diversion."

"What kind of diversion?" Tews asked.

"Get them to shoot at you, Captain, so they don't shoot at us," Magnus replied.

Tews blanched, but he nodded.

"Everyone understand?" Magnus said. Nods. He pulled his pocket watch. "We've got about thirty minutes to pull this off or Harkevich drops Stryker in the river."

"What's the rush, then?" Harrow said with a grin, eliciting a murderous glare from Tews.

"That's enough," Magnus said. "If the lord general doesn't succeed, then we're trapped behind enemy lines. How badly do you want to get reacquainted with Khadoran torture methodology?"

The smile disappeared from Harrow's face. "I think I learned all I need to from those bloody bastards the last time."

Magnus turned away. "Captain Tews, you're in command while Xavius and I go for the bridge."

Everyone looked shocked at that, but Tews was the senior officer, and despite the Stormblade's loathing of him, he was reliable.

"The clock is ticking, gentlemen," Magnus said. Let's get to it."

— 22 —

Eastern Riversmet, Occupied Llael

THE SCREECHING WHIR OF THE CYCLONES' chain guns was a welcome sound as Stryker and the Storm Lances rode out from beneath the cover of the first tower toward the third, having dealt with the second already. The surface of the tower ahead bloomed with showers of sparks as hundreds of bullets smashed into it. Some of the bullets found more than steel and stone, and a few of the projecting rifle barrels disappeared from the various slits.

Despite the covering fire from the Cyclones, Stryker's arcane shield lit up around him as bullets slammed against it. Some of them penetrated, but the power field generated by the arcane turbine in his armor drained enough of their lethal energy that they failed to penetrate the armor beneath.

Their attack on the second tower had gone very much like the first. They'd breached the portcullis, fought a furious battle in the courtyard beneath the tower, and had been victorious. They'd lost more men, but holding two towers allowed him to move more men and warjacks onto the bridge. With Maddox and a bevy of warjacks that included Defenders and their long-range cannons holding the second tower, Stryker had more faith in taking the third and final tower. The problem was that they were doing well, they were winning, and that meant Harkevich's decision to detonate the bridge was getting easier with every passing minute. Stryker was forced to put his faith in Magnus, and it was an ill fit.

He couldn't dwell on Magnus now, however, so he let his mind be pulled into the familiar chaos of combat. Rowdy was charging alongside them, smoke billowing out behind the big warjack in a black stream. The warjack's enthusiasm, even joy, at the coming battle was infectious, and it flowed back through the connection they shared. Rowdy would make the work in the final tower easier.

They were nearly upon that third tower. He ordered the charge and sent Rowdy forward to assault the portcullis, but, unexpectedly, it rose. The movement confounded Stryker for a moment, but then he understood.

Kommander Izak Harkevich was a huge man with a great black beard, and as he stepped out onto the bridge, his crimson warcaster armor gleamed in the morning sunlight. Beside him was a towering warjack, its hull painted black. Stryker recognized the chassis, a Destroyer, the long-range bombard on its left arm leaving little doubt. However, this warjack had been customized; instead of the axe most Destroyers carried in their right hands, this one's right appendage had been replaced with terrible ripping talons.

Man-O-War flowed out behind the Khadoran warcaster and formed a line in front of him, their shield cannons aimed at the charging Storm Lances.

There wasn't time to break off the charge, and Stryker gritted his teeth as Harkevich's arm rose and then fell sharply. Fire rippled across the Man-O-War shields as their cannons discharged, and behind them Harkevich's warjack loosed a blast from its bombard. There was a moment of eerie silence that seemed to stretch time as the shells howled toward their targets.

The shells struck, and Stryker felt more than saw one of the explosives hit Valorous, his horse, beneath him. Then he was flying forward, weightless, as the explosive force hurtled him through the air. He hit the ground ten feet away, his armor and power field absorbing most of the impact but not all of it. His breath was smashed from his lungs, and he heard the terrible screeching of horses and men blasted apart by explosives.

He tried to reach out to Rowdy, but his brain was a jumble of pain and panic. The big warjack was no stranger to warfare, though, and he and Stryker had fought together for more than a decade. Rowdy was suddenly looming over him, angling his hull to deflect bullets and even artillery shells targeting his master.

Stryker regained his senses quickly and climbed to his feet. Many of his Storm Knights were down, including Bartlett, but there wasn't time to count the dead. The Man-O-War were advancing to finish the job.

Stryker cast his mind back to the other warjacks in his battlegroup, pushing the Defenders forward. Maddox would have seen what had happened as well, but her warjacks would take time to arrive, and Harkevich was taking his shot now to remove the head of the Cygnaran Army with one stroke.

Stryker snatched Quicksilver from the ground where it had fallen and turned to see the wall of red armor closing in on them. He ordered the Defenders to open up with their cannons, but the locked shields of the Man-O-War deflected the shells well enough that few of the heavily armored warriors fell. In the middle of the advancing Man-O-War came Harkevich himself, armed with a brutal-looking mechanika mace that glowed an icy blue. His warjack was close behind him.

"To me!" Stryker cried. "Form a line!"

The remaining Storm Knights heeded his call and moved to him. A quick count told him there were seven. Seven against fifteen Man-O-War, a warjack, and a warcaster.

They managed to form a ragged battle line before the Khadorans plowed into them. Stryker parried a blow from an annihilator axe and kicked out at its owner, knocking him back. He sent Rowdy forward, and the warjack hammered a Man-O-War with one fist, sending the Khadoran flying off the bridge to drown in the river below.

Stryker slashed with Quicksilver, cleaving a Man-O-War shield and the man behind it. He was trying to reach Harkevich, and to his surprise, the Khadoran warcaster obliged him.

He saw through Rowdy's eyes that the warjack had found its own counterpart and had engaged Harkevich's Destroyer. Stryker channeled some of his will into Rowdy's initial strikes against the enemy 'jack, and the Khadoran machine's hull buckled beneath the blow. He kept moving the Cyclone chain guns up to the tower above, shredding masonry and keeping Khadoran soldiers from firing down on them. Then he pulled back and focused on Harkevich.

They were in the middle of the fighting, and a ring of combatants had formed around them both. Whether this was intentional, Stryker couldn't tell, but there was nowhere to flee. He glanced back; Cygnaran warjacks and troops were rushing toward them, but Harkevich had obviously planned for this. From atop the tower behind him bloomed a bright flare of orange fire—more Man-O-War firing their shield cannons at the charging Cygnarans. The Khadoran warcaster had decided to risk shelling the bridge if he could cripple the Cygnaran offensive right here. The shells were inaccurate but effective en masse, and the Cygnaran advance was halted for a moment to avoid what was essentially a firing squad above. Stryker urged the Cyclones to concentrate their fire on the Man-O-War atop the tower. They couldn't adequately form a shield wall up there and were forced to seek cover from the hail of bullets.

Harkevich rushed forward, aiming a heavy blow with his mace at Stryker's head. He was quick for a large man, and Stryker snapped Quicksilver up into a high guard to knock the blow aside, turning his body to lessen its impact. He riposted, rotating his wrists and bringing Quicksilver around in a swiping cut at his enemy's midsection. Harkevich leaped back, but he was a fraction too slow, and Stryker's blade flared against the warcaster's power field, penetrated, and scraped across the Khadoran's breastplate, leaving a vivid white line.

Harkevich grinned, his white teeth showing through the tangle of his black beard.

"Well struck, Lord General," he said in heavily accented Cygnaran. Then the Khadoran warcaster bulled forward, spell runes forming around his left hand as his right brought his mace down in an overhead smash.

The spell struck first, an icy blast of arcane wind that plowed through Stryker's power field and then through his left pauldron, cutting and freezing the flesh beneath. He staggered back, the pain forcing him to take one hand off Quicksilver as he brought it up to parry Harkevich's mace. The Khadoran's weapon hammered down, blasting through Stryker's parry and into his breastplate. The steel crumpled, pushing jagged shards of metal into his flesh, and he was knocked backward off his feet.

Stryker landed in a heap a few feet away from Harkevich, and the force of the blow saved him. It gave him enough time to summon his own magic. Runes flashed around his body, and he pointed his fist at Harkevich, charging forward to finish the job. Azure lightning flashed from Stryker's outstretched fist, and jagged bolts of electricity rained down from the sky around Harkevich; one struck him in the chest and sent him reeling away, his armor smoking. More bolts struck two Man-O-War nearby. One of them went down, his body jerking in the terrible throes of voltaic power.

Stryker got to his feet and summoned his magic again, filling his limbs with arcane strength and fury. He charged, smashing a shoulder into Harkevich as the warcaster turned to meet him. The impact sent bolts of agony up his injured arm, but it had the intended effect. Harkevich staggered back and his guard dropped for a moment. Quicksilver licked out. The blade arced low and bit into Harkevich's right leg above the knee. The steel parted, then the flesh beneath, and Quicksilver's blade thudded against bone.

Harkevich did not cry out or even give ground. Instead, he gritted his teeth and smashed Stryker in the face with a gauntleted fist. The cartilage in Stryker's nose crunched and warm blood splattered his face. He stumbled, his eyes blurring as they filled with tears. He brought Quicksilver up to fend off Harkevich again, but the warcaster was limping away through the line of Man-O-War, which closed ranks behind him.

Stryker cast his mind out to find Rowdy, and fear raced through him. The warjack's cortex was a dim spark, not the vibrant fire it usually was. He couldn't see through the warjack's eyes, so he used his own. Rowdy was lying on his side, the black Khadoran warjack standing over him. Stryker could sense the damage Rowdy had suffered—the huge rents in the warjack's hull, the severed hydraulics in both legs and the right arm. Rowdy was seconds away from the scrap heap.

Stryker pushed forward toward his 'jack. The Khadoran warjack was withdrawing with Harkevich and the Man-O-War. The remaining Storm Knights were letting them go.

Another fusillade of cannon fire from the top of the tower drew Stryker's attention upward. The Man-O-War were still peppering the advancing Cygnarans, braving the Cyclones' chain guns, but the Cygnarans had pressed on regardless, and now Maddox, flanked by a pair of Defenders, appeared through the smoke and clouds of debris. The Defenders fired together and the top of the tower burst apart in a shower of masonry. One of the Man-O-War, too close to the edge, fell forward, plummeting fifty feet to the bridge below. He hit like a red meteor, exploding in a shower of armor and blood.

"Get Rowdy out of here," he shouted as Maddox ran up to him. Her face went pale when she saw Stryker's injuries, but she began shouting orders. He'd already lost Valorous, and he sure as hell wasn't going to abandon Rowdy.

The portcullis of the third tower rattled down behind the retreating Harkevich, and Stryker realized his victory here would cost him. There was no reason for the Khadoran warcaster not to blow the bridge now.

"Hurry, Magnus," Stryker whispered into the smoke-filled air.

— 23 —

Eastern Riversmet, Occupied Llael

ALTHOUGH THE LOSS OF HIS ARM OFTEN PAINED HIM and reminded him of other things he had lost, there were times when Magnus was grateful for its mechanikal strength. He was currently dangling beneath a massive stone bridge by a sturdy rope, the thunder of cannon and gunfire shaking the foundations of the structure above him. He held the rope with his mechanikal hand, letting its strength take most of his weight.

He and Xavius were strapped into a climber's harness, something a man might use to scale a mountainside. The rope assembly worked just as well on the bridge, and the Rhulic-forged pitons bit into the stone with just a tap from a hammer. The Khadorans had been sufficiently distracted by the attack above that they hadn't seen him and the former Golden Crucible alchemist scaling the underside of their bridge and not as a neighborly gesture of greeting. *Count as blessings small favors*, he thought.

"Can you see it?" he called out to Xavius, who was dangling a few feet from the underside of the bridge above him.

"I can," the Ordsman called back. "But these aren't Khadoran explosives."

"I don't care. Just disarm the bloody thing."

Xavius didn't answer for a moment, and the bridge shook again, this time not with gunfire, but from the heavy tread of warjacks. Things were likely getting desperate up there. "It's more complicated than that. The explosives *are* linked, but they're much more sophisticated than I anticipated."

"How long?" There wasn't time to dwell on the implications of Xavius' discovery.

"Ten minutes," Xavius called back.

Magnus dangled his pocket watch so he could glance down at it. They might have that long or he might end his days hanging from the underside of a bridge just before it fell on his head.

"Stop talking to me and do it," he said.

A shower of stone chips suddenly slashed across Magnus' face as a bullet ricocheted off the bridge a few inches from his head. He was suddenly very aware of the absence of the power field generated by his warcaster armor. He looked down; a group of Winter Guard was standing on the shore, their rifles pointed up at him.

He quickly summoned his magic, the runes forming around his body in a protective barrier. He let the spell encompass Xavius, too, and the outline of the Ordsman's body wavered and became blurry and indistinct. More bullets slammed underneath the bridge, missing but filling the air with chips of stone.

"Can you do something about that?" Xavius called down, irritated. He was clinging to the bridge like a giant spider, his face pressed against what Magnus guessed to be enough explosives to reduce him to little more than red mist.

Magnus didn't answer; instead, he pulled his hand cannon from its holster with his left hand and took aim. He'd left his scattergun behind, knowing the hand cannon's increased range would be of more use. Another shot whizzed by, and Magnus sighted on one of the Winter Guard on the shore. He channeled arcane power into the shot, and his aim steadied. His target was a good two hundred yards away—an incredibly difficult shot under normal circumstances. He pulled the trigger, and the gun bucked in his hand. The heavy slug, guided by his magic, found its target. The head of the Winter Guard snapped back, and he collapsed to the ground.

Magnus' hand cannon, although powerful, was a single-shot model, and he didn't want to let go of the rope with his other hand to reload. More shots rang out from below, but they weren't aimed at him or Xavius. Another of the Winter Guard collapse to the ground. Three men were charging up the narrow strip of beach toward the guardsmen—they were outnumbered, but Magnus had little doubt that Harrow, Tews, and another of his men, a brutish ex-Steelhead named Silus, would make short work of the soldiers. He had a birds-eye seat, quite literally, to the slaughter that followed.

Tews hadn't bothered to draw his gun, and he cut down the first Winter Guard he encountered—the Khadoran tried to parry the big Caspian battle blade with a short-hafted axe. Tews cut through the axe and then through the man's neck behind it. Harrow shot two guardsmen dead with his repeater, and Silus took care of the last one with his blunderbuss.

Harrow waved up at Magnus after the last guardsman had fallen. They remained on the beach, likely in case any additional Khadoran troops showed up. Given the noise on the bridge, Magnus didn't think that likely.

"Where are you with that bloody bomb?" Magnus called up.

"Nearly there," Xavius said. "We got lucky. The detonator relay is linked to this one. If I can remove it . . . There."

"Are you done?"

"Not quite yet. I want to take the device with us."

"Wait. That sounds like a bad idea. Have you even identified the chemical agent?"

"I have, and trust me, General, you'll want to see this."

More gunshots rang out from below. Magnus knew he'd been wrong, and now it wasn't just that more guards were on the way.

Man-O-War were escorting what looked like a pair of snipers to take up firing positions. Harrow, Tews, and Kalen were retreating, unloading their weapons on the enemy as they went.

Magnus holstered his pistol and drew Foecleaver. "Xavius, we need to leave now. Can you swim?"

The Ordsman looked down at him eyes wide. Magnus didn't give him a chance to answer and slashed through the ropes holding them to the bridge.

They fell.

— 24 —

Eastern Riversmet, Occupied Llael

A BRIGHT GREEN FLARE ROSE UP over the city of Riversmet, and a wave of relief washed over Stryker. It was the signal he'd been waiting for. Magnus had done it.

The medic seeing to Stryker's wounds grunted in irritation. "Sir, please hold still," he said. He had removed Stryker's left pauldron and was seeing to the wound beneath. Harkevich's spell had both frozen and cut the flesh, and the medic was doing his best to close the wound. Stryker had let Maddox set his broken nose soon after they'd retreated back to the second tower, after Harkevich had withdrawn. She'd taken some pleasure in snapping the cartilage back into place and the pained wince it had elicited.

"Well, maybe you won't duel the next warcaster you encounter like you're some kind of green-horned cadet, sir," she'd said.

The medic finished and helped Stryker put his pauldron back on. He moved his arm. It was tender, but he could swing his sword with both hands now.

"Maddox," Stryker said, turning to where the commander was standing over the wreck of Ol' Rowdy, taking stock of the damage. They'd used the Cyclones to drag the warjack back beneath the shelter of the second tower. Stryker tried not to look at the wreckage—it was like looking at the corpse of an old friend. "Get the Stormwalls up here. I want to neutralize those Conquests right away. They might not be able to blow the bridge with explosives, but the cannons on those things might do that job for them. And move the artillery up to the shore. I want to start hitting the Khadoran gun emplacements immediately."

Maddox turned and shouted orders to a pair of trencher commandos, and they rook off toward the Cygnaran front line to deliver Stryker's orders. Stryker sent one of his Cyclones with them. The warjack would provide cover for the trenchers until they could reach Master Sergeant Halverson, the experienced trencher ⊠jack marshal currently in charge of the Cygnaran colossals.

The remaining Cyclone and Defenders made the courtyard beneath the tower more than a little crowded, not to mention choked with smoke from the warjacks' stacks. What remained of Stryker's Storm Lances were also here; he'd lost more than half of them, including Major Bartlett. She'd been struck by a Man-O-War slug and they couldn't find enough pieces of her to recover. It made him sick; she'd been a hell of a soldier and a respected leader, and her loss would hurt them. But he couldn't focus on that—she wouldn't be the last good soldier he was going to lose in the coming days and months. He could only honor their memories by fighting with every ounce of courage and conviction he possessed.

In addition to the Storm Lances, he still had a full squad of rangers, and they had stormed the upper level of the tower, killing the snipers and Winter Guard they found there. They were now the snipers, firing back at the Khadoran soldiers in the third tower.

Stryker said, "I'm going forward with the Defenders and the Cyclone to crack that third tower. Stay here and take command of the Stormwalls when they arrive. Then I want you to throw everything you've got at those Conquests. Understood?"

"Yes, sir," Maddox said with a grin. "This will be the first time

I've controlled two of those monsters. Looking forward to it."

"Lieutenant Sims," Stryker said, turning to the experienced ranger who would have been the man to interrogate Vasko Aleshko if Magnus hadn't intervened. "Give me some cover; I'm going to go knock on the door of the third tower."

"Absolutely, sir." He moved to relay the orders to the rangers in the tower above.

Stryker closed his eyes and concentrated, strengthening his connection to the three warjacks he commanded. He'd controlled as many as seven at once, but more than four or five tended to stretch even a veteran warcaster's abilities; it was like trying to solve complex mathematical equations in your head while simultaneously trying not to get shot, stabbed, or exploded.

Stryker dug into his arcane reserves and cast one of his most potent spells. Runes enveloped him and the warjacks under his command, filling the great machines with furious energy that would ultimately conserve his own power.

"Let's go," Stryker shouted, and ran out onto the bridge. His warjacks followed, and behind them the rest of his Storm Lances, now afoot, came along with a full squad of Stormblade infantry that had been brought forward.

Bullets began pounding the stone in front of and around Stryker, and he urged his Defenders to open fire on the tower ahead. Their heavy cannons swiveled and took aim then discharged in a blast of flame and fury. The shells struck the tower dead center, blasting apart stone and steel and creating a gaping hole in the wall, exposing the forms of Khadoran soldiers within.

The Cyclone fired next, its lighter, more accurate chain guns targeting enemies within the building, sending a hail of shredding bullets through the breach the Defenders had made and reducing men to gory paste.

The rain of bullets from the tower ahead slackened, and Stryker targeted the portcullis next. He sent the Defenders forward to assault the iron and steel portcullis with their shock hammers. The portcullis buckled, but it wasn't Man-O-War beyond that threatened the warjacks—they were men in heavy baroque plate, not steam-powered, and were armed with shields and long pikes with conical tips, shaped charges that could punch a hole in warjack armor. The Defenders' hammers had done their work. The portcullis crashed down, but not before half a dozen Iron Fangs struck one of the warjacks with their lances. Blossoms of fire burst around the Defender's hull, steel and hydraulics ruptured, and then abruptly the Defender's presence in Stryker's mind disappeared as a lucky strike from an Iron Fang blasting pike destroyed the warjack's cortex.

There wasn't time to worry about the fallen Defender. "Charge!" Stryker cried, and he and the rest of the Storm Knights surged forward behind the remaining Defender to engage the Khadoran troops in the courtyard of the third tower.

As they pounded toward the enemy, the ear-shattering report of a Stormwall's heavy cannons sounded, sending a massive projectile whistling over the bridge. It struck one of the Conquests, knocking the gargantuan machine back a step and leaving a scorched crater in its hull. Stryker smiled as more shells followed and were joined by the booming thunder of Cygnaran artillery.

The Iron Fangs were waiting for them in a wall of shields and pikes in the third tower. Behind them came a pair of warjacks, massive Juggernauts, the terrible workhorses of the Khadoran military. Each was armed with a fearsome mechanika axe that generated freezing cold. Harkevich was not with the 'jacks; they were following the shouted orders of an Iron Fang officer.

The Cygnarans did not slow their charge. Instead, they ran headlong into the arrayed pikes of the Iron Fangs. A series of explosions rattled Stryker's teeth, even as he avoided the end of a pike and cut down the man behind it. He pushed the Defender into the fray. It swept aside pikemen to get at the two Juggernauts. His Cyclone now came forward as well, using its fists to smash aside troops, though a few blasting lances exploded against its hull as it barreled through the enemy. Luckily, the damage was not critical.

Stryker drove himself through the Iron Fangs and found himself face to face with the officer, a large man wielding a heavy two-handed axe. The officer was more than a skilled veteran—he was likely controlling the Khadoran warjacks as a 'jack marshal, a non-sorcerous way of commanding the machines with verbal instructions and hand signals. Stryker hoped removing him would make the Juggernauts far less effective. He cut at the man's legs, but the Khadoran nimbly leaped over the cut and brought his axe down in an overhand slash. Stryker twisted to the side, and his power field flashed as the axe struck him a glancing blow. He pressed forward, inside the range of the Iron Fang's axe, and rammed Quicksilver's pommel into the enemy's throat. The Iron Fang's gorget, the piece of metal protecting his throat, crumbled, and he staggered, gasping. Stryker steppe back, flipped his blade's direction, thumbed the firing stud on Quicksilver's handle, and fired a bolt of lightning at the man from point-blank range. The Iron Fang officer was flung backward, a smoking hole in his breastplate and his chest. He hit the ground a corpse, and Stryker returned his focus to his warjacks. The Defender was pounding one of the Juggernauts with its shock hammer, sending surges of damaging voltaic energy through the enemy warjack's cortexes. The Cyclone wasn't faring quite as well with its fists, and Stryker felt the shuddering impact of an ice axe against its hull. He channeled more of his will into its strikes, guiding them, making them more accurate and impactful, then he returned his attention to the battle around him. His knights were locked in brutal combat with the Iron Fangs, but it was clear that once they were past the Khadoran troops' lances, the Cygnarans were more skilled in hand-to-hand combat. Corpses in red armor were piling up.

More thunder echoed overhead as the Stormwalls continued their assault. Then another sound overwhelmed all others. One of the Conquests, its hull pockmarked with ragged, scorched holes, teetered on the edge of the bridge like an enormous drunken sailor. Then it crashed through the stone railing and plummeted into the river below. As the colossal's boiler hit the chill waters of the Black River, it detonated like a bomb, throwing a one-hundred-foot geyser of water and debris into the air.

A ragged cheer went up from the Cygnaran troops, a cheer that echoed across the bridge. They were winning.

— 25 —

Eastern Riversmet, Occupied Llael

MAGNUS HANDED THE FLARE GUN back to Harrow and shook the water from his hair. The river had been cold, and the weight of his prosthetic limb sent him straight to the bottom. They'd landed in a relatively shallow part of the river, and Magnus had pulled himself up the riverbed quickly, dragging the half-drowned Xavius to safety. The Ordsman hadn't helped much to resolve his own plight and had clutched the Khadoran explosive he'd liberated from the bridge to his chest the entire way.

He'd let the current take them both farther downstream to avoid the Khadoran troops who'd been shooting at them. Harrow, Tews, and the rest of his men quickly found them. With the battle raging above, they hadn't been pursued.

"Our own men should have seen that as well," Magnus said. "They'll be attacking the eastern half of the city soon."

"We going back through the town to reach them?" Tews asked. The man's tone had softened, and the rancor that tinged his every word hours before had all but disappeared. His soldier instincts had taken over, and he was following orders now.

"Yes. The Khadoran forces are going to be in disarray and likely panicked now that the bridge will remain intact. We'll just blend in and push through." In addition to the soldiers awaiting his return, there were four warjacks, potent Stormclads armed with voltaic swords that would be devastating in the close confines of the city. Magnus' armor was there, too, and he ached both figuratively and literally to get back into it.

"Sir, have a look at this," Xavius said. The man looked like a giant, waterlogged insect. His clothes clung to his spindly limbs and enhanced his gaunt appearance. He was holding out the explosive device he'd pulled off the bridge. It was a pair of glass tubes filled with a green viscous liquid. A mechanika detonator and a length of detonation cord topped each tube. Both had been cut.

Magnus accepted the device and turned it carefully in his hands. He had some knowledge of explosives, and he understood that whatever was in those tubes was highly volatile.

"It's safe," Xavius said, as if reading his thoughts. "A voltaic charge is necessary to ignite the substance."

"Why am I looking at this?" Magnus asked. "Do you know what kind of alchemical agent this is or not?"

"Look at the marking on the first tube."

A wide bowl topped by a five-pointed flaring star had been stenciled onto the tube. It was faded, but Magnus recognized it.

"The Order of the Golden Crucible," he said, naming the order of arcanists Xavius had once belong to.

"Just so," Xavius confirmed. "But more than that, do you know what this is?"

Magnus was getting irritated. This was the kind of game Xavius liked to play, lording his knowledge over those without it. It always made Magnus want to shoot him. He resisted. "Just tell me. Now."

A delighted grin spread across Xavius' face. It made Magnus very uncomfortable.

"This is devil's gasp," he said.

Magnus frowned. "I thought the Order had banned its creation," he said. He'd heard of devil's gasp; he'd even seen it used once. It wasn't just a potent explosive—when detonated, devil's gasp created lingering gas clouds of insidious potency. The gas dissolved the tissues of the lungs in the men who breathed it, ensuring a slow, agonizing death that ended with victims drowning in their own blood.

"Oh, they have," Xavius said, "but the existing stockpiles weren't destroyed. Just hidden. I think Harkevich found one of those stockpiles in the ruins of Riversmet. If we could find—"

"This is a discussion for another time," Magnus said and handed the devil's gasp back to Xavius. If they could find more of the substance, it might make a potent ace in the hole. Stryker would never agree to its use, of course, but it would be foolish to overlook a possible advantage. That, too, was a discussion for another time when one of Stryker's most trusted officers was not among them.

A huge sound from above pulled their attention to the bridge. One of the Conquests was suddenly struck by two massive artillery shells, likely fired from the Stormwalls advancing up the bridge. The massive warjack gave what sounded like a pained gasp of escaping steam and tottered sideways, crashing through the guardrails on the bridge. Over it went. Fifty tons of steam and steel crashing into the river, then exploding in a huge burst of water and debris as red-hot boiler met icy river water.

"That's a good sign," Harrow said.

"Agreed," Magnus said. "Now let's get out of here and see if we can't make things a little worse for the Khadorans."

— 26 —

Eastern Riversmet, Occupied Llael

STRYKER SURVEYED THE DAMAGE to the buildings across the bridge. It was bad but not as bad as it could have been. Once they'd taken the bridge and moved the artillery up close, Harkevich had pulled most of his men and guns deeper into the city. The Khadoran commander had done his share of damage as well, and one of the Cygnaran Stormwalls had joined its Khadoran counterpart in the river.

Still, Harkevich was outnumbered and outgunned, and reports were trickling in that Magnus had been hitting the Khadorans hard all day with hit-and-run guerilla-style attacks.

Cygnaran troops were moving up and securing positions across the river, largely using the Khadoran fortifications left abandoned after the enemy had retreated. They would soon be ready to strike deeper into the city, something Stryker was not looking forward to. That kind of fighting, in the close quarters of a city, meant a lot of collateral damage. There were still thousands of innocent

Llaelese citizens in Riversmet, and they would undoubtedly suffer in the fighting to come.

"Lord General," a voice said from behind him.

Stryker turned to see Maddox. Her armor was dented and gouged in many places; she'd been front and center in the last bit of fighting that it had taken to secure the bridge. Her command of the Stormwalls had been exemplary, and she'd destroyed both Conquests with help from Cygnaran artillery.

"You should head back to base camp, sir," she said. "Get something to eat, and get that arm looked at."

He nodded, and a powerful, aching weariness settled over him. He was not a young man any longer, and the rigors of combat took their toll on him for days, even weeks, after the fact. "Right, you've got the command then. There'll be reports coming in from the forward lines. Send a runner if Harkevich decides to do anything more than lick his wounds."

She seemed to consider whether or not to continue Finally, she added, "Magnus has returned. He's looking for you."

He smiled wearily. "Why didn't you say that in the first place?"

"Slipped my mind," she said evenly. "You should also check in with Halls; he's been working on Rowdy."

A wave of concern hit Stryker. Sergeant Major Halls was the senior warjack mechanik in the Cygnaran invasion force, and if he was working on Rowdy instead of assigning one of his many assistants to do it, things could be bad.

Maddox reached out and put a hand on Stryker's arm. "He'll be fine," she said. "That old 'jack is tougher than dragon spit."

"Thanks, Beth," he said. He couldn't quite vocalize his attachment to the warjack. Some warcasters considered their machines to be little more than tools, despite the fact their cortexes grew and learned. Stryker had always seen them as soldiers first and machines second. Rowdy had been with him for over a decade, and the big 'jack was more comrade-in-arms than many of the flesh-and-blood soldiers he'd fought alongside.

"Go," Maddox said. "We fought the good fight today, sir. Revel in it a bit."

He agreed, though he couldn't take much pleasure in the victory. There was still more blood and fire on the horizon.

...

THE CYGNARAN ARMY HAD MOVED the bulk of its military camp up near the river. It was risky—Khadoran artillery might still reach them—but the ability to move men and machines quickly across the bridge made it a credible risk.

Stryker moved through the rows of tents, greeting the soldiers moving busily among them. There were many smiles and shouts of encouragement—they'd won today, and the casualty count had been low. They'd lost only 127 men, though many of them had been Storm Knights in the initial assault on the bridge. The loss of Colonel Bartlett still pained him and would for years to come. He'd managed to find her dog tags on the bridge, and he'd personally send them back to her family in Corvis.

He made his way to the rear of the camp, where the sound of hammers on metal echoed. Sergeant Major Nathaniel Hall's workshop was swarming with activity, and no fewer than six warjacks stood silently nearby awaiting the master mechanik's attentions.

The workshop itself was one of the more permanent structures on the camp, a portable workshop and foundry set within four railcars that could be pulled overland by horse or laborjack. Once assembled, they created a square some thirty feet on a side complete with a forge, a 'jack hoist, various worktables, and more racks for tools than could easily be counted. Of course, the workshop was more of a base of operations, as most of the actual repair work happened on the field, especially on the monstrously huge Stormwall.

Halls was shouting orders at his underlings, many of whom were the diminutive humanoids known as gobbers. The short green-skinned creatures had narrow heads with oversized ears, sharp teeth, and big yellow eyes. They moved quickly, almost bird-like, darting around one another as they hastened to follow Halls' orders. Although gobbers had a well-earned reputation as thieves, they were also naturally skilled with machinery, and the Cygnaran Army employed hundreds of them as mechaniks, often to the consternation of their human overseers.

As he got closer to the workshop, a bolt of panic ran through him. Hanging from the 'jack hoist was Rowdy—or what was left of him. The big Ironclad had lost both legs and his right arm. His hull was torn open in multiple places, exposing his mechanikal guts within. Guilt made a knot in Stryker's stomach. He'd forced Rowdy to leave his quake hammer behind when they assaulted the bridge. The warjack's fists were potent, but the quake hammer was a devastating weapon, and it might have given Rowdy an advantage over Harkevich's modified Destroyer.

Halls had seen him coming, and he set down a heavy hammer, shouting something to one of his gobber underlings. He walked out of the workshop and approached Stryker.

The sergeant major was a burly man, his wide chest and arms slabbed with muscle from hours without end spent swinging heavy tools and lifting pieces of warjack hulls into place. His face was red and soot stained, and he had the appearance of a common laborer. Nothing could be further from the truth, though. Halls was an arcane mechanik, and he commanded the gift of magic the same as Stryker, though his skills were focused on the arcane intricacies of mechanika rather than the battlefield.

"How is he?" Stryker asked, trying to keep the worry from his voice.

"He's beat up something fierce, sir," Halls said. "But his cortex is intact."

Relief flooded Stryker. If the cortex, the mechanikal brain of a warjack was intact, the jack could be salvaged, even if the cortex was moved to an entirely different chassis.

"Sorry to worry you, Lord General," Halls said. "I should have come right out with that."

Stryker shook his head. "No, no. You've got a lot on your plate. How long before Rowdy is up and running again?"

Halls considered the question. "We've got more than enough extra Ironclad parts. Whole limbs even."

"Then I'd like you to give Rowdy special consideration."

"Yes, sir, we can't have our lord general without his personal warjack. Give me two days."

Stryker reached out and shook Halls' hand. "You're a bloody miracle worker, Halls."

The mechanik chuckled. "Just remember that when my parts requisition rolls across your desk."

. . .

MAGNUS WAS WAITING FOR HIM in his tent when Stryker arrived. Food had been set out on the small table inside, and the warcaster was eating when Stryker entered.

"I heard Rowdy was torn up a bit on the bridge," Magnus said, putting down his knife and fork.

Why Magnus had chosen to open their conversation with that, Stryker couldn't say, but it was likely the first shot in an impending salvo. "Yes, he was damaged. Halls has it under control."

"And Bartlett?"

Stryker turned away from Magnus so he couldn't see his face twist with anger. He began unbuckling the straps on his armor. "Yes, we lost the colonel on the bridge. She died bravely. Did you plan to read the entire casualty report to me, General?"

"I'm sorry," he said. "I just knew Bartlett's father; he was a good soldier, like she was." He sounded genuine, and it made Stryker's next words a bit easier.

"You did well with the bridge," he said, though still with some difficulty.

"Well, it was either disarm the bloody things or let the Khadorans kills us both," he said. "But thank you . . . sir."

"Surely you can find somewhere else to rest and eat than my tent," Stryker said as he lifted his breastplate over his head and set it on the wooden stand in front of him. He wouldn't bother with the leg armor—the cuisses and greaves were a pain to take on and off, and they didn't bother him as much as the heavy breastplate and pauldrons.

Magnus chuckled. "Quite right, but I'm not here to break

bread with you." He reached down to a leather satchel at his feet and pulled a cloth-wrapped bundle from it. He set the bundle on the table, and it made a heavy *thunking* sound. "We recovered one of the explosives from the bridge, and it is of remarkable origin and quality." He unwrapped the bundle, revealing two glass cylinders filled with greenish fluid. A mechanikal device—a detonator Stryker guessed—had been fitted to the tops of both cylinders.

Stryker stepped closer to have a look. He could see the symbol of the Order of the Golden Crucible etched into one of the cylinders. "There are of Crucible manufacture?" he said, surmising Harkevich had likely raided the Order's guildhall when the Khadorans had taken Riversmet.

"They're more than that, Lord General," Magnus said. "This is devil's gasp."

Stryker snatched his hand away from the cylinders. He'd been part of the council that had outlawed the use of the terrible weapon in Cygnar, even before the Golden Crucible had stopped manufacturing the stuff. But he'd never actually seen devil's gasp in person.

"Xavius tells me it's inert unless a voltaic charge is applied," Magnus said.

"I wouldn't think Harkevich would use a weapon like this," Stryker said, suddenly reassessing the Khadoran warcaster.

"My thoughts as well," Magnus said. "Yet he is Khadoran, and they tend to be . . . pragmatic with such things."

Stryker grimaced. "Magnus, don't even suggest it."

Magnus drew in a deep breath and put his hands flat on the table. "Look, I've seen this stuff in action, and despite what you might think of me, I'm in no hurry to use it, even on the Khadorans. But I think we should keep our options—"

"No," Stryker said. "I was on Leto's council when we decided to prevent the use of this . . . this *substance*, and do you know what the deciding factor was?"

"Enlighten me, sir," Magnus said. His tone was an inch away from insubordinate.

"That it was no better than a Cryxian weapon; in fact, it was eerily similar to some of the horrible weapons they've employed on our *own* troops. You've seen that firsthand too, haven't you?"

Magnus mouth twisted into a hard line, and anger flashed in his eyes. "You do not need to remind me of the horrors of the Nightmare Empire, *sir*. I fought during the Scharde Invasions . . . along with your father."

"And he returned with a burn so terrible on his leg from a Cryxian bile weapon that it never healed and left him in pain for the rest of his life. To use a weapon like this is inhuman, Magnus." Here it was again, Magnus proving he was no different than the ruthless warcaster Stryker had known and deposed all those years ago. That he would even consider using something like devil's gasp on other human beings, even enemies, was unconscionable.

"Coleman," Magnus said, his tone softening, "we are looking at a long and hard fight in the weeks ahead. We cannot overlook an advantage, even one as terrible as this."

"General, I gave you no leave to call me familiar," Stryker said stiffly. Hearing Magnus use his first name set his teeth on edge. It reminded him of a time when he'd trusted the man, and that time was long past. "You will call me 'sir' or 'Lord General.' Do you understand?"

Magnus said nothing.

"Good. Then you are dismissed." He pointed to the devil's gasp on the table. "Leave that, and send a team of engineers to destroy what remains under the bridge."

Magnus stood but left the explosive on the table. "This is a mistake, Lord General, sir," he said, not making any attempt to hide his disdain for Stryker's decision.

The tent flap opened before Stryker could say anything further. It was a trencher corporal, a young man, with a frightened look on his face.

"Sir," he said, "I'm sorry to intrude, but Major Maddox sent me from the bridge."

"It's fine, Corporal," Stryker said. "Report."

"We've received an envoy from the Khadorans."

Even Magnus seemed surprised. "What are you talking about?"

"Kommander Harkevich, sir. He sent an envoy. He wants to meet with the Lord General to discuss terms."

"What terms, Corporal?" Stryker said, his mind awhirl with the implications of the Khadoran warcaster's message.

"That's the amazing thing, sir. He wants to discuss terms for his withdrawal from the city."

— 27 —

IT RAINED THE FOLLOWING MORNING, and the drops spattering down on the boilers of the two Defenders walking behind Stryker made an incessant sizzling sound. He, Magnus, and Maddox had crossed the bridge and made their way through the portion of the city the Cygnarans occupied, coming at last to a no man's land between the western and eastern halves of the city.

Stryker had no additional troops with him—the warjacks were for show, a statement of strength, not for combat. Still, snipers moved atop buildings in their wake, among them Sharp and Horgrum, and although Stryker did not expect treachery from Harkevich, the thought of the trollkin sniper's Raevhan Express watching over him was a comforting one.

Harkevich was waiting for him at an intersection that seemed to form a line of demarcation between the largely intact eastern half of the city and the largely ruined western half. There were no Riversmet citizens on the street, though a brave few peered through open doors or looked through windows to witness the meeting that would decide the fate of their city.

Harkevich had only one warjack with him, the fearsome black Destroyer with the talon-like right hand. There were two other men with him, however, one wearing the uniform of high-ranking Khadoran soldier; the other was clearly not a soldier, an older man with short greying hair and a stout physique that spoke of a life of hard labor. Harkevich, like Stryker, Magnus, and Maddox, wore his warcaster armor. He was armed with his mechanika mace, which he held before him, its head planted in the middle of the street.

"Lord General," Harkevich said as Stryker and his group drew near. The Khadoran warcaster took a few paces forward, and Stryker noted with some satisfaction that he limped on the leg Stryker had wounded during their short duel. Harkevich held out one huge hand in greeting.

Stryker stepped forward and took Harkevich's hand. The man squeezed, and there was immense, crushing strength in his grip. He had little doubt that Harkevich could break his arm with that grip, armor or no. "Kommander Harkevich," Stryker said and released the Khadoran warcaster's hand.

"May I present to you my senior officer, Kovnik Alexi Krupin," Harkevich said, and the uniformed man stood straighter. "And this is Andrei Ladislav, an elder in this city, a man who represents all that is good about its citizens."

A pity play? Stryker wondered. Ladislav's presence was important. It would undoubtedly factor into their negotiations.

"This is General Asheth Magnus and Commander Elizabeth Maddox," Stryker said, introducing the two warcasters.

Harkevich smiled, something he seemed to do quite a bit, especially for a man with such a fearsome reputation. "Asheth Magnus in the flesh," he marveled. "I had always hoped to face you in battle someday, but I never thought you would be under the banner of Cygnar."

"Your surprise is not unwarranted, Kommander," Magnus said. "I can scarcely believe it myself some days."

"Hah!" Harkevich laughed.

"Kommander, let us not get distracted. We should discuss why we are here," Stryker said.

"Of course, Lord General," Harkevich said. "But first a question."

Stryker waited.

"What have you done with Lord Vasko Aleshko?" He said the name with obvious distaste. Stryker could hardly blame him for that; the kayazy prince was a detestable human being.

Stryker saw no reason to lie. "He is currently a guest of Cygnar," he said. "And will remain so."

Harkevich sneered at the answer. "I have no doubt it was he who gave you the information you needed to disarm the explosives on the bridge. Do with him what you will. The Empire has no need of traitors."

"He will not be treated poorly," Stryker said. *Anymore.*

"Put him in the darkest dungeon you have, so he may enjoy the company of other vermin," Harkevich replied and spat.

"Kommander, you said you wanted to negotiate a withdrawal from the city," Stryker said, urging the Khadoran to get to the crux of their meeting.

"You have the bridge, you have more men, more warjacks, and more artillery. And I am no fool," Harkevich said. "I *could* stay and fight you"—he pointed one thick finger at Stryker—"and make no mistake, I could cost you dearly."

"Your battlefield prowess is not in question, Kommander," Stryker said. "I have no wish to battle you further if I do not have to."

Harkevich put one broad hand on Andrei Ladislav's shoulder. "I could fight you, I could hurt you, but men like Andrei would suffer the most. True, he was not born in Llael, but Riversmet is his home, and he and thousands like him have bled to restore her."

"What are you saying, Kommander?" Maddox said, stepping forward.

Harkevich's jaw worked, as if he was chewing something tough. The words he wanted to say would not be easy for him. "I will withdraw from the city, if you will allow the people of Riversmet to remain, even those of Khadoran origin."

Stryker sometimes lamented the fact that he was often forced to fight men who he might gladly call friend under other circumstances. Kommander Izak Harkevich was one of these men. Stryker could see in the warcaster's face how difficult it was for him to admit defeat, and without a fight no less, but his concern was not his own martial pride, but for the innocent men and women who had been under his care.

"Kommander, you have been a worthy adversary, and I salute your concern for men like Andrei," Stryker said. "Any man or woman who wishes to remain in Riversmet may do so and enjoy the protection of the Cygnaran Army. Any who wish to leave and relocate elsewhere will also be allowed to do so."

Harkevich tipped his head. "That is noble of you, Lord General. Then here are my terms. I will leave the city at once, taking every Khadoran soldier, gun, and warjack with me. By tomorrow evening, we will be gone."

"Lord General, a word in private," Magnus said. Both he and Maddox were staring at him, and to Stryker's surprise, they both had the same look on their faces: disapproval.

"A moment, Kommander, while I confer with my senior officers," Stryker said.

"Of course, Lord General," Harkevich said.

Stryker, Maddox, and Magnus walked a few yards away and stood close together. The rain had picked up, and the downpour would mute their voices. "All right, tell me," he said.

"We can't let him go," Magnus said. "If we let him march out of this city, he's going to head straight for Rynyr, join up with the two battalions there and likely the *five* battalions in Laedry, and we'll be fighting him again inside of two weeks. But this time, he'll have an entire army at his back."

"I agree, sir," Maddox said. "I don't like the idea of fighting in the streets, and there will be collateral damage, but we jeopardize too much if we let him go."

"Harkevich will bleed us," Stryker said, feeling undermined by

Maddox. He'd expected this from Magnus, perhaps, but not from her. "He's got enough men and arms that it'll take weeks to root him out, and we'll lose men, not to mention the hundreds or even thousands of Riversmet citizens who will die in the crossfire."

"There may be a way to minimize the damage," Magnus said, "but we give up a huge strategic advantage if we let him go. Not only will his resources be added to those in Rynyr and Laedry, but he knows the composition and abilities of our army. That alone is enough to make the battle worth it."

Maddox swallowed and looked away. "Again, I agree with the general, sir," she said when she looked back. He could see the war going on behind her eyes between her loyalty to him and what she considered to be sound tactical advice.

Stryker looked back at Harkevich. Andrea Ladislav was standing beside the hulking warcaster. He looked small and miserable next to the kommander, a man with no voice to add in the decision of his own fate. Stryker had seen men like him a thousand times, in every city he'd fought in, in every village he'd seen razed by Cryx or the Protectorate of Menoth. He'd rarely had a chance to help such men, and he looked back at Magnus, a man who rarely found the *need* to help those like Andrei Ladislav.

"No," Stryker said. "We will allow Harkevich to withdraw. A battle in the city will be too costly."

"Sir, please," Maddox said. "This is not—"

"This is not a committee," Stryker said. He didn't want to argue this point with her or with Magnus, who, for once was silent. "I understand your misgivings, and I will not let Harkevich walk out of here without leaving something on the table."

"As you wish, sir," she said.

Stryker glanced at Magnus. "I've said my peace," the warcaster said. "Listen or do not, sir."

Stryker turned away and walked back to Harkevich. Maddox and Magnus followed.

"Kommander, here are *my* terms," Stryker said. "I will allow you to leave the city, but you will leave your artillery and your warjacks behind, taking with you only your personal arms."

Harkevich's eyes widened. "That is ridiculous!" he said, spreading his arms wide, making him look even more bear-like. "You ask too much, Lord General."

"Or stay and fight, and I'll burn you out of Riversmet if it takes me a month to do it. You can't win; you're outnumbered and outgunned. You might make things difficult for me, and, yes, men like Andrei would suffer, but so would your soldiers. You can spend their lives here needlessly, or let them fight another day, when their deaths might mean something."

Stryker didn't look back at Maddox and Magnus; he didn't care what either of them thought of his terms. It was the best course of action—he'd rather fight Harkevich and whoever else he might bring with him outside the city than deal with a costly guerilla battle that could drag on for months.

Harkevich's subordinate officer, Kovnik Krupin, leaned in and said something in Khadoran.

"A moment, Lord General," Harkevich said and stepped away with Krupin, leaving Andrei Ladislav behind.

"I'm sorry, Mister Ladislav," Stryker said. "I'm not here to cause more suffering to you and the people of Riversmet, and I will do what I can to help you."

"You and the kommander are not so different," Ladislav said and gave Stryker a tired smile. "But at the end of the day, you have but one mistress, and her name is war. *She* does not care what happens to men like me."

Stryker didn't know how to respond to that, but Harkevich had returned, a grim look on his face. "I agree to your terms, Lord General," he said, "though I will not leave Black Ivan behind." He looked back at the Destroyer warjack, standing in the rain, steam rising off its hull like clouds of poison gas.

Ladislav was right; he and Harkevich were a lot alike. This Black Ivan was likely as important to Harkevich as Rowdy was to Stryker. "Agreed. Black Ivan, and only Black Ivan, may go with you."

Harkevich put his hand out again, and Stryker shook it. "We will meet again, Lord General."

Behind him, Stryker heard Magnus' voice pitched just loud enough for him to hear. "Of that, I have no doubt."

• • •

THE WALK BACK THROUGH THE CITY was a tense one. Magnus excused himself shortly after the meeting with Harkevich, stating he needed to brief his men. Stryker was more than willing to let him go, but that left him with Maddox, and her anger lanced through the rain at him like a storm of knives.

"Just tell me one thing, sir," she said after they'd walked in silence for some time, weaving through the city, watching the buildings change from burnt-out hulks to intact and even beautiful structures. "Tell me you let Harkevich go because you thought it was the right thing to do and not because Magnus suggested otherwise."

Her words shocked him, and he stopped and turned to her. "Major, I am the Lord General of the Cygnaran Army. I do not make decisions that could cost men's lives out of spite. If you recall, you suggested the same thing." He was annoyed as well, mostly at being challenged this way, but a part of him sincerely hoped she wasn't right.

"With respect, sir," she said. "He was right; he is right. We're going to fight Harkevich again, and he'll have an advantage next time."

He saw no reason to continue to explain his decision, but the words came anyway. Maybe he needed to hear them himself.

"Do you remember the fighting in Caspia and Sul?" he said. It was a low blow; she'd been captured by the Protectorate in the Caspia-Sul War. "Do you remember the fighting in the streets, the men burning alive?"

Maddox face twisted into a rictus of disgust. "How can you ask me that? I was there, in the middle of it, breathing the same stink of burned flesh as you. But Harkevich is not the Protectorate, and this is not Caspia."

She was right, of course. This was no Caspia, but a battle in the streets would be brutal nonetheless. He adjusted his approach. "I will not risk men when we don't have to, Commander, not when we'll need them desperately in the days and months to come. This is just the beginning, remember; we'll be moving on to Rynyr soon, and I need as many healthy soldiers as I can manage."

"You know you don't have to explain yourself to me," Maddox said, though her tone said differently. "I'll follow your orders, without question, and I won't speak on this again, but Magnus has value, something to offer that we need, if you can get past your distrust of him."

Stryker tipped his head. "I listen to General Magnus' counsel the same as I listen to yours."

"I don't think that's so. You listen, but you don't *hear* it. You still hear the voice of the man who betrayed you all those years ago, the man who supported king Vinter—"

"Stop," Stryker said. "That's not a necessary line to cross, Commander." He was frustrated, the rage and doubt that seemed to surround Magnus at all times crackling through his brain like an electric storm. "I don't need you to dredge up the past every time we speak about Magnus. He is here, and he has the king's favor. There's nothing I can do about that, but I *will* do my duty."

Maddox looked at him unflinchingly. There were tears in her eyes, but they weren't from terror or sorrow; they were tears of rage. He'd brought up her past, as painful as it was, and he'd struck out at her when she'd returned the favor. His own frustration evaporated, leaving him cold and empty.

"My apologies, Major," he offered lamely. "That was not . . . seemly of me."

"Yes, sir," she said, her voice level and ice cold. "Will there be anything further?"

"No," he said. "You are dismissed."

He stood there in the rain for some time as she moved on, if only to avoid catching up with her on the way back to the camp.

— 28 —

Western Riversmet, Occupied Llael

MAGNUS AND THE ALCHEMIST XAVIUS MOVED through the ruins of western Riversmet to the sound of hammers on stone. Work on the crumbling outer wall had resumed after Harkevich and the occupying Khadoran forces had pulled out. Stryker had allocated hundreds of men and a handful of warjacks to aid the citizens of the city in rebuilding Riversmet's western fortifications.

Magnus sighed. Stryker was expending men and resources on the wall because that's where the next attack would come. From Rynyr or Laedry, and it would surely be bolstered by Harkevich's largely intact force. Yes, they had forced the Khadoran warcaster to leave behind warjacks and artillery, and that would blunt Harkevich's strength some but not enough.

Stryker had ignored irrefutable tactical advice, to Magnus' mind, from both him and Maddox, but for what? To save a few peasants? Or was it just to exert control over him, to take any action so long as it countermanded Magnus' own? He sighed again. No, Stryker wasn't stupid, and he hadn't survived fifteen years of active combat duty by ignoring sound tactical strategy. He valued the lives of the men and women of Riversmet as much as he did those of his own men. It was that kind of thinking that had cost Cygnar so much: soft-hearted foolishness they could not afford. Magnus didn't consider himself a cruel man, no matter what men like Stryker might believe, but they had a mission, one that would ultimately *serve* the people of Llael even if they suffered in the serving. If a few thousand of them had to die to achieve a stronger Cygnar and through *that* a stronger Llael, it was a worthwhile sacrifice.

He didn't miss exile, but he sometimes missed the freedom it had granted him. At that time, it had been him making the tactical decisions, and men followed his orders, not the other way around. Fitting back into the constraining chain of command of the Cygnaran Army was maddeningly difficult at times.

"It should be up ahead," Xavius said, pointing to a collapsed building, possibly a tower, near an intact portion of the outer wall.

They'd been walking the northwest quadrant of the city for hours. He, Xavius, and a small contingent of men loyal to him. He'd told Stryker he would oversee the rebuilding of the west wall, and he had left Harrow and some of his other officers behind to do that. But he had accepted oversight of the construction efforts so that he could explore this section of the city with Xavius, looking for the ruins of the Order of the Golden Crucible guildhall.

"We've been searching for hours, Xavius," Magnus said. "Do you know if there even *was* a guildhall in Riversmet?"

The spindly Ordsman nodded vigorously. "Had to be. Devil's gasp is not the kind of thing the Order would let out of their sight unless they had no choice."

"Fair enough," Magnus said. "That means Harkevich or his men must have found the stockpile, so we should find evidence of construction or at least a clearing, but there is always the possibility that the Khadorans took what was left with them."

"I don't think so. They had to get out too fast," Xavius said. "We've got enough eyes in the city that we'd have seen it."

They approached the ruined building Xavius had indicated, and Magnus turned to the six men following closely behind them. They were armed and armored like trenchers, but they were men who'd served him in exile, mercenaries who owed him personal allegiance.

"Spread out, and keep any one from disturbing us or approaching these ruins," he said. The city was a beehive of activity now. The bulk of the Cygnaran invasion force had moved into the city, and the citizens of Riversmet were venturing forth from their homes, trying to live their lives again amid the chaos.

The ruined building looked like it had been hit with artillery fire. Many of the white stone blocks that made up its foundation were scorched and blackened. It might have been as tall as three stories, and it appeared to have fallen over rather than simply crumbling. Much of the white stone debris lay across a pair of houses to the east. The symbol of the Golden Crucible was plainly visible on some of those stones. So, they'd at least found the guildhall then.

"There," Xavius said and pointed.

Magnus looked to where he was indicating, to the orderly piles of debris,—the kind made by men excavating.

Magnus followed the alchemist to the site. The heaps of debris were high, but Xavius wasn't paying any attention to them. He was searching between them and the ruined tower.

"It wouldn't have been kept in the guildhall," Xavius said. "Most had subterranean vaults for housing the more dangerous and volatile substances we used." He began walking the perimeter of the ruins, eyes on the ground. Magnus followed him, intrigued.

Something black against the piles of white stone drew Magnus' eye, and he moved deeper into the ruins. It was a black canvas tarp, spread out and weighed down with stone. It bowed in the middle, as if it were covering a depression or a hole.

"Xavius," he called out, "here. Help me move some of this stone."

Magnus was wearing his warcaster armor, and he could move large chunks of stone with ease. Xavius, on the other hand, skinny and unused to hard labor, struggled to move much at all. They had the tarp uncovered quickly enough, and Magnus pulled it back, revealing a stepped passageway of worked stone descending into the ground. A faint smell rose from the opening—dust and something acridly chemical.

Xavius stepped back, covering his mouth and nose with a bit of cloth he'd brought for just that purpose. "We need to be careful," he said. "Some of the vessels may have been broken during the initial attack or even the most recent one. We don't want to breathe in those fumes."

Magnus wound cloth around his own mouth and nose.

Xavius reached into a pouch at his side and produced a small vial of clear liquid. He shook it, and it began to glow brightly. A minor bit of alchemy, bottled light was common in the marketplaces of most large cities.

"Shall we?" he said, his voice taking on a nervous quiver. The alchemist was getting excited, and that made Magnus uncomfortable.

Magnus held out a hand. "Give me the light. You'll follow me."

Xavius handed over the bottle light, and Magnus moved onto the first step, shining the light down into the passageway. It descended for about ten feet then ended in a wider hall or room below.

He moved down the steps, adjusting the boiler on his warcaster armor to reduce the amount of smoke it produced. At the bottom of the steps was a great empty chamber, maybe thirty feet to a side. It was built of solid stone, and a chill radiated from the rock. There were three heavy wooden doors along the east and west walls, all shut, and all barred save one.

Magnus moved to the unbarred door, his footsteps echoing in the gloom. He stopped and stepped out of the way. "*Now* you can go first, Xavius," he said.

The alchemist stepped up to the door and ran his hands over the wood. He blew some dust away to reveal a symbol, a circle ringed with spikes. "This is it," he said. "This symbol means *pericula*, 'great hazard' in old Caspian. It means there are very dangerous substances beyond, the most dangerous elements the Order works with."

"Well, Open it, then," Magnus said.

Xavius turned to him, visibly shaking with excitement. "If it's in there, if there's enough, we'll use it, right? It has been a dream of mine to see devil's gasp in action."

Magnus frowned. He already *had* seen the vile stuff in action, and he was not eager to see it again. "As I told you, we're just confirming if it's here, and if it is, we'll secure it." The next thing he had to say was like a serpent biting his tongue. "It is the Lord General's call if we use it in combat. Based on our last conversation, I'd say that's unlikely."

"No, no, no," Xavius said, his face crumbling into a pout. "I can't be so close to this and not see it used. How can you let that trumped-up fool command you like this. I remember—"

Magnus shot out his right hand, the mechanika hand, like a piston to catch Xavius by the throat. The Ordsman gave a frightened squawk as Magnus slammed him against the door and then pushed his face into the alchemist's.

"You need to listen to me because I'm only going to say this *once*," Magnus said, hissing the word. "So, are you listening?"

The alchemist nodded, at least as much as Magnus' grip would allow.

"That 'trumped-up fool' is the Lord General of the Cygnaran Army, and I follow his orders . . ." He grimaced. "Because that is what the king commands. He commands it of me, and he commands it of you. Do not mistake my adherence to the chain of command as weakness or inability to see the king's will done. We will secure the devil's gasp, and if there is a need to use it, I will convince the lord general it is the best course of action."

Magnus released Xavius and stepped back. The alchemist rubbed his throat and swallowed. "My apologies, General," he said. "I am still adjusting to a more . . . legitimate profession."

The implication was clear enough; when they were in exile, they did what Magnus thought was best. No doubt Xavius wasn't the only man who'd noticed a shift in Magnus' personal influence.

He'd likely have to "correct" more of them in the future, as he'd done with Xavius.

"You are forgiven," Magnus said. "Now open the door."

Xavius turned and put his hand on the pull handle. His arm tensed, and sudden alarm stabbed through Magnus' brain. . It wasn't quite precognition, but death seemed to leave some trace of its passing for him, and he saw it now.

Magnus heard the tension trigger give way with a sharp crack. He hurled himself to the side. The door came open, and the blast was small, but still strong enough to fling Xavius backward and down. The explosion was only a delivery device, however—the plume of greenish mist that enveloped the alchemist was the trap's real payload.

Magnus backpedaled toward the steps leading to the surface, his ears ringing. He had dropped the bottled light, though he could still hear Xavius nearby. The alchemist was making terrible coughing and retching noises. Magnus had heard something like it before. Devil's gasp was heavier than air, so after the initial explosion, it tended to settle like mist above the ground. It was doing that now, and Magnus could see through the door Xavius had opened. The bottled light had rolled into the chamber beyond, illuminating rows of wooden crates, each marked with the circle and spikes symbol. They'd found the stockpile, but someone among Harkevich's men, maybe Krupin, had ensured its discovery would be a costly one.

There was no air current in the underground chamber, and the gas had largely settled. Magnus moved back toward the exit, toward the safety of the afternoon sun streaming down from above. He turned, crossed the room in three quick strides, and bounded up the stairs. Xavius hacked and coughed behind him.

He emerged onto the surface and drew in a deep breath of fresh air, then turned and ran down the steps again. Devil's gasp would not soak through the skin; it had to be breathed in to be effective, and he could hold his breath long enough.

Magnus could see the shadowy form of Xavius slumped against

the wall opposite the rigged door and moved to the alchemist's side. He scooped up the Ordsman, threw him over his shoulder, and raced up the stairs again.

When Magnus reached the surface, his men were waiting for him. They'd heard the explosion below.

"Move away!" he said and hurried from the subterranean opening carrying Xavius. He set the alchemist down on his back twenty feet away.

Xavius face and chest were blackened, and much of his clothing had burned away. The burns were bad, but they were survivable—the poisonous compound in his lungs, however, was another matter. Xavius' mouth, neck, and chest were covered in blood. He was no longer coughing, just struggling to draw breath through his rapidly disintegrating lungs. His eyes were wide as saucers—he *understood* what was happening. He also likely understood he had five, maybe ten, more agonizing minutes before death claimed him.

Magnus stood and drew his hand cannon. He held it out so Xavius could see it. "It's quicker," he said softly.

The alchemist stared up at him, then coughed violently, spraying blood from his mouth in a plume of red mist. He nodded weakly.

Magnus did not hesitate. He took aim, pushing some of his magic into the shot. He wasn't likely to miss at this range, but he wanted a one-shot kill. He pulled the trigger, and the hand cannon unleashed thunder and smoke. The heavy bullet struck Xavius in the forehead, where Magnus had aimed, and blood splashed beneath the alchemist's head. He was still after that.

Magnus holstered his gun and realized his men were staring at him. There was grim acceptance in most of their eyes, though fear and even disgust were evident in a few.

"I'd have done the same for any of you," he said. "To save you from a death like that."

Some of the men nodded; they were hard men, but they had also seen Xavius, seen what was happening to him, and most of them would have accepted the bullet just as he had.

"Make sure no one comes near these ruins for the rest of day," Magnus said. "The gas should dissipate after that."

He looked down at Xavius, the alchemist's eyes wide and staring in death. He had gotten his wish after all.

— 29 —

Eastern Riversmet, Occupied Llael

STRYKER STARED DOWN AT A PAIR OF CORPSES in front of an open prison cell and tried to maintain his composure, tried not to scream and rage at the pointless deaths of two good soldiers. He had an audience that included Maddox and Magnus, as well as Lieutenant Sims, to whom these men had reported.

The two slain soldiers, both rangers, had been guarding Lord Vasko Aleshko, standing outside the holding cell in one of the Riversmet Watch garrisons. The building had still been intact, and its holding cells were perfect for detaining such an important prisoner. Stryker hadn't wanted a large guard detail on the kayazy, mostly because he didn't want word to spread of what had been done to him. Now, with Aleshko gone and two men dead in his wake, it was clear it had been a mistake to leave the man so lightly guarded.

Stryker bent down over the bodies—each dispatched with a blade, a sword or knife—and collected the men's dog tags. He stood and walked over to Sims, pressing the tags into his hands. "I'm sorry, Lieutenant. They were brave men, and they died fighting." That much was also true, because there was a third corpse, the body of a man named Tibbs, a man who had joined the Cygnaran military only a few short months ago, a man who had served Asheth Magnus while the warcaster was in exile.

"Were there any survivors?" Stryker asked Sims.

The young lieutenant nodded. "Yes, sir, Private Conners. He's hurt bad—the bastards ran him through—but he's tough, and he's holding on."

Stryker looked past Sims to where Magnus stood. The warcaster did not avert his gaze, but there was a crack in his usual mask of stony indifference. This mess had rattled him. Maddox looked angry, and she was staring at Magnus, fists clenching and unclenching at her side.

"We'll need to speak with Conners right away," Stryker said. "We'll be quick."

"He was taken to the main infirmary," Sims said.

"All right. See to your men. I'll take it from here. Maddox, Magnus, you're with me."

Stryker walked out of the watch garrison with Magnus and Maddox in tow, and they made their way to the infirmary, which as luck would have it, was set up in the only intact hospital in Riversmet.

"It was Harrow, wasn't it?" Stryker said after they'd moved away from the garrison.

Magnus said nothing for a time, likely weighing his answer. "Probably," he said. "That looked like his knife work."

"I hold you responsible for this, General," Stryker said, trying to rein in his emotions and maintain a professional demeanor. He succeeded. Mostly. "You trusted this man, knowing what he was capable of, and *you* put him in a position to hurt us."

"I accept that responsibility, sir," Magnus said, surprising Stryker. "He was my man." The warcaster's lips were a tight line, and there was real rage behind his eyes. Stryker could likely guess why. Harrow had surprised Magnus. He *had* trusted the former mercenary.

Stryker said nothing else until they reached the infirmary, a large three-story building in the center of the eastern part of the city. The medics took them to Conners immediately, in a wing of the hospital reserved for the critically injured. They passed rows of beds containing men with terrible wounds, most sustained in the short battle with Harkevich. There were men with missing limbs, horrible burns, and bodies that had been riddled with bullets. Those who could acknowledged Stryker as he passed, but it wasn't he that drew the wounded to prop themselves up or whisper greetings. It was Maddox.

The faces in the room lit up as soon as she walked in. She was the Liberator of Llael, the woman who had survived the Protectorate of Menoth and had been reborn stronger from the ordeal. Leto and the Army's work to promote her as a figure of empowerment and national pride had worked brilliantly.

She often resented this role, but here, in this place, Stryker did not see that. "Sir, go ahead," she said to him. "I'll stay and talk to some of them."

"Of course." Stryker watched her move to the bedside of a man who couldn't be older than twenty. Both his legs ended in bandaged stumps below the knees, but the pain and despair on his face disappeared, if just for the moment, as she approached.

Stryker and Magnus followed the medic to the south end of the room, where a white curtain had been drawn across the injury ward, separating it into two halves. The black smell of putrefaction and death struck them as they neared the curtain. He braced himself for what lay behind it—men so gravely wounded they had no chance of survival.

The medic pulled the curtain aside; there were only six beds beyond—their casualties had been light so far. The men in these beds made no note of his presence; most were far past making note of anything.

Conners' bed was at the end, and he lay atop the sheets, stripped to his small clothes. His chest was a mass of bandages, stained crimson from the hideous wound they covered.

"There's nothing more we can do for him," the medic said. "I honestly don't know how he survived this long."

Stryker turned to Magnus, catching the warcaster's eyes and holding them. *Here* is the result of your handiwork, your misplaced trust, he wanted to say, but there were more immediate concerns.

He moved to Conners' bedside. The man's eyes were open, his face ashen, the flesh slack. "Sir . . ." he said weakly, and blood ran down his chin.

"Don't speak, Private," Stryker said and held out a hand to the medic. The man passed a clean white cloth to him. Stryker gently wiped the blood from Conners' mouth and took the soldier's right hand in his own. "I'm going to ask you some questions, and you just squeeze once for yes and twice for no, Can you do that, soldier?"

One squeeze.

"Good man. Did you see the men who attacked you?"

One squeeze.

"Was Captain Harrow among them?"

One squeeze. It confirmed what was already a fact in Stryker's mind, but he needed Magnus to see it.

"Did they take the prisoner with them?"

One squeeze. It was also a question he already knew the answer to, but it was still more confirmation.

"Did Lord Aleshko leave with them willingly?"

One squeeze. Stryker grimaced at that. It meant the kayazy had struck some kind of deal with Harrow, the man who'd tortured him. It made a sick kind of sense—inflicting torment was just the cost of doing business for both men.

"One more question, Conners, and then you can rest. Did they give any indication of where they were going?"

Two squeezes.

"I know where he's going," Magnus said. "The ships."

Stryker looked up at Magnus, who was standing at the foot of Conners' bed. The warcaster was doing his best to avoid looking at the mortally wounded soldier. Was it guilt on his face, guilt that caused him to avert his gaze? Stryker wondered. The thought of it made Magnus appear almost human. "Wait for me outside,

General," Stryker said.

"Yes, sir." Magnus walked away. He seemed relieved.

Stryker turned back to Conners to tell him how brave he'd been, to tell him how much he appreciated his sacrifice, but the young man was past hearing. The trencher private was staring up at the ceiling, his eyes sightless in death.

Stryker laid Conners' hands on his chest, and then closed his eyes. He leaned close and whispered, "It won't be for nothing. I promise."

• • •

"HE'S GOT A THREE-HOUR HEAD START," Tews said.

"How many men are with him?" Stryker asked, turning to Magnus. They were in his tent again, just the people he trusted most . . . and Magnus. He couldn't let news of Harrow's treachery spread through the camp.

"Looks like twenty or so," Magnus said. "All career mercs, tough men, among the best I had."

"The best!" Tews said. "That's bloody rich. Best what? Traitors? Thieves? Murderers?"

Stryker raised a hand for silence. "There are no horses missing, so they're on foot. We can still catch them if they're heading where you think they're heading."

"The ships are the only thing that makes sense," Magnus said. "Harrow needs to cross into occupied Llael, and he can't do that through the city."

"I agree," Vayne di Brascio said. Everyone present had agreed to include the fierce Llaelese gun mage in this meeting and in what would follow. "It's their best and only chance at escape."

The ships they'd taken from Vasko Aleshko were docked farther up the river, away from the city. They'd been left there during the battle with Harkevich, as they would have made for tempting targets, but Stryker still needed them. "So, he can crew, what? One of them?"

"With the men he's got with him, I think so," Magnus said.

"This isn't just about Harrow's treachery," Maddox said. She'd been silent since they'd left the infirmary. "That bastard has a lot of valuable information to sell. He knows the intimate details of our operation in Llael."

Stryker turned to Magnus. "How much?"

"All of it."

"Blood and hell," Tews said. "And you trusted him."

The big Stormblade was being insubordinate, and Stryker had allowed it thus far. His own anger at Magnus overrode his devotion to duty and protocol, but he couldn't let it continue. Magnus wasn't going anywhere. He certainly wouldn't court martial him; Magnus had committed no crime beyond putting his faith in the wrong man. "Captain, that's enough out of you," Stryker said. "You will address the general properly, do you understand?"

Tews' eyes went wide. "Yes, sir."

"We've wasted too much already," Stryker said, weary of the discussion and the weight of it. "Maddox, find ten Stormblades you trust. I'll see about horses. We'll meet at the Great Gate."

— 30 —

North of Riversmet, Occupied Llael

THEY POUNDED DOWN THE NARROW ROAD running along the river, heading north and deeper into Protectorate-controlled territory. It was unlikely the Menites would notice such a small force of thirteen, but Stryker felt exposed without any warjacks at his command. They had to move fast, and no 'jack could keep up with a horse at full gallop.

The ten men Maddox had recruited were good soldiers and honorable knights. Stryker knew most of them by name, and he'd fought alongside many of them. They understood the gravity of their mission, and they would give their lives to complete it. It disgusted Stryker that some of them might die because of Harrow, because of the trust Magnus had placed in him. A terrible waste. But there was nothing else for it now.

"Sir, look," Maddox shouted and pointed to the north, in the direction they were riding. A subtle red glow hung on the horizon, lighting up the early morning darkness.

"Fire," Stryker said. "The Protectorate?"

Soon they came to the small dock where Vasko's ships were moored, the same docks where they'd captured the kayazy. All but one of those ships were on fire, their masts blazing like great lurid candles in the dark. Stryker uttered a short, pained cry. Bad enough Harrow had turned traitor, bad enough he'd freed Aleshko, but the man had also made sure to undermine their mission in Llael, no matter what happened in the next few minutes.

There were men moving on the docks, next to the single intact ship, men in Cygnaran armor who had no right to wear it.

"At them!" Stryker shouted and drew Quicksilver.

They came down a steep berm as gunshots rang out. Stryker could now see that some of the mercs had formed a gun line and were firing slowly, methodically. Bullets slammed into his power field, and sparks flew as they impacted Magnus' and Maddox' fields as well.

Stryker spurred his horse into a gallop and then spotted the architect of this calamity standing at the top of the gangplank of the remaining ship, screaming orders at the men below. Harrow had his sword and pistol in hand, and he was pointing at Stryker's position.

Then he saw the cannons and realized it had been Harrow's plan to lure him close, out in the open between the road and the river. Sudden thunder and a ripple of bright flares burst from the gunwale of the ship, and the telltale scream of artillery shrilled toward them.

"Down!" Stryker yelled a mere second before the shells struck and detonated. He threw himself from his mount as his power field flared, but the force of the blast sent him flying. He crashed to the ground, wincing as his breast plate was driven painfully into his side.

He had been closest to the pier and had taken the brunt of the cannon barrage\. Stryker climbed slowly to his feet, wincing as a dozen bruises and cuts made their presence known. A number of his knights were down, and most of the horses had scattered. The knights were moving but were clearly stunned.

"Pull them back!" Stryker shouted hoarsely, and those knights still on their feet, including Tews and Maddox, began pulling their stunned compatriots back toward the berm.

Movement on the deck of the ship heralded yet another cannon barrage, and Stryker caught the bright spiral of runes forming around di Brascio's magelock, then the sharp crack of its discharge. A man about to touch off another cannon blast aboard the ship stiffened as the ensorcelled bullet struck him in the chest, and it seemed his entire body had seized up like a damaged steam engine. He fell forward on his face.

The cannons fired again, minus one, and the shells whistled toward the Cygnarans. They had made the safety of the berm and had thrown themselves flat behind it. The cannon shells struck just in front of it, billowing up a shower of dirt. The shockwave smashed against the warcasters' power fields and the protective spells they had cast. The blast rattled teeth and reduced hearing to a high pitched keening, but no one was injured.

Tews rolled over to lay next to Stryker. "They don't have the range to hit us from there," he said, shouting. Their ears would take time to adjust.

"Yes, but they've got enough range to blow us to pieces before we can reach the ship," Stryker said. Some of them might make it through, and it was unlikely Harrow and Aleshko would fire the cannons so close to the ship or at the pier where a number of their men were still waiting for Stryker and his men to close on them.

"If we let Harrow and Aleshko escape, they'll go straight to the Khadorans," said Magnus. The warcaster had moved next to Stryker as well.

"You would know; he's your man," Stryker said.

"You're right. I *do* know him," Magnus said, his voice even, though his eyes shifted away from Stryker's glare. "More the reason we stop him."

Stryker couldn't argue with that. He turned his mind to their immediate problem. "Options?" he said, then summoned his magic and renewed the arcane shield above them. The cannons had not fired again, but the extra protection the spell provided would blunt their impact considerably if Harrow opened up on them more.

"I hate to say it," Maddox shouted from farther down the line of Storm Knights clinging to the ground on their bellies. "But we need to rush him, get close enough to use our storm glaives and too close for him to fire at us."

"You may be right," Stryker said. "But there's no cover, and thirteen Storm Knights are a big target."

"What about one warcaster," Magnus said. "I can weather a cannon blast, and I'll be harder to hit."

"No," Stryker said. "No one is going out there alone."

It was a truth that hid a lie. He wouldn't send one man on such a suicide mission, but he didn't care much for the idea of Magnus getting that close to the ship alone. He doubted he was acting in concert with Harrow, especially given how genuinely surprised Magnus had seemed by the man's betrayal, but Stryker didn't trust him enough to test that notion under such duress.

"They're making preparations to leave," di Brascio said. "We don't have much time."

"All right. Here's what we're doing. Magnus, Maddox, the three of us will lead, and I want protective enchantments over the entire unit." Stryker was well acquainted with the spells Maddox had her disposal and he was familiar with Magnus' repertoire as well. Together, they could likely shield themselves and the ten Storm Knights from the worst of an inevitable cannon bombardment. Both warcasters nodded, and Stryker turned to Tews. "Captain, you lead the unit behind us. As soon as you get within range with the storm glaives, let the cannon crews on that ship have it. I don't care if you hit them—just keep them from firing the bloody things."

"I can also keep a few of them from firing," di Brascio said. "I'll come up behind the Storm Knights." The gun mage was the only member of their force who could hit the men on the ship at this extreme range, and Stryker was grateful to have him.

"Thank you ," Stryker said. "As always, any assistance you can provide is more than welcome."

Stryker looked from knight to knight; there was steel and determination in their eyes. These were good men and women, brave and steadfast. He was proud to command them. "Maddox, give us a little protection."

Runes formed around Maddox's hand, bright blue motes of power, and her spell settled over the Storm Knights. Stryker's men were now as protected as Stryker could make them.

The lord general took Quicksilver in one hand. "On my signal." A few seconds passed, and the adrenaline spike of upcoming battle flowed through him. "Go!"

He sprang to his feet, Magnus and Maddox beside him, and charged. A fierce cry echoed behind him as the Storm Knights followed.

The cannons went off almost immediately. Harrow had been waiting for them.

Roughly a hundred yards of open ground lay between Stryker's Storm Knights and the pier, and they were hit by the first volley with three-quarters of that distance to go. The protective spells blunted the impact somewhat but not nearly enough. Plumes of dirt and debris cascaded into the air, and Storm Knights were thrown to the ground.

Stryker managed to keep his feet, as did Magnus, but Maddox was knocked down. The sharp crack of di Brascio's magelock rang out, but there was too much smoke and debris to see if he'd hit anything.

Harrow was likely reloading now.

Someone grabbed Stryker by the back of his armor and spun him around. It was Tews. There was blood running down the big Stormblade's face, but his eyes were hard and steady.

"We're not going to make it as a group," Tews shouted. "Magnus was right. One man is a smaller target."

"No, Captain," Stryker said immediately. "I'll go."

"Bugger that, sir," Tews said. "You're a lord general; I'm just a captain."

Then he was gone, disappearing into the lingering smoke from the cannon shells.

"Move! Move! Move!" he heard Maddox shouting, and the Storm Knights—all of them, thankfully—got up from the ground.

They were running again, out of the smoke and into the clear. He could now see Tews had nearly reached the pier, and the cannons were still trained on Stryker and his group. Harrow was now onboard the ship, shouting orders to the men who were reloading the cannons. Aleshko was standing next to him, unmoving, his hands bound before him. Whatever deal Aleshko had made with Harrow clearly did not involve his total freedom. At least not yet.

"Give the captain some cover," Stryker shouted. They were still too far away from the ship to hit with their storm glaives, and the blasts from their weapons fell well short as the Storm Knights fired them on the run, but they still had some positive effect, as two of the cannon loaders stopped what they were doing and ducked.

They were close enough for Maddox to fire off a blast from Tempest. She pointed the great sword at the ship, and its blade split down the middle, separating so it looked like a massive bladed tuning fork. Storm accumulators within the interior of the blade flared, and she launched a bolt of lightning. One of the men loading the cannons was limned in blue fire and fell over the side of the ship.

di Brascio fired his magelock again, and another loader went down.

Now the mercs on the pier were adding rifle fire to the mix, though with the wards Stryker and his force had erected, the bullets were harmlessly deflected.

Some of the mercs had drawn swords as Tews reached them. Stryker was not overly concerned for his friend. He'd seen Tews in action many times, and the man's skill was superlative. In battle, Tews whirled like an armored tempest, his storm glaive licking out in a bright azure arc as the power coil in the blade flared with power. He cut down two men with the first heavy strike and then a third with the next. He was moving forward all the time, pushing toward the gangplank and the ship above.

The cannons went off again; this time, there were fewer shots and their aim was more erratic. Tews was clearly giving them something to think about. The blasts fell to the sides and behind the charging Storm Knights, spattering them with dirt but doing little else.

Tews had made the gangplank, and the Storm Knights were now in range.

"Gun line!" Stryker called out, and the Storm Knight ground to a halt and aimed their glaives. Stryker leveled Quicksilver as well. "Aim at the pier."

Some of the mercs were attempting to come up the gangplank behind Tews.

"Fire!" Stryker commanded.

Twelve bolts of lightning slammed into the mercs on the pier, hurling many of them into the water. Magnus' scattergun went off, as did di Brascio's magelock, and two more corpses fell.

Tews was now aboard the ship, and he was weaving ruin among the cannon loaders, kicking their corpses over the side of the ship. He'd neutralized the cannons but not Harrow. Stryker watched as the deadly merc descended on the Stormblade with his saber.

He couldn't leave Tews on his own much longer. "Move!" he called out. "Take the ship!"

They sprinted toward the pier again. A number of mercs were still assembled there, armed with rifles, and they began to fire as they moved toward the gangplank.

Only ten yards separated the Cygnarans from the pier now, but a huge burst of smoke belched from the ship's main stack as its steam engine powered up. It wouldn't take long for it to reach full steam and move up the river, taking Harrow and Aleshko away.

Bullets bounced off Stryker's power field or thudded against his armor as he ran. One lucky shot scored his cheek, but he kept moving. On the deck of the ship, Tews' glaive flashed, and Harrow checked the blow, riposted, and struck sparks off Tews' left pauldron.

They had reached the pier, and the mercs had boarded the ship, leaving the docks empty. Stryker sprinted toward the gangplank, but before he could reach it, the ship began to move. They didn't bother to pull up the gangplank as the ship drifted away from the dock. The gangplank fell into the water with a splash, leaving Stryker stranded on the pier.

Tews was fighting for his life, his glaive a living thing that slashed and hewed. He was holding Harrow at bay, using the reach of his glaive to keep Harrow's shorter weapon from making an effective attack.

"Fire at will," Stryker called out to the Storm Knights who had not joined him on the pier.

Bolts of electricity arced up from the pier, but the angle was wrong. They were too low and the ship too high. Most of the Storm Knights' blasts simply charred the vessel's hull.

Panic crept into Stryker's mind as he fired at the retreating ship. Tews was alone, and he couldn't reach him. All he could do was watch as Tews backed up to the forecastle deck. Harrow was letting him retreat, and his men were massing behind him.

It was clear what was going to happen, but Stryker could do nothing to stop it. Over a dozen rifles were trained on Tews, and Harrow stepped behind the gun line and raised his sword.

Stryker didn't hear Harrow say the word as his sword fell, but it seemed to be all around them, amid the burning ships slowly sinking into the Black River.

Fire.

The rifles discharged a single fusillade, and Tews stumbled backward. His armor would turn some of those bullets, but not all of them.

Around him, the Storm Knights kept firing, and he heard a terrible, wrenching cry. He turned to see Maddox firing Tempest at the fleeing ship. di Brascio and even Magnus were still firing, but it was futile.

Tews sank to his knees, holding himself up with his glaive. The riflemen parted and Harrow walked between them, across the deck to stand in front of the Stormblade captain. He sheathed his saber slowly, casually, like a man who knows he has an audience. He pulled his pistol, the heavy repeater he never seemed to be without. Tews tried to stand as Harrow aimed the pistol at his head.

"Garvin!" Maddox cried out and ran toward edge of the pier.

Stryker heard the sharp crack of the pistol, saw Tews head snap back, and then the big Stormblade, a warrior with few equals and a man more loyal than any he'd ever known, toppled forward onto the deck.

Stryker had faced death on the battlefield a thousand times; he'd fought and survived the necromechanikal horrors of the Nightmare Empire. He'd learned to live with all of it. But as Harrow's men tossed Tews' body overboard, Stryker knew this wound would never heal.

...

THEY PULLED TEWS' BODY FROM THE RIVER. It had been dumped unceremoniously in a relatively shallow area, and the weight of the Stormblade's armor had taken him straight to the bottom. It had been di Brascio who dove into the frigid water with the end of a rope in his hands. He tied it around Tews' body ten feet down, and one of the horses had pulled Stryker's friend from the dark waters.

They gathered around the body, and Stryker crouched down over Tews. He could hear Maddox softly weeping, and even Magnus wore a look of quiet remorse. Harrow had shot Tews above his right eye, and his breastplate was riddled with numerous bullet holes.

di Brascio squatted down next to Stryker, his eyes full of sympathy. He understood what it was to lose a friend in battle.

"I am sorry, my friend," he said. It was a simple statement, and di Brascio didn't adorn it with more pointless words or platitudes. Stryker was grateful, and the sincerity of the gun mage's words moved more than just him.

"Coleman . . . Stryker, I'm . . .," Magnus began, then seemed to fumble for words, as if simple compassion was an alien state to the man. "He was a good—"

"You don't to say anything, General," Stryker said. "Nothing at all." His gift itched in the back of his brain, wanting to be unleashed, to strike out at the man responsible for so much pain in his life. But it would be a meaningless gesture of spite. Magnus sensed it; he fell silent.

Tews stared up at the night sky, at the stars, and Stryker hoped death had taken him painlessly. Had he not just been here? At the side of another good soldier cut down pointlessly. Conners' death had affected him, but this was a spike through his heart.

He reached out and closed Tews' eyes, wanting nothing so much as to close his own, to shut out the pain of his world turning upside down. He looked up; the rest of the Storm Knights were standing a respectful distance away. They had all removed their helmets, and their faces were masks of grief. Some of them were openly weeping.

"Brothers," Stryker said. "Take him to the horses."

The Storm Knights moved forward and gently lifted Tews from the ground and carried him away. di Brascio went with them.

"You did this," Maddox said suddenly, wheeling on Magnus. "He was your . . . creature. You brought him among us, and now a good man is dead." Her fists tightened around the hilt of Tempest, and Stryker wondered if she might try to cut Magnus down. He wondered if he would try to stop her.

Magnus didn't move. He faced down her wrath with a kind of stoic resignation. "You're right," he said at last. "I failed him. I own that."

"Maddox," Stryker said.

She turned to him, tears streaming down her face. They made her look even more terrible than the emotion that had twisted her features into a mask of grief. She had been close to Tews, and there had been more between them than simple friendship and camaraderie at some point in the past. She took a step back and wiped furiously at her eyes.

"I'm sorry, sir," she said. "I was out of line." The rage that been there a moment before disappeared, leaving the mask, the wall she had erected to protect herself from all the grief and horror she had suffered. One more bright sliver of pain to hide away in the dark.

Stryker looked at Magnus, but the warcaster refused to look him in the eye. So, he turned to Maddox. "No, Beth. Don't apologize. Let him live with it a while."

"I would," Maddox said, "but I don't think he'll even notice."

— 31 —

Eastern Riversmet, Occupied Llael

THEY RODE OUT IN SILENCE, Tews' body lashed to his horse. Stryker tried not to look, tried not to see his friend hung over the saddle like nothing more than cargo.

There was a temporary cemetery in Riversmet. They'd started it after taking the city, and it would soon grow. Tews would be put to rest there until his remains could be sent back to Caspia for a proper burial.

No one spoke as they rode back to Riversmet, and a pall of sorrow hung over their small party. Magnus hung back, riding at the rear. Maybe he did feel some responsibility for what had happened; Stryker couldn't say. He *hoped* the warcaster was suffering under such staggering guilt that kept him from looking any of them in the eye, but he knew Magnus better than that.

When they reached Riversmet, Stryker broke the silence. "Magnus, brief the senior officers on what happened today," he said as they reined up beyond the Great Gate. "I'll take Tews to the

. . ." His voice shook. The next words were difficult. "I'll take Tews to the morgue in the infirmary. Those who wish to accompany me may do so."

They entered the city, and Magnus veered off toward the main camp, while Stryker, Maddox, and the rest of the Storm Knights escorted the fallen to the infirmary.

. . .

WHEN STRYKER LEFT THE INFIRMARY, he did not go to his current quarters, a small well-kept home near the river that had been abandoned by its owner, though he ached to close his eyes for a while, perhaps after a few glasses or the entire bottle of Caspian brandy he kept there. Instead, he sought out Sergeant Major Halls' foundry. Again, the eastern side of Riversmet had provided them with unexpected resources, in this case a fully functional 'jack foundry. All the tools of the trade were there, and Halls had been quite content to set up shop in the building.

As he neared the foundry, a familiar presence stirred in the back of his mind. Rowdy greeted him with a mixture of enthusiasm and irritation—the warjack had been kept out of much of the fighting while he was being repaired, and the cantankerous old 'jack loved nothing more than a good scrap.

The foundry was a large brick building with a vast set of sliding doors that faced the river. Inside, the glow of furnaces could be seen, and the clatter of hammers and tools drifted out.

Harkevich had leveled some of the nearby buildings and had had the rubble removed. The reason for this was clear: it allowed him to move his colossals closer to the foundry for repair. Halls was using the space for the same reason, and the gargantuan form of a Stormwall loomed over the building, its hull pockmarked with bullet holes and dents. Gobbers were swarming over the huge warjack, tools in hand, making repairs in a frenzied green-skinned tide. One of the gobbers, standing at the foot of the huge machine, was shouting orders to the rest in the rapid-fire gobber tongue.

The Stormwall's cortex was markedly different from Rowdy's.

He'd commanded colossals many times, and their minds were direct and without nuance. This had much to do with the fact that Stormwalls and the even newer Hurricanes had not been in service for more than a few years and had not had the chance to develop the quirks and personalities many warjacks gained during service. It was like controlling a twenty-foot child, a child with the power to level buildings and kill men by the hundreds.

"You come to see Rowdy, sir?" asked the gobber mechanik at the right foot of the Stormwall. He had a crew chief's stripes on his apron. Gobbers in service to Cygnar wore their mechanik's aprons as uniforms.

"That's right, Chief . . .?"

"Sergeant Filk, sir," the gobber said then turned and shouted something indecipherable to a gobber riveting a hull plate on the Stormwall's left leg.

"He give you any trouble?" Stryker asked.

The gobber grinned, exposing a forest of needle-like teeth. "Plenty, sir," he said. "He's mean as a gatorman, and he don't like to listen to 'jack marshals, that's for sure."

Stryker chuckled. "He's a handful, no doubt."

"It was honor to work on him, sir," Filk said. "He's the most famous warjack in the Army."

Stryker liked that Filk referred to Rowdy as *him* and not as *it*. Stryker did the same; Rowdy had ceased to be an *it* for him a decade ago. "Thank you, Chief."

"Sir," the gobber said, and he turned back to the Stormwall, shouting again in gobberish.

Stryker made his way into the foundry and was instantly struck by memories from his childhood. His father had been a 'jack mechanik and had worked in a place much like this one. When his mother had grown ill, Stryker had often seen the foundry as a refuge, a warm, safe place where sorrow could be masked by the clatter of hammers and the uncomplicated presence of 'jack cortexes.

Rowdy was suspended in a 'jack hoist, a heavy rig that suspended a warjack off the ground so mechaniks could work on it. It also held unpredictable warjacks like Rowdy immobile. It was good to see the warjack whole again; Halls had replaced his damaged limbs and welded plate steel over the tears in his hull. The Sergeant Major hadn't bothered to repaint Rowdy, but Stryker preferred his warjack like his soldiers—looking rough and combat ready.

"Lord General," Halls said, coming out from behind Rowdy. "Glad you're here. Maybe you can get this cranky son-of-a-bitch to hold still while I adjust his cortex relays."

"Of course, Sergeant Major." He reached out to Rowdy, and the warjack's irritation bloomed in the back of his mind. No soldier liked to convalesce when there was fighting to do; Rowdy was no different. *Be still*, Stryker thought at the big 'jack. *It's for your own good, you ornery hunk of steel.* Resignation flowed back through his connection with the warjack, and Rowdy's arms lowered to his sides. The warjack vented a low whistle of steam that sounded very much like a sigh.

"Go ahead," Stryker said to Halls.

The sergeant major disappeared behind Rowdy.

Rowdy's memories flowed into Stryker's mind, and he tried to focus on the battle with Black Ivan. It was like viewing the world through the lens of a dream, distorted and jumbled, mostly the raw emotions of the warjack rather than actual images. It had been as Stryker thought—without his quake hammer, Rowdy had been at a disadvantage, even with Stryker actively guiding him in places.

The memories of the battle faded, and then something unexpected came through the link. It was an image, crystal clear, of Captain Tews, charging up the bridge, storm glaive flashing as he slashed into a pair of Man-O-War. He looked defiant and strong and indestructible. It wasn't his own memory he was seeing; it was Rowdy's. More astounding yet, the warjack had reached into *his* mind to retrieve it.

Stryker's breath caught in his throat, and he watched, stunned, as the image of Tews changed from the battlefield vision that was clearly Rowdy's memory to the cold, lifeless body on the docks that was Stryker's own memory. Something else came through the link, something he had previously thought the warjack incapable of: a sense of questioning, as if Rowdy were trying to understand the two memories in relation to one another.

Raw emotion clawed its way through Stryker's guts, and tears sprang to his eyes. He'd managed to put Tews' death out of his mind, or at least isolate it, so he could go about his duties. But Rowdy's childlike query had brought all that emotion to the fore, and Stryker pushed the warjack's cortex away from his mind, severing the link. Warjacks developed personalities, even rudimentary emotions, but he'd always thought understanding of abstract concepts like life and death were beyond them. He'd just learned this was untrue in the most painful way possible.

"Sir, are you all right?"

Sergeant Major Hall was staring at him, Hall's face a mixture of surprise and concern. He realized what he must look like from the mechanik's point of view. His lord general was standing, staring at nothing, with tears brimming in his eyes. "I'm fine. Just a bit tired."

"Of course, sir," Halls said. "Maybe a bit of rest is the best thing, then."

"You're right. I'll retire and leave you to your work." He left immediately, Rowdy's presence and the memory the warjack had unearthed fading mercifully into the night.

• • •

THEY BURIED TEWS THE NEXT MORNING, just as the sun was breaking over the horizon. The makeshift cemetery was near the river on a plot of land that might have been marked by Harkevich for construction at some point. It was a bare patch of earth, soft enough to dig, and the sound of the river nearby and the calls of waterfowl had a soothing quality. There were already too many laid to rest here.

The grave had been dug the night before, and Tews had been placed in a wooden coffin, the Cygnus hastily burned into the top. It wasn't a fitting caskets for a man like Tews, but it was what they had at the moment.

All the knights in Tews' company, over two-hundred soldiers, were present for the funeral. They surrounded the cemetery in a sea of steel and blue. Maddox was also present, as well as others who had known and fought beside the Stormblade captain. Stryker was not surprised to see Vayne di Brascio there. The Llaelese gun mage had become more than an ally, and Stryker wasn't alone in his favorable appraisal of the man. Many of the knights offered a quiet word of greeting to the gun mage, who, under normal circumstances, might be considered an outsider.

Battle Chaplain Dominic Hargrave stood at the head of both grave as the coffin was lowered into it. The Morrowan knight wore the archaic white armor of his order, the sun burst of Morrow on the breastplate in gold. He held an immense metal-bound book in his right hand, the *Prayers of Battle*, the sacred tenets of war handed down by Morrow and his blessed ascendants. Hargrave had long served as the company's chaplain and had fought beside Tews and his knights for years. There was no better man to send Tews on his way to Urcaen, the realm of the dead where the gods of men held their domains.

Stryker and Maddox stood at the foot of the grave, and Stryker could see the top of the coffin. Magnus was absent, and though Stryker hadn't ordered him to stay away, news of who had killed Tews had spread through the camp. Likely, most of the knights present wouldn't blame Magnus for Tews' death, but Stryker was relieved the warcaster hadn't created an opportunity for an ugly scene. More than that, to him, Magnus *was* to blame, and his presence would be an insult to the man who'd died for his mistakes.

"Brothers and sisters," Chaplain Hargrave said, his low, clear voice carrying over the assembly like a comforting blanket. There had been little talk among the men, but what there was ceased and all eyes turned to the chaplain. "Today, on this most somber of occasions, we lay to rest one of Morrow's most ardent soldiers, a man who fought and died bravely to uphold the beliefs we all hold dear."

The chaplain paused and smiled, his gaze sweeping over the silent men and women before him. "But we must not grieve, brothers and sisters. No, we must rejoice, for while our friend and brother-in-arms has been taken from our lives, he lives on in Urcaen. He is the truly blessed, as he will enter into the presence of our lord, who shall welcome a great warrior into a battle far greater than any in this earthly realm. Captain Garvin Tews shall stand forth with Morrow, in his domain, his sword joining those of their righteous brothers and sisters in the eternal struggle."

Hargrave paused again, letting his words sink in. Stryker was not overly religious, but he was aware of the war in Urcaen for the souls of man to which the battle chaplain was referring, the struggle against the tyrannical Menoth and the twisted darkness of the Devourer Wurm. In truth, it all seemed like a fanciful tale to him, and one that offered little comfort. But he could see on the faces of the men and women around him that Hargrave's words did offer succor to some, and he heard whispered prayers throughout the assembled knights.

Hargrave opened the *Prayers of Battle*, and read. "As Ascendant Katrena sacrificed herself to protect the first primarch, we honor the valor and nobility of our fallen brother."

"We honor him," came the reply from the assembled knights. Stryker echoed their response. He'd been to far too many funerals like this.

"As Ascendant Markus held off a barbarian horde with nothing more than his faith and his sword, we honor the devotion and loyalty of our fallen brother."

"We honor him," came the response.

"And as Ascendant Solovin, who offers healing and comfort to all, we grant to our fallen brother his due rest until his sword is needed once more."

"Rest now, brother." The final response heralded a long silence as all bowed their heads and offered prayers to Morrow for safe passage to Urcaen for Tews. Stryker couldn't bring himself to pray; his friend's death was too senseless, too fresh for him to simply assign him to Morrow's will.

"Lord General," Hargrave said as he closed the *Prayers of Battle*, "do you have anything to add?"

All eyes were upon him now, and the expectation of more comforting words weighed heavily on him. He glanced at Maddox. Her face was streaked with tears, but her eyes were steady, hard. She expected something of him as well.

"My brothers and sisters," Stryker began, using the more archaic form of address as was appropriate for the occasion. "I have fought beside Captain Tews for many years, and he was among the bravest and most steadfast men I had the pleasure to command. His loss is a stone around my heart, and I know there is but one remedy for my sorrow and for yours as well."

The words began to take shape in his mind, and although there was a lie behind them, they kindled something within him, a fire that had been long missing.

"Brothers and sisters, we must take our pain, our sorrow, our grief and forge it in the heat of righteous anger. Let it become the blade with which we strike at the enemy, the oppressor, the tyrant. Our brother died for a cause, one that we all hold sacred—to protect the innocent and to fight darkness wherever it is found."

Nods and whispers of agreement moved through the soldiers, and their emotions became a wave of heat that drove him on.

"Now, draw your weapons and hold them aloft."

The clatter of steel on steel thundered over the silent cemetery as two hundred storm glaives were drawn and lifted high. Stryker raised Quicksilver over his head.

"Now light up the sky and remind this world that though one light dims, a thousand others still burn!" He thumbed the trigger on Quicksilver's hilt and a bolt of brilliant electricity blasted from the weapon's tip. It was joined by two hundred more, and the steel grey sky arced with Cygnaran fury.

And now Stryker did offer a prayer to Morrow. *See our light, and give me the strength to keep it burning.*

— 32 —

Western Riversmet, Occupied Llael

GENERAL ASHETH MAGNUS STARED at a hole in the western wall large enough to ride an army through, which is exactly what he'd been looking for. He stood on a pile of rubble twenty yards from the hole, imagining Khadoran heavy horse streaming through the breach. The area was too rubble-strewn to make an easy entrance for horsemen. He'd need to remedy that.

He'd avoided the funeral of Captain Tews, not out of any sense of guilt or responsibility about the man's death but because he needed an opportunity to scout out certain sections of the city without Stryker asking him a lot of questions.

"Captain Silus," he called out to a broad-shouldered man with a shaved head nearby. The man was brutish, but he'd served Magnus for many years, and he'd been a Steelhead captain at one point in his long mercenary career. Magnus had promoted him to captain in the Cygnaran Army to replace Harrow. "I want the rubble cleared in this area as soon as possible. Within the day, if it can be done. Requisition as many men and warjacks as you need."

Silus looked around, confused. "Sir, I don't mean to second guess you, but why? There's nothing here but a bunch of wrecked houses. Nothing important. Plus, don't we want to make it harder for the Khadorans to get in?"

Magnus smiled. "I understand your confusion, but I need you to follow my orders. Without question."

Silus glanced behind him, where a dozen more of Magnus' men were carefully moving crates, each marked with a spiked circle. Understanding dawned in the man's eyes. "Good Morrow," he said under his breath.

"Do you see a problem?" Magnus wasn't keen on being questioned by any of his men. After Harrow's treachery, he was more than a little sensitive about any malcontents among those that had served him in exile. He had never trusted Harrow, but he'd believed he had the man measured and that he'd understood what drove him. He'd been wrong, and it had cost them all. Tews' death was unfortunate. Despite the man's annoying bluster, he was a skilled battle leader. They would feel his loss. But it was losing Lord Aleshko's ships and Lord Aleshko himself that filled Magnus with rage very time he thought about it. The tactical advantage they'd lost and likely handed to the enemy was a significant blow. Harrow and Aleshko would go directly to Rynyr, and Harrow would offer up the intelligence he had on the Cygnaran invasion force to their enemies. Aleshko was his ticket, and the kayazy had likely offered Harrow a deal of some kind for his freedom, a deal that was better than what Magnus was offering.

"Sir, I've seen that stuff used on the field," Silus said. "My chapter deployed it during a contract for Ord against a trollkin kriel in the Olgunholt. I have no problems killing a man or a trollkin, for that matter, for duty or for gold, but no one deserves to die like that."

Gods, this one would be right at home with Stryker, Magnus thought. It was irritating, but it said something about Silus. It said he had a conscience, a limit to what he'd do for coin or country. It was something Magnus could use. The problem with men like

Harrow was they had no limits, no boundaries, and predicting what they might do could be difficult. Not with men like Silus; their edges firmly established, you just needed to push a little.

Magus approached the newly minted captain and put a hand on his shoulder—his flesh-and-blood hand. The former merc flinched but did not draw away.

"I understand you reticence, Captain," Magnus said. "I've seen it too, and devil's gasp is terrible, no doubt. But you understand what's at stake here, yes?"

"Of course, sir," Silus said. "I've served you a long time, and you know I couldn't give two shits about Llaelese freedom. But I'd like to live a little longer. You've been good to me, kept my purse full, and I go where you go, but I won't lie to you: this doesn't sit right with me."

"You're a good soldier, Silus," Magnus said, noting the subtle look of pleasure that crossed the man's face. Most mercs, even the bad ones, liked to think of themselves as soldiers first, especially ones like Silus who'd served in organized mercenary outfits like the Steelheads. "I appreciate you being honest with me. I tell you this. I have faith the lord general will lead us to victory, and we'll crush the Khadorans outside these walls."

"Apologies, sir, but I thought you hated Lord General Stryker," Silus said, exposing his mercenary roots. No honest soldier would say something like that to his commanding officer.

"I don't *hate* the lord general," Magnus said. "He and I have a history, and we don't see eye-to-eye on things, but Stryker's a good fighter and a good leader." He had pulled Silus close, making their conversation intimate, even conspiratorial.

"So why do we need the devil's gasp," Silus asked, "if you and the lord general will lead us to victory?"

"Because I don't like to hang all my hopes on one strategy, no matter how competent those implementing the strategy may be. The devil's gasp is our last resort, our all-is-lost measure. Certainly you can see some wisdom in that?"

Silus rubbed his stubbled chin. "I guess I can," he said. "I'm sorry for questioning you, sir. If it's a last resort, if it's all that's standing between us living or dying, then maybe it's an advantage we ought not to ignore."

"My thoughts exactly, Captain," Magnus said. "Now, let's get this rubble cleared so we can plant these explosives."

Silus frowned. "Without that crazy Ordsman, who's gonna prime the damn things?"

"I'm an attentive student," Magnus said. "I had Xavius show me how to prepare the devil's gasp before his . . . accident."

Silus shuddered. "That was bad, sir," he said, and then looked up at Magnus, his eyes questioning. "That was mercy you gave him, wasn't it?"

"You've seen devil's gasp at work," Magnus said evenly. He had to be cautious here—it *had* been mercy when he'd shot the alchemist, but he'd killed one of his own men with his own hand, and such things had to be handled delicately.

"Right," Silus said. "I'd take the bullet, too."

"One more thing," Magnus said. "Make sure there are no civilians in this area."

Silus brightened at that. It sat well within the moral boundaries the man had established for himself. "Of course, sir. We'll do a thorough sweep."

"Good, and choose your men wisely. Men who can keep their mouths shut. This is supposed to be a trap, a surprise, so we can't have too many knowing about it, even within our own ranks. We'll do this in two stages. First we'll detonate half the devil's gasp behind Vlad or Harkevich or whoever comes when they enter far enough into the city. That will cut them off as well as inflict demoralizing casualties. Then we'll detonate the rest right on top of them. You'll need two men with the detonators, you and one other. Pick a man you can trust."

"Yes, sir," Silus said, then turned to get about the duties Magnus had assigned him. Magnus watched him go. Such men were useful, and it was clear he needed more like Silus. Harrow and his ilk had been a mistake. One Magnus would not repeat.

— 33 —

Western Riversmet, Occupied Llael

STRYKER STOOD ON ONE OF THE FEW intact battlements remaining on the western side of Riversmet. It looked out over the great plain that stretched for miles in all directions. A single road ran through the emptiness, disappearing over the horizon toward Rynyr and Laedry.

"How far?" he asked the man next to him. It was Sergeant Sharp. Horgrum, Sharp's trollkin companion, loomed nearby.

"We spotted them about ten miles from here," Sharp said. "We hadn't been patrolling much father out than that."

"Numbers?" Magnus asked. He, too, had joined Stryker on the battlements after reports of an approaching Khadoran army had reached Stryker. Their advance scouts, led by Sharp, had been looking for signs of the inevitable for two weeks.

Sharp's face blanched.

"That bad, huh?' Stryker said with a grim smile.

"Sir, we counted three full battalions of infantry and more

heavy horse than I thought there were in all the goddamn world. Ten thousand would be my guess."

"Did you see warcasters? Warjacks?" Stryker asked.

"We did, sir," Sharp said. "They've got plenty of heavy warjacks and a pair of Conquests. Harkevich is with the army, but he isn't leading it."

The name that followed Harkevich's was no surprise to Stryker.

"It's Tzepesci," Magnus said.

Sharp said, "The great prince leads them, and it looks like he's brought most of his heavy horse from Umbrey."

"How long do we have?" Stryker asked.

"It's a big army," Sharp said. "They're moving slow, but they'll be here in two days."

"Thank you, Sergeant," Stryker said. "You are dismissed. Go get some food and rest. You're going to need it. I'll want a full briefing in an hour."

"Sir," Sharp said and left, taking the steps to the city below. Horgrum followed.

Stryker turned to Magnus. The warcaster was staring out over the battlements, his hands gripping the stone. Stryker expected him to gloat, to again take Stryker to task for letting Harkevich leave.

"We can't keep him out of the city," Magnus said.

"No," Stryker agreed. They'd managed to continue some of the work Harkevich had done on the western fortifications, but there were more gaps than standing walls. "We'll have to meet him in the field, beat him there."

He's got more heavy horse than we do," Magnus said, "and likely both battalions from Rynyr as well, not to mention more warjacks and colossals. I don't like our chances in a straight-up fight."

"What do you suggest then?" Stryker asked, wondering where Magnus was going with this. His eyes glittered in the way they did when he was scheming, and that worried Stryker. He wanted to heed Maddox's advice and listen to Magnus, to use his martial expertise, but the events of the last few days made it difficult for

Stryker to be anything other than suspicious. Magnus had taken action to alleviate some of that suspicion; he'd ruthlessly gone through his own men, questioning them and looking for anyone's involvement with Harrow. Now there were currently fifty former mercs locked up in the rebuilt brig in the center of town. Magnus had assured him everyone else was trustworthy, but Stryker wondered if that was because they were loyal men or if they just feared Magnus.

"I don't know," Magnus said, and Stryker saw the lie in his eyes. He was hiding something. "We need more information before we can decide on a course of action."

"Then assemble the senior officers in the town hall," Stryker said. "I'll join you there shortly."

"As you wish, sir," Magnus said and left him there on the battlements.

Stryker put his hands on the crenellations—the late-summer heat had warmed them—and leaned forward. It was mid-afternoon, and the sky was clear. He could see a plume of dust far away on the horizon. It was small now, but it would grow and grow until it became large enough to swallow them all.

PART III

— 34 —

A SEA OF CRIMSON LAY BEFORE the battlements of eastern Riversmet: thousands of men and machines armored in the unyielding steel of the Motherland.

Stryker had seen armies this size before, but there was something about this one that sent a chill down his spine. Perhaps it was the presence of Great Prince Vlad Tzepesci, a devastating warrior with whom Stryker had crossed blades once before. If he was being honest with himself, it wasn't Vlad; it was actually Harkevich, the warcaster he'd let leave the city, who troubled him. He couldn't see Harkevich, but with the two Conquests that loomed over the great Khadoran army was where the warcaster would likely be.

Had Magnus been right? Should he have risked the lives of innocent Riversmet citizens to avoid this overwhelming force he faced now? He clenched his fists. No, he wouldn't go down that road. He'd done the right thing, and if they emerged victorious, he could put his head on the pillow at night without guilt or remorse about the war he'd waged here.

"I count at least ten full companies of Iron Fang uhlans," Magnus said, naming the military order to which most of Vlad's horsemen belonged. "No drakhun." Magnus' tone suggested he thought this was odd.

"I have no truck with that," Stryker said. He was grateful his enemy had not brought the heaviest and arguably the most devastating cavalry in the Iron Kingdoms. The drakhun were Man-O-War mounted on massive warhorses, the strongest in the Iron Kingdoms, encased in heavy armor like their riders.

"Still, it is odd the greatest cavalry commander in the Khadoran Army would leave one of his most potent weapons behind," Magnus said.

"I agree," Stryker said. "Perhaps he could not muster enough of them for this attack."

"What do you think they're waiting for?" Maddox broke in. She was standing next to Stryker, staring over the battlements alongside most of his senior staff. He wanted them all to get a good look at what they'd be fighting. There could be no illusions about what was at stake.

"Vlad will send an envoy," Magnus said. "He's here to protect what he believes is his."

Stryker agreed. "We beat him to the punch with this invasion, set him and his new bride back on their heels. He won't have taken kindly to that. It makes him look weak and slow."

"I can't imagine he's going to offer us terms," Maddox said.

"None we could keep," Magnus said. "He'll come with some of his top men so they can hear him threaten us while he shows us his strength."

As if Magnus were speaking prophecy, a small group of horsemen broke away from the main body of the army and rode toward the western gate of Riversmet. The riders were carrying a billowing white banner, indicating they wanted to parley.

They were far away, but Stryker could see that one rider in particular moved ahead of the rest. His crimson armor was bulky and magnificent. Unlike most warcasters who wore modern steam-powered armor, Vlad wore the ancient plate and mail of his ancestors. The armor was rumored to be enchanted in some fashion and protected the great prince as well as the most modern galvanic prototype.

"You'd think he'd be worried we'd take him hostage," Maddox said with a grim laugh.

Magnus shot her a crooked smile. "No, the great prince knows his enemy well."

• • •

THEY MET VLAD AT THE GATE, one of the few intact and fully fortified structures left in the western half of the city. Stryker had assembled a greeting for the great prince, an entire company of Storm Knights lining the wide road leading from the gate into the city. He'd also had a small pavilion set up in the middle of the street a stone's throw from the gate. He wouldn't let the Khadoran warcaster go farther into the city than that—Vlad already knew too much about their defenses. Stryker had also moved the vast majority of his troops into the western half of the city, along with nearly all his warjacks. He sent Maddox to command in his stead, primed to get their army moving immediately if the Khadorans tried anything during their parley.

"Open the gate," Stryker said to a pair of Storm Knights next to the great winch that operated the massive aperture. It rose slowly, creaking and grinding. Beyond were ten horsemen, and as soon as the gate was high enough, they rode forward, their horses' hooves clattering on the cobblestones.

Vlad rode in the lead. He was a large man, made even larger by his baroque armor; its oversized pauldrons made the warcaster appear both wider and taller. Vlad's lineage was steeped in strange occult practices, and his armor was enchanted to function much like the warcaster armor Stryker was familiar with, protecting its wearer from all but the most determined attacks. The great prince wore no helmet, revealing his aquiline features and black hair, which streamed behind him as he rode.

After Vlad rode Harkevich, and Stryker grimaced at the sight of the big Khadoran. He sat his mount oddly, and Stryker was struck by the image of a great black bear atop a horse. Behind Harkevich came eight Iron Fang uhlans, members of one of Khador's most skilled cavalry orders. Each of these men wore heavy plate armor and carried lances tipped with blasting charges—dangerous weapons that required incredibly brave men to wield.

Vlad reined up in front of Magnus and Stryker. He smiled down at them, his face that of the beneficent autocrat, which he was purported to be—as well as an honorable if ruthless warrior.

"Lord General Stryker," he said, his Cygnaran flowing, his own accent making the language sound more regal somehow. "It is a pleasure to see you again."

"I cannot say the same, Lord Tzepesci," Stryker said. He wasn't going to be anything but honest with this man. This meeting was for show, and he wanted to get it over with.

"And *General* Magnus is it now?" Vlad said. He still hadn't dismounted.

"That's what they tell me," Magnus said.

"I said we would meet again," Harkevich said and climbed down from his horse. Stryker noted he dismounted first, but whether this was a sign of respect to Vlad or to him, he wasn't certain.

"You did," Stryker replied. "Perhaps our second meeting can be beneficial to us all." It was little more than words, but diplomacy demanded some adherence to protocol. "Lord Tzepesci, if you will dismount, we can meet in comfort and privacy." He indicated the pavilion behind him.

"Ah, of course," Vlad said. "We Umbreans are born and bred in the saddle. I sometimes forget I'm mounted." He slid from his saddle with expert grace, and Stryker noted he was armed with an ornate longsword. He'd seen that blade up close, and it bore powerful enchantments.

"This way," Stryker said.

Vlad turned and said something in Khadoran to his horsemen.

One of them laughed. Then in Cygnaran, he said, "Kommander Harkevich, join me please."

The four of them made their way into the pavilion, Magnus and Stryker leading the way. Inside the spacious tent were four stout chairs, the kind that could support the weight and bulk of a man in armor. They were arranged around a low wooden table where a decanter of Cygnaran brandy and four glasses had been placed.

Magnus and Harkevich adjusted the boilers on their warcaster armor to reduce the smoke to a trickle. Vlad and Harkevich sat while Magnus and Stryker took the seats opposite them.

"I'm not going to bandy words here, Lord Tzepesci," Stryker said. "You are trespassing on the sovereign soil of the nation of Llael, a Cygnaran ally."

Vlad laughed softly. "Perhaps my memory is flawed, but I remember your presence during the signing of a treaty that ceded this land and this city to the Khadoran Empire. Am I wrong?"

"Perhaps you recall the portion of the treaty that stated you would forfeit those claims if a legitimate heir to the throne of Llael was found," Magnus replied. "That has happened."

Harkevich snorted derisively. "This girl is nothing more than a ploy devised by your king and his council"—he threw a dark look at Magnus—"to take all of Llael for themselves."

It was a perceptive observation and half-true. The princess *was* a legitimate heir, but her marriage to Julius was clearly a ploy to expand Cygnaran territory.

"We provided you with all the necessary documentation verifying her lineage and the legitimacy of her claim," Stryker said.

Vlad waved a hand dismissively. "Such documents are easily forged, especially by one as skilled as your Scout General Rebald. To my mind, *you* are in violation of the treaty by bringing an invading army into lands rightly owned by Khador, attacking one of her cities, and killing her brave soldiers."

Magnus filled two glasses with brandy. "Morrow, I don't know about you, Lord Tzepesci, but I need a drink to wash away that load of horse shit."

Stryker had to repress a smile. True, he generally loathed Magnus, but the man had put words to his own thoughts exactly.

Vlad was unfazed by Magnus' comment, and he took up the proffered glass of brandy, sniffed it, and took a regal sip. "I'm more partial to the uiske of my country," he said. "But this is quite good."

"You can take a case of it with you when you leave here . . . with your army," Stryker said. "My gift."

"That is most generous, Lord General, but my army is not going anywhere. You know that," Vlad answered. "That said, you can save many lives, both Cygnaran and Khadoran, if you quit Riversmet and march your army back to Cygnar. Do that, and the empress will consider the treaty we signed still in effect, to the benefit of all."

"Except to the benefit of the people of Llael, of course, who will be denied their rightful monarch."

"Bah, this is foolish, Lord Tzepesci," Harkevich said. "I tire of throwing words across this table when we both know it will be bullets and blood that must pass between us."

"Quite right, Kommander," Magnus said and raised his glass to the warcaster.

"Very well." Vlad leaned forward. His dark eyes focused on Stryker. "You will leave Riversmet or you will be destroyed. I have enough heavy horse and warjacks to crush you in the field, but if you prefer a siege, I have enough artillery to bring this city down around you."

Stryker noted Harkevich's deep frown. He suspected the kommander was a good man, and he was well aware of what a siege meant—thousands of innocent dead. He said nothing, however.

"Do you think it will be that easy?" Stryker asked.

The great prince shook his head. "I would not insult you so. You are a worthy enemy, and the blood of many a loyal son of the Motherland will mingle with that of his Cygnaran foes. Make no mistake, though, you cannot win here, and I will burn Riversmet to the ground, if I must."

Stryker looked over at Magnus. "Anything to add, General?" he said.

"No, I think it's time we get to it. Talking is thirsty work; I much prefer swinging a sword."

Vlad stood. "No doubt you will have many opportunities to do so in the coming days."

Harkevich stood as well, and the big warcaster still looked uncomfortable, as if he had more to say. Stryker wondered if the kommander had actually hoped for a peaceful resolution.

"Despite what you have said here, I will give you one day to consider my terms," Vlad said. He was playing the noble autocrat again, showing mercy from a position of strength. No doubt his magnanimity was more for Harkevich's benefit than that of Stryker or Magnus. "Send an envoy at dawn if you agree; otherwise, I will see you on the field."

"We'll show you out, Lord Tzepesci," Stryker said. They walked the two Khadorans back to their horses, where the enemy commanders mounted immediately.

"One day," Vlad called over his shoulder as he rode through the gate. It clattered down behind him, obscuring Stryker's view of the mammoth army outside the city.

"Assemble the senior officers," Stryker muttered to Magnus. "We're meeting in the town hall in thirty minutes."

— 35 —

Eastern Riversmet

"I WANT THREE PLATOONS from the 32nd here," Stryker said, pointing to one of the larger breaches in the eastern wall on the map. "Captain Adkins."

Stryker turned to a middle-aged Storm Knight, one who had received a field promotion after Tews' death. "I want you there as well. I'll give you a pair of Fireflies to hold off anything that comes through that hole."

"Sir," Adkins said. He was standing at the other end of the huge round table that held the detailed map of Riversmet, recently updated with the state of the eastern walls.

"Magnus, I want you here with most of the 82nd rifle company outside the western gate." Stryker indicated areas marked with deep lines that showed where trenches had been dug. Each was six feet wide and seven feet deep and manned by the soldiers who took their name from them, trenchers armed with rifles and grenades. The trenches would serve as further protection for the strongest portion of the eastern wall. "We'll need a warcaster there to support the trenchers. They've got a complement of Grenadiers and Sentinels, but take two of the Stormclads. You'll provide fire support to the cavalry, and if Vlad gets past me, it'll be up to you to stop him."

"I concur," Magnus said, surprising Stryker. He'd expected Magnus would chafe at defending the city rather than riding out to meet Vlad with Stryker.

"Maddox, you're with me, along with every Storm Lance we've got," Stryker said. "The rest of the 32nd will go with us, and we're going to hammer down the middle of Vlad's line. He'll ride out to meet us, and we're going to give him something to remember."

"That's exactly where I want to be, sir," she said.

"What about artillery, Lord General?" Said Major Trenton Hughs, a grizzled trencher who had spent the better part of twenty years as an artillery commander.

"The western gate is the most fortified," Stryker said. "I want our heavy guns and mortars there. Focus your fire on Vlad's flanks to keep the bulk of his infantry off us while we hit him on the field."

"You leaving me the Stormwall?" Hughs asked.

"No, I'll need it on the field," Stryker said. "They've got a pair of Conquests, and while Harkevich will probably hold one back to pound the walls, Vlad will probably have the other with him. I can give you some Defenders and as many riflemen as we can spare on the battlements to keep infantry at bay."

"It'll do, sir," Hughs said.

"Chaplain Hargrave," Stryker said to the Morrowan knight who had overseen Tews' funeral. He was more than a spiritual leader; he also led three platoons of Precursor Knights, holy warriors armed with archaic weapons and armor yet deadly effective due to their faith and the Morrowan blessings on their weapons and armor. "I'll need your Precursors with me. The enemy has Iron Fangs and Man-O-War aplenty, and you and the Stormblade infantry can blunt their advance while we drive horseflesh and Storm Lances down Vlad's throat."

"Of course, Lord General," Hargrave said. "You will have Morrow's strength at your side."

Stryker looked over at the one member of the assembly who was not part of the Cygnaran Army. Vayne di Brascio stood quietly at table, studying the great map of Riversmet. "Again, Captain di Brascio," Stryker said, "I cannot give you an order, but I'd be glad for any help wherever you'd like to give it."

The Llaelese gun mage nodded and ran his hand down his goatee. "Well, I'm not much of a horseman, so I won't be joining you on your little jaunt." He smiled. "I might be useful on the western wall, however. Perhaps giving Commander Hughs and his boys a little cover fire if Vlad gets up close and personal."

"We'd be bloody grateful to have you," Hughs said. di Brascio had become a popular figure among the men and women of the Cygnaran invasion force. He was a soldier's soldier: loyal, dependable, and very skilled. Those traits were always admired by fighting men, no matter which uniform they wore.

"Then it's settled," Stryker said. "I'd only ask that you follow Commander Hughs' directions. He knows his business."

"I am at your disposal, Commander," di Brascio said to Hughs.

Magnus said, "I have a suggestion."

Suspicion stirred within Stryker. "What is it, General?"

"Our preparations and strategies as you've outlined them are impressive, and you may well carry the day on the field."

You don't fool me, Stryker thought. *You're paying me lip service so you can suggest something more to your liking.* "The point?"

"Vlad's army is primarily heavy horse. But he's light on infantry. If we ride out and meet him, he'll have the advantage."

Stryker could easily see the wisdom in this. Magnus was putting into words some of his own doubts and fears. "What do you suggest, then?"

"Lure him into the city, draw him into the ruins, where his horseman are at a disadvantage and our trenchers and heavy infantry are right at home."

All eyes were on Magnus, and Stryker could see in the faces of some of his officers that they agreed with the warcaster. But a fight within the city walls would be a disaster for the citizens of Riversmet, worse than an artillery bombardment. It was the same discussion they'd had about Harkevich, and his opinion had not changed on the matter. "While I agree with your assessment to some degree, a drawn-out guerilla war within Riversmet itself is *not* within our charter of protecting the citizens of Llael."

Magnus was silent. No one spoke for long moments. Magnus had already convinced some of the officers that his plan was the right one, so Stryker needed to countermand that. He couldn't have his senior officers divided on such an important matter.

"Yes, he has more heavy horse, but they are largely Iron Fang uhlans, skilled horsemen, but they are not the equal of our Storm Lances." The uhlans' blasting lances were better suited for cracking heavy armor, and they lacked the ranged attack of the Cygnaran heavy cavalry.

There were nods and mutters of agreement from many of the knights in the room as Stryker continued. "If we can keep the infantry occupied, our Storm Lances, with the help of the Stormblades and the Precursor Knights, will overcome Vlad's horsemen, despite his numbers."

Magnus held his hands up in a placating gesture. "I concede our heavy horse is better equipped and trained, but it is a risk to meet Vlad in the open. It's what he wants."

"I have made my decision," Stryker said.

"And I will not argue with you. But let me propose a fallback point, in case things do not go as planned on the field."

They faced a mighty foe, and as much as Stryker hated to admit it, retreat was a very real possibility. "We would fall back through the western gate. It is the most heavily fortified."

"A sound strategy," Magnus agreed, "but I think here would be a better position." He pointed to the huge breach in the western curtain wall, easily the largest. It was in a section of the city that was entirely ruined and of little strategic value.

"Why there?" Stryker demanded.

"It's large enough that a good portion of Vlad's horsemen could be drawn through it," Magnus said. "And if we position trenchers

and Storm Guard there, we can bloody his nose if he follows you."
The Storm Guard were counterparts to the Stormblade infantry,
armed with voltaic halberds instead of glaives. They were highly
effective at holding fortified areas.

Maddox agreed. "It makes sense." She put her finger on the
map where Magnus had indicated. "This was a residential district,
and once past the breach, there are still many small buildings intact
that would provide cover for our infantry and pose a difficulty for
cavalry to negotiate. If we fall back there, we could pass through
our own troops and rally while Vlad would be stopped cold."

"Until he pulled his warjacks up and started leveling those
buildings," Hughs said with a frown.

"I don't disagree," Magnus said to the artillery commander.
"But that would take time, and we could hurt him *and* allow our
Storm Knights to pull back safely."

Stryker nodded. It *was* a good plan, but he could not disregard
a certain wariness when it came to trusting Magnus' counsel,
though he could see no good reason to refuse it. "Very well,
General. Divert two companies of trenchers to this area and three
platoons of Storm Guard."

"At once, sir," Magnus said, and for the first time the "sir"
sounded sincere to Stryker's ears. *Good.* Maybe it was one less
thing to worry about.

"All right, you know what to do," Stryker said to the room of
officers. "Let's get to it."

— 36 —

Western Riversmet, Occupied Llael

THE KHADORANS LAUNCHED the first volley of artillery at dawn, fired from the massive cannons of the two Conquests. Stryker and two hundred Storm Lances were behind the eastern gate, mounted and ready. Through the portcullis, Stryker watched the shells descend, smashing into the trenches before the wall, sending dirt and broken bodies into the air.

It had begun.

He reached out and touched the cortex of the Stormwall standing behind his assembled knights. The huge warjack responded with a surge of primitive anger and vented a shrill blast of steam, a battle cry if he'd ever heard one. The Stormwall's heavy cannons usually didn't have the range of the Conquests' guns, but it had other capabilities. A hidden firing port near the top of the Stormwall's hull concealed special galvanic pods, and it was these Stryker ordered the colossal to launch. With an explosive blast, three lightning pods sailed over the walls and landed in front of the trenches to the left and right of the eastern gate. They hit the ground, their tips digging deep into the earth, and opened like strange metallic flowers. Lightning flashed as the pods powered up, and arcs of deadly electricity raced between them, creating a lethal galvanic fence. Vlad's cavalry and infantry were already advancing, and the lightning pods would keep him from hitting the wall before Stryker was ready for him.

"Storm Knights," Stryker called out and raised Quicksilver aloft. He pulled hard on the reins, and his horse reared. It was well trained, but he missed Valorous. "With me!"

It was the signal they had been waiting for. The portcullis rose with a screeching rattle. Beyond were rows of trenches, each manned by the trenchers who made up the backbone of the Cygnaran military. There were warjacks in the trenches as well, Sentinels armed with chain guns and Grenadiers armed with heavy picks and grenade launchers. Most of these warjacks were controlled by a 'jack marshal, but he spied the bright blue light of a Stormclad's galvanic blade to the right of the wall. That's where Magnus was, ready to enter close combat using some of Cygnar's most potent warjacks.

The heavy thuds of Cygnaran artillery sounded, and shells began whistling over the walls toward the Khadoran Army. They fell short, but their psychological impact on the enemy could not be underestimated. Artillery was terrifying.

Stryker spurred his horse and galloped through the gate, the thunder of nearly a thousand metal-shod hooves followed him as the Storm Lances fanned out behind him, placing him at the head of a wedge.

There were four warjacks under his command, including the Stormwall. Rowdy's excitement flowed through their connection as the warjack came through the gate behind the Storm Lances, quake hammer in hand. Flanking the big Ironclad were a pair of Defenders and, looming behind them, the Stormwall. The warjacks would follow Stryker's charge and provide cover for Maddox as she advanced with her Stormblade infantry. She also controlled a group of 'jacks, lighter Chargers and Fireflies. They would hit the Khadorans as a second wave while the trenchers poured rifle fire and artillery into the enemy infantry.

The Khadoran horsemen were advancing, a tide of red armor and glinting steel pounding toward the Cygnarans. Vlad's warjacks were farther back; the heavy Khadoran machines were not known for their speed, but once they reached the melee, they'd be devastating.

Wind whipped through Stryker's hair as his horse picked up speed. He summoned his magic and cast a protective ward around himself and the horsemen closest to him. They were the point of the spear, and he needed to keep it intact. Flashes of blue light at the head of the approaching Khadoran cavalry told him Vlad was working magic of his own.

The world sped by, and the symphony of war began to fill the air: gunshots, screeching artillery, the clatter of armor, the screams of the dying, and the exultant shouts of the victorious. They were covering ground rapidly. They were now beyond the trenches and hundreds of yards from the walls of Riversmet. He could see Vlad astride his magnificent charger, his archaic armor glinting in the morning sun. The warcaster was armed with a notable flail and a great spear, and he, like Stryker, rode at the head of a deliberate spear, a wedge larger than the Cygnarans'. They were the points on which their armies would collide, two great arrows smashing into one another.

They were close enough now that Stryker could showcase his cavalry's technological superiority. He raised Quicksilver above his head, the signal for his Storm Lances to ready their electro lances. Around him, lances came down, couched and braced for impact. Then he brought Quicksilver down in a sharp stroke, a signal of another kind.

The front rank of Storm Lances rippled with blue galvanic power as they fired their electro lances, unleashing gouts of deadly electricity into the enemy. The first rank of Khadoran horsemen took the brunt of the attack. Men and horses tumbled backward, scorched and dying. Dozens were hit and killed. Their compatriots rode over them, trampling their corpses into the ground. Stryker had seen a few bolts strike Vlad, only to be deflected by the warcaster's enchanted armor.

There was no time for a second volley; the enemy loomed before them, a red wall of men and horses. Stryker let go of his reins. He was guiding his mount with his knees, but he hardly needed to. The warhorse was well trained, and it *wanted* to charge straight at the enemy.

Vlad flashed toward Stryker, his spear leveled, and the two armies came together with a deafening crash of metal on metal. Stryker lashed out with his heavy blade as he closed on Vlad, twisting his body away from the barbed tip of the warcaster's spear as it sought the center of his breastplate.

A hard thump against his armored side told Stryker Vlad's lance had struck but failed to penetrate. The Khadoran ducked low in his saddle as Stryker's sword stroke came down. It, too, was repelled, scraping harmlessly off Vlad's right shoulder.

Then Stryker was by the warcaster and plunging into the heart of a thousand Iron Fang uhlans. He slashed left and right, his blade cutting through armor and flesh, even as he avoided the broad tips of uhlan blasting lances. Behind him, the thunder of those lances exploding against the bodies of his Storm Lances was like an eruption.

He pushed forward, not wanting to lose the momentum of his charge, and cut down two more uhlans directly in his path, splashing his armor with crimson. He pulled hard on the reins and wheeled about, finding himself in the center of a maelstrom of red and blue. He had cut a bloody swath through the enemy, but his Storm Lances hadn't fared as well. They'd slain many uhlans, but now they were in close quarters, thrusting with their longer lances, while their foes resorted to shorter weapons more maneuverable in the confines of hand-to-hand combat.

Stryker spurred his mount forward, looking for Vlad. He found the warcaster easily enough. He was a storm of steel and blood in the center of a tight knot of horsemen. Storm Lances tumbled from their mounts with each thrust of his spear.

Stryker charged up and summoned his magic, letting the runes form around his body as the lightning spell gathered. A jagged bolt of electricity shot from the sky and struck the horseman directly behind Vlad. The uhlan shuddered and fell from his saddle, a hole burnt cleanly through his mail. The lightning jumped, striking Vlad and the uhlan next to him. The uhlan was killed, but Vlad was merely rocked back in his saddle as the spell spent its energy against his armor.

Vlad wheeled around and kicked the flanks of his huge black destrier. He came across the field at Stryker at a full gallop, his spear leveled. Stryker hunkered down in his saddle, holding Quicksilver in one hand like a short spear.

As they closed, Stryker thumbed the stud on his weapon's haft, loosing a voltaic blast. It missed, passing over Vlad's head, but it caused the enemy warcaster to duck, and this likely saved Stryker's life. Vlad's aim was thrown askew a heartbeat before they slammed together. The spear thrust aimed at Stryker's heart slipped low and scored his horse's neck. Blood splashed, and Stryker's mount reared and screamed, then toppled over, pinning Stryker to the ground under its immense weight. The warhorse so wounded regained its feet, but before Stryker could grasp its reins, it bolted away through the throng of warriors.

There were hooves all around him, and Stryker rolled over onto his back just in time to see a blasting lance coming at his chest. The grim face of the uhlan behind it was set in a fierce snarl. Stryker desperately batted at the weapon with his own, knocking it off-target so it smashed into the ground next to him and detonated. The blast was blunted by the earth, but it was enough to lift him from the ground and fling him away. He hit the ground again, but his armor and power field absorbed most of the impact. He climbed to his feet in a no man's land, surrounded by the corpses of horses and men. The uhlan who had attacked him earlier took advantage of his vulnerability and charged, reversing his spent blasting pike and using the spike on its butt like a short spear.

Stryker took Quicksilver in a two-handed grip. There wasn't time to blast the uhlan with lightning; all he could do was wait for him to close. The Khadoran's spear lashed out, and Stryker spun away from it, using the momentum to slash upward. He struck the uhlan below his right arm, biting through the chain mail and deep into the Khadoran's body. Blood sprayed as the uhlan passed, nearly pulling Quicksilver from Stryker's hands. He yanked backward, pulling the critically injured uhlan from his saddle. He landed at Stryker's feet and tried to rise. Instead, Stryker finished him with a heavy downward stroke that opened his foe from neck to waist.

His enemy dispatched, Stryker sprinted toward the churning mass of horsemen still fighting a hundred yards away. The Khadoran infantry was advancing and was nearly on top of them. They were now in range of the Cygnaran artillery; the shells were taking their toll, but it did little to impede the enemy's progress. Worse, the Khadoran warjacks were closing, including the hulking shape of a Conquest.

Stryker let his consciousness drift into his warjacks, and through their eyes he saw the Cygnaran infantry was moving in. That surging sea of blue was a welcome sight. Magic runes forming in the air over the forward ranks of the Stormblades told him where Maddox was. He pushed the 'jacks forward as he rushed to join her.

He moved through the field, around dead horses and men, avoiding the brutal press of the two cavalries battling it out. Without a horse, he wouldn't be of much use there. He reached his own infantry just as the Khadoran footmen slammed into them, mostly Iron Fangs armed with blasting pikes and shields and Man-O-War armed with terrible annihilator axes and shield cannons.

The front rank of Stormblades opened to allow him inside, and he made his way quickly to where Maddox and Captain Adkins were calling out orders or sending runners to convey them.

Relief softened Maddox's face as he approached. "Morrow, I saw you go down," she said, shouting so she could be heard over the din of battle. "I feared the worst."

"I'm harder to kill than that," he said. "Take your 'jacks and hit their right flank. I'll take the left with the Stormwall and Rowdy,"

He pointed to the left side of the Khadoran infantry line; the Conquest loomed behind it. "Captain Adkins, I'm leaving the Defenders with you. Go up the middle—the Defenders will give you some cover."

"Yes, sir," Adkins said.

Stryker turned and moved to the front of the infantry line, along the left flank. He reached out to Rowdy and the Stormwall as he ran, urging them to join him.

He reached his position, and the faces of the Stormblades around him brightened. Their confidence in him lent their strength to his own.

The two armies were converging on a central point, the tight knot of horsemen still fighting in the middle of the field. Infantry and warjacks advanced to the left, right, and behind the morass of horsemen. The artillery had slackened, as both sides now feared hitting their own troops. Mortar volleys on the outskirts of the enemy flanks still fell, keeping the two sides fairly compact. The Khadoran guns were being moved up now, behind the advancing infantry, so they could begin targeting the walls of Riversmet.

A mere twenty yards now separated the two advancing infantries, and Stryker called out to the men around him. "On my signal, charge and fire!" He held Quicksilver up, then swept it down. The Stormblades around him moved as one, breaking into a charge, and the front rank fired their storm glaives at the enemy, arcing lightning bolts into the locked shield of the Iron Fangs and Man-O-War shocktroopers. A few of the heavily armored Khadorans were slain, but the true purpose of the galvanic volley was to blunt their advance, setting them back on their heels. It was effective enough for now.

They hit the Khadorans hard, and Stryker shoved through a forest of blasting pikes to slash at the men behind them. He heard the roar of the Iron Fang's weapons detonating to his left and right. Each likely heralded the death of a Storm Knight.

Stryker and the front line of Stormblades pushed against their foes, but the Khadoran shield wall was too strong, and Stryker's troops were taking stiff casualties. He needed to make a hole.

To me, Rowdy, he thought at the big Ironclad. The warjack responded by running through the ranks of Stormblades, a smoke-billowing engine of destruction. They let the warjack pass, but even so, Rowdy would be careful to avoid running into or stepping on them as he barreled forward.

Rowdy arrived in the front ranks with a trumpeting blast of steam and swung his quake hammer. The massive weapon sent Iron Fang pikemen flying and crumpled Man-O-War armor like cheap tin.

"After Rowdy!" Stryker called, and he and his Stormblades surged into the opening the Ironclad had made. They were in tight quarters now where the storm glaives of his infantry would be more useful than the long pikes of the enemy.

Stryker lost track of time in the melee. His world was reduced to little more than instinctual reaction fueled by the adrenaline spike of combat. Almost without thought, he slashed out at foes with his sword and parried incoming strikes. Men fell around him, Khadoran and Cygnaran, and he pressed on.

His consciousness was split between his own mind and that of the two warjacks he controlled. He'd didn't need to guide Rowdy much in combat; the old warjack was an experienced combatant and was still effective on his own, but Stryker urged the Stormwall on, keeping it back until Vlad or Harkevich moved one of their own colossals into the melee. He ordered it to fire its cannons and chain guns over the heads of the Stormblades, blasting holes in the enemy formation that were quickly filled by Cygnaran troops.

The startling shock of a heavy impact on Rowdy's hull came through the link he shared with the warjack. It brought the world back into wider focus, breaking him out of the almost trance-like state of sustained combat. He parried a blow from a Man-O-War annihilator axe, riposted, and removed the top half of the enemy's head with a two-handed reverse cut. He then turned his attention to Rowdy.

The Khadorans had brought their own warjacks up, and Rowdy was trading blows with a Juggernaut, a huge warjack armed with an ice axe.

Rowdy was ten yards away, close enough for Stryker to augment the warjack's strength with magic. He stepped back, letting two other Stormblades take his position in the fighting line, and cast his spell. Runes formed around Rowdy's hull, as the spell infused the warjack with power, lending arcane strength to his blows.

The Juggernaut had damaged Rowdy's right arm but not critically, and Stryker channeled his will into the Ironclad's next strike. The quake hammer came down, fueled by Rowdy's immense strength and his own arcane augmentation. It struck the Juggernaut's left leg, destroying steel and hydraulics, and the quake hammer's mechanika triggered, sending a tremor of energy through the Juggernaut's body. The multi-ton Khadoran warjack was knocked off its feet by the blow, crashing down atop a line of Iron Fang pikemen, smashing them flat.

Rowdy did not relent. He strode forward and hammered the downed warjack with his left fist. Rowdy's rage and joy, mixed into one swirling emotion, was a bright mote in Stryker's mind. The warjack's fist came down and punched through the Juggernaut's hull, crushing the cortex underneath. The Khadoran warjack stopped moving, and Rowdy yanked his fist out of its innards, trailing shredded metal, conduit piping, and hydraulic hosing.

One warjack was down, but the Khadorans had just brought their 'jacks into play. One of the Conquests was striding forward, the wave of crimson-armored bodies separating before it. Spell runes formed around its body, and its cannons discharged twice in rapid succession. The first volley struck the Stormwall, but the damage was minimal—just dents and scorching. The second shot was expertly placed, however, falling in the middle of the Cygnaran center line and vaporizing dozens of Stormblades.

Let's get him, Stryker thought to both of his warjacks.

Bolts of electricity arced up from the Cygnaran line, as those Stormblades not engaged in melee fired their storm glaives at the advancing Conquest. It was like trying to blow down a mountain with a gust of wind. The colossal's heavy armor deflected the lightning easily and with little damage.

Rowdy was closing in on the Conquest, battering aside

any Khadoran troops foolish enough to get in his way. Stryker pulled him back—a one-on-one confrontation with a colossal would destroy him. The warjack's irritation at the delay was not surprising.

Hold on, Stryker told him. *Help is on the way.*

He glanced around for one of the Khadoran warcasters. Vlad was likely still in the center of the Khadoran line, fighting among his horsemen and commanding the warjacks there. But Stryker had seen the spell runes around the Conquest, and he looked for Harkevich, trying to spot the trail of smoke that would indicate warcaster armor. He found that trail quickly enough and then the man beneath it. Harkevich was ten yards away from the Conquest surrounded by a group of Man-O-War, his protective escort.

The presence of Harkevich meant the Conquest would be fighting at the peak of its capability. So, Stryker's Stormwall had to do the same. The Cygnaran colossal was a mighty machine, but the Khadoran colossal was larger, bulkier, and stronger in a hand-to-hand fight. He'd need both Rowdy and the Stormwall to win this one.

"With me," he called out to the Stormblades around him. "Keep them off me."

A half-dozen knights closed ranks around him, their glaives forming a lethal galvanic hedge.

The Stormwall had reached the Conquest, and Stryker cast a spell on it to augment its strength. Its massive fists were charged with energy that lent galvanic power to its strikes, and he urged the colossal to lash out with its right fist, pushing his will into the blow to empower it further. The Conquest was a ponderous machine despite its strength, and it could not move away in time. The Stormwall's blow landed, making a sound like a storm on top of a train wreck. Bolts of jagged electricity shot out in all directions, some striking Khadoran troops nearby for lethal results. The Conquest staggered back beneath the force of the blow, but it recovered quickly and lashed out with its own fist.

Stryker felt the blow through the connection he shared with the colossal, felt the shuddering impact and the crumpling steel.

His machine couldn't take many more hits like that. *Get in there, Rowdy.*

The Ironclad charged eagerly toward the enemy colossal, trailing a thick black plume of smoke as he advanced. He was nimble for a heavy warjack; he ducked under one of the Conquest's fists as it descended to pulverize him. Stryker picked Rowdy's target for him—the Conquest's right leg—and the Ironclad struck it soundly with his hammer. At the same time, Stryker brought the Stormwall's left fist around in another haymaker blow that landed like a meteor, destroying one of the secondary cannons on the Conquest's hull.

The Stormwall shuddered as the Conquest returned the blow, this time annihilating one of the Stormwall's chain guns.

Stryker turned his attention back to Rowdy just as a squad of Man-O-War arrived, each man armed with a heavy two-handed maul. These were part of the powerful Man-O-War demolition corps, and their heavy ice mauls could inflict terrible damage on warjacks. Harkevich was trying to get Rowdy out of the fight.

Stryker pulled Rowdy back, away from the colossal, but the Man-O-War followed. Rowdy came reluctantly, but Stryker ordered him to retreat, hoping to lure the Man-O-War closer to the Stormblade line. Instead, they changed direction and barreled toward him instead. Their goal was clear: take out the warcaster, take out the warjacks.

Another crushing blow from the Conquest rang through his connection with the Stormwall, and his colossal's left arm now dangled useless at its side.

The Man-O-War were closing in, but they were intercepted by four Stormblades who had seen the danger and had moved to intercept. Stryker returned his attention to the Conquest as two explosive shells impacted against its right leg, fired from the pair of Defenders he'd left with Adkins. Stryker looked toward the center of the Cygnaran line; the two warjacks had been moved closer to the left flank, putting the Conquest in range of their heavy cannons. The Conquest's armor was thick, but the damage Rowdy had done increased their efficacy. The leg buckled, but the

Conquest did not fall. It limped forward, and now Stryker had the advantage.

He pulled the Stormwall back, out of melee with the Khadoran colossal, and opened fire with its heavy cannons at point-blank range. He pushed arcane power into each shot, increasing its penetration and explosive yield. The Conquest tried to close, but its ruined leg made it all but immobile.

Shell after shell struck the Khadoran colossal. Pieces of its armor flew in all directions. He let Rowdy back into the mix again, and the Ironclad closed in, smashing at the Conquest's hull and legs.

The Conquest shuddered as Rowdy's quake hammer smashed something vital beneath its hull. It was nearly finished. Stryker sent the Stormwall to end it. The Cygnaran colossal charged and delivered a brutal strike with its right fist. The Conquest's right side collapsed completely under the blow, smoke and sparks bursting from the ruined metal. It staggered, the smoke from its stacks coming out in irregular bursts like the gasps of a dying man. Then the smoke stopped altogether, and the gargantuan machine toppled backward, now nothing more than fifty tons of wreckage. The ground shook as it crashed down, and a cheer went up from the Cygnaran ranks.

Stryker breathed a sigh of relief then refocused. The enemy was far from defeated, and this war had just begun.

— 37 —

Western Riversmet, Occupied Llael

MAGNUS HATED TRENCH WARFARE. He hated the confining nature of it, the way it restricted his ability to view the entire battlefield. It had its uses; he'd more than learned that in his time as a Cygnaran officer in Vinter's Cygnar. But right now he needed to see what was happening. He looked through the eyes of the warjacks he controlled, but they were in the trenches as well and, despite their height, still gave him a limited view of the battlefield. Muttering to himself, he climbed out of the forward set of trenches so he could see, with his own eyes, the swirling chaos of the battle unfolding before Riversmet.

"Sir," Captain Silus said beside him, ducking as the shrill whine of an incoming artillery shell shrieked by overhead. It impacted behind them. Dirt and, in all probability, pieces of the soldiers it had killed bounced off Magnus' power field. "What are your orders?"

Magnus studied the battle before him for a moment and

then turned to his captain. "They're locked in a stalemate for the moment." He gestured to the crush of red and blue five hundred yards away. "Bring the snipers and all the express teams to the forward trenches. I want them to pick their shots, wounding but not killing. Let's see if we can slow their infantry down a bit."

Silus hurried off to relay Magnus' orders.

Magnus let his mind move to the cortexes of the three warjacks under his command, a pair of Chargers and a Grenadier. The Charger's light cannons and the Grenadier's grenade launchers did not have the range to affect the Khadoran Army yet, but he urged them forward and out of the trenches just the same. The tide of battle often changed, and targets would come his way.

A bullet struck his power field, penetrated, and bounced off his breastplate. The arcane force field around him had robbed the projectile of most of its energy, but it hit hard enough to stagger him. The Khadorans had snipers, too, some of the best in the world, and all of them would love to claim a warcaster kill.

Reluctantly, he turned and climbed down the ladder behind him and into the forward trench. Trenchers lined the deep furrow in the earth, bracing their rifles over the top, waiting for the enemy to move within range. Their role here was largely defensive for the moment, at least until they were forced to pull back into the city. A battle in the tight confines of Riversmet would put their skills to good use.

The trencher rifles were silent at the moment; they, too, did not have the range to reach the enemy yet. Officers watched the battle with spyglasses, waiting for the moment when the battle might shift and bring the enemy closer to the walls and the trencher guns.

It was hard to tell if Stryker was winning or losing. Magnus had seen the Conquest go down, and that boded well for the Cygnaran Army, but something bothered him, an itch in the back of his mind, a lingering sense of danger and doubt. He'd survived as long as he had by paying attention to that feeling, and he was alert for any sign that might indicate he had missed something.

What bothered him was the composition of Vlad's army. The man had brought a lot of horsemen—naturally, the Great

Prince of Umbrey would do no less—but it wasn't enough. With Harkevich's intel, Vlad should have had a clear idea of the enemy he would face at Riversmet. The truth was he wasn't prepared for a siege, and his only hope to avoid one would be to draw the majority of the Cygnaran Army out, which he'd done. But if that was the case, why wasn't his army overwhelmingly large? It seemed comparable in size to Cygnar's and destined for the stalemate currently unfolding on the field.

That sense of alarm intensified as Magnus continued to watch the battle from the trench. Something was most certainly off. Something was absolutely *wrong*.

"Sir," a trencher sergeant said to Magnus' right, "look at this."

Magnus turned, his gut lurching with that sense of impending doom, and he accepted the spyglass the trencher offered him. "Where?"

"Northeast, sir." The trencher officer pointed.

Magnus saw nothing at first, just the plains fading into the looming mountains to the north. Then, a massive plume of dust appeared on the horizon. It could indicate only one thing—men and horses moving at high speed in their direction.

"Bloody hell," Magnus said and took the spyglass from his eye. "Send a runner for Major Hughs. Tell him to train half his guns on the northeast corner of the city."

The trencher nodded sharply, then chose a man and sent him running. Magnus glanced down the trencher line. The ranking officer here was a captain. Magnus hurried down the trench toward the man. The captain looked more than a little surprised when Magnus placed a hand his shoulder and wrenched him around.

"Captain, start moving men and weapons to the forward trenches; leave just a skeleton crew here. Pass that down the line."

The trencher looked confused, and something passed across his face Magnus didn't like. It was not just doubt; it was defiance. Magnus had seen that look on the faces of men who had once considered him a traitor and likely still did.

"Now, soldier!" Magnus said.

Discipline kicked in, and the man started shouting orders, the first of which was to send runners to the other trenches to convey Magnus' orders.

Magnus turned back to the battlefield and brought the spyglass to his eye again. The plume of dust to the east had gained a terrible nucleus, a blot of crimson that would soon become a secondary force of Khadoran horsemen. Vlad had held them back, knowing Stryker would ride out to meet him. The lord general was about to be outflanked.

He kept the eyeglass on the approaching enemy until they began to take on more definite and terrible composition. Leading hundreds of additional uhlans were massive armored horsemen, the steam-powered drakhun, a terrible and deadly melding of man, horse, and mechanika. There were enough of the brutes to plow through the unwitting Cygnaran ranks like the tip of great red lance.

There wasn't time to get any word to Stryker or Maddox; Magnus figured he'd just have to hope they'd seen the threat. All he could do was prepare for the inevitable collapse and retreat of Stryker's advance attack. He cursed. If the fool boy had listened to him, *trusted* him, they wouldn't be standing here with their asses hanging out in the wind for Vlad's secondary attack.

"General," Captain Silus called out as he came racing up the trench, "there's a huge force of horsemen—"

"I know," Magnus said, cutting him off. "Gather the necessary men and make sure we are prepared for Stryker's withdrawal."

Silus blanched. "Good Morrow, we're going to use it then?"

"Do you see another option?"

The former Steelhead shook his head.

"Then get to it, Captain. We don't have much time."

The arrival of the secondary Khadoran force had been seen by all the Cygnarans now, and the trenches were abuzz with activity as men and machines moved to bolster their defensive line.

Magnus brought the spyglass up once more as the drakhun hit the right flank of the Cygnaran Army. Then he let it fall and handed it to the nearest trencher before he began toward the eastern gate.

"Take it," he said. "I've seen enough."

— 38 —

Western Riversmet, Occupied Llael

STRYKER HEARD THE DRAKHUN-LED horseman hit the right flank before he saw the damage it had done. There was a tremendous sound, like the crashing of a great wave, and the entire Cygnaran army was *shoved* to the right beneath the brutal impact of the drakhun.

Stryker summoned Rowdy to his side and moved away from the front line. He urged the Stormwall back toward the walls of Riversmet, where its cannons could help stem the tide of enemies if they broke through.

The fighting there had slowed as Stormblades and Khadoran infantry battled at a horrifyingly slow pace, due in large part to the excellent defensive capabilities of the heavily armored Iron Fangs and Man-O-War.

He needed to reach Maddox on the right flank; she would be taking the brunt of the drakhun attack. He cursed himself silently for not expecting the ploy. But Vlad's army had been so large, he couldn't imagine the great prince had held *anything* in reserve. Then a sour thought struck him, and it struck him hard.

But Magnus had.

Stryker pushed that thought away. It would do him no good now.

Rowdy had been pulverizing a unit of Man-O-War but now joined Stryker. The warjack reacted to the alarm in Stryker's mind, and his excitement spiked. The big Ironclad had long ago linked his master's emotional state with the opportunity for more destruction and mayhem.

They pushed through the ranks of Storm Knights, and Stryker called out orders as he moved. Tasking his officers with holding the center and left, he collected men and warjacks to bolster the right.

He found Adkins still in the center, the two Defenders Stryker had left with him looming behind him.

"Report," Stryker shouted at the Stormblade captain.

"They're getting hammered, sir," Adkins replied. "The Storm Lances have largely retreated, and we're getting heavy pressure from the uhlans. If Maddox collapses, we'll be routed."

Stryker rubbed at his face, panic beginning to wash over him. He clenched it down, set is aside for later consideration. He needed to think, to see the solution that would save his army. Again, Magnus loomed large. He'd bolster the right flank, but he had to make sure they could still retreat without being routed.

"I'm taking the Defenders with me," he announced, "and I'm going to the right flank. I want you to keep pushing, but don't advance farther up the field. Hold them here."

The captain looked pale. "Are we going to retreat, sir? Draw the enemy into Riversmet?"

"I hope not," Stryker said. That meant going with Magnus' fallback position. "Just hold them."

He reached out and took control of the Defenders, then he began pushing through the ranks toward Maddox and the right flank. He could see the massive forms of the drakhun rising above the army, their annihilator axes swinging down to cut through

Storm Knights with ease. They were still in formation and still pushing forward.

He'd dragged an entire company of Storm Knights from the left and center, thinning their ranks there, but he'd had little choice. He needed to stem the bleeding on the right.

Spell runes forming in the air and the towering forms of Cygnaran warjacks told Stryker where Maddox was and that she was still alive. The troops on the right were a mingling of Storm Knights and Precursor Knights.

He reached Maddox and watched her cut the legs out from under an armored drakhun mount and then cut the head off its rider with a strike from Tempest.

She was largely alone in the middle of a field of dead Storm Knights. Only her warjacks and her own magical abilities had allowed her to survive this long. The drakhun charge had been blunted, but now the Iron Fang uhlans behind them hit the Cygnaran Army.

Stryker watched the front ranks of the left flank disappear beneath a tide of hooves and steel. The right was taking it from two sides: horsemen on its flanks and infantry on the front. They'd be pinched between them, annihilated, and then the Khadoran Army would be in a great position to hammer the rest of the Cygnaran forces.

Stryker charged forward, shouting at the Storm Knights with him to separate and bolster the weak spots in the right flank. He headed straight for Maddox, urging his two Defenders to fire their cannons at three drakhun charging straight for the warcaster.

The shells hit two of the drakhun, blasting one off his horse while the armor of the second absorbed most of the impact, and the man stayed mounted and fighting ready.

Maddox saw Stryker coming and quickly retreated, pulling her lighter warjacks, a pair of Lancers and a heavily damaged Charger, with her. The Lancers closed ranks in front of her, creating a shield wall that was soon struck by the charging drakhun.

One drakhun was skewered from his saddle as Maddox's Lancer drove an arcane-enhanced thrust completely through his body. The second drakhun fared better. His annihilator axe slammed into one of the Lancers, driven by his charge and the steam-powered strength of his armor, removing the warjack's head entirely. This was not necessarily crippling damage to a warjack, as the cortex, the brain of the machine, was housed deep within the hull, but it blinded the Lancer and rocked it.

Stryker urged Rowdy into the mix, and the Ironclad rushed forward, quake hammer leading. The big weapon came down on top of the drakhun rider, smashing him and his horse to the ground and mingling their splintered bones and armor into what seemed a single pulverized corpse.

"We can't hold them," Maddox said as she reached Stryker's side, slashing off the arm of an Iron Fang pikeman who tried to intercept her.

Stryker finished the pikeman with his own blade and kicked the body away. "I've brought knights with me. They're shoring up the holes."

"We lost nearly half our men here. They can't hold." Maddox pointed to where the Iron Fang uhlans were pulling back, leaving the drakhun to harass the left flank. "They've taken the heart out of us, and Vlad is going to take advantage." She was looking to the center of the Khadoran line.

Stryker followed her gaze there and realized what was going to happen. The newly arrived uhlans were riding through the Khadoran left flank, which was opening before them, so they could meet up with Vlad and the horsemen in the center. Then they were going to smash right through the middle of the Cygnaran Army, split it in half, and crush both sides independently. Stryker glanced back at the gaping hole in the walls of Riversmet that Magnus had identified as a place to pull back. He gritted his teeth; the thought of letting the Khadoran forces bring the fight into the city, even if they were headed into an ambush by Magnus' forces, sickened him. It could too easily fail—especially if Magnus proved to be as unreliable as Stryker continuously feared he would be. He needed to make a decision, and he needed to make it now.

The uhlans had largely gathered behind Vlad, and Stryker

could see the center of the Khadoran Army swelling further as warjacks and infantry moved to support the coming offensive push.

"What are your orders, sir?" Maddox said beside him. Her tone was worried—not desperate but definitely concerned.

There was only one path for him to take if he was going to preserve his army on the field.

"We're going to pull back," he said, "to the point General Magnus identified." The words were ash on his tongue, but it was the right course. The ambush had to work.

Maddox looked relieved. The battle had slowed around them as the Khadorans gathered.

"I want you to join up with Adkins," Stryker said, "and pull the left flank back toward the eastern gate. I'll take what's left of the Storm Lances and the Stormblades on the right and center and see if I can get Vlad to follow me. I'll have Rowdy with me, and you you'll have your 'jacks."

"We'll have to be quick," she said. "Good luck, sir."

She waded back through the sea of armored men and women toward Adkins and the center of the Cygnaran line.

Stryker began giving orders to the officers he could find for the general retreat. Maddox would do the same. The army, huge and ponderous, was slow to move, an immense shifting tide of men and machines, but it began to split and pull back.

If Maddox could reach the western gate, the trencher corps and the artillery there would likely keep Vlad and Harkevich from following her. Stryker, his more-vulnerable force, and the gaping hole in the wall of Riversmet would be a much more tempting target.

His orders had been passed along, and the Storm Lances began to gather around him. One of the knights was leading a riderless horse, the mount of a fallen knight. Stryker accepted the reins from the Storm Lance and swung up into the saddle. "Storm Knights," Stryker called out. "With me."

The Khadoran Army was moving, the great mass of horsemen at its center driving forward. The Cygnaran Army, however, was pulling back, an orderly retreat that stole some of the momentum from the Khadoran charge. Stryker and the Storm Lances were riding toward the walls of Riversmet, and the Stormblade infantry and Precursor Knights were falling back steadily in tight formation. They would take the brunt of the punishment when and if Vlad followed.

He glanced to where Maddox and the left flank of the army had pulled away and were retreating toward the eastern gate. The staccato thunder of trencher chain guns now sounded along with the whine of artillery.

To Stryker's immense relief, the Khadoran infantry harassing Maddox left off and turned to join the large part of the army that had pursued Stryker. Vlad was following, and now his life and the lives of thousands were in the hands of Asheth Magnus.

— 39 —

Western Riversmet, Occupied Llael

MAGNUS WATCHED MADDOX and a third of the Cygnaran Army break away from the main body of the army and head toward the western gate. She was retreating in an orderly manner, dissuading pursuit from the Khadorans with cannon fire from her warjacks or blasts of lightning from her Stormblades. She had most of the warjacks with her, including the hulking Stormwall. Stryker had likely abandoned all but Rowdy in his mad dash for the wall.

Most of the Khadoran Army had spilt off to follow Stryker and the larger force he commanded. Vlad was no doubt tempted by the thought of crushing Stryker *and* gaining access to the city. Magnus nodded to himself. Stryker had chosen the right path.

Trencher chain guns sputtered to life as Khadoran Man-O-War and Iron Fang pikemen came within range. Magnus reached out to his own warjacks, and the Chargers began adding their light cannons to the deterring firepower in front of the western gate.

It had the desired effect. The Khadorans broke off the chase and moved to rejoin the main army chasing Stryker.

Maddox reached the trenches and made a beeline for Magnus. "Is everything in place? Stryker won't have much time."

Magnus said, "I've sent Captain Silus to oversee the deployment of the trenchers beyond the breach. He's a good man; he'll get it done." A lie, but not one Maddox would suspect. Silus *was* in position, but only to make sure the devil's gasp was properly detonated.

"A good man like Harrow, sir?" she said. The barb was well thrown, and he hadn't expected it from her. It was likely born of her concern for Stryker. That much was obvious.

Magnus let it slide. "I made a mistake with Harrow; I didn't with Silus. He's a former Steelhead, a real soldier, if you will. He'll follow orders."

Her eyes glazed over for a moment as she sent a command to her warjacks, and her Lancers took forward positions near the chain guns, protecting them from incoming fire with their heavy shields. Then clarity returned to her eyes, and she nodded. "Very good, sir," she said. "What are your orders?"

"I want you to stay here, hold this position. I don't think the Khadorans are going to come this way, but I don't want to leave our most fortified position under-defended. Hold your Stormblades in reserve behind the gate. We may have need of them soon."

"Yes, sir," Maddox said. "And where will you be?"

"I'm going to the western gate to move some of Major Hughs' guns. We might need to shell the northwestern part of the city if the men we have there don't stop Vlad."

"Understood," Maddox said and saluted. She hurried away to follow his orders.

Magnus turned to watch Stryker nearing the hole in the eastern wall, a sea of red close behind him.

• • •

THE BREACH IN THE EASTERN WALL was massive, large enough to let twenty fully barded warhorses ride through breast to breast. Stryker and his Storm Lances reached the hole and burst through without issue. Magnus had cleared much of the rubble from the area, and they rode smoothly over largely intact cobblestone streets.

Stryker expected a sea of blue on the other side of the breach, hundreds of Cygnaran soldiers waiting to reinforce his Storm Lances. The ambush. But the space beyond the breach was empty. There were no trenchers, no Storm Guard, nothing; Stryker's retreating forces were alone. Had Magnus betrayed him? There was no time to consider such things as his Storm Knights and Precursor Knights moved slowly backward through the breach, blunting the Khadoran advance as well as they could so as many Cygnaran soldiers could make it through as possible. Rowdy was with them, and Stryker urged the big 'jack to aid the retreating infantry by forcing the Khadoran horsemen to keep their distance. That would all change if Vlad or Harkevich sent a warjack or two after Rowdy. That hadn't happened yet; Vlad seemed to want to make a point with his cavalry.

Many of the Cygnaran infantry had come through and were fanning out, creating a defensive line behind the wall. Most of them likely hadn't recognized that they were alone. The knights were only doing what they'd been trained to do.

If he was going to save them, Stryker needed them to let the Khadorans in, not to hold the breach like a bottleneck. He needed them to run, and that meant someone else had to hold back Vlad while they retreated.

"Storm Lances," he said, wheeling his horse in a circle. There were roughly a hundred of the heavy Cygnaran cavalry left, and they were gathered around him. Their faces were grim; they knew what was expected of the ambush and they had anticipated riding into a sea of Cygnaran soldiers that would cover their retreat, just as he promised. "We need to give the infantry a chance to retreat, and that means we need to give Vlad another target."

Stiff nods greeted his pronouncement; they would follow him. Into death, if need be.

Stryker held Quicksilver aloft. "Form a line, three ranks deep," he said, and his knights quickly obeyed. "Forward!"

The triple line of Cygnaran horsemen moved forward at a trot. Ahead, more Stormblades and Precursor Knights were flowing through the breach.

"Pull them back!" Stryker shouted, grabbing the shoulder of a nearby lieutenant as he rode past. The man began passing the order.

Soon the infantry was streaming around the cavalry, pulling back and firing their storm glaives to keep the Khadorans at bay until the cavalry could get into position. Stryker and the rest of the Storm Lances added their own galvanic blasts to the fusillade.

The Khadorans were coming through now, and leading them was Vlad, magnificent and deadly astride his huge charger. He held his spear aloft, pointing it at the line of Cygnaran horsemen riding at him. Behind the great prince were thousands of horseman and infantry. They would drive through the wall and into the city like a needle piercing a boil.

The area around the breach had been largely residential. There was evidence of wealth as well. The burnt-out wrecks and crumbled masonry suggested a former grandness to the ruined buildings. Those ruins were now providing cover to the retreating Cygnaran infantry.

Stryker signaled for the Storm Lances to halt. They stood in three lines of roughly thirty horsemen. He rode in the center of the forward rank. They were a hundred yards from the breach. He reached out to Rowdy, who had been nearer the wall, and drew him back, behind the treble line of Storm Lances. He wanted to hold the warjack in reserve and give his fleeing infantry the best chance of escape.

Vlad had seen them, and he rode slowly forward, flanked by a pair of drakhun. His own horsemen fanned out behind him, and Stryker could almost feel the crushing weight of the thousands to come.

"Do you think to hold back an army with only one hundred horsemen?" Vlad called across the space between them. "Unless you have come to formerly surrender the city to me, that is."

"We're not here to surrender," Stryker called out. "We're here to fight." There were still infantry forces behind them, moving toward safer parts of the city, where the Cygnaran Army had fortified. Unlike where he had expected to find Magnus' forces. Just the same, he needed to keep Vlad busy.

Stryker summoned his magic, invoking the arcane shield across the front rank of horsemen. Then he pointed his sword and spurred his horse. One hundred knights followed suit, and one hundred electro lances dropped into place.

Vlad spurred his own mount, and behind him came a crimson storm.

Stryker aimed his horse at Vlad's. He'd come up short in their first clash and had suffered for it; he meant to repay the debt this time.

The city echoed with pounding hooves, and the smaller space forced the Khadorans to match the line of the Cygnarans, with roughly thirty horsemen in each rank. Like Stryker, Vlad rode at the center of the first rank.

They sped together, and the Storm Lances triggered their electro lances, unleashing bolts of electricity into the Khadorans. A handful of uhlans tumbled from their saddle. A pebble in the ocean.

Stryker fired his own weapon, unleashing a burst of electricity from Quicksilver. He pushed arcane force into the blast. He didn't aim for Vlad; instead, he aimed for the armored horse of the drakhun next to the great prince. The bolt of lightning struck the big drakhun mount on its right leg, shredding armor and the flesh behind it, blasting the leg off at the knee. The huge horse crashed forward and to the right, smashing into Vlad's horse and causing the great prince to pull hard on the reins just to keep his seat.

Stryker hated intentionally injuring the animal, but he needed the great prince to think about something, anything, while Stryker closed on him.

He took Quicksilver in a two-handed grip as he streaked toward Vlad and the Khadoran line. The great prince regained control of his mount just as Stryker reached him. Quicksilver lashed out, driven by Stryker's momentum and every bit of magical augmentation he could transfer to the blade. The weapon smashed into Vlad's breastplate with the force of a 'jack fist. The enchanted armor buckled. Vlad was smashed from his saddle and disappeared beneath the churning hooves of his own horsemen.

Many of the Khadorans had seen what had happened, and panic swelled among them. They suddenly had more to deal with than the charging Cygnarans—they had to avoid trampling their prince to death.

A hole opened in the center of the Khadoran line, and Stryker took advantage of the enemy's momentary lapse in concentration. The Storm Lances pushed forward, slashing and spearing the uhlans and drakhun in their way.

Stryker glimpsed Vlad climbing to his feet ten yards away, blood running from a broken nose and a split lip. His breastplate bore a huge dent—Quicksilver hadn't penetrated the armor, but the force of the blow had likely cracked a few of Vlad's ribs. Stryker held his blade aloft at the enemy warcaster, a mocking salute that was not returned. Vlad snarled and swung back up into the saddle of his horse one of his uhlans had retrieved for him.

The fighting intensified, and the momentary advantage the Cygnarans had enjoyed turned into a vicious slog as horsemen, their mounts side by side, hacked and thrust at one another.

Stryker was hemmed in by his own men and no small number of enemies. He struck out with his sword or blasted the enemy with bolts of arcing electricity. Despite the pitch of the battle, they were holding. Could he force Vlad back through the breach, then perhaps fortify it? Magnus had wanted him to lure the great prince here to ambush him, but if he could still win despite Magnus' failure to back him...

A blast of icy wind hit Stryker, and the Storm Lance next to him suddenly came apart as if an invisible blade had cut him in half. Blood fountained, and Stryker ducked low in his saddle. It had been a spell, and it had come from Vlad. He'd seen the razor wind in battle before; Vlad wasn't the only Khadoran warcaster to make use of the deadly enchantment.

Vlad withdrew, and Stryker saw why. The hulking forms of Khadoran warjacks had moved up and were pressing through the knot of horsemen. Vlad's spell was aimed at the giant machines, and crimson runes spiraled around two towering Juggernauts. Already quick for their size, the machines gained terrible speed and power from Vlad's spell. The Storm Lances nearest the huge warjacks wheeled their mounts around and tried to pull back.

Vlad would use the Juggernauts to punch through Stryker's Storm Lances, and then the great prince's army would follow. Stryker could sound a retreat, pull back, but if he could hold and reinforcements could be brought up, they might inflict enough damage to Vlad to push him back, out of the city. They'd be faced with a siege, but now that he'd had a look at Vlad's army, that might not be the worst choice before him.

First he had to do something about the Juggernauts. Rowdy's presence loomed in the back of his mind, ready and eager to join the fight, but it would be certain destruction for the Ironclad if Stryker let him face down two Juggernauts. Instead, Stryker reached deep within himself, finding the primitive core of his magical ability, remembering the first manifestation of his magic all those years ago. That manifestation had caused him a lot of trouble until he'd harnessed it and turned it into a weapon.

The spell runes formed around him, comforting, familiar. He hadn't cast this spell in some time, and as it flowed through him, it was like the embrace of an old friend. He unleashed the magic, aiming for a spot just beneath the Juggernauts.

The magic struck, and the ground heaved. The earthquake spell was one of his most potent arcane weapons, and as the ground buckled beneath the Khadoran warjacks, they were smashed to the ground along with half a dozen uhlans. The Juggernauts flailed about, trying to heave their monstrous bodies upright again.

The fighting resumed, and now they were holding. They were keeping Vlad at bay. Stryker turned to one of the Storm Lances next to him, a young lieutenant named Lissa Archer. "Ride for the western gate, find Maddox, and tell her to get reinforcements here at once. We can hurt him here."

He struck out at an uhlan closing in on Archer's flank, tumbling the enemy from the saddle and clearing the way for her. "Go!"

She spurred her mount and streaked off, away from the fighting. Stryker returned his attention to the battle and pressed forward again, closing ranks with the nearest Storm Lances. The world faded around him into familiar territory: blood, steel, and magic.

o

Western Riversmet, Occupied Llael

MAGNUS STOOD ON THE BATTLEMENTS above the western gate, looking over the lines of trenches that stretched for nearly a thousand yards, a formidable obstacle. The fighting had largely moved farther north, to the huge breach in the Riversmet wall where Stryker had retreated with two-thirds of the Cygnaran Army.

Reports were coming in that the lord general was locked in combat with Vlad there, and this worried Magnus. Stryker had sent most of the infantry, Stormblades, and Precursor Knights back to him, to the fortified area behind the western gate. But Stryker had not yet joined them.

More alarming still were the other reports he was receiving from Silus. The former Steelhead couldn't detonate the devil's gasp with Stryker and a hundred Storm Lances still in the blast radius.

Movement behind him caused Magnus to turn. A bedraggled Storm Knight climbed up the ladder to the battlements. Her armor was dented and scratched, and her face was covered in dirt and blood, some of it probably her own.

"General Magnus, I was told to find Major Maddox," she said, breathing heavily.

"I don't care who you were told to find, Lieutenant. Report," Something akin to panic was growing in his belly. She'd come from Stryker. There could be no doubt.

"Sir, the lord general commands that reinforcements be sent to his position at once," she said. "He believes we can hold Vlad at the breach."

The stupid fool, Magnus thought. He had expected Stryker to make the more pragmatic choice when he realized there were no troops waiting for him on the other side of the breach and flee along with his infantry. Instead, he was fighting with his heart instead of his brain.

Magnus was careful not to let his anger manifest on his features or in his body language. He'd long ago learned to stifle such impulses, especially when subterfuge was necessary.

"Thank you, Lieutenant," he said. "I'll take it from here." He let his face soften, and he reached out to put one hand on her armored shoulder. "You look tired, soldier, and you're wounded. Get to the infirmary, and get some food in you."

"Sir, I can fight," she said. Her eyes conveyed a different message. She was exhausted and terrified. She only needed one more small push.

"That's an order, Lieutenant," he said gently. "Go."

"Yes, sir," she said and climbed down from the battlements.

Magnus watched her go and clenched his fists in frustration. If he didn't relay Stryker's order, the fool would die there, and as much as that would remove a painful thorn in Magnus' side, he couldn't let that happen. He was surprised to find that he didn't *want* that to happen, even after everything. It was a confusing revelation, one he could not worry about at the moment.

Magnus turned and looked down on a battery of mortars that had been steadily firing over the walls but that had now fallen silent with the Khadoran Army so close to the city. Major Hughs was there shouting orders, and soldiers were swarming over the huge guns, getting them ready should the Khadorans assault this part of the wall.

Magnus hurried down the ladder behind him and moved swiftly to Hughs. As he approached, he noted another figure standing next to the trencher commander. The Llaelese gun mage Vayne di Brascio had been shadowing the gun crews since the fighting began; he'd be a formidable deterrent to any enemies who managed to reach the guns. Nonetheless, his eyes narrowed as Magnus drew near. di Brascio was just another on the long list of men and women who didn't trust him.

"Major Hughs," Magnus said as he reached the first of the mortars. It was one of the biggest, and its massive multi-ton bulk was mounted on a reinforced wagon some twenty feet in length. The huge gun fired shells that could only be loaded with the aid of a laborjack, and each mortar had one of the heavy machines to manage its gargantuan ammunition.

"Sir," Hughs said. Magnus detected no disrespect or reticence in the major's voice. This was a career soldier, a grunt who'd worked his way up the ladder through a combination of luck and skill. He followed orders, no matter who they came from.

"Do you have a map of the city?" Magnus asked.

"Of course, sir," Hughs replied. "Torrance! Bring the map!"

A man brought a rolled-up diagram, a smaller version of the blueprint they'd studied during their war councils.

Magnus took it and spread it out on the wagon. "I want you to train these guns on this point here." He pointed at a section of the map.

Hughs' brows wrinkled. "But, sir, Lord General Stryker has fallen back to that area, and we have troops there to cover his retreat. In fact, you'd be putting mortar shells almost right on top of them."

"General Magnus, I do not understand what it is you're trying to accomplish," di Brascio said, his tone suspicious.

"Since you are not part of the Cygnaran Army, Captain di Brascio, you do not *need* to understand," Magnus said flatly.

He could deny di Brascio but not Hughs. The man's expression said he was more than a little confused. He had been in the war council and had heard Magnus outline his plan to Stryker. This was a man who would refuse his order instantly if he thought Magnus had betrayed Stryker. "Major, I've just had word from Stryker." The major had undoubtedly seen Lieutenant Archer, battered and bloody, report to him, but it was impossible that he'd heard *what* she reported. "They're falling back. Vlad's force was too overwhelming."

Hughs opened and closed his mouth, very much like a fish. "I can't—"

"Are you about to disobey a direct order from a superior officer, or am I mistaken?" Now Magnus would find out if he had guessed the true measure of the man.

"Major, think about this," di Brascio said.

"Captain, if you do not shut your mouth, I will have you removed. Do you understand?" Magnus said. He'd had enough of the gun mage's meddling. While the man had his uses, Stryker had indulged him far too much.

di Brascio snorted in disgust and stalked away.

"Major? If you don't get your men moving, I will, but I guarantee you, my artillery skills are nowhere near the caliber of yours."

That seemed to push the man where he needed to go. Hughs swallowed. "Yes, sir," he said. "Load one and two!"

Magnus moved on and returned to the battlements. He climbed up the ladder where trenchers lined the walls, looking for signs of the enemy. There were more than trenchers here, though. Magnus had made certain some of his own men, those who had served him in exile, were here as well. He went to one of them, a man named Garret, a former mercenary who'd specialized in smuggling and getting into and out of occupied territory quickly and quietly.

Magnus pulled the man aside. "Find Silus and tell him to trigger the explosives as soon as Stryker is clear of the area. Go."

The man hurried away. Magnus looked to the east and the

mass of Khadoran soldiers pushing through the breach there. One of the mortars behind him fired, a thunderous blast that shook his bones.

He couldn't rely on Stryker to make a pragmatic decision, but he could count on one thing from the man that *would* drive him.

Hatred.

· · ·

STRYKER HEARD THE FIRST SHELL coming in as a shrieking demon of destruction. It struck the wall near the breach, blasting apart masonry and vaporizing the Khadoran uhlans in that area. Where had the shell come from? Was the Khadoran Army firing at them from behind the wall? No, they wouldn't put Vlad at risk like that. Then the angle of impact became clear to him—that shell had hit the *inside* of the wall, which meant it came from within the city.

The fighting around him seemed to slow, as both sides tried to take stock of what was happening. None of them had much time to consider. The terrible howling scream of another mortar shell came whistling out of the sky. This one landed behind the Cygnaran line, blasting apart a ruined house and creating a shockwave that rattled Stryker's teeth.

"Sir, that's our gun!" the Storm Lance next to him shouted, his eyes wide with terror.

Why would Hughs fire so close to them? The answer slammed into Stryker like a punch to the stomach.

Magnus. Magnus was firing on him.

Another shell hit, this one close enough to the Cygnaran line to blast Storm Lances from their saddles. The way one of them landed said he wouldn't be getting up again.

Damn him! Stryker seethed. He had no choice; he could hear the distant thunder of the mortars firing again. Was this Magnus' plan all along, to put him in a vulnerable position, alone, facing impossible odds so he could bomb him and his med? Magnus had hoped Vlad would crush him, but Archer had likely told him otherwise, and he had turned to a more direct method. He could tell Major Hughs any lie he liked at that point.

"Retreat!" Stryker cried and brought Quicksilver up. His order was followed immediately, and they took advantage of the momentary confusion the falling mortar shells had created among the Khadorans, wheeled about, and sped east, toward the safe point Magnus had indicated.

He reached out to Rowdy and urged the warjack to retreat as well. The warjack's disappointment was undeniable.

Stryker was in the lead of the Storm Lances who remained. They galloped through the city, moving as swiftly as possible through the cluttered ruins. More mortar shells fell behind them; Stryker looked back to see if they had deterred the Khadorans. They hadn't. Vlad was too close now. He could pull his entire army into the city, including his own guns.

Like blood from a burst artery, the Khadoran Army flooded through the breach in a jet of crimson. He could see the uhlans and drakhun leading them, but infantry and warjacks were close behind.

The ruins were becoming thicker as they rode forward, pushing their mounts hard. Gunshots rang out behind them as some of the Khadoran infantry, likely Winter Guard or snipers brought up from the rear, fired at the retreating Storm Lances.

The Storm Knight riding to Stryker's right suddenly pitched forward in his saddle and tumbled from his mount—a sniper's bullet gouged a hole in the back of his helmet. Stryker summoned his magic and shielded as many knights as he could with an arcane shield. It would save some of them.

They were nearing a portion the city marked by a separation of ruins and more intact buildings, where the damaged part of the city gave way to parts that had been rebuilt. They thundered through, and Stryker turned back to see that a huge portion of the Khadoran Army had come through the breach.

Then everything came apart.

It began with a bright flash from behind them, like the sun itself had fallen from the sky into their midst. The sound followed, and it was if the bowels of Urcaen had opened and unleashed a howling clamor of the damned. There was no way to describe it properly; it was simply too huge.

The shockwave hit next. His breath was crushed from Stryker's lungs, and his power field activated, trying to hold the pressure wave at bay. It helped some, but it didn't keep him in the saddle. He was hurled forward over his horse's head, and many of his knights tumbled through the air after him.

The ground came up hard and fast, and what little breath remained to him was knocked savagely out of him. He lay there, ears ringing, his body a mass of aching misery. When he finally summoned enough strength to move, he climbed to his hands and knees with a groan. Around him lay knights and their horses, some moving, some who might never move again.

He looked up and saw men in trencher armor and uniforms approaching. They were Magnus' men; he recognized the man leading them, a former Steelhead name Silus. There was something wrong with Silus' face; his mouth was hanging open and his eyes were wide to the point of insanity. He was staring at something behind Stryker.

Stryker struggled to his feet. Silus made no move to help him; the man looked paralyzed. Stryker turned and instantly understood the former Steelhead's shock.

The northwest corner of Riversmet was a scorched wasteland, a crater-pocked hell-scape covered in a foul greenish fog. Within this tormented landscape, men moved like dying insects, crawling toward him, gasping, strangling. It made no matter they were the enemy—their agony was horrifying to behold. Stryker stumbled and grabbed Silus by his breastplate.

"What did he do? What did he do?" he shouted into the man's face, spraying him with spittle.

Silus closed his eyes. "He said it was a last resort . . . " he said. He looked up at Stryker, and the pain and sorrow in his eyes told Stryker he was telling the truth.

Stryker released him. "It's devil's gasp, isn't it?"

Silus nodded. His face was ashen, and he looked like he was going to be sick. Stryker wanted to hate him, wanted to lash out at anyone for the horror that was unfolding around them, but that hatred would be misplaced. Silus was as much Magnus' pawn as he was. "Is there more?"

That seemed to snap Silus back to himself, at least for a moment. "Yes, sir. There's another batch farther ahead . . . Martens has the detonator; he'll blow the rest as soon as he sees the Khadorans."

A portion of the Khadoran force had already recovered, and horsemen were skirting the massive bank of fog and riding toward them. Vlad was in the lead. There wasn't much time.

"You're going to have to stop that next detonation," Stryker said to Silus.

The man groaned. "But the Khadorans . . ." he said, pointing at the uhlans and the other Khadoran troops moving toward them. Their progress was slowed by the ruins and the necessity of avoiding the devil's gasp. How many had Magnus killed already? There were thousands within the walls when the first blast went off. To punctuate this thought, a terrible sound rose from the fog-shrouded ruins, the cries of men dying, hoarse and wretched. Those who had been lucky enough to survive the blast were now drowning in their own blood as the devil's gasp liquefied their lungs.

"I'll hold them," Stryker snarled.

"If I get near him," Silus said, "Martens'll just set it off. I can't stop him. You shouldn't send me."

Stryker urged Rowdy to his side, and the warjack came swiftly through the dense fog of the devil's gasp. It would have no effect on him. "You show Rowdy where the bomb is. If you don't think you can find this Martens and stop him from detonating the rest, Rowdy can destroy the bomb. Do you understand me?"

"Sir, I'm sorry . . . I didn't think—"

"Captain, if you want to atone for some of this atrocity, do as I say. Now."

"Yes, sir." The former merc hurried off deeper into the ruins. Stryker sent Rowdy after him, viewing the world through his warjack's eyes and splitting his attention.

Soldiers began to move in and carry away wounded knights or help along those that could still walk. There was no way to tell how many they'd lost, but whatever that number was, the Khadoran casualties had to eclipse it by unthinkable orders of magnitude.

Vlad was closing, leading a stream of horsemen. Infantry was visible behind them. They were forced into a narrow column to avoid the devil's gasp on one side and the intact ruins on the other.

"Those of you who can still stand and fight," Stryker called out, "you're with me. The rest of you, mount up. We're not done here."

The remaining Storm Lances stirred and found what mounts they could. There were no more than twenty-five still in fighting condition. Along with the horsemen, perhaps fifty Stormblades and a handful of Storm Guard answered his call.

His horse, or at least the one he'd been riding, had come through the devastation and was standing near a ruined house, stamping at the ground, its eyes rolling. Stryker went to it, soothing it with calm words.

The horse calmed enough for him to mount it, and he swung up into the saddle, held Quicksilver high, and kicked the horse's flanks. The mount surged forward, followed by what remained of Stryker's knights.

He couldn't defeat Vlad; Stryker and his men were overwhelmed and outmatched, but they could delay him and possibly save the rest of his troops from the awful fate Magnus had in store for them. He would not likely survive this battle, but at least he could go to his death knowing he'd done his best for king and country. For what was right. For Cygnar.

For a moment, Stryker checked in on Rowdy. He saw Silus moving ahead of the big warjack, picking his way through the ruins on what seemed a deliberate course. Stryker had no way of knowing how far away Martens was, however, so he pulled his attention back to the battle at hand.

Vlad was coming at him like an arrow, the weight of hundreds of horsemen behind him. He'd rallied his forces quickly after the detonation of the devil's gasp, a testament to the man's leadership skills. The blast had not left him entirely unaffected, however; somewhere along the way, the Khadoran warcaster had lost both his helm and his spear. He gripped a long-handled flail in his right hand as he raced toward Stryker.

As they came together, Vlad's face twisted into a snarl of hatred. His flail whipped out, the three steel balls whistling through the air. Stryker raised Quicksilver to parry. The flail's chain wrapped around the wide blade, and one of the balls struck his right arm with numbing force.

Their mounts wheeled around one another. Stryker lashed out with his blade, channeling his will into the blow. He would kill Vlad if he could—his goal was to save him and his men from an ignoble death, but not from an honorable one. In the end, they were still enemies. Vlad ducked low in the saddle, letting Quicksilver pass over his head. The man was a born horseman, and his skill was far beyond Stryker's own.

Their mounts came apart biting and kicking at each other, and Stryker took the momentary reprieve to check on Rowdy. His vision blurred and then doubled; he saw through the warjack's eyes again. He was still following Silus, but his connection with the warjack was waning as Rowdy traveled farther away. They had not reached their destination yet.

The rest of Stryker's knights had engaged the enemy, and the narrow confines meant no more than a dozen or so of Vlad's horsemen could come at them at any point. Steel rang against steel, and the snarling discharge of voltaic blasts filled the air with static.

Stryker pulled away from Rowdy as Vlad summoned a spell in a flash of fiery runes. Freezing cold assailed Stryker's power field, blue on blue, and he clenched his teeth against the arcane assault.

"You have no honor, Stryker!" Vlad said as he whipped his flail forward again.

Stryker smashed away the strike with his blade. He riposted. Vlad jerked away from the blow, and Quicksilver came down on the great prince's horse's neck, denting the heavy plate armor there. The beast screamed and reared, but Vlad kept his saddle.

"I didn't do this," Stryker shouted back. "I wouldn't." He knew his enemy wouldn't believe him; the man had just witnessed the horrific death of thousands of his men.

"Lies!" Vlad snarled and charged forward, slamming his horse into Stryker's. He reeled in the saddle and was forced to take one hand off of Quicksilver to grab the pommel and keep his seat.

Vlad took advantage of the opening and swung his flail at Stryker's head. Luck more than skill saved Stryker; his horse chose that moment rear and kick at Vlad's, and his enemy's flail crashed into the horse's body, denting the armor.

A sudden flash of emotion from Rowdy filled Stryker's head. He could see that the warjack and Silus had reached the area where the additional explosives were planted—Silus appeared to be directing Rowdy where to go next—but now they were being confronting a tall gangly man in battered trencher armor. Silus was shouting at him, but Rowdy was too far away to pick up the words. The man, Martens, Stryker suddenly realized, was shaking his head, and Stryker could see he held a short, cylindrical device in one hand. A length of wire ran from one end of it back into the ruins.

Martens appeared to realize why Rowdy was there, and he moved to intercept the warjack. While it wasn't clear what he was capable of doing to stop Rowdy, he clearly felt he was capable—he moved with ease and confidence. As if recognizing the threat to the warjack, Silus interposed himself between the man and the machine, still shouting, still bent on preserving their sole hope of decommissioning the bomb.

Martens drew a pistol from his belt.

Kill him, Stryker sent to Rowdy.

Before the warjack could respond, Martens had aimed at Silus and pulled the trigger.

Rowdy charged forward as Silus collapsed to his knees, a bright splotch of blood at his throat, and the warjack brought his quake hammer down on Martens.

Stryker didn't feel the blow connect because his senses were suddenly overloaded with blinding light and crashing thunder. He tumbled from the saddle, severing his connection with Rowdy, but it didn't shut out the sound. It wasn't just coming through the warjack. To the south, a ripple of massive explosions went off, followed by a cloud of heavy gas that spread over the ruins like the tendrils of some monstrous octopus.

Martens had triggered the devil's gasp.

The fighting stopped around Stryker, and he climbed to his feet and carefully picked up Quicksilver from the ground. Vlad was towering over him, still mounted, his gaze locked on the aftermath of the second explosion. His soldiers and Stryker's were transfixed by the spectacle as well.

Vlad looked down at Stryker, his noble face a confused tangle of emotions. Rage still burned behind his eyes, but he was in control. "I would have led my men directly into that to take the city," he said. It was a statement, not a question.

"I know," Stryker said, reaching out to grasp the reins of his horse. He steadied the animal and swung himself up into the saddle. He would have this conversation eye to eye with Vlad.

The Khadoran's eyes narrowed. "You could not have prevailed here with so few. We have fought before; you are not so recklessly brave as to throw away your life in such a futile effort."

Stryker locked eyes with Vlad. The man was putting it together. "I fought for something I believed worthy."

"We are enemies, Lord General," Vlad said. "I would have been destroyed, and you would have been showered with the glories of victory."

"There is no glory in such a victory," Stryker said, "but the men who would use such a thing as devil's gasp do not care."

Vlad cocked his head and grimaced. "Do you think me one of these men?"

"I don't know," Stryker said. "The bridge was rigged with it."

"I had no knowledge of this," Vlad said. "Kommander Harkevich had charge of the city and its defenses."

"And then I left the defense of the city to another as well," Stryker admitted. He didn't need to say the name.

Vlad shrugged. "I suppose not all warriors are as noble as you and I," he said.

"No, Great Prince," Stryker said, "they are not."

"What shall we do now, Lord General?" Vlad leaned forward in his saddle. "I still have many men in the city."

"And many dead as well," Stryker said. "You will lose here if you continue to fight."

"A wise tactician would advise me to fall back to Rynyr, rally my forces, and fight you there," Vlad said. "What do you advise?"

"Pull your men out of the city and return to Rynyr," Stryker said. "Leave Harkevich and a token force to collect your dead."

"And if I simply kill the lord general of the Cygnaran Army here and now and then fight on?" Vlad said.

"Then you are *not* the man I believed you to be," Stryker said.

Vlad stared at him for a moment, searching his eyes, perhaps for duplicity. He found none. The great prince wheeled his mount about and shouted orders in Khadoran. Hundreds of uhlans and drakhun followed his example. They retreated as one.

"I will see you in Rynyr, Lord General," Vlad called over his shoulder as he rode away, a stream of red steel in his wake.

Stryker glanced around him at the haggard faces of the men and women under his command who had come so close to death today. There was relief in their eyes, and he was glad of it.

Rowdy's presence bloomed bright in his mind, and he turned to see the warjack approaching. Stryker let out of a grateful sigh; Rowdy had survived the blast. Silus, he realized, had not, if he had any hope of surviving being shot trying to protect the warjack. Rowdy carried the man's limp corpse in his left hand; the former merc's face and chest were covered in blood. He'd obviously succumbed to the devil's gasp, if not to the bullet Martens had put in his throat.

"Put him down," Stryker said. Rowdy gently laid Silus' corpse on the ground. Stryker squatted down next to the body, looking into the man's sightless eyes, frozen in horror and pain. He reached out and closed them. The man had atoned for his crimes. Stryker stood and looked to west. There was still one more who had yet to do so.

— 41 —

Western Riversmet, Occupied Llael

SMOKE AND ASH ROSE ABOVE the northeastern part of the city, obscuring everything from view. Magnus didn't need to see it, though; he knew how much of the devil's gasp had been used and he knew the destruction it would yield. But something was wrong; the Khadoran army was not leaving the city in tattered clumps. Instead, it was streaming from the breach in the wall in an orderly formation. A retreat. He could see Vlad had suffered casualties, but it was nowhere near the number it should have been.

The Khadorans were still vulnerable, and Magnus pulled aside a trencher sergeant. The man had been staring at the smoke, his eyes wide. The entire square behind the eastern gate was filled with equally stunned Cygnaran soldiers.

"Sergeant," Magnus said, "relay these orders to Major Maddox at once. I want the trencher units out of their holes and attacking the Khadorans *now*."

"Sir, I—" The man stammered.

"Pull yourself together," Magnus said and leaned close. "We're *winning.*"

The man headed for the sally port in the eastern gate. Magnus looked around at the Storm Knights and Precursor Knights who were still streaming in from Stryker's position. Magnus needed to get them onto the field again immediately. But first he needed to get the artillery working again.

"Major Hughs," he shouted, moving to the big mortars that had once more fallen silent. The master artillerist looked as stunned as the rest of the soldiers in the square.

"Good Morrow," Hughs said. "What *was* that?"

"The sound of victory, Major," Magnus said. "Now, train those guns on the Khadoran position and let loose. Send runners to the other artillery batteries with the same orders. I want you to hit them until either Lord General Stryker or I close with them. Understood?"

Hughs swallowed. "Yes, sir."

Magnus opened his mouth to issue further orders to the knights in the square, but the clatter of hooves on stone drew his attention to one of the main roads leading up to the eastern gate.

Stryker came galloping toward them, the galvanic nodes on his armor the only thing to break up its outline of dark soot. He made a beeline for Magnus.

The lord general leapt from his horse while it was still cantering, hitting the ground at a dead run. Magnus let him come, hands at his sides. This part was inevitable, unavoidable.

"You *traitor!*" Stryker said as he advanced on Magnus.

Storm Knights and Precursor Knights moved in behind him, their faces filled with doubt and worry.

Magnus stared Stryker dead in the eyes. The lord general was a fountain of rage, and lightning crackled around his head and fists as that whirling emotion tapped into his magical ability.

"Lord General," Magnus said, "if I have given offense in some way, I apologize." He had to be careful here. Stryker would be completely within his rights to have Magnus taken into custody, especially once Lieutenant Archer was interviewed.

"Draw your sword," Stryker said, lifting Quicksilver to a fighting stance. The warcaster's face had calmed, and there was something quiet and terrible behind his eyes.

"You cannot be serious," Magnus said, glancing around the square. The soldiers and knights had all taken multiple steps away from them. A curious hush had settled over the area.

"You disobeyed my order and murdered thousands of men and women," Stryker said, pointing his heavy sword at Magnus. "You will pay for that crime."

"*Murdered*, Lord General?" Magnus said. "We are at war, and our enemy was *killed*."

"I am within my rights to have you dragged away and beheaded," Stryker said. "But I will see justice done here. *Now*."

"As you wish, Lord General," Magnus said and reached over his shoulder to grasp the hilt of Foecleaver. He drew the weapon from its scabbard, and slipped into a fighting stance of his own. In some ways, they had been heading toward this moment ever since he'd returned to Caspia. And what would happen if he killed Stryker? Would the army turn on him? Would Julius pardon him? He didn't have time to ponder the consequences as Stryker leaped forward, leveling a heavy rising cut at Magnus' right leg.

Magnus brought his sword down in a crisp parry, halting Stryker's blade before it connected. The strength behind the blow was immense, and the shock of it traveled painfully up his arm.

He danced backward and summoned a spell. He pointed his fist, and a bolt of blue fire shot toward Stryker. The spell impacted the lord general's power field and penetrated, knocking Stryker back a step with a smoking burn in the center of his breastplate.

Stryker responded with a spell of his own, one very similar to Magnus'. But the arcane bolt he fired was faster and stronger, and it struck Magnus high on his right shoulder, piercing his power field, spinning him around. Magnus heard Stryker's heavy footsteps behind him and whirled in time to catch a downward stroke with Foecleaver, angling the blade and twisting his body so the force of the strike was deflected downward.

Stryker recovered instantly, and he snapped Quicksilver out

in a short cut, powered by a simple flick of his wrists. Magnus had been unprepared for the speed of the blow, and Quicksilver gouged a deep furrow in his breastplate, pushing him back.

Stryker pressed in, his blade humming through the air in one strike after another, the speed and power of each one growing as he hammered against Magnus' defenses. Stryker had always been a skilled fighter, but the force behind his blows was not practice or experience—it was anger, familiar and hot, that drove his heavy blade with blinding quickness.

Magnus desperately parried each strike, giving ground each time. The wide eyes and nervous faces of the men and women watching the battle loomed around him. They owed him no loyalty; they had fought for Stryker for years. They would not weep to see him fall here.

Magnus managed a single riposte from one of Stryker's cuts. It was strong and well executed, and he sliced through the armor on Stryker's right leg, cutting into the flesh beneath it. If Stryker noticed the injury, he gave no indication of it, and he lashed out with the other leg in a powerful front kick that caught Magnus in the belly and drove him back, gasping for air. His defenses dropped for a heartbeat, but it was long enough for Stryker to spin in a complete circle, bringing Quicksilver around in a murderous arc. There was no parrying this blow—Magnus could feel the electric crackle of magic drive it toward him. The blow caught him below his right arm, staved in his breastplate, and cracked the ribs beneath. His power field and armor had kept the blow from being fatal, but it didn't really matter. He was thrown sideways, his breath driven from his lungs, and he found he could not draw another.

Stryker closed, smashing Quicksilver into Magnus' weapon and sending Foecleaver spinning through the air away from them. Magnus might summon a spell or reach for the scattergun at his hip, but it would make no difference. Stryker would cut him down now just the same.

With a sigh, Magnus prepared himself for the end. It was fitting that it be Stryker, the boy he had plucked from obscurity and set on the path to glory and power, who did the deed. The boy who had betrayed him once, long ago, would now finish the job.

Unexpectedly, Stryker's blade hammered in low, and the lord general turned his wrists to strike with the flat of the broad sword at the last moment. Magnus' legs were knocked out from under him, and the ground rose up to bludgeon what little strength he had left.

He lay on his back, gasping, blood running down his armor, and watched Stryker advance. The lord general held his sword in both hands, pointing it like an accusing finger at Magnus. He lifted it to deliver the final blow. And then he stopped. Some of the fire went out of his eyes, and he let out a long ragged breath. He let his sword fall and stepped away.

No one dared move. Magnus just waited.

Stryker finally looked to his left where a group of Storm Knights stood. "Take him. Lock him up."

If Magnus had any doubts about the Storm Knights' allegiance, they disappeared as two men rushed forward and grabbed him by the arms, lifting him from the ground. The absence of any sort of gentleness convinced him that things had changed.

"I want an entire squad on him," Stryker said. "Major Hughs, you go with them. I'll send Rowdy as well."

Magnus let them drag him away, the massive form of Ol' Rowdy shadowing them every step of the way. They would kill him if he struggled, he already suspected, and the death blow would come from Rowdy, guided by Stryker's hand. Once they left the square, it became clear the Storm Knights escorting him would take no chances. A mailed fist struck him soundly in his jaw, and he welcomed the darkness it brought with it.

— 42 —

Western Riversmet, Occupied Llael

STRYKER FOUND MADDOX ensconced behind the trencher line. She'd already given the order to cease fire and let the Khadorans pull back. The first thing Stryker had done after his duel was to countermand all of Magnus' orders to continue the attack on the Khadorans.

"Did you know?" he asked when he reached her.

Anger flashed across her eyes, and it gave him his answer, but she spoke anyway. "No, sir. General Magnus certainly did not tell me what he had planned."

"I'm sorry," he said. "I knew that. Of course I did."

She nodded, accepting his apology.

"He lied to me, to all of us. It's treason, plain and simple."

"I won't argue that," Maddox said, though it was clear she had more to say on the matter but was holding back.

"All right, Beth, tell me what you think," he said. "Please. I want to hear it."

"We won," she said flatly. "We protected Riversmet with minimal damage to its people or the rebuilt sections of the city. It's what you—what we—wanted."

"But not like this," he said. "Not like this."

"We've been here before, both of us. We're lucky to be alive, all that we've been through. I'll lose sleep over what Magnus did, the way those men suffered, but I'll also thank him a little every time I put my head on the pillow. I won't be alone in that feeling, sir."

Her meaning was clear to him. "And if I execute him?"

"He'll be martyr to some," she said evenly. "His crimes will diminish as this war continues, and there are men and women who are alive now who wouldn't be because of him. You can't deny that."

The truth behind her words was knife-sharp, and it cut to the center of the anger and outrage he felt over Magnus' action with childish ease. "What do you advise then?" he said. "I may not be thinking as clearly as I'd like to be when it comes to this issue. When it comes to Magnus."

"Strip him of his rank," she began, "but don't send him back to Caspia, sir. If you want to keep him from gathering strength, he can't be near the king."

He agreed with that. Magnus' influence over Julius was unquestionable, and who knew what the king would do. Pardon him? Promote him to Lord General? No, she was right—he needed to keep Magnus close. "You think he still has some value, then."

"He's a gifted soldier and a brilliant tactician," she said with a shrug. "If you can control him."

"If I can control him," he echoed. He had nothing to say to that, and she offered no further advice. She left him there, standing in the middle of the battlefield, counting the dead.

...

THE DESTRUCTION WAS WORSE than Stryker could have anticipated. The devil's gasp had lingered for days, making it impossible to search the area for survivors. He had men and medics posted on the outskirts of the area to help anyone who came out of the blighted ruins. Some did, and there was nothing that could be done for them. The quick mercy of a bullet was all they could offer those unfortunate souls.

Once the gas had dissipated, Stryker had men combing the area, pulling bodies out and carrying them to an area designated for them. Stryker and Maddox were among those searching; he'd ordered Magnus to stay behind and keep watch on the Khadorans.

The enemy had pulled back two miles from the city, and Stryker's forces hadn't seen any sign of them for the last twenty-four hours. Still, reinforcements could come from Rynyr or Laedry.

As he and Maddox picked through the site of Magnus' atrocity, they were silent, both struck nearly dumb by the destruction. There were so many bodies, and conservative estimates put the death toll at close to three thousand. The lucky ones had been killed in the explosion, so it was almost a relief to find a body that was badly scorched or blasted to pieces. Much, much worse were those victims who had succumbed to the devil's gasp. Often it was clear they had crawled some distance, dragging themselves over the corpses of their compatriots looking for salvation when there was none to be had. The faces of these poor soldiers were frozen in pain and horror, their features and chests caked with their own blood. Each time the searchers found one—and they found many—it drove a spike of guilt into Stryker's heart. He hadn't known what Magnus would do, but he was the lord general of the Cygnaran Army. What had happened here would bear his mark, not Magnus'.

He and Maddox spent the day loading bodies into carts. Their warcaster armor and the increased strength it provided allowed them to do the work of two men each. They also each controlled a pair of warjacks, using the big machines to clear away rubble and recover yet more corpses. Rowdy was one of these warjacks, and the normally cantankerous 'jack was oddly compliant, as if he somehow recognized the somberness of the occasion.

Just before sunset, a rider came through the ruins toward them. It was the young Storm Knight officer Lieutenant Archer.

She rode up to them and saluted.

"What is it?" Maddox said.

"Ma'am, sir," she said. "There's a delegation of Khadorans approaching under a banner of parley."

Stryker sighed. This was inevitable. It was only a matter of time before the Khadorans sent a delegation to negotiate the recovery of their dead and the release of their survivors. It was time to tell them he had plenty of the former and none of the latter.

— 43 —

Western Riversmet, Occupied Llael
Katesh 4th, 611 AR

THE KHADORANS BEGAN TO COLLECT their dead the next morning, loading up wagon after wagon of corpses. Stryker ordered some of the trencher corps and a few warjacks to help them. It took two days to remove all the corpses—it seemed an endless stream of death flowing through the gates of Riversmet.

Not all was horror and despair, however. A delegation of the citizens of Riversmet asked to meet with Stryker the day following the Cygnaran victory. He had been pleased to see this delegation led by Andrei Ladislav, the man who had represented the people of Riversmet in their first meeting with Harkevich.

Andrei had asked to resume efforts to rebuild portions of the city, which Stryker had granted immediately and promised aid where he could provide it. They discussed how the town would operate under Cygnaran occupation, and Stryker assured the man they were there to protect the people of Riversmet until the country was once again ruled by a Llaelese sovereign. This seemed to satisfy Ladislav, and before he and the other citizens departed, he pulled Stryker aside.

"War is terrible business," he said, his eyes hard. "But you were true to your word. You protected us when others would not have. For that, I thank you."

The man's words lifted some of the weight off Stryker's shoulders. It was true: there had been virtually no casualties among the citizens of Riversmet. He'd at least succeeded in keeping the fighting from their doorsteps. Of course, that success had been due in large part to a vast portion of the Khadoran Army being destroyed by the devil's gasp. By Magnus.

Over the next few days, reports began to filter in from their scouts that Vlad's army was, indeed, moving toward Rynyr. In addition, casualty reports had been compiled, and the news was better than he could have hoped. They'd lost just under two thousand men, many of them from the Stormblade infantry. The Khadorans had lost an estimated four thousand, nearly half their number. Stryker still had over six thousand men at his disposal, and he needed to get them moving. He still had a city to hold, and he'd need to leave some of those men behind for that purpose.

He ordered light duty for all those in the Cygnaran Army over the next few days to let them recover from the battle. Four days after their victory, he summoned his senior staff to the Riversmet town hall to plan the next phase of the invasion.

"Rynyr is our next target," he said, running his finger down a map of the region, tracing the road between Riversmet and Rynyr. "Khador produces much of their blasting powder here, and if we can take it quickly, we can cut one of their vital supply lines and strengthen one of ours."

Maddox nodded. "Agreed. If you can get there soon, they won't have much more to defend themselves than what was left of Vlad's army." She pointed to a city on the map west of Rynyr. "Laedry could be a problem. There are still troops there, and it's not far from Rynyr."

"I'd expect troops to be moving up from Merywyn as well," Captain Adkins added.

"More the reason we need to get there quickly," Stryker said. He turned to Maddox. "As planned, you'll stay behind in Riversmet and hold the city. We'll need to maintain a foothold in the area."

"Of course, sir," she said. "I'll hoist the first banner of freedom over Llael."

"Word has already been sent back to Caspia, and I expect reinforcement to arrive in Riversmet in two weeks. I'll leave behind two full companies and some of Major Hughs' artillery. I don't expect trouble, but it should be enough to hold you until reinforcements arrive from Caspia."

"We'll hold, sir," she said.

"Perhaps it is time to speak more plainly about the Resistance's role in your invasion, Lord General," Captain di Brascio said. The Resistance put Stryker in a difficult position.

"You know very well I would like nothing more than to fight beside the brave men and women of the Resistance, Captain, but if we are to speak plainly, your involvement with the Protectorate of Menoth has some in Caspia nervous," Stryker said. "I understood why you felt the need to cooperate with the Protectorate. Fighting a war on two fronts with two powerful enemies is suicide."

"Our ties to the Protectorate are not unbreakable," di Brascio said, "with certain promises from your king."

"Perhaps another meeting with Colonel Jarov is in order then," Stryker said. "Maddox, I'll leave that to you and to relay what comes of it to Caspia."

"I look forward to working with you, Commander," di Brascio said to Maddox.

"It's a three-day march to Rynyr," Stryker continued. "I want to move out in forty eight hours." He glanced at the men and women in the room, experienced officers all. "You know what to do. Make it happen."

The room emptied quickly. He stopped Maddox as she was leaving the tent. "Major, have Asheth Magnus brought here. It's time for us to talk."

Magnus arrived a short time later flanked by two Storm Knights. His armor had been removed, and his hands were manacled before him. He looked old and tired without that armor.

"Remove his bonds and leave us," Stryker said. There was no danger—he wore his warcaster armor, and Quicksilver hung from his back.

"We're going to talk now," he said.

Magnus rubbed at the red marks left by the manacles around his wrists. "Of course, sir. I would welcome such a discourse."

"First, I will ask you a question," Stryker said. "You may speak freely. This will be off the record."

"You don't need to ask it," Magnus said. "I'll tell you. I found a cache of the devil's gasp in the ruins."

"Then you disobeyed my orders to destroy what you found?" Stryker said.

"No. If you will recall, you ordered me to destroy the explosives under the bridge. I did that."

"You would hide behind semantics as a defense for your actions?"

"Are we truly speaking freely?" Magnus said.

"I won't have you executed for a crime I already know you committed. If I'd wanted that, I would have killed you in the square."

"Fair enough," Magnus said. "I did what I knew to be best, what you could not do. We could not have held Vlad at the breach, and our best option to defeat him was the one I chose."

Stryker considered. "You're right. I would never have agreed to condemning so many men and women, enemies or no, to a lingering, torturous death. That is the difference between you and me."

Something flashed in Magnus' eyes, something Stryker had not expected. It looked like remorse. "I take no pleasure in that, and if I had thought there was another path to victory, I would have gladly followed it."

"I'll speak as openly as I asked you to: I don't believe you," Stryker said. "Instead, I believe your promises are as meaningless as they were twenty years ago."

"Coleman," Magnus said, and for the first time Stryker didn't feel like the warcaster was using his name to goad him, "there was a chance you would defeat Vlad in the field, and I would not need to use the devil's gasp. War is a cold, practical business. I prepare for as many eventualities as I can, even the ones I'd rather not face."

"There is a line you do *not* cross," Stryker said. "If you can't see that, then you haven't changed at all. You're still the man who served Vinter all those years ago until he was no longer useful to you. How long until you put a blade in Julius' back?"

"I was wrong to put so much faith in Vinter," Magnus conceded. "Whatever you may think of me, you have no idea what that man was capable of."

"I have some idea, but I remember you serving him readily, even eagerly," Stryker said. "And now you have another king to serve. Maybe this one will be more to your liking. Maybe this one will be easier to control."

"Julius is *not* his father," Magnus said, and his eyes grew flat and hard. "He is a worthy king, and he will make Cygnar strong again, if men like you don't stand in his way."

"Where would Cygnar be now had good men not stood in the way of his father?"

A weary smile crossed Magnus' face. "We want the same thing. Peace for Cygnar."

"Not if it means compromising what Cygnar stands for," Stryker said.

"Cygnar has stood for different things at different times."

Stryker changed tact. "We are marching on Rynyr in forty-eight hours," he said, "and you have a choice. You can stay here and rot in a prison cell. Or you can come with me. I won't deny you have talents I can use."

Magnus said nothing for a long moment. "Come with you as what? I assume my commission as a general has been revoked."

"Yes, I'm demoting you," Stryker said. He and Maddox had discussed Magnus' role at length. "You will command a small force of specialized operatives and serve me in scouting and infiltration roles." There was no denying Magnus success at disarming the bombs beneath the bridge. He'd executed it perfectly, regardless of what had happened after.

"Who will this force be comprised of?"

"Mostly men loyal to you, those you brought with you, plus men of my choosing who can tolerate serving under your command."

"Watchdogs," Magnus said.

"We view the world differently, even though our goals are aligned. You see solutions I won't even consider. You *will* be watched, but I *will* listen to your counsel and do my best to weigh without judgment based on your past." Stryker paused. "I warn you, if you work around me, or against me, then we are enemies, and I'll put you down like any rabid cur. So, which will it be, Magnus: the cell or a fight in Rynyr?"

"I never knew you could be so . . . sensible, Coleman," Magnus said and smiled thinly. "I will accompany you, Lord General, and you can count on me to follow your orders to the best of my ability."

Stryker digested Magnus words. Their meaning was clear. "That will have to do. You are dismissed, Major," he said. There was nothing left to say.

— 44 —

Western Riversmet, Occupied Llael

THE TEMPORARY CEMETERY near the river had grown considerably. The makeshift grave markers—mostly bits of masonry taken from the rubble-strewn western half of the city—thrust up from the bare earth like old, gray teeth. Each irregular headstone bore a name and a regiment in red paint. Stryker moved through the orderly rows of graves carrying a long cloth-wrapped bundle. It pained him there were so many dead, but part of him was grateful there weren't more. He was alone; the rest of the army was busy preparing for the march to Rynyr.

He found Tews' grave near the center of the cemetery, surrounded by the resting places of other Storm Knights. It gave Stryker some comfort that his old friend was among his brothers and sisters, the Storm Knights he had spent his life fighting alongside.

He put one hand on the jagged piece of stone serving as Tews' marker and set his bundle on the ground. He stood for a moment, trying to sort out the tangle of emotions that clawed their way into his mind. Anger and sorrow, equally powerful. Tews' death had been such a waste, shot down by a man who should have never had that chance, who should never been anywhere near the Cygnaran Army. Harrow had been a monster, but it had been Magnus who'd set that monster loose among them. He thrust the anger away; it was pointless. The sorrow was more fitting, and he let it flow over him, washing away everything else in a tide of heartache. The power of it staggered him, and he sank to his knees, the tears he'd been holding back for weeks running down his face. His chest tightened with wracking sobs, but he choked them back. He put his head down and silently wept.

His face burned from the shame of losing control in such a way. He clamped down on his emotions, overriding the pain by sheer force of will. His tears stopped as he regained control. In time, he drew in a deep, ragged breath and rose, wiping at his eyes with the back of his hand.

He turned his attention to the bundle on the ground and unwrapped it. Steel gleamed in the early morning sunshine, and Stryker removed his practice Caspian battle blade, its blunted edge still nicked from the last time he and Tews had sparred in Caspia. It seemed like a hundred years ago, in a land he could scarcely believe existed any more. He leaned the sword against Tews' grave marker, point down.

"I'll get another," he said. "I don't think I could swing this one without seeing your big, ugly face." He put his hand on the grave marker again. "I hope you're giving them hell in Urcaen. Morrow is lucky to have your sword at his side."

"Sir," a soft voice said. "Am I interrupting?"

Maddox was standing a few yards away. She had something in her right hand—it looked like a sheaf of bound letters.

"No, Beth," he said. "You're fine. Just came to say goodbye to our friend." If it were anyone else, he might have been ashamed, but Beth Maddox was more to him than a fellow soldier. She was his friend.

She made her way through the headstones to stand beside him. She stared at Tews' gravestone for a moment, and then said, "We were together before Sul. After that . . ." Her voice faltered.

"It's all right," Stryker said. "I understand."

She held up the sheaf of letters. "We wrote each other a lot in the beginning," she said mechanically. "When I was on my journeyman tour."

Stryker waited. Tews has never spoken of his relationship with Maddox, though Stryker had suspected much about it. Such things were frowned upon in the army, but it happened, and usually the senior officers looked the other way.

"These are the letters he wrote to me after Sul, after I told him I couldn't be with him." She swallowed, and he could see bright tears standing in her eyes. "It seems so cruel now, so low. He only wanted to help me, but I couldn't let him."

The wall Maddox had erected to protect herself from the emotional trauma of her ordeal with the Protectorate of Menoth had come down, if only for a brief moment. The pain behind it left him speechless, and he stood silently, wanting to reach out to her, to comfort her, but knowing it would break this single moment of openness she had chosen to share with him.

She set the letters on the ground next to Stryker's sword. "I don't want these anymore," she said. "I'm just keeping the good ones, the happy ones. To remember him."

She inhaled deeply, and the subtle buzz of magic filled in the air. She extended her hand toward the pile of letters on the ground, and a ring of spell runes formed around her arm. They disappeared, and a small but bright bolt of lightning shot from her hand and struck the letters. They were instantly incinerated, erased from the world.

"He would have liked that," Stryker said. He took her hand and squeezed it gently. She didn't pull away, but her body tensed at the contact, so he let her go. The walls were falling back into place, sealing away the hurt once again. He understood that; he had walls of his own.

They stood quietly for a few moments, then left the cemetery together. The time for grieving was done, though it still loomed on the horizon, a specter of the many deaths to come.

...

STRYKER RODE THROUGH THE STREETS of Riversmet, thankful the sounds of death and war had been replaced with the steady, comforting sounds of men and women working to restore their city rather than tear it down.

Andrei Ladislav had been instrumental in getting the people of Riversmet back to something resembling normal life. Stryker heard glad voices and even occasional laughter as men carried rubble away from the site of a ruined house or a shopkeeper greeted a longtime customer, welcoming him back for the first time in many weeks.

The Cygnaran soldiers were often given a wide berth by the townsfolk. It was understandable they might be wary of men in uniform, but they were polite when circumstances forced them together. Stryker had passed along strict orders that Cygnaran soldiers were to comport themselves with the utmost dignity and respect, and any injustice or crime committed against a citizen of Riversmet would be dealt with both harshly and publicly. He wanted the Llaelese to know they were safe, and though their city was currently occupied by a foreign power, they were in better hands with Cygnar.

Maddox and Vayne Di Brascio rode beside Stryker, flanking him. Behind them came a long and winding ribbon of blue and white, two battalions of Storm Knights and Precursor Knights and nearly two full regiments of the trencher corps. Warjacks moved along with the tide of men, and Rowdy's impatience at the slow, steady pace of it all was a thorny sensation in Stryker's mind.

He'd sent Magnus and a force of roughly fifty men ahead to scout out the way to Rynyr. He couldn't bear the sight of the man, but he could at least put him to good use.

They were moving down the main road that ran through the center of Riversmet and terminated at the eastern gate. Some townsfolk had turned up to watch the procession, but most stayed away, busying themselves with rebuilding their lives.

The army passed the blasted heath that used to be the northwest corner of the city. Most of the rubble had been cleared, and the bodies were gone, but the scorched earth, the chunks of blackened masonry sticking up like rotten teeth, and the lingering acrid stench of the devil's gasp drove a spike of regret into Stryker's guts. He had also left strict orders to keep everyone out of the area until the alchemists he'd left behind said it was clear.

Maddox must have felt his discomfort. "They can rebuild there soon. The devil's gasp will dissipate before long."

"Though I doubt anything will ever grow there again," di Brascio said gravely. Maddox shot him a dark look, and the gun mage shrugged. "I know what happened, Lord General, and I do not personally hold you accountable. I will also ensure others in the Resistance know the truth of what happened."

"That one of my generals disobeyed a direct order and leveled half the city with poison gas?" Stryker said and grimaced. "But I thank you for the consideration, Captain."

"In the end, Khador is gone from Riversmet, Vlad's army was crippled, and the Llaelese here have been spared much suffering. That, I think, will carry more weight with the Resistance, and the Llaelese people, than anything else."

"I hope you're right," Stryker said, and he meant it.

They had reached the eastern gate, and the portcullis clattered up into its mountings. "Luck and victory in Rynyr," Maddox said as they reined in.

"Thank you, Beth," he said. "I'll sleep better knowing Riversmet is in good hands." He turned to di Brascio and extended his hand. "You are a brave and honorable man, Captain," he said. "It has been my privilege to fight beside you."

di Brascio smiled, a rarity for the man, and gripped Stryker's hand. "I feel the same, and I hope we may fight together again soon under the twin banners of Cygnar and Llael."

"May Morrow make it so," Stryker said and turned toward the gate. Ahead lay the battered plains of Llael, which had seen so much bloodshed of late. And beyond that gate lay Rynyr and Laedry and thousands of Khadorans intent on killing him.

Stryker pulled Quicksilver from his back and held the big blade aloft.

"For Cygnar. For victory!" he cried and spurred his mount forward. Behind him a fierce cry echoing his own went up, and the wheels of war rolled on.

— ABOUT THE AUTHOR —

Aeryn Rudel, who has recently signed a deal to write multiple books for Skull Island eXpeditions, also contributes fiction to the Iron Kingdoms setting and writes WARMACHINE, HORDES, and RPG articles for No Quarter magazine. He is also a notorious dinosaur nerd (ALL theropod dinosaurs had feathers!), a rare polearm expert (the bec de corbin is clearly superior to the lucerne hammer), and has mastered the art of fighting with sword-shaped objects (but not actual swords). Check out his blog on writing and rejection (mostly rejection) at www.rejectomancy.com.